A Homeplace

By

Steve Goshey

This book is a work of fiction. Except for my grandparents, the names, characters, places, and incidents are products of the authors imagination or are used fictitiously. Any resemblance to actual events or locations or people, living or dead, is entirely coincidental.

Copyright 2000 by Steve Goshey

All rights reserved, including the right to reproduce this book or portions thereof in any form whatsoever.

Library of Congress Cataloging-in-publication Data Applied For.

ISBN—0-9701452-0-9

Published by Steve Goshey

Printed in the **United States of America**
by
Bang Printing. Brainerd, Minnesota.

**Cover and Illustrations by
Janis Gallagher Young**

Acknowledgements

    I wish to thank my wife, Debora, and my children for their saintly toleration of my long and frequent periods of neglect when writing this story.
    I must also thank my good friends, Amy Sharpe and Andrea and Brian Gaffney for publishing my early attempts at writing in their wonderful little magazine, "Homespun," which gave me the confidence and courage to forge ahead. I also thank them for their assistance with the final touches on my manuscript, along with my brother, Dan, and his wife, Julie, for their invaluable assistance in helping me with refinements from the rough draft. I must also thank my brother, Jim, for minding the store while I wrote this story.
    I've heard it said that music gives life to a motion picture. I believe that a similar relationship exists between a story and it's illustrations, and I wish to express my sincere thanks to Janis Gallagher Young for her work on this project.
    Most of all, I thank God, who has so richly blessed my life through my parents and grandparents. It hadn't occurred to me until I was nearly finished with the manuscript, that the inspiration necessary for me to write this story is, in reality, a tribute to my upbringing. There is no doubt in my mind that without the fond, sentimental recollections of family values, faith, and the loving guidance of parents and grandparents, I would not have been able to imagine this story.

A Homeplace

The Early Years

From the Red Pine Weekly Herald, Thursday, October 13, 1921.

News from in town:

Don't miss the fourth annual Fall Festival at Emmanuel Lutheran Church of Red Pine this Saturday, October 15, from noon until seven. Many homemade gifts and baked goods will be offered for sale as well as the delicious Sausage Dinner put on by the Ladies Altar Guild. Located in the church basement hall.

Gustav Schmidke caught a 26-pound pike while fishing on the north end of Crystal Lake last Monday with his brother, Henry who is visiting from St. Paul. It was reported to be a real beauty, according to Rudy Nelson.

Father Keith Branigan is the new priest at St. Gabriel Catholic Church replacing Father Jerome Sherman who has retired near St. Cloud. Father Branigan will be celebrating his first Mass at St. Gabriel this Sunday.

News from the country:

Mrs. Oliver Carlson was an afternoon luncheon guest at the farm of Mr. and Mrs. Reginald Larson last Sunday where much fun and conversation was enjoyed by all before returning home that evening.

The County Sheriff was called to the Younghans farm south of town on Tuesday of this week to investigate an apparent wolf kill. This is the second cow in two weeks to be found dead in his pasture.

The Red Pine Weekly Herald appreciates the news items our friends and subscribers furnish to us each week. If you have any news items please call phone 66 and we'll take care of the rest.

The Early Years

On a chilly Friday afternoon in mid-October, in a small northern Minnesota town, the colors of autumn surrounded the deep blue lake, and a light westerly breeze created the perfect chop on the water for the sunlight to transform the waves into shimmering diamonds. The sweet scent of fallen leaves from aspens, oaks, and maples filled the air. Perched high up among the crimson leaves of a sprawling oak beside the road, a dove with radiant white plumage, cocked its head inquisitively at an approaching group of children.

The serenity of the moment gave way to the clattering engine of a vehicle as it approached from around the bend. "Ahoooogha!" sounded the horn of the Model "T" Ford truck, as it lugged its way past the young pedestrians beside the road. The truck, laden with a delivery of lumber, made its way into the town of Red Pine, sending up a cloud of dust that rolled like a spiral over the group as they walked home from the one-room schoolhouse.

"I'll bet that's the lumber that my father ordered for the cabin," said John Nelson, addressing his stocky, blond-haired friend.

"You're right," replied Ray. "My dad said he would probably have the order cut this morning and try to deliver it before supper."

"Well, now I know what I'll be doing this weekend," said John, as an eager smile developed on his tan face.

"What?" asked Mary.

"Bringing the lumber out to the island so my father and I can start construction of another cabin this fall."

Mary flipped her long black hair behind her shoulder and looked up at her tall boyfriend asking, "Will it take you all weekend?"

"Probably," he answered.

A look of disappointment came over Mary's face, and in a pouty voice she replied, "You said you would come to church with me for the Fall Festival on Saturday afternoon, *remember?*" Her disappointment quickly turned to anger as she recalled the numerous diligent hours she had spent over the last two weeks making a new dress just for this occasion. It was nearly three weeks ago when John had suggested he accompany her to the Fall Festival, inspiring Mary to purchase the pattern and material for the dark blue dress with a white lacy collar that she had been admiring at the general store for so long.

Quickly losing his grin, John swallowed hard when he realized he had forgotten about his earlier commitment to his girlfriend. Lately, he was torn between his relationship with Mary, and his desire to build the new cabin out on the island.

The attraction between the two childhood sweethearts had reached a new level in the last few months, and he was well aware of his recent negligence of romantic responsibility to Mary. Sensing that it was about to come to a head, he cringed and said, "Well, yeah, but that was three weeks ago. How did I know that the lumber would be ready to move this weekend?"

Out of the corner of his eye he verified the tension he felt, as the warmth from Mary's fiery Scottish personality claimed the soft, fair skin of her face. Oh shoot—I wish I could rephrase that statement, he thought, realizing that his response sounded rather callous.

For a moment the group continued to walk from the schoolhouse toward town in their usual formation, John in the middle, Mary on his right, and Ray on his left, with several younger children following behind. Mary stopped abruptly, and like a seasoned military marching unit everyone behind them came to a sudden halt and watched her as she turned to face John. She snatched her school books from his arm, saying in a huff, "Very well, John Nelson, it's obvious to me that you would rather spend time with your friends than with me."

"But, Mary, please let me explain. I'm doing this for us," he pleaded.

She scolded back quickly—his plea ignored by ears deafened with anger. "All I know is that all you seem to care about lately is that stupid cabin, and you don't spend any time with me anymore because you and Ray are always out on that island doing whatever it is you do out there. So if you want more time for yourself, fine! You can have it!" Mary turned and stormed away from the rest of the group as John watched in astonishment. She stopped, turned back to him and said in an elevated, tear-filled voice, "I hope when you get out to the island your boat drifts away, so you're stranded out there and I never have to see your ugly face again!"

"But, Mary! Please listen to me," John shouted as she turned and ran toward home.

"Huh," said Ray with raised eyebrows as the group resumed their walk. "What did you do to deserve that?"

"I've got a pretty good idea," John replied. His face reddened in response to the snickering by the young children behind him. "I think I'll just let her stew about it for a while and then try to talk to her on Sunday after church services." Outwardly he seemed confident in making that statement, but in his mind, he was already scrambling for a solution that would accommodate both commitments. As they continued on their way home from school, the group gradually diminished in size as they dispersed toward their homes. While walking along, an idea suddenly came to John, and in a hopeful tone he asked Ray, "Would you be able to help me move the lumber out to the island this weekend?"

"I'm really sorry, John, but my dad needs me to help cut up a lumber order tomorrow."

"Oh, well, that's okay, I'll manage." Now he regretted asking him for his help. He felt guilty for even thinking of it because Ray was always so generous with his time, and it was so easy to take advantage of his reliable friendship. John always believed that Ray was the kind of person who would give the shirt off his back and then apologize if it didn't fit properly. John could see by the look in his sparkling blue eyes, that Ray wanted to say yes and come to his aid, as if their friendship was now somehow in jeopardy. But Ray's loyalty to his parent's needs was second to none. Reassuringly, John put his arm around Ray's thick shoulder and said, "And by the way, thanks a lot for helping me put the foundation in last weekend. I don't know how I'd have done it without you."

"Glad to help," said Ray with a rejuvenated smile. "Maybe sometime the two of us can use the cabin when you don't have it rented. It would sure beat sleeping in a tent."

"It's a deal," said John, tightening his grip on Ray's shoulder and giving him a hearty shake as they continued to walk along.

John and his father were planning to finish construction of the cabin on the island in Crystal Lake over the winter months as time and weather permitted. The island, about a quarter of a mile out from the shoreline where John's father kept his rental boats, had been a life-long attraction for the two young men. John and Ray had camped out on the island many times as young boys. Their favorite fishing spot was a little drop-off on the north side of the island where, in the spring of the year when the water clarity was at its best and the lighting conditions were just right, you could see all the way to the bottom of the 20-foot hole where the walleyes were suspended in layers like stacked firewood.

A Homeplace

John's father, Rudolph, had purchased the two-acre island a year earlier and had decided to build a small one-room cabin similar to the ones that they had built behind their store. The design of the 16-by-24-foot cabins was simple and rustic, but "perfectly comfortable," it was said, at least by the men whose primary concern was fishing.

In the middle of each cabin stood a small wood stove for heating and cooking. A table and four chairs next to a large window overlooked the lake. The only other window was in an area designated as sleeping quarters at one end of the cabin, which was partitioned off from the rest of the room by a curtain suspended from a rope between the two walls. The curtain could be closed when necessary for privacy, but it was usually left open during the night to allow the heat from the wood stove to circulate throughout the cabin. Kerosene lamps were used for light.

The kitchen consisted of a countertop that was merely a series of thick pine planks attached to the wall with a large metal wash basin recessed into the counter. Above the counter were two shelves for plates, cups, utensils and canned goods. The interior of the cabin was lined with knotty-pine paneling, and a six-foot wide covered porch overlooking the lake was attached to the entire length of the cabin.

John and Ray had grown up together and had become best friends. They were both seven years old when their families moved to Red Pine in the summer of 1910. At six feet, John was slightly taller than his friend Ray and fairly thin in comparison. He owed his wide, square shoulders to years of vigorous work around the resort and general store. His dark brown hair and thick eyebrows were striking against his sun-darkened skin, and his narrow, chiseled face already showed faint evidence of wrinkles around his eyes from the squinting reflex when working around the sunlit water.

John's parents, Rudolph and Sarah Nelson, had moved their family to Red Pine from Minneapolis and reopened the general store that the previous owner had lost due to his poor financial management. John and his younger sister, Rose, lived above the store with their parents. The store was located at the east edge of the two-block-long business district. The property that the store was located on also abutted the shoreline of Crystal Lake, and the wide, deep, grassy lot behind the store sloped gently to the lakeshore where Rudolph Nelson kept a dock and several wooden rowboats that he rented by the day or week.

Every fall for the past seven years, Rudy, with the help of his son, had built a new cabin near the waterfront—an undertaking that John fervently awaited each year. At the age of 12, John had been given the responsibility during the summer months to take care of the resort grounds and help his parents clean the cabins after checkout time. It was a job less than cherished by John—at that age he would much rather have been fishing or exploring the island with his friend, Ray.

Rudy was aware of his son's annoyance with the demands of the resort business, but his concern was offset by the fact that John was building a nice little nest egg in the bank while learning some valuable entrepreneurial skills. As John matured, however, he came to realize the wisdom in his father's guidance. The Nelsons had gradually built up a loyal clientele, and seldom was there a week during the summer when all of the cabins were not occupied.

Ray's parents, Pete and Alice Hanson, had relocated to the area upon the successful purchase of a sawmill and storage ice business from Mrs. Oliver Carlson, the widow of the former owner. Previously, Pete had been employed by a lumber supplier in St. Cloud. Before the unexpected passing of her husband, Oliver, the Carlson's lived on a small farm outside of town, where they had started a small sawmill and lumber enterprise to supplement their storage ice business in town.

Located diagonally across the street corner from the Nelson's general store was the Red Pine Hotel, owned by Andrew and Ellen McCulloh. Over the years, the Nelsons and McCullohs had developed a strong working relationship as well as a friendship. The McCullohs purchased most of the food and supplies used in their hotel from the general store. During the summer months, many people from St. Paul and Minneapolis came to vacation in the area and would rent boats from the Nelsons. When there was no vacancy at the resort, the Nelsons always referred people who arrived without reservations to the hotel for meals and lodging.

Eleven years earlier, the McCullohs only child, Mary, had suffered through a bout with rheumatic fever, but not without casualty. The subtle damage to her heart would remain hidden for a lifetime, but its effects would never impair her faith in God and the love of her family, friends, her hometown of Red Pine and life itself. Mary was a year younger than John, and growing up across the street from each other, they had become close friends over the years. They could usually be seen walking to school together, and there was little doubt by most folk, that someday they would be husband and wife.

A Homeplace

    John and Ray continued walking toward the general store on their way home from school, and when they noticed that their fathers were still unloading the delivery truck down by the docks, they ran to help. When the truck was nearly unloaded, John walked to the water's edge and stood for a moment, just staring out at the island with his hands on his hips. A wide gleaming smile appeared on his face as he pondered a solution to his dilemma. I'll move this lumber out to the island tonight, then tomorrow morning, after she's had a chance to cool off, I'll apologize to Mary and ask her to go to the Fall Festival, he decided. With fresh enthusiasm, he stooped over to right one of the overturned rowboats, slid it into the water and started loading some of the lumber into the boat.
    "You're not thinking of bringing a load out yet this afternoon are you, Son?" asked Mr. Nelson.
    "I thought I would, Father, if you don't mind."
    "That's fine by me, John, but it'll be dark before too long you know. You've got all day tomorrow if you'd rather wait 'til then."
    "Yeah, I know, but I forgot about the Fall Festival at church tomorrow and I promised Mary I'd go with her. There's a full moon tonight, and if it stays clear and I work steady, I can be done by morning."
    "Suit yourself, Son," Rudy replied, beaming with pride at his son's ambitious approach to such an enormous task. "What about supper?"
    "Do you think Mother would make me a sandwich so I can keep going?"
    "I'm sure she will. I'll ask her to make you one while you take this load out."
    "Thanks."
    Rudy looked on with his hands on his hips as John began rowing out toward the island, while Pete and his son, Ray, unloaded the last of the wooden planks from the truck.
    "What some men won't put themselves through for a woman," Pete said, smiling at Ray and shaking his head in disbelief.
    Rudy turned and started back toward the truck saying, "I figure it's going to take him 'til five in the morning to get all that lumber out there. That is, *if* the weather holds for him. It must be nice to be young and so full of vinegar."

"Well, there was a time when we were too," said Pete, followed by a deep hearty chuckle.

Ray waved to John and shouted, "See you at church on Sunday."

John returned the wave and glanced over his shoulder to line up the bow of the boat with the island. He lowered the oars deep into the water and with a mighty pull began to row. The boat was so heavily loaded that the gunwale was only a few inches above the waterline. He realized that if the wind picked up, he wouldn't be able to load down the boat so much. It'll take about an hour per trip, he figured, as he continued to row toward the island.

After nearly half an hour of rowing, the bow of his boat scraped upon the rocky shore of the island and came to an abrupt halt, causing John to lose his balance and fall backwards off the seat and onto the floor of the boat. He rubbed his head as he stood up and mumbled, "This could be a long night."

After carrying a bundle of two-by-fours up the bank and stacking them near the foundation, he realized his endeavor was going to take longer than he thought. Six more trips up and down the slippery bank and he was ready to start back toward the docks. The sun was sinking low on the horizon as he pulled up to the dock where his mother met him with a sandwich and an apple. "Are you sure you want to do this, Son?"

"Sure, Mother. If the weather turns bad or I get too tired, I can always quit."

"I'd feel a lot better about this if you'd bring a lantern with you in the boat so we can tell where you are by looking out our window."

"That's a good idea, Mother. I think I'll bring two so I have a spare. I may need one on the island to light my trail a little better; there's a few places where the roots are sticking up out of the ground."

After retrieving the lanterns from the shed, he finished loading the boat, ate his simple supper and started off once again. It was dark now, but a large amber moon rose behind a stand of towering pine trees on the island enabling him to guide the boat with an occasional glance over his shoulder.

As he made his way across the water he could see the light come on in Mary's bedroom window. Her curtain was open, and he could see her figure move about in the room. He wondered if she was still angry with him and if she could see his boat in the glistening beam of moonlight that lay across the water. As John continued to row, he noticed that his breath was now visible in the crisp October air. He began to consider what Mary said about not spending time with her anymore and being preoccupied with the construction of the new cabin. "She's right," he said, mumbling to himself. "But if only she would have let me explain why I am doing it, I know she would understand."

Nearly all of the money generated by the rental cabins was returned to John by his father as wages for managing that enterprise. John, like his father, was frugal, and over the last two years was able to put over 80 percent of his earnings into a savings account that was beginning to compound into a nice nest egg for him.

Mary was sitting in a chair next to her bedroom window watching John as he made his way to the island when her mother entered her room. She had noticed that her daughter seemed rather distraught when she came home from school—briskly walking unannounced through the hotel lobby, past her parents, and up the stairs to her room.

"Mary, it's almost time for dinner. Would you come down and set the table please?"

"I'm not very hungry, Mom," she answered, continuing to look out the window to conceal her emotions.

Her mother easily detected the weepy tone in her daughter's voice and said, "What's wrong, dear?"

"Nothing, Mom, I'm just not very hungry."

"That's no reason to cry, is it, Mary?"

Mary turned to face her mother. "Oh, Mom, I think John is losing interest in me," she anguished, dabbing the tears from the corners of her reddened eyes.

Her mother smiled at her with reassuring comfort, resting one hand on her shoulder while raising her daughter's chin with the other.

"Now, Mary McCulloh, what gave you that idea, Dear?" her mother asked condescendingly, confident that her daughter's concern was unfounded.

"Because lately he's always working out on that island with Ray and never seems to spend any time with me anymore. Whenever he does have time, it seems like I'm needed here to help with the hotel. We just can't seem to find time for each other anymore. Then on the way home from school today he told me that he couldn't go to the Fall Festival at church tomorrow because he had to move that pile of lumber out to the island."

"Well, did you talk to him about it?"

Through gritted teeth she replied, "No! When I thought about all the time I've spent on that dress, it made me so mad that I told him I never wanted to see his face again."

"Oh, Mary," said her mother as she rolled her eyes "You've made a terrible mistake."

"Why do you say that, Mom?" she asked, irritated by her mother's apparent lack of support.

"Now listen, Mary, you must promise not to repeat what I'm about to tell you."

"What, Mom?"

In a secretive voice she said, "Last night after you left for Mrs. Carlson's house for your piano lessons, John came over to talk to your father. They sat out on the back steps for the longest time and I overheard part of their conversation."

"What conversation, Mom?" she asked impatiently.

Ellen took a deep breath and sighed with a last moment of hesitation deciding whether or not to disclose her deviously-attained information.

"MOM! What conversation?"

Confident that she could rely on her daughter's pledge of secrecy, she said, "Mary—John asked your father for your hand in marriage."

"...OH—NO!" Mary gasped. Quickly rising from her chair with her hand over her mouth, she stood in silence for a moment, staring into her mother's eyes. Then, as she recalled the hurtful words she had spoken to John, and the vivid image of the heartbroken look on his face when he said, 'I'm doing this for us,' the tears welled in her eyes, backed by an avalanche of guilt.

"What did Dad say?" she asked, drying the fresh collection of tears.

"I don't remember word for word, but something to the effect that he would be proud to have him for a son-in-law, but insisted that his daughter should finish school first. He went on to say that he knew that John would be done with school next spring, and he realized that it would be hard to wait another whole year for you to finish school, but that is what he wanted for his only child."

"What did John say to that?"

"He said that he understood and he would be willing to wait, and besides, that way he could save up some more money. Then your father asked that John not propose to you until you are almost done with school, so you wouldn't be tempted to skip your last year."

Mary lowered her head onto her mother's bosom and said, "Oh, Mom, what can I possibly say that will enable him to forgive me?"

"I am sure that he will forgive you, Dear, it's obvious he loves you very much, but you better go and talk to him when he comes back to the dock. I spoke with Mrs. Nelson a short while ago, and she said John was going to work all night so he could go to the festival with you tomorrow."

"Oh, I do hope he didn't tell his mother about the way I acted this afternoon. I don't think I could ever look her in the eye again if she knew the way I treated John."

"She didn't mention anything about it, Mary. I'm sure John just kept it to himself."

Mary lifted her head and looked at her mother, "Oh Mom, I'm such a fool."

Her mother realized that this was one of those helpless moments that parents occasionally find themselves in, when their children get caught in a predicament that they must resolve for themselves—if they ever hope to make the transition to adulthood. "Well, Dear," said her mother in a comforting voice, "We all make foolish mistakes once in a while. Look, Mary," as she pulled the window curtain aside. "John's boat is returning. I think you'd better go to him right now. I'll set the table and hold your dinner for you."

"But, Mom, what shall I say to him?" She asked in a panic.

"That's something you'll have to figure out for yourself, Mary. My only advice is to be honest with him and speak from your heart." She gave her daughter a hug, and the two women hurried down the stairs and through the lobby where Mr. McCulloh sat in a chair reading the paper. A thin cloud of smoke from his pipe hovered around his shiny black hair, barely visible above the "Red Pine Weekly Herald." He lowered his newspaper, peered over the top of his half-frame reading glasses and asked, "What's going on?"

"Nothing, Dear," said Ellen.

"When will dinner be ready?"

"Shortly, Dear," she sighed, annoyed by his questioning.

"Why is Mary crying?" he asked.

"Just never you mind, Andrew!" she said firmly. "It's a female concern. Now go back to reading your paper, and I'll call you when supper is ready!"

Andy sat for a moment in silent astonishment as the two women departed from the room. He shook his head in confusion, shrugged his shoulders and returned to his newspaper. As Mary put her coat on and went out the door, her mother set the table, held off the meal, and went back up the stairs to her daughter's bedroom. Turning out the light so she couldn't be seen, she sat by the window and watched her daughter as John's boat came to shore.

Mary waited near the lakeshore in the shadow of a small shed used to store equipment associated with the rental boats. When John stepped out of the boat, he stood with his hands on his hips and arched his back trying to relieve the stiffness that developed while rowing. He turned to pull the boat further onto the beach when he heard a sniffling sound coming from the shadows. "Who's there?" he asked. "Is that you, Mother?"

When Mary stepped out of the darkness and walked toward him into the lantern light, John's face immediately beamed with happiness. "Oh, Mary," he said with a sigh of relief, rushing to her with open arms. "I'm so glad you came down here. I need to apologize to you for the way I talked this afternoon."

Mary stopped short of his arms, and he could now see that she was weeping, almost uncontrollably.

"Mary, what's wrong?" he asked, his brow furrowed with concern. John went to her, took her into his arms, and could feel her shake as she cried. She put her arms around him, and as she embraced him, she felt that his shirt was soaked with sweat. Again he pleaded, "Mary, please tell me what's wrong."

When she finally regained some of her composure, she raised her head from his chest and said, "I am just a stupid, foolish schoolgirl. That's what's wrong."

"What do you mean?" asked John.

"You have no reason to apologize to *me*," said Mary. "Everything that went wrong this afternoon is *my* fault. I didn't even give you a chance to explain. I'm so sorry, John, and now I'm afraid that you'll never forgive me for the way I acted today."

John tightened his embrace and again she began to cry. He gently cradled her face between his hands, looked intently into her watery eyes and said, "Mary, I know I've never really told you this before, I guess I just thought you knew. Mary, I love you with all my heart, and I would never do anything to hurt you. It just tore me up inside when I saw how angry you were with me today. When you told me you never wanted to see me again, I felt a terrible ache inside, and that's when I discovered just how much I love you, and how much I need you."

In an instant, Mary's tears were transformed to those of joy as they hugged and kissed each other tightly on the lips. Looking up at the moon, which was now just above John's shoulder, she noted the thin vapor rise from his warm, sweaty shirt in the cool night air. "Please go home and forget about the lumber until morning," she pleaded. "It's so cold and lonely out here tonight."

John replied, "Mary, I'm so happy now that I couldn't sleep a wink anyway. I think I'll just keep going until I am finished. It's not that cold when I'm rowing, in fact, I've worked up quite a sweat. Besides, then we can go to the festival tomorrow."

"Work if you want, John, but if you're tired tomorrow, let's just skip the festival. I really mean it. It's not that important to me now."

"I won't be tired if I sleep in late tomorrow morning. How about if I pick you up at noon?"

"That would be wonderful."

They gave each other one last kiss and embraced.

Her mother, who had been watching the whole time, dried the emotion from her eyes as she looked up and whispered, "Thank You."

Mary ran back to the hotel, and John continued to load the boat for another trip to the island. When she came in the door and went up the stairs, she was met in the hallway by her mother who asked, "Well?"

Mary looked at her and said with a smile, "Oh, Mom, I just love him." Then she hurried into her room with her mother at her heels.

"You didn't mention anything about his talk with your father, did you?"

"Of course not, Mom," she said. "But I feel so terrible that he's going to work all night long just so he can be with me tomorrow."

"Well, Mary McCulloh, I hope you learned something by this. You need to ask yourself—are you in love with John for the man he is now, or for the man you hope to change him to."

"I realize that now, Mom. And yes, I am in love with him because of what he is now, and I never want him to change. I just realized tonight that he is the kindest, most sincere, and dedicated man I know, besides Dad, that is."

The two women hugged each other, then Mary's mother said, "You'd best get cleaned up and come down to dinner now."

"Could I please just skip dinner tonight? I am really not hungry anymore. I would just as soon sit here, watch John for a while, and get ready for bed. I'll get up early and help you and the other ladies finish decorating the church hall tomorrow morning while John sleeps late."

"Very well, I'll see you in the morning. Sleep well, dear."

"Thank you, Mom, I will." Her mother closed the door behind her as she left the room, and Mary went to the window and began brushing out her long black hair. She watched John return from the island as his boat passed through the sparkling ripples on the moonlit lake.

After a while she went to her dresser and took out her favorite flannel nightgown, a white full-length gown with a dark blue ribbon woven in the collar. Behind her changing screen, she dressed for bed. Lifting her long hair from inside the gown, she let it fall behind her shoulders and returned to the window where she continued to brush her hair and watch John maneuver his boat toward the island. As she contemplated the sacrifice he was willing to undertake for her, she wished that they *were* married so that she could express her love for him at a higher level. She was so thankful that they had worked things out, and wondered if the feelings of guilt and embarrassment from the way she had acted that afternoon would ever go away. She returned the hair brush to her dresser drawer and brought a sheet of paper and fountain pen back to the small table by the window and began to write.

Friday, October 14, 1921

I was overjoyed when I learned today that John has asked Dad's permission to ask for my hand in marriage. I am so ashamed that my first entry in this journal must include a confession of my own foolish behavior. If only I had known that John's feelings for me were so strong, I could have spared myself a terrible embarrassment. Or, perhaps, the more truthful statement would be, if only I had more control of my detestable Scottish temper. He tried to explain why he wanted to start construction of the island cabin instead of attending the Fall Festival,

A Homeplace

but foolish as I was, I didn't give him a chance. I realize now, that after his conversation with Dad, his thoughts had changed to those of our future together while mine still dwelled on a single afternoon together. It must have been terribly difficult to keep his conversation with Dad a secret while I scolded him in front of his friends. I can't seem to escape the image of heartache and despair on his face that I caused this afternoon; perhaps that is just punishment for my foolish behavior. Somehow, simply telling him I'm sorry, seems far too little for the anguish I caused him and the effort that he is undertaking tonight just to keep our date. I know that I will never do such a thing again, and if fate should ever bring your eyes to read this journal, John, I hope by then you'll know just how sorry I am. But more importantly, I hope you'll know how much I love you.

She rose from the chair, and went to bed. Lying on her pillow, she realized that today, she had made the transition from girl to woman. Never again will I jump to conclusions and act so immature, she promised herself. She reached for the lamp and turned out the light, closed her eyes, and in her mind gave John a kiss on the lips.

John was nearing the island when he saw the lights go out in Mary's bedroom. He stopped rowing for a moment, puzzled by a sudden feeling of warmth around his mouth. He wiped his lips with the back of his hand and inspected it in the lantern light. Seeing nothing, he continued to row and the sensation passed after a few moments. The boat lurched forward with each powerful tug of the oars.

John worked with a renewed vigor, from a spirit refreshed by the happy reconciliation he had with Mary. "If only we *were* married," he thought, "then I'd really show her how much I love her." He considered how it seemed like such a long time to wait until they could be married. Mary had another full year of school left after this one. He respected Mr. McCulloh's desire for his daughter to finish school, but he desperately wanted to propose to her. That would certainly prove my commitment to her and end any more concerns about my love for her and my intentions, he figured. He was so preoccupied by the thoughts about their future that rushed through his mind, that he was oblivious to the blisters that were forming on the palms of his hands. He worked through the night and finished his task by five-thirty the next morning.

The Early Years

When Mary woke, she hurried to the window and saw that the lumber pile was gone and John's boat was pulled up on shore and turned over. There had been a heavy frost during the night, and the thick fog rising from the lake hung like ghostly capes around all but the tops of the giant pines on the island. Mary dressed and hurried downstairs to join her mother for breakfast. Her father was busy serving breakfast to a young couple who were traveling to Duluth for a wedding

Mary and her mother finished their breakfast, and as they were leaving, Ellen informed her husband that they would be at the church hall setting up for the Fall Festival. "Do you need any help, Andrew, before we leave?"

"I don't believe so," he said. "The young couple is checking out this morning, and I'll clean the room while you two are gone."

Mary was waiting on the front porch of the hotel while her mother went back to the storeroom to get some table decorations for the church festival. The young woman came out on the porch to wait as her husband brought their luggage down to the car. Mary smiled at her and they exchanged "Good mornings." Mary thought that the woman was about her age, so she sat by her and engaged her in conversation. They talked for several minutes until Ellen returned through the front door with a large paper bag of decorations. Mary said goodbye to the young woman, wishing them a safe trip.

While Mary and her mother walked down the edge of the road toward the church, she told her mother that in her brief conversation with the young woman, she learned that she was from St. Cloud and they were on their way to her cousin's wedding and had decided to stop and spend the night. The young woman, well advanced in her pregnancy, had become fatigued from the rough ride over the gravel roads in their Model T. She also learned that she was only eighteen years old and that they had been married for just over a year.

"Mom," said Mary. "That means she was about the same age as I am when she got married."

"I think I know where this conversation is leading," said her mother as they briskly walked along. "Mary, I realize that you and John

A Homeplace

are in love with each other, but I am in complete agreement with what your father wants for you. True, you and John have known each other since their family moved to town eleven years ago, but you have only been serious with each other for a few months. For goodness sake, you're both still in school. You two need more time to let your love continue to grow and strengthen. Tell me, Mary, do you think you would have gone on your own to see him at the dock last night and apologized if I hadn't told you about his conversation with your father?"

Mary paused for a moment and said, "I don't know, Mother."

"See what I mean? This is what I am talking about, Mary. Give yourselves time to really get to know each other's feelings better. If you really knew John, you wouldn't have had the misunderstanding with him that you did yesterday. Your father and I were engaged for well over a year before we were married, and this gave us time to work through some of the same kinds of difficulties that you and John just had. I think that right now, you're still feeling guilty about what you did and said to John, and are looking for a quick way to set things right with him."

Mary thought about her mother's words for a moment before conceding with a hint of dejection in her voice, " You're probably right, Mom. But don't you understand how hard it is for me now, to know that John wants to marry me, and I want to marry him?"

Ellen replied with raised eyebrows, "Please don't make me sorry that I told you that John asked your father for your hand, Mary."

"I'm sorry, Mom." Their pace gradually slowed to a stop, and they turned to face each other at the side of the road.

"I'll tell you what, Dear. Just be patient and allow your love to blossom at its own pace. If you and John continue to grow closer, and really get to learn each other's thoughts and feelings, and how to work through and avoid these kind of misunderstandings—when school lets out next spring, I'll talk to your father and see if he won't change his mind about John proposing to you sooner. Will you at least agree to that?"

"Yes, Mom, yes I will," she replied with excitement.

Putting her arm around her daughter's waist she said, "Now let's get into the hall and help the other ladies."

Mary felt a sense of reassurance. She knew that her parents were right about finishing school first, but was delighted that her mother offered to talk to her father about reevaluating the terms of their engagement next spring.

The Early Years

Mary and her mother walked into the church hall where the air was buzzing with conversations and laughter as the church women decorated and set out their food and crafts for the festival. The aroma inside the church hall was a blend of apple and pumpkin pies, hot apple cider with cinnamon sticks, homemade sausages and sauerkraut. Mobiles of turkeys, pilgrims, and large maple and oak leaves cut from autumn-colored paper, gently turned in air currents from the hustle and bustle below them. This was the fourth year for the fund raising event that continued to gain in popularity each succeeding year. People came from as far as thirty miles away for the big dinner and for the handmade goods donated for sale by the members of the church.

Mary had high hopes of winning the wildflower pattern quilt made by her piano teacher, Mrs. Carlson, that would be drawn for at the festival. Mrs. Carlson worked on her quilt in the same room where Mary took her instruction, and with each lesson, Mary was able to keep track of her progress as the weeks went by.

Mrs. Carlson moved to town after her husband passed away and she sold the farm and sawmill to the Hansons. She had no children of her own, but gave piano lessons to many of the children in the area. She had also played for church services each Sunday for nearly fifteen years. Mary had been taking lessons from her for four years now, and even though they had no piano at the hotel, she was able to practice on the one at the church whenever she wanted to.

It was late in the morning, when Mary said to her mother, "I think I'll go home now and get ready for the dinner, if that's all right with you, Mom. I want to take a bath before I get dressed, and John said he'd come by for me at noon."

"Go ahead, Dear, it appears that everything is ready. I'll see you later. Now make sure you check with your father to see if he needs any help."

"I will—and Mom," she said, pausing until she had her mother's full attention. "Thanks for all the advice you've given me lately."

Ellen looked at her and smiled. "You're welcome, Dear. I'm glad I could help." She watched with pride as her daughter turned, and quickly walked out the door with her long hair flowing behind her. She thought to herself how mature Mary seemed to be all of a sudden. She seemed more willing to listen to her mother and take her advice. Mary was always a helpful, obedient child to her parents, but now, suddenly, it seemed the child was gone.

A Homeplace

Mary walked into the hotel and found her father at the desk busy with some paper work. "Need me for anything, Dad?" she asked.

He turned to her with a smile and lowered his glasses saying, "No, not right now, Honey." His daughter seemed so different all of a sudden, more mature perhaps, he thought. "Do you have a minute?" he asked.

"Yes, Dad, what is it?"

"Sit down, Mary, I'd like to talk to you."

She pulled a wooden chair up beside him and asked, "What do you want to talk about, Dad?"

"Well, Mary. I've noticed that you and John Nelson have been seeing quite a lot of each other the last few months and I just wondered how you felt about him. You know, for some reason, it seems like fathers and daughters never talk about such matters, but I just want you to know how much your Mother and I really care about you," he said as his face warmed. "And if you ever need any advice about men," he cleared his throat, "I want you to feel comfortable with coming to me and talking about that sort of thing."

Mary was moved by what her father had said. She never thought she would hear those words pass his lips, and could see that he was uneasy with the conversation he had just initiated. She realized that his determination to communicate with her on such a foreign topic stemmed from his deep love and concern for her, and she decided to match his candor.

"Dad, I'm certain I'm in love with him. I know that he is my first love, and that you probably think it's foolish of me to suddenly feel that way about someone I've known for so long, but he has always been a perfect gentleman to me. I can't explain it really, but when we're together, he makes me feel so special. He's always kind, and I feel so safe and comfortable when I'm with him. As far as I am concerned, there is no other man for me."

The sincerity of Mary's response both delighted and relieved her father. "Well, Mary, it's true that many people end up falling in love with someone they didn't know as a child, but in a small town like this one, it really isn't so unusual. Actually, if you think about it, at least you know what you're getting when you grow up with someone. Your mother and I have always felt that the Nelsons are a very strong family and have done a good job raising their children. I don't think you could ever meet anyone nicer than John."

For a moment, Mary thought she could sense her father's desire to tell her about his conversation with John last Thursday evening and hoped to entice him into a revelation. "Do you think that John will ever ask me to marry him?"

After a long pause he held her hand and said with a guilt-ridden blush. "Well, I don't know, Mary, but I hope you finish school before we need to think about that. Something tells me though, that things will work out the way you want them to. Just give it some time. You're both still young."

Mary stood up and said, "Thank you, Dad. I am glad we could talk like this. It's nice to know that you approve of my seeing John. I had better get upstairs and get ready for the festival. John said he would come by for me at noon." She scurried up the stairs to her room thinking about what her father had said. She was not disappointed that her father didn't reveal to her his discussion of matrimony with John. She knew that he was right about waiting until she was done with school and that he was only trying to protect her by keeping the conversation confidential. For now, her knowledge of it would remain a secret she shared with her mother.

Responding to a knock at the back door, Andy rose from his chair at the front desk. Looking down the hall he saw John standing on the porch in his Sunday suit. He smiled and motioned for him to come in as he walked toward the door. John returned Andy's smile as he entered, saying, "Good afternoon Mr. McCulloh. I've come for Mary."

"Come on in, John. You must be worn out after the night you put in."

"Just a little sore in the back, Sir. Raised a pretty good blister on my palms too," he said as he lifted his hands up to display the gauze bandages.

"Ouch!" Andy winced. "That must hurt like the devil."

"Only when I close my fist, Sir. Is Mary ready?"

"She should be down shortly. I could hear the water drain from the tub a while ago. Before she comes down though, John, I would like to talk to you about our conversation the other day." He put his arm

A Homeplace

around John's shoulder as they walked back toward the front desk. He took a moment to light his pipe and gather his thoughts. With Mary's candid response about her feelings for John still fresh in his mind, he shook the wooden match until it went out and blew a long stream of fragrant smoke into the air.

"John, I've been doing some thinking the last couple of days, and I have come to realize that the attraction you and Mary have for one another is stronger than I thought. Now, I still want to see my daughter finish school before she gets married, but if you two still have strong feelings for each other next spring, you have my permission to become engaged to her. Just don't set a wedding date until after she graduates. Fair enough?"

"Yes, Sir, Mr. McCulloh," John said with a smile. "And thank you for being so understanding."

"You're welcome, John," he said with a smile and a wink. "I haven't forgotten what it's like to be young and in love."

Just then, Mary started down the stairs wearing her new dress. The close fitting ankle-length gown had white lace around the collar and at the end of the long sleeves, and the gathered waistline accentuated all the curves and contours of her maturity. Both men turned their attention to the stairway and stared with anticipation as she became more visible with each descending step.

Andrew rescued the pipe from the corner of his mouth just before it fell to the floor. He and John stood awestruck with their mouths open, watching as she left the last step and turned to approach them. *She's—beautiful*, John thought, observing the way her long black hair seemed to flow beside the soft, fair skin of her face as she moved toward them. When Mary entered the room, she became aware of their mesmerized expressions and displayed a bashful smile. Then she noticed John's bandaged hands and hurried to his side saying, "Oh my goodness, John, what happened to your hands?"

Still somewhat dazed by her overwhelming beauty he replied, "Ah—oh, ah—well, I ah—raised a devil of a blister on my palms last night rowing that boat." With a slightly blushed face from an awareness that his good Sunday suit now seemed rather plain and ordinary when Mary stood next to him, he continued, "That's the trouble with a blister, by the time you feel the pain it's too late."

John and Mary said goodbye to her father and walked out onto the porch with her arm in his. They stood for a moment at the top of the

A Homeplace

stairs where John surveyed the town with a big, proud smile, like a king overlooking his domain.

Mary looked up at him inquisitively and asked, "What's the big smile for?"

"What do you mean?" asked John.

"You look as though someone has just handed you a pot of gold."

Still uplifted by the good news he had just received from Mary's father, and her breathtaking beauty, he replied in an unintelligible murmur, "Someone did."

"What did you say?" Mary asked.

"Never mind." He put his arm around her and held her close to his side as they walked down the steps, into the street, and toward the church. Feelings of guilt returned to Mary as she looked down at the bandages on his hands and considered what John had gone through for her last night.

"Does it hurt very much?"

"What?" John asked.

"Your hands."

"No, not really, only when I close them tightly. It's just a bad spot to have an open sore. Darn things will take forever to heal, 'cause there isn't much a person can do without using their hands."

After a short pause, Mary smiled when a clever reply came to her. "I can think of something you can do without your hands."

"What would that be," he asked. Mary stopped and turned to face him. Standing up on her tiptoes she gave him a long, hard kiss on his lips.

From the Red Pine Weekly Herald, Thursday October 20, 1921

News from in town:

Winner of the quilt drawing last Saturday at the Emmanuel Lutheran Church Fall Festival was Mary McCulloh of Red Pine. The beautiful quilt of a wildflower pattern was made by Mrs. Oliver Carlson, also of Red Pine, and donated to the church drawing as she has done for many years.

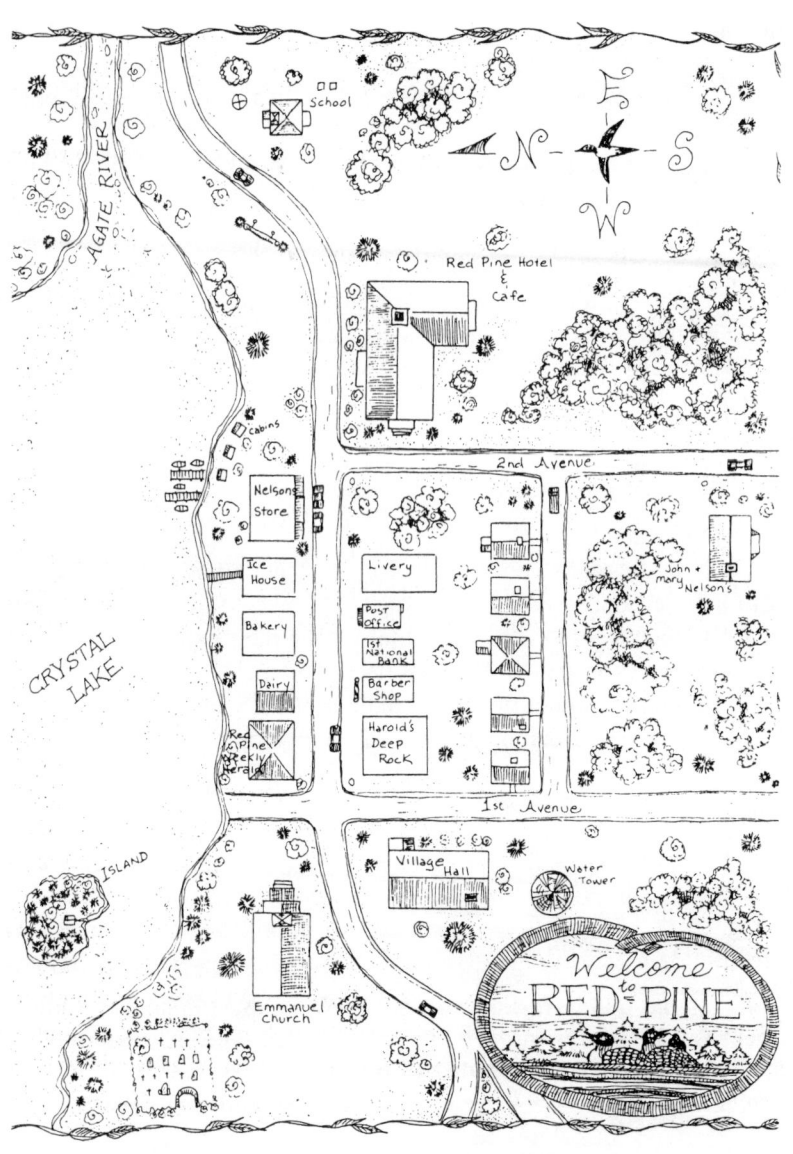

A Homeplace

The Town

In 1921 Red Pine was a quiet little village, with just under 600 inhabitants of predominantly Scandinavian and Scottish descent, the balance being from German and other eastern European heritages. Although the population had steadily declined in step with the once-booming timber harvest, it struggled to remain fairly constant the last several years, unlike its much larger neighbor, Agate Falls, a thriving railroad town. But the growing interest shown by the sportsmen of Minneapolis and St. Paul in the abundance of game fish in Crystal Lake and in the peace and quiet of the north woods, had given hope for the development of a new kind of business in the area, tourism. This new-found interest was enough to raise the optimism of the existing residents, as well as attract a few gambling visionaries who hoped that the recent trend of the big-city sportsmen would continue to grow.

All of the buildings along the hard-packed dirt road of Main Street were once again occupied, thanks to the addition of the first barber in town in over two years. Gustav Schmidke chose to relocate his business to Red Pine, from Agate Falls, after his wife of ten years had run off with his best friend. His inability to recover from the shocking departure of his wife had driven Gus into becoming a lonesome and bitter man, the effects of which, slowly destroyed his once-thriving business. When he finally realized that his own scornfulness had driven his customers away, it was too late to reverse the damage done to his once loyal clientele. He woke one morning, and decided he wanted to start over—new building, new town, new neighbors and new customers. He purchased the little two-story building located next to the First National Bank of Red Pine. Formerly a saloon, the tall, narrow, flat-fronted building had living quarters above the business area, as did most of the businesses in town. After a fresh coat of white paint on the outside and a few modifications within, Gus moved his barbering equipment from his old shop in Agate Falls to his new location in Red Pine, and started his new life.

From the Red Pine Weekly Herald advertisement pages.

PINOL
For itching scalps---Instant relief.

Three preparations complete one treatment.

Pinol Germicide Kills the Dandruff Germ. Contains no acids, no Alkalies nor Artificial Coloring.

Gus' Barber Shop

| Red Pine | Phone 31 | Minnesota |

At the east end of town, and on the north side of Main Street, stood Nelson's General Store. The front of the store had two large show windows separated by a set of double doors. The doors and trim around the multiple panes of glass in each window were dark green and set into the red brick façade. A continuous green and white striped awning above the windows and entrance was lowered when the bright afternoon sun became a nuisance. Two smaller windows above the entrance overlooked Main Street from the living quarters above the store.

Upon entering the store, the customers were greeted by a large "Monarch" cast-iron cook stove located in the center of the sales floor. The black stove with nickel-plated oven doors, could be fueled with either coal or wood. The Nelsons were dealers for that line of stove and used it as a working display. In the winter months, it was used to help heat the store as well as a pot of free coffee and a small kettle of hot apple cider laced with cloves and cinnamon sticks. On Saturdays Mrs. Nelson would bake an apple pie or a few loaves of bread in order to demonstrate the cooking ability of the stove, the aroma of which usually inspired the patrons to add to their grocery list. The clean, but well-worn hardwood flooring creaked beneath the customers' feet as they strolled through the store, passing through an aromatic blend given off by apples and oranges, spices and soaps, coffee beans and teas.

A Homeplace

From the Red Pine Weekly Herald advertisement pages.

Make Your Hens Lay

Feed your chickens ground bones to make them lay eggs. We have them here at 5 cents per pound.

Prepared Lutefisk 3 pounds for 25 cents.

Specials for Saturday
Good Quality Bacon per lb.
24 cents
Fresh Prunes per lb.
11 cents
Good Green Tea per lb.
49 cents
Calumet Baking Powder per lb.
29 cents
High Grade Pea Berry Coffee
34 cents
Canned Sweet Corn per can
12 ½ cents
Jonathan Apples per box
$2.85

Nelson's Store
Phone 60
Delivery Available
MAIN STREET
RED PINE   MINN.

Along the west wall of the store was the stairway that led to the hardware items in the basement. While the wives shopped upstairs, men

The Town

could usually be found there visiting with each other, standing beneath the blue haze of pipe and cigarette smoke that stratified around dim, open light bulbs.

The hardware section of the store had everything from nuts and bolts, to nails and screws, chain or rope, snowshoes and shovels, paint and ladders, light bulbs and small appliances. It was not uncommon on a Saturday to have several male customers from Agate Falls come to purchase items that were unavailable in their town.

The general store and icehouse were carved into a hillside that gently sloped to the lake, giving these two businesses the unique advantage of a basement with ground level access as well as accessibility from the interior stairway.

The icehouse was a large red building with a steep gabled roof. The large vented cupola atop the ridge, designed to vent the build-up of summer heat, was topped with a black metal weather vane. The trim around the doors and the solid wooden shutters over the very few windows were painted white, matching the lettering of the sign that proudly displayed the name of the proprietors: "Hanson's Ice Company." The shutters over the windows were opened only to allow light for working within the cold, clammy building.

In mid-January, when the ice harvest began, a flurry of activity sent block after block of neatly cut pale-blue ice up the long wooden trestle that stretched from the lakeshore to the large double doors of the basement entrance. The ice was then packed away under a fresh aromatic blanket of pine sawdust from the sawmill.

Standing in front of the store and icehouse, and facing west, the other businesses on the north side of Main Street were the Bakery, Schroeder's Meat and Dairy, and a building on the corner of Main Street and First Avenue that housed the offices of Doctor Stevenson and of Phillip Lewis, owner and editor of the "Red Pine Weekly Herald." Dr. Stevenson's office overlooked Main Street, while the entrance to Mr. Lewis' office was around the corner on First Avenue.

Samuel Hopkins and his wife, Laura, lived above their bakery business with their five- year-old daughter, Elizabeth. If it wasn't for the fact that they referred to each other as "mama" and "papa," Sam and Laura would appear more like brother and sister than husband and wife. They both had sandy brown hair, rosy red cheeks and contagious smiles. They were both rather short and stout, and with their constant giggling and good-natured teasing of each other, it was impossible for anyone to leave their store without a smile. Five years ago, they had moved to Red Pine from Duluth where Mr. Hopkins had been employed as a cook at a large hotel. The brown brick veneer on the front of their building closely matched the fresh coat of reddish-brown paint that Sam had recently applied to the narrow lap siding on the remaining three sides of his building. Laura had decided that the window trim and doors should remain beige, the same color as the awnings.

From the Red Pine Weekly Herald advertisement pages.

THE

Pride of the Household

Is the wife when she knows she has good clean up-to-date groceries to cook from. Our meat line is absolutely complete.

We carry only the best meats and sell at a close margin. The main thing is to dispose of it fast and again receive fresh meat.

Our delivery service is at your disposal

Schroeder's Meat and Dairy
Phone 77

Main Street   **Red Pine, Minn.**

Delicious *Velvet* Ice Cream

Eat more Velvet Ice Cream every day. It's your guarantee to better health. Doctors tell you to drink more milk and Velvet Ice Cream is made out of rich pasteurized cream and imitation fruit flavors. Its food value is greater and is very satisfying.

Available At

Hopkins Bakery

Main Street   Phone 20   Red Pine, Minn.

The Town

The last building on the north side of Main Street belonged to Phillip Lewis. Last spring, after graduating from the University of Minnesota with a degree in journalism, he had finally convinced his father to lend him the money to buy a building and start his own newspaper, the "Red Pine Weekly Herald." Phillip's father, Jacob, owned the daily newspaper in Agate Falls, the "Daily Crier," where Phillip had worked since he was twelve years old, before going to college. After buying the large white building, which formerly housed a boat building business that had failed, he discovered that it was much more space than he needed for his newspaper business. All of the printing for the Red Pine Weekly Herald, which came out on Thursdays, was done on a contract basis at his father's presses, saving him from the expense and space requirements for his own equipment.

**It Pays to
Advertise
in the
Red Pine
Weekly
Herald**
Call for prices
Phone 66
**1st Ave.
North
Red Pine**

Phillip Lewis was a tall, awkward, young man with neatly-combed red hair and thick glasses. He was somewhat reserved and appeared to be in a constant state of deep thought. He was friendly enough, but when met on the street, he seldom engaged in conversation beyond "hello" or "good morning." He worked alone, spending many hours in his office typing and writing and preparing his paper for printing every week. Mr. Lewis' ambitious approach to successfully building his newspaper business just as his father had done, left him with no social life to speak of, nor did he seem to care. Until he was able to find a renter for the front half of his building to help defray the payments, he was unable to hire someone to assist him with his business.

A Homeplace

That day finally came when a young doctor from Agate Falls decided to open a practice in Red Pine. Philip Lewis and Dr. Stevenson came to an agreement on the terms of the rent, and Dr. Stevenson hired a carpenter to make the necessary modifications to the front half of the building. Walls were built to create two examination rooms, an office for himself and a small reception and waiting room.

From the Red Pine Weekly Herald, Thursday November 10, 1921

News from in town:

The Red Pine Weekly Herald wishes to welcome to our community Miss Milicent Harper. Miss Harper has accepted the position at the Weekly Herald as Assistant Editor. She is a recent graduate of the University of Iowa and comes to us from her hometown of Storm Lake.

    James Stevenson, originally from Pennsylvania, married a woman he met while attending the University of Minnesota nearly ten years prior. Dr. Stevenson's wife, Cynthia, and their two daughters lived in Agate Falls.
    Originally from St. Paul, Cynthia, an only child, was raised by her mother's parents in Agate Falls. When she was just a toddler, her parents traveled to attend her paternal grandmother's funeral in Chicago. The night before they were to return home, her parents tragically lost their lives in a house fire.
    Dr. Stevenson's practice in Agate Falls was well established, allowing the opportunity to open an office in Red Pine for the convenience of his patients there.
    At the intersection with First Avenue, Main Street skewed in a southwesterly direction between Emmanuel Lutheran Church and its cemetery, and a large fieldstone building housing the fire department, the village hall, and a small library. Behind the village hall, a small, gray, wooden pump house stood beneath the four steel legs of a silver water tower with its bright red top. Painted in large black letters around the cylindrical portion of the tower, the words RED PINE were visible for miles away above the tree tops.
    Across Main Street from Dr. Stevenson's office was Harold Nyberg's garage and filling station. Above Harold's blue and white

painted building stood a large yellow sign, and in blue lettering the words "DEEP ROCK."

Harold was active in the community and on the council of St. Gabriel Catholic Church. He was a friendly man and, as a mechanic, there was none better. A year ago, his wife Madeline, now pregnant with their sixth child and hoping desperately for their first daughter, had finally convinced Harold to sell their little two-bedroom house in the country, and build a new four-bedroom home in town. She was overheard in church one Sunday after moving into their new home, "It's like ve're livingk in a castle comparet to da olt house." Besides the additional room, she thoroughly enjoyed the convenience of living in town. Harold's growing reputation of being excessively thrifty no doubt stemmed from the size of his rapidly growing family, but his worst fault was that he cussed on the same level as any sailor. Fortunately, though, he had the uncanny ability, as if flipping a switch, to control his swearing in the presence of women, children and clergy.

From the Red Pine Weekly Herald advertisement pages.

Harold's Garage

Dependable Petroleum Products

Lasts Longer

DEEP   ROCK

Goes Farther

HIGH TEST GASOLINE

It's Good All The Time

TRY IT !
Phone 301
RED PINE

A Homeplace

Next door to Harold's Garage, and facing east, was Gus' Barber Shop, the First National Bank of Red Pine, the Post Office and the livery stable. The Postmaster, Charles Goshea`, resided in the living quarters above the post office with his wife Pearl and their two young sons. The livery was owned by August Rutger, who also sold and repaired horse-drawn wagons, cutters and carriages.

Three vacant lots stood between the livery stable and the intersection with Second Avenue. Across Second Avenue, was the Red Pine Hotel and Café. The narrow lap siding on the large hotel that overlooked Crystal Lake was painted a soft yellow with white trim around the windows and doors. The doors and shutters added accent with a light peach color.

Equally as impressive as the beauty and cleanliness of the hotel itself, was the lush, green, manicured landscape outside. In recent years, Mary's parents had given her complete responsibility over the grounds surrounding the hotel. She was very fond of her gardens, and the weed-free, colorful flowerbeds were a testimonial to that fact. Her diverse selection of flowers and shrubs ensured a summer-long blend of color and fragrance for the hotel guests as they strolled along the brick paved walkway that meandered throughout the property.

From the Red Pine Weekly Herald advertisement pages.

Spring Chicken Dinner
****
Sundays
12:30 to 2:00 PM
RED PINE HOTEL
&
CAFE

The little white schoolhouse, located just beyond the town line on Main Street, was only four blocks east of the hotel, the last business establishment on that side of the street. Main Street ran east and west about three hundred feet from the southern shore of Crystal Lake. The clear, spring-fed lake was also the source of the Agate River. Traveling east on Main Street toward the school, the road gradually faded northward and ran between the banks of the river and the schoolyard before leaving the town limits. It was an ideal setting for the school and playground. The dense stand of spruce trees on the north side of the school protected it from the howling winter wind and drifting snow. The tall windows on the south side of the building captured the warming effects of the low-angled winter sun, assisting the little wood stove in heating the interior of the schoolhouse. The playground offered a picturesque view of the lake and river, and in the warmer months, many of the children would cross the road and eat their lunch while dangling their bare feet into the cool water of the river.

From the Red Pine Weekly Herald Thursday, November 10, 1921

PROCLAMATION
PRESIDENT HARDING

The nation will stand in silent prayer for two minutes from 12 o-clock noon until 12:02. The occasion will be the burial of an unknown soldier—representative of all unidentified American dead of the world and whose body is being brought from a battle field of France to rest in the central amphitheater of Arlington National Cemetery.

The Red Pine and Agate Falls Posts of the American Legion request the people of Red Pine and Agate Falls and vicinity observe and help celebrate.

ARMISTICE DAY
Friday, November 11, 1921

A Homeplace

From the Red Pine Weekly Herald advertisement pages Thursday, November 10, 1921.

---

100 Laborers Wanted

Buick Motor Company
Flint Michigan

50c Per. Hour
Board 8.50---Free fare if you stay 90 days
For Information apply at
International Labor Agency

525 Michigan St.   Duluth, Minn.

Just Approved !

Nelson's General Store is Now
The Agency for

OLD TOWN CANOE
Main Street

Red Pine,   Minn.

Just Received
New Fords **$663.00**
Equipped with self starter

Meyar's Ford Garage
Located on Cedar Avenue

Agate Falls   Minn.

A Homeplace

Disappointment, Waiting, Wondering

The vibrant colors of autumn that so briefly shared the landscape with the towering evergreens were replaced by stark brown limbs against a gunmetal-gray November sky. Crystal Lake was now completely frozen over, a dusting of snow covered the ground, and the town had settled back into its quiet winter pace. School had been in session for nearly three months and all of the crops were harvested. Construction in the area slowed to a trickle and the tourist trade was over for the season.

Since the delivery of the lumber, John and his father had been working on the island cabin every Saturday except for one when they were waiting for a layer of ice to form on the lake, thick enough to safely support their weight. The shell of the little cabin was framed up and the shingles were on the roof. All that remained was to install the narrow lap siding and the interior finishing work.

After enjoying the Thanksgiving Day holiday, Sarah and Rose minded the store for the remainder of the week so John and his father could spend long hours working on the cabin, taking advantage of the brief vacation from school. Rudy decided to install the small wood stove that would be used for heating and cooking, and early that Friday morning, he and John brought the stove down to the lake and skidded it out across the glass-smooth ice on a makeshift sleigh. Once they arrived at the island, they carried the little cast iron stove up the bank and into the cabin. After installing the stove pipe and roof cap, they lit the stove to break it in, allowing the thin oily film to burn off.

"There," Rudy said, smiling with a sense of accomplishment. "Now we can warm up when we're out here working on the siding. We'll even be able to make a hot lunch and coffee."

John continued to work on the cabin throughout the winter, occasionally assisted by his father and Ray. The following spring, before the resort opened for business, the only task that remained would be to paint the exterior.

Disappointment, Waiting, Wondering

From the Red Pine Weekly Herald, Thursday January 26, 1922

News from in town:

Hanson's Ice Company is making preparations to start the annual ice harvest on Crystal Lake. The severe cold weather of the past two weeks has put the ice in the best of condition for packing.

Mrs. Gunnar Halversen entertained the Norwegian Ladies Aid yesterday afternoon. There was a large attendance and a most pleasant afternoon spent.

The home of Harold Nyberg was quarantined this week due to scarlet fever, one of the little ones being sick.

In late April, the first truly nice day of spring just happened to land on a Saturday, and Red Pine suddenly sprang to life after the long winter. The sun's strength in the cloudless sky would eventually send the temperature soaring to 60 degrees, inspiring a flurry of springtime rituals. All over town people were busy raking in their yards, sweeping their walks, removing storm windows in favor of screens and shaking rugs from their porches, while young children played around remnant puddles of melted snow. Neighbors visited across their white picket fences, and in the background, the crisp, clear song of a bright red cardinal, a rarity at this latitude, seemed to proclaim the beginning of spring from its sunny perch high atop a stately elm tree on the hill above town.

John was working down by the lakeshore preparing the wooden rental boats for the season. Every year the hulls of each boat were inspected for wear and if required, scraped and repainted. It was a boring, tedious job that John hated with a passion, but it had to be done. 'Those boats cost a lot of money,' his father would say. 'We've got to make them last as long as we can.'

A Homeplace

John was busy scraping on one of the boats when Mary noticed him from a second story window of the hotel. She and her mother had started the spring cleaning chores at the hotel. Mary tired rather quickly with the strenuous chores such as flipping mattresses and carrying the heavy rugs down the long flight of stairs and outside to be hung and beaten in the back yard of the hotel. For the last few years, her mother had become increasingly suspicious that Mary's illness as a young girl was related to her loss of stamina, and despite her daughter's stubbornness, tried her best to guard against her over exertion. Ellen knelt to roll up one of the braided rugs and looked up to see her daughter pull the curtain aside with her hand, smiling as she watched John through the window. "Why don't you rest for a while, Mary," her mother offered. "Take this rug down to the back yard and then go across the street and visit with him."

"Thanks, Mom. I think I will. Perhaps I'll see if he'd like to eat lunch together."

"Whew!" said Mary, trying to catch her breath as she approached John. "I remember when I used to look forward to spring. Now it has a whole new meaning."

John looked up to see her smile as she removed her scarf. and fluffed her hair with her fingers. "I know what you mean," he answered, wiping his brow with his forearm. "We finally get a chance to enjoy some nice weather and here we are, working like there's no tomorrow," he added, tossing his scraper on the hull in disgust.

His downcast attitude changed quickly when she said, "Oh well, just think, John, school will be over in less than a month."

"Well, it'll be over for me for good, but you'll have to go back again in the fall," he teased, now smiling.

"Very funny," she replied with a playful jab to his stomach that widened his grin. "How much longer will you be working on these boats?"

"Probably all day. Why?"

"I was wondering if you'd like to have a picnic lunch together?"

"Sure would," he said. During their brief conversation, John watched half attentively as a man stepped out of a truck and started walking toward them. He noted the slight limp in his walk, and a sudden gust of wind toppled the hat from the man's head revealing his bright-red

Disappointment, Waiting, Wondering

curly hair. Returning the hat to his head, he approached them with a smile and said, "Good morning. I'm looking for a young lad by the name of John Nelson. I was told he and his father operated a boat rental business down here."

John noticed that the man's accent seemed similar to Mary's and her parents. "That would be me, Sir," said John. "But we're not quite ready for business yet. It will be a couple more weeks before the fish start biting anyway."

"Oh, I'm not here to rent a boat, Lad. I just wondered if I could have a few minutes of your time."

Mary smiled at the man and excused herself, "I'd better get back to work, John. See you at noon."

"Okay, Mary," said John as she turned and walked away.

"Is that your wife?" asked the man.

"Oh, no, Sir," he chuckled. Someday soon I hope, he thought to himself. "That's my girlfriend."

"Well, you're very lucky to have the interest of such a fine looking lass."

"Yes, Sir, I sure am," he said with a proud smile. They watched as she crossed the street with her long hair swaying rhythmically with her feminine stride. Turning his attention back to the man he asked, "What can I do for you, sir?"

"John," said the man, reaching out and offering his hand. "My name is Patrick Delaney. Pete Hanson and his son Ray from the sawmill referred me to you. I'm an electrician from Duluth, and I am going to start up an electrical business near here this spring. The reason I came to you is that I'm looking for a young man who would be interested in being my apprentice and learning the trade, and, quite honestly, I would like to hire someone who is also familiar with the area and the people. You come very highly recommended as a good worker, reliable, and good with your hands. Is that true, Lad?"

"Well," said John with a blush of modesty. He was no stranger to hard work, but this was the first time he had received such an uplifting compliment from someone other than his parents. It made him feel good to know that Ray and his father thought so highly of his work ethics.
"I suppose so. I do love construction. My father and I built these cabins and just finished the one out on the island," he said, proudly pointing to the cabins in front of them. "But I have to be honest with you, sir, I don't know much about electricity."

A Homeplace

"Well, John, that's what an apprenticeship is all about. What I am proposing to you is this: Come and work for me this summer and find out if you like this type of work. You'll get plenty of experience. Now, if you like it, and decide that you'd like to make it a career, I strongly recommend that you go to a trade school in Minneapolis in the fall. There you'll learn the theory of electricity, and some other things that I can't teach you but are important to know if you are going to be a good journeyman someday. So, what do you think, Lad? Are you interested?"

"Yes, Sir," John replied excitedly. This could be just the job I need to support a family, he thought. "Do you think there'll be enough work to make a decent living?"

"I wouldn't be here if I didn't believe it my boy," replied Mr. Delaney. "I plan on serving about a thirty-mile radius of here. More and more people are putting in electricity, especially on the farms, and the way this country is growing lately, I'm sure we'll have plenty of work. Winter tends to slow down the construction industry up in this neck of the woods, but summers are so busy it easily makes up for it. That's been my experience anyway. I'm a fair man, and all I ask is an honest day's work for an honest day's pay. If you make money for me, I'm not afraid to share it with you. There are no other electrical contractors in this area, and that's why I'm in a bit of a hurry, Lad. I want to get my business set up and going before someone else has the same idea.

"Now, I've given you a lot of information in the last few minutes. I want you to think about it for a while before you make a final decision. I'll be back in town at the end of May. When my children get out of school this spring, we will be moving down here. I'd have liked to get started sooner, but my missus wasn't very happy with the idea of moving the children to a new school with only a month left." Mr. Delaney put his hand on John's shoulder and said with a smile, "I'll give you a little advice you can use if you get married someday. When the women aren't happy, nobody's happy." They both exchanged a chuckle as Mr. Delaney reached for his pocket and withdrew a small piece of paper with his address and phone number on it. Handing it to John he said, "If you have any questions, you can reach me here. Otherwise, I'll see you in about four weeks, okay, Lad?"

"Yes, Sir," said John. "And thanks for the opportunity, Mr. Delaney."

"You can call me Pat," he said as they shook hands again.

Disappointment, Waiting, Wondering

John's mind raced with excitement as he watched Pat Delaney walk back to his truck and drive away. He couldn't believe that an opportunity like this could fall into his lap so unexpectedly. He had always resigned to the idea that he'd be taking over the store and resort from his father someday. Although he wouldn't say he hated it, he was never really enthused about working in the store very much. And except for maintaining the boats each spring, he had grown to enjoy most of the chores associated with the resort because it allowed him to be outside. But now, thanks to Mr. Delaney, he had an option. Working as an electrician would fit well with his love of construction he thought. But most importantly to him, this would be an opportunity to strike out on his own, to be independent and prove that he could start a career and raise a family just like his father had—and the thought made him feel good.

While John labored away on the hulls of the boats, he continued to contemplate his conversation with Mr. Delaney. Two concerns surfaced to cloud his excitement about the opportunity he was considering. How would he explain to his father that he wanted to start a career as an electrician? So many times he recalled, his father had said, 'Someday you'll be running this business, John.' He knew that this would hurt his father's feelings. But I have dreams and desires too, he thought.

Even more troubling to him though, would be the arduous task of telling Mary that he would have to go to Minneapolis for training and not be able to see her. Just when I was about to propose to her too, he thought. I am so in love with her, I can't imagine a day going by and not seeing her. The fact was, because they had grown up across the street from each other and attended a one-room schoolhouse, there was seldom a day in the last several years that they hadn't seen one another. There's no need to say anything to her at this point, he told himself. I've still got lots of time to think this over.

John looked up to see Mary walking toward him with a lunch basket and blanket. The sun was shining brightly, but the slight breeze off the lake was still cold since the ice had only been absent for four days. They spread the blanket next to one of the overturned boats using it to shield themselves from the cool wind. Mary took the sandwiches out and handed one to John.

"Who was that man you were talking to this morning?"

A Homeplace

"His name is Patrick Delaney."

"Oh, well that explains the accent," said Mary.

"What do you mean?"

"Couldn't you tell he was Irish by his accent? she asked while unpacking their lunch.

"I don't know. His accent didn't sound a whole lot different than yours," he said, scratching his head beneath his hat.

Mary rolled her eyes and giggled at his naivete about such matters and said, "What did you two talk about when I left?"

"Oh..." hesitating because of his uncertainty to Mary's reaction, John struggled with whether he should reveal the complete content of their discussion and decided to be selective about what he would tell her. "Mary, you won't believe this," he said. "He offered me a job opportunity as an apprentice electrician."

"Oh, John! Aren't you excited?" she asked as she sprung to her knees and whirled around to face him. Then, puzzled by his lackluster response she asked, "That is *good* news isn't it?"

"Well, yes and no, I guess."

"What do you mean?"

"Well, if I take the job, which I really want to do, my father is going to be very disappointed. I'm sure he's counting on me to work full time with him and become a partner in the store and resort after school is out."

"Oh, I see what you mean," she said as her excitement quickly faded.

"I just have to think about this for a while before I tell him. Please keep this just between you and me."

"I will."

John wanted to tell her that if he took the job he would have to go away for a while but he just couldn't bring himself to that conversation right now. I'll just wait for a better time to tell her, he figured. And who knows? Maybe I'll change my mind about taking Mr. Delaney's offer anyway. No sense stirring up a bee's nest until I'm darn sure about my decision, he thought.

"Oh, by the way, Mary, my mother asked me to tell you and your folks that we are having a little get together after graduation at our house and you're all invited. It's just cake and coffee."

"That's sounds like fun. We'll be there"

Disappointment, Waiting, Wondering

The days and weeks drifted by, and finally the last day of school arrived. The Nelsons and Hansons had decided to combine a graduation celebration for their two boys. Because most of their acquaintances were mutual and lived in town, they would hold the party at the Nelsons. Sarah and Alice had prepared the refreshments in the Nelsons' residence above the general store. After the commencement ceremony at the school, the friends and family gathered in the yard behind the general store. Mary and her parents arrived, as well as Pastor Hansen, a very close friend of the family. Mary's best friend, Diane Larson, who held a secret fondness for Ray, was also there with her mother, but her father had to return to the farm after the ceremony and tend to their dairy herd.

Everyone was seated at the long row of picnic tables pushed together end-to-end when Mr. Nelson stood to make a toast to the future success of the two graduates. Next, Pete Hanson stood up and spoke with a smile saying, " Well, I guess it's no secret what my son, Ray, will be doing in the future. I would like to announce formally that beginning tomorrow, Hanson's Sawmill and Ice Company will now be known as Hanson and Son." At that, everyone clapped their hands in approval as Pete gave Ray a hearty pat on the shoulder.

Not to be outdone, Mr. Nelson stood again to address the gathering, "Although I haven't formally discussed it with John, I think I can safely assume that the same holds true with my son. He knows everything there is to know about our business and I am looking forward to having him as a partner on a full-time basis. Lord knows my back could use the help," he said with a chuckle. Once again everyone applauded and congratulated John, patting him on the back and shaking his hand. Mary, who was sitting across the table from him and could read his face better than his own parents could, watched as he blushed with embarrassment. She could see by his hollow smile how uncomfortable he was with his father's announcement. John's eyes met Mary's, and he could tell that she, too, was uneasy with the secret between them.

The party continued and when it was nearly dark, the guests thanked the Hansons and Nelsons for the refreshments and offered

A Homeplace

congratulations to the two young graduates. After everyone left, Mary helped Mrs. Nelson clean up and bring the dirty dishes up the back stairs to the kitchen. She could see John and his father down by the lake having a talk, and because of the way John was gesturing with his arms, she knew what the conversation was about. She juggled her attention between her conversation with Sarah, and the father-son discussion she was watching through the kitchen window. The two men walked along the beach and then stopped to face each other. Mary watched Rudy turn and walk away as John lifted his arms in disgust, then put his hands in his pockets, walked toward the dock, kicking away at the sand on the beach. Mary finished helping Sarah with the dishes and excused herself saying, "I really should be getting home now, Mrs. Nelson, but thanks for inviting me and my family to such a wonderful party. The food was very good. You and Mrs. Hanson put on a very nice get-together."

"Oh, Mary you're so welcome, and thank you for helping me clean up. I do think the party went very well. Good-bye, Mary."

As Mary descended the last two steps she noticed Mr. Nelson through the window, seated at his desk beneath the soft yellow glow of lights in the basement storeroom. Knocking softly while slowly opening the door, she walked in undetected as he sat with his back to her, both elbows on his desk and his forehead cradled in his hands. Mary subtly cleared her throat to get his attention. When Rudy looked up at her, she could see that he was distraught, yet he smiled at her and said, "Hello, Mary. Did you enjoy the party?"

"Yes, Mr. Nelson, it was very nice. Thank you for inviting me and my folks."

"You're very welcome," he said. Then his frown of concern returned and he said, "Mary, I'm glad you stopped in. Please sit down. I have something I'd like to discuss with you," he said as he pulled another chair beside his desk. She sat down next to him nervously holding her hands, knowing full well what the discussion would be centered on.

"Mary, did John ever tell you what his plans were after school was out?"

"Yes he did, Mr. Nelson," she replied, in a voice so calm it surprised her. "I was there when Mr. Delaney came to talk to him, but I had to get back to work. John explained everything to me later that day."

"Mary, I know that you and John have become very close over the years, so tell me, how do you feel about what he wants to do?"

"....Well, to be honest with you, I was very excited for him. He told me how lucky he was to have an opportunity like this just fall into

Disappointment, Waiting, Wondering

his lap. You know how much he loves to work with his hands and build things. I know how proud he is of the cabins you two have built over the years. In fact, I found out last fall just how much he enjoyed working on the island cabin. He was so excited to start building it, that he forgot all about taking me to the Fall Festival because he wanted to move the lumber out there. Unfortunately, though, I made a fool of myself about it."

Rudy smiled with raised eyebrows at her remark and said, "Yes, I remember that, Mary. He ended up working all night just so he could be with you the next day."

Mary looked down and blushed, embarrassed that Rudy had become aware of her childish temper tantrum from last fall. Then she looked up at Mr. Nelson and continued her appeal, "Mr. Nelson, I will probably never be able to forget how guilty I felt when I put him in a position to have to choose between what I wanted and what he wanted that day. As it turned out, he found a way to do both, even though it cost him a decent night's sleep and blistered hands. To him that was a small price to pay. I know he loves you and Mrs. Nelson very much, and has been agonizing over this decision for weeks. But this time he can't find a way to please everyone, and it's breaking his heart. Mr. Nelson, I don't mean to sound disrespectful, but I think you should try to remember back to when you were young and had an opportunity to move up here and fulfill your dream of starting your own store. Were you put in a position of having to choose between disappointing someone you love and pursuing your dream? You took a risk and won. You have a very successful business. Please, let John have a chance to pursue his opportunity without any guilt attached."

Rudy sat in his chair staring down at the floor, humbled, as the wisdom in Mary's words started to sink in. After a few minutes Rudy looked up at her and said, "You know, Mary, you're right. I've forgotten what it was like to be young and chase my dreams. I have just assumed all these years that he would want to take over the business. I guess I thought I was just being a good parent by working hard to build this business so that my son would be spared the same trials I went through. I'll go to John right now and set things right between us. I can see now that the best thing I can do for my children is to help them realize *their* dreams, not mine." As he stood up he put his arm around Mary's shoulder and said, "Thank you, Mary, for opening my eyes, and my

A Homeplace

mind. You're a very wise young woman and, just between you and me, I wouldn't mind having you as a daughter-in-law."

Blushing, Mary smiled and said, "I'd like that too, Mr. Nelson."

As he walked out the doorway toward the lake, he turned back to her and said, "From now on, you call me Rudy." Mary smiled and nodded affirmatively. She watched from the doorway as John and his father talked and then embraced each other. Her eyes welled with emotion as she realized what a huge burden must have been lifted from John's heart just then.

Mary walked back to the hotel and sat on the front porch overlooking the lake where John and his father continued to talk. When Rudy walked back to the store, John sat on the hull of one of the overturned boats with his knees tucked under his chin, agonizing over how Mary would respond to his leaving for school in the fall. His hair tossed in the gusty northwest wind as he sat facing the tangerine glow of the setting sun behind the silhouettes of towering pines.

The sound of the waves lapping the shoreline and the wind in the trees, silenced Mary's approach as she walked up behind John. Looking back to make sure no one could see, she reached inside his untucked shirt and gently massaged his warm muscular back.

"A penny for your thoughts," she said.

Her touch startled him for an instant and then he smiled at her saying, "Thank you, Mary. Thank you for talking to my father. He is really impressed with your wisdom and so am I. You knew how to explain my feelings better than I could have. Thanks to you, everything is back to normal between my father and me."

"Then why the glum look?"

John swallowed hard then said, "Mary, there is one more thing you need to know about my job opportunity—this fall I will have to go to Minneapolis for the school year to get some training."

She stopped rubbing his back for a moment and he knew that Mary was hurt by what he told her. Then she resumed his gentle back scratch and rested her head on his shoulder. He lifted her chin to look at her and could see the sadness in her moistening eyes.

"Don't you have anything to say to me?"

Mary replied, "There's nothing I can say, John. I meant what I said when I spoke to your father."

"What do you mean?"

Disappointment, Waiting, Wondering

"I told him not to make you choose between your love for him and your dream. The same goes for me too."

He slid down off the hull of the boat and took her into his arms. He gave her a long kiss on the lips and tasted the saltiness of her tears. She put her arms around him and hugged with all her power, nuzzling tightly to his chest. The mournful cry of a loon could be heard from across the lake, and the last band of a chalky, orange sunset disappeared behind the dark tree line.

The following Monday, John started working for Mr. Delaney. The hours were long but he loved the work and quickly decided that he would make arrangements to attend trade school the coming fall as Mr. Delaney had recommended.

John continued to court Mary whenever their busy schedules allowed the opportunity. On windless evenings, he would take her out in the boat where they talked and laughed while rowing back and forth across the bay in front of the resort. Sometimes they sat for hours in the hotel porch swing, watching red sunsets form over the dark glassy water. Their love for each other continued to grow, but as June became July, Mary's impatience over the lack of his marriage proposal increased daily, fueled by the haunting reality that the time was rapidly approaching when John would be leaving for Minneapolis. One morning, her patience exhausted, Mary asked her mother if she had spoken to her father yet about the possibility of an earlier engagement like she had promised last fall. "Yes, I have, Mary. I talked to him about a week after school was out—but I just didn't know what to tell you."

"Why, Mother?"

Reluctantly, because she too was puzzled why John hadn't yet proposed, Ellen explained to her about the conversation she had with her father. "Your father told me that he had already changed his mind and had spoken with John last fall. He said it was the same day as the Fall Festival at church and you were still upstairs getting ready when he came for you. He said he would agree to an earlier engagement, after John graduated, so long as the wedding date would be after you finished your last year of school.

Mary thought for a moment and then said, "So that's what the big smile was about when we left for the church."

Confused, her mother asked, "What in the world are you talking about?"

"When we left for the Fall Festival at church that afternoon, he had the biggest smile on his face that I have ever seen. I thought how it seemed so unusual, especially when he had just put in such a long night and had hurt his hands. I asked him what his big smile was about, and he just said, 'Never mind.'" Then she said, "I wonder why he hasn't proposed to me yet?"

"Maybe he's not sure if he should wait until he's done with trade school," her mother offered.

"Oh, well, I can't worry about it. The last thing in the world I want to do is pressure him into a proposal. He's probably trying to decide when to set a wedding date." Mary smiled as she walked out onto the front porch, considering all the possibilities about when John would pop the question. Her mother was relieved at Mary's mature reaction, saying to herself, "She truly has become a woman."

In her room that evening, Mary lay on her bed and made another entry in her journal.

Thursday evening, July 20, 1922

What on earth is he waiting for? The suspense is becoming more than I can bear. I learned today that John has had Dad's permission to ask me to marry him since school let out in May. Is he trying to decide if he should wait until his schooling is over? I hope not. I'm certain he hasn't changed his mind. He's so romantic. Yesterday, I happened to notice when Mr. Delaney dropped him off after work, and I watched as he frantically worked to help his father finish the daily chores at the resort, just so we can spend some time together. I will be patient, however, for as strong as our love is for each other, I will not risk tarnishing the preciousness of this blossoming relationship by trying to influence him into a proposal before he is ready.

Disappointment, Waiting, Wondering

The summer passed by quickly and Mary continued to wait and wonder. She and John saw each other nearly every evening, and sat together every Sunday at church. Their love continued to deepen, but still John did not propose to her. School would be starting in three weeks, and John would be leaving for Minneapolis soon.

One Friday night in early August, John and Mary were sitting down by the lake on a blanket, hidden from view behind the wide trunk and sprawling crown of a large oak tree. They had been there for over an hour, talking and reminiscing about their childhood and when they first met. John sat with his back against the tree and Mary sat between his legs, leaning back against him with her head resting against his chest. As they looked out over the water, John nervously looked back to make sure they wouldn't be seen as they sat together in the twilight. He was confident in the trust shown by his parents, as well as Mary's, about their being alone together, especially of late, but he understood the wisdom of not fueling the rumor mill and raising the eyebrows in Red Pine.

Mary giggled mischievously as she recalled one of her stories. "I can remember one Saturday afternoon, about five years ago, I stayed for the weekend at Diane Larson's farm. It was a hot afternoon and her older sister, Carol, talked us into going swimming in the Tamarack Creek where it flowed through their pasture. At first, Diane and I didn't want to because we were afraid to be seen by some boys. Carol assured us that there wouldn't be any boys around. 'Its private property,' she said, 'and I do it all the time. The swimming hole is behind a hill and nobody will ever see us.' So we went down to the swimming hole and took off our clothes in the bushes. We took turns swinging out on a rope that Diane's father had put up for them. All of a sudden Carol yelled, 'BOYS!' We started screaming and ran back into the bushes to get dressed. When we looked up, we saw two boys running with their fishing poles as fast as they could go. We never saw who they were and I remember being really nervous about getting teased at school the following Monday."

Snickering with a reddened face, John said, "It just so happens that I know who those boys were."

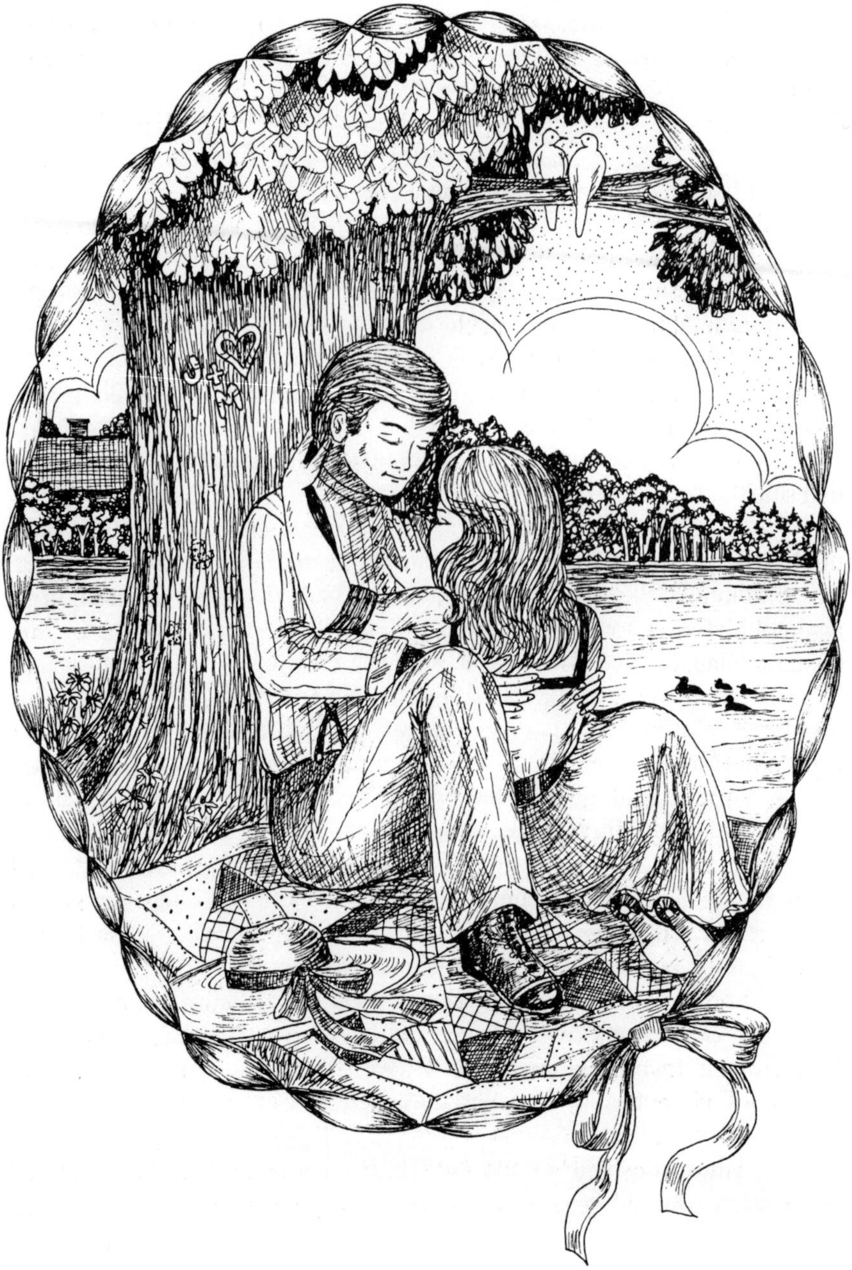

Disappointment, Waiting, Wondering

Mary spun around to face him on her knees and said demandingly, "Who?"

John started laughing and said, "It was—it was me and Ray."

"You're teasing!" said Mary as she thumped John on the chest with her fist. John was now laughing uncontrollably as Mary blushed and continued her affectionate punches. "How did you know we would be there?" she asked, as a smile began melting through her fabricated anger.

"We didn't! We were just following along the bank, trying some different fishing spots. When we came around the bend we saw you girls swimming so we hid in the bushes and watched. When Ray tried to get a better position he slipped into the water. That's when Carol saw him and yelled. We turned around and ran like hell." John's laughter brought tears as he held his aching stomach.

Then Mary asked, "How much did you see?"

John dried his eyes with his sleeve and said, "It'd be easier to tell you what I didn't see."

Mary's blushed darkened and she asked, "Okay then, what didn't you see?"

John fought to hold back his laughter and said, "Well, let me think now. Hmm. Come to think of it about the only thing I didn't see was the bottom of your feet." Immediately, Mary started punching him again while John fell back to the ground helplessly disabled by his hysterical laughter.

"John Nelson, you should be ashamed of yourself for peeking at us. I've a mind to give you a good close look at the bottom of my feet right now!" They began to wrestle on the blanket and then he pinned her on her back, straddling her waist with his legs and holding her arms above her head. She tried bucking him off as their laughter gradually transformed into a tender stare. John slowly lowered his head and kissed Mary on the lips. He kissed her on both sides of the neck as she sighed with pleasure, then he whispered in her ear, "Mary, would you be my wife?"

She lay still for a moment, and then John lifted his head to look her in the eyes. Tears rolled down her cheeks and she said, "Yes, John. Yes, I would love to be your wife. I was so afraid that you would leave for school without asking me."

"I love you, Mary."

They sat on the blanket and talked a while longer. Mary revealed to John that she and her mother knew about the conversation he had last fall with her father about asking for her hand in marriage. It was dark when Mary made her suggestion, "Let's go and tell our parents the good news."

"Okay," said John. "We'll tell your parents first. They have been waiting and wondering just as long as you have."

When John and Mary entered the kitchen of the hotel, her parents were just finishing up some of the dishes. When Ellen saw the smile on Mary's face, she knew right away what had happened. No words were spoken at first. The two women just embraced and then her mother said, " I am so happy for you two."

As soon as Andy heard those words he, too, knew what had happened and reached to shake John's hand. "Finally, it appears that now I will have a son," said Andy. Even his eyes were moist with joyful emotion as their news began to sink in.

"Have you told your parents yet, John?"

"No, Sir. That's our next stop."

"Well, congratulations, you two. When's the big day going to be?"

"We haven't talked about it yet, Sir. Probably sometime next summer when we're both done with school."

"Well good, good. I'm glad you're waiting until then," he said as he gave John a wink of approval. "Let us know if there is anything you'd like us to do in the mean time. We'd like to help any way we can."

"Thank you. That's very kind, sir," said John.

"We had better get over to your folks and give them the good news, John."

"You're right, Mary. My father is usually in bed by ten. He gets up very early you know."

They said goodnight to Mary's folks and crossed the street to the store. Through the window, Sarah could see the couple walk up the back stairway to the kitchen. As they entered the glow of the outside light at the top of the stairs, she knew by the smiles on their faces that something good was about to happen. "Don't go to bed just yet, Rudy! Mary and John are here and I think they'll have something to tell us." Rudy entered the kitchen just as John closed the door.

With his arm around Mary and beaming from ear to ear, John said, "Mother, Father, I have something to tell you that will make you very happy. Mary and I are engaged to be married."

Disappointment, Waiting, Wondering

Sarah's intuition told her that this was going to happen, but she was still overcome with emotion by the reality of their happy announcement. "Oh, I am so happy for you two, this is truly good news. We will be so lucky to have you for a daughter-in-law, Mary. I just knew that someday you two would get married. Didn't you, Rudy?"

"Yeah, I hoped it would work out that way someday," he said with a smile as he winked an eye at Mary. "When's the big day?"

"We haven't set one yet. Probably next summer when we're done with school."

Sarah took a position next to her husband and looked up at him saying, "Well, Rudy, now is as good a time as any to tell them what you told me the other day, don't you think?"

He looked at her with a frown of confusion for a moment until she whispered in his ear. "Oh, yeah," he said. "Yes, I think you're right, Sarah. John, you know those lots up on the hill I bought from old Mr. Younghans several years ago?"

"Yes, Father, I know them. Why?"

"Well," said Rudy. "Your mother and I would like to give them to you and Mary for a wedding present. I've always thought that would be a pretty place to build a home someday. It has such a nice view of the lake and town below."

John smiled with delight at the thought of building a home up there. He remembered how much he enjoyed building the cabins. This would really be a fun challenge, he thought. He looked at Mary and said, " What do you think, Mary? Would you like to live in a new house up on the hill?"

"Oh, John, that would be wonderful. When can we start?"

"Well—we'll have to figure out how much money it would cost but we could start clearing trees tomorrow if we wanted," said John.

"Speaking of trees," said Rudy. "I talked to Pete Hanson about two weeks ago and he said that there are more than enough big pine trees on that acreage to provide all the lumber you would need to frame up a nice size house. He said he would work out a deal where you give him the stumpage, and in exchange, he'll give you all the dry, ready to use dimension lumber you'll need."

"That would be great!" said John. "I'll talk to Ray and Pete tomorrow and see when they can start cutting. It would be nice if we could get the trees cleared yet this fall." He turned to Mary and said excitedly, "I have a set of plans for a house that Mr. Delaney and I wired

A Homeplace

in Agate Falls about a month ago. It's not a very big house, but I really like the layout even though there are a couple of changes I would make if I built it. Would you like to see them?"

"I sure would, John. Bring them out here."

Rose, who was awakened by all the commotion stepped into the kitchen doorway shielding her eyes from the bright light. "What's going on?" she asked .

Mary went over to her and gave her a hug saying, "How do you feel about having me as your sister-in-law?"

Rose looked to her mother for some sign of confirmation and when she saw the glisten of happiness in her mother's eyes and the look of joy on her face, she smiled with delight and returned Mary's affectionate embrace. "Does this mean I get to be in a wedding?" she asked hopefully.

"I was certainly counting on you to be my flower girl, Rose. Will you do that for us?"

"Oh yes, Mary! I'd love to," she said as she shared a proud smile with everyone in the room while rubbing the sleep from her eyes.

John returned to the kitchen with the house plans and spread them out on the kitchen table.

"Oh, John! A two-story, with a front porch and a balcony. I love it!" said Mary.

Rudy and Sarah watched the couple's excitement grow as they turned each page of the blueprints and John carefully explained each detail to Mary. Mary looked back at his parents, smiling with an emotional sparkle in her eyes and said, "I can't believe this is happening to me. In less than an hour we've become engaged, had a building site given to us, and now I have seen what our house is going to look like. This is the happiest day of my life!"

From the Red Pine Weekly Herald, Thursday August 31, 1922

Mr. and Mrs. Andrew McCulloh of Red Pine, announce the engagement of their daughter Mary, to John Nelson, son of Rudolph and Sarah Nelson, also of Red Pine. A wedding date has not been set.

A Homeplace

BACK TO SCHOOL

The next morning, John rose early and hurried up the hill to the land his father had given him. Using his blueprint, measuring tape, and a ball of string, he staked out an approximate location of where the house should be situated on the lot. Ray met him at the building site later that morning to discuss which trees should be removed for the house and the trees that would be included as part of the exchange for framing lumber.

Mary joined them at the noon hour, and over a picnic lunch, John explained to her everything that had been discussed earlier. She was delighted with the way the house would be situated on the lot, but her excitement quickly faded when she learned how many trees would be coming down. She realized that there would have to be some trees removed to accommodate the house but was shocked at the number that would be lost to satisfy the agreement with Ray and his father for the lumber exchange. Her fondness for nature and the beauty it provided, stirred an internal conflict when she realized that some of the trees that would be lost, had stood there for over a century. "In a way it seems so sad, John, that all these trees will be lost just so we can build our house."

Her sudden deflated enthusiasm was unsettling for John, whose mind had been reeling with the thoughts of building a new home. He was at a loss for words about what to say to her, and turned to Ray with a look that pleaded for a clever explanation that would restore the elation that he and Mary had enjoyed the night before. "If we want to start construction next spring we'll have to let Ray take this timber, Mary. We simply don't have enough money saved to make an outright purchase of the framing lumber we need to build," John replied.

Ray understood Mary's concern about the loss of the mature, stately trees and stepped in diplomatically. "Come here you two, I want to show you something." Ray led them into the center of their property among the big stand of red pine that Ray proposed to harvest. "Look up into the crown of these big trees. Notice all the dead branches underneath the canopy of each tree? I can guarantee you that at least some of these trees are already starting to rot deep inside the trunk. Dad and I have taken down many a tree just like these that are hollow near the base. Now look down here on the ground," directing their attention to several waist-high evergreens. "These trees are actually starving for sunlight.

When we remove the big trees, it will be an enormous benefit to these saplings, and you will see the difference next spring when they candle. They will grow much quicker because they won't be in competition for sunlight and moisture. Also, a much wider variety of wildlife will benefit when the bigger trees are removed, and the under-story is allowed to thrive. You need to keep in mind that before man settled here, the trees just blew over or burned naturally in forest fires. All we are really doing is managing a crop like corn or potatoes for example, and using it for our own benefit. The next crop will be the trees and seedlings that are presently waiting patiently for a chance to thrive. The only difference between trees and vegetables is that instead of being ready to harvest each year, it takes trees many decades to become ripe, so to speak."

"I know you're right, Ray," said Mary. "And I have seen places that have been logged off and have grown back quickly, just like you said. It just makes me feel a little guilty to think that something that has been a part of the land for so long will have to be removed to make way for our house."

"I understand how you feel, Mary," Ray replied. "Many times I've thought about the same thing myself. But I have come to realize that this thing we call progress doesn't come without a price."

As John and Ray walked back to the building site, Mary lagged behind, taking a few moments to admire the large stand of red pine, as if to capture the beauty offered by the towering trees and lock it into her memory forever. The scattered intrusions of sunbeams filtering through the dense evergreen boughs reflected off the pink patches of scaly bark, creating a rosy translucent glow that seemed to suspend just above the sparse under-story. She imagined how this small cluster of magnificent flora could be like a temple as she stood among the towering pillars of wood supporting the expansive green dome. As Mary walked back to join Ray and John, she said a silent prayer of thanks for the beauty of nature, and for the harvest they were about to use for their new home.

John was impressed with Ray's knowledge of the timber industry. He was so professional in his explanation to Mary about the tradeoffs when considering the harvesting of trees and the impact on nature. This was a side of Ray that he had never seen before, and even though it sounded like he was reciting from a book, it was obvious that his father was doing an excellent job of grooming him in all aspects of their business.

A Homeplace

When Mary rejoined them, she asked John, "Couldn't we try to leave a few more trees close to the house? I think we would be sorry if we cut too many down. I'm sure we would want some shade during the hot summer to help keep the house cool."

"You're probably right, Mary. I didn't think of that. We can leave some of them until the house is done, and then if we think they're too close we can take them down. I just don't want any to come down in a windstorm and damage the house. Let's mark the ones you want to try and save and I'll tell Ray to leave them."

The remainder of the evenings and Saturdays before John left for Minneapolis were spent helping Ray cut down the trees and move them out to the sawmill. Once the trees were down, John re-staked the area that would be excavated for the house and spread a thick layer of straw over the ground.

John and Mary spent their final day together and had dinner at her parent's house that evening. The following day his father would drive him to the train station.

"Where are you going to stay while you're at school in Minneapolis?" Andy asked during the meal.

"I'll be staying with my aunt and uncle in Minneapolis. Their house is only a mile from the school and I'll be able to walk. My uncle, Richard, and his wife own the house that he and my father grew up in. Their children are grown and gone now, so they have a couple of extra rooms. At least I won't have to pay rent. My uncle said that once I get settled in school I could probably get a part-time job washing dishes or cleaning at one of the restaurants close by. I should be able to earn enough to pay for my schooling and books."

"Well, it sounds like everything should work out pretty well for you John. Will you be able to come home for the holidays?"

"I'm not sure Mr. McCulloh. School will be out for about two weeks around Christmas, but it depends if I have a job that I can get away from and if I can save up enough money for the train fare."

When they finished their meal, John and Mary walked out onto the front porch of the hotel and sat in the swing that overlooked the lake.

Back to School

They sat close to each other, staring straight ahead in an awkward, unfamiliar silence, as if it were their first date. The quiet was occasionally interrupted by the faint clattering of dishes being washed by Mary's parents. John took hold of Mary's hand and when she turned to face him, she noticed the emotional glisten in his eyes and the ripple in his neck as he swallowed hard and began to speak. Still facing forward, he said, "Mary."

"Yes, John."

"Remember the time that I forgot about taking you to the Fall Festival and you were so angry with me you said you never wanted to see my face again?"

"Yes, John, I remember. And I remember you saying how hurt you felt. I'm sorry about that, John. Please forgive me."

He looked at her and smiled, "Don't worry, Mary, I have. But that heartache was nothing compared to what I'm feeling now," he said with a trailing crackle in his voice. She rested her head on his shoulder, and they tightened the grip of their interwoven fingers. The remainder of the evening was spent talking about their future and the construction of their house next spring—anything to avoid the eventual painful word: goodbye.

Early the next morning, Mary watched from a window as John and his father carried John's luggage to the car as they prepared to leave for the train station. She opened her journal and began writing.

September, 1922

I watch as John and his father prepare to leave for the train station this morning. I truly hope everything goes well for John, for I know that he is excited about continuing his training. I wonder if his heart aches as mine does at the thought of such a long absence from each other. I pray that the love we have together that has grown so strong these last months, will not be diminished during our separation.

As their car disappeared from her sight, Mary closed her eyes, and in her mind, gave John a kiss on the lips.

A Homeplace

John was staring out the window of the car, nervously wondering about what lay ahead for him, when he was suddenly distracted by a warm sensation that developed around his mouth. Frowning with bewilderment, he wiped his lips with the back of his hand, examining it as if expecting to find something on the surface of his skin. After a few moments, the sensation passed and the distraction gave way to a supportive conversation initiated by his father.

"I'm very proud of you, Son," said Rudy, as they drove along. "I know how hard it must be to leave Mary behind for so long, especially after all the plans you two have made these last few weeks. But time will go by quicker than you think, and before you know it, you'll be home again. And, you'll have had the schooling you need to make you a better tradesman, which will benefit you for the rest of your life."

"I know you're right, Father," said John. "And I've been excited about going to school almost all summer, but ever since Mary and I became engaged, I've been—well—I suppose you could say, a little worried about leaving. That, and the thought of building a new house, makes me wonder if I shouldn't just stay home and start working on it. I could probably get the cellar dug and foundation in before freeze up."

"I can understand your excitement about getting started on your house, John, but I'm not sure what you mean about being worried about leaving."

"Oh, I'm not worried that something will happen to me, I'm just afraid that Mary's feelings for me might change while I'm gone. You know, like when some of the men went into the army and their girlfriends lost interest in them after awhile. It just seems strange to think that I won't see her for such a long time."

"Well, Son, there are no guarantees in life, especially where people's feelings are concerned. But take it from me, she's very much in love with you, John, believe me, I just know it."

"I know she is, Father, but don't you think that it's easier to stay in love when we see each other everyday? What will happen to those feelings when we're apart for so long? I just hope that she'll keep feeling that way until I get back."

"I think you're getting all worried over nothing, John. Remember, you two are engaged, you've already started to clear the land for the house you're going to build next spring, and she's just as excited about it as you are. Besides, John, what's to say she isn't just as worried about your feelings for her? Remember, you're going to be in the city where there are thousands of girls to meet. I'll bet she's worrying about the same thing you are," Rudy offered, then chuckled.

"Well, maybe you're right. For some reason though, for the last few days I've been thinking that maybe it wouldn't be so bad to stay home and help you with the store and resort."

"I thought you were so excited about being an electrician. Didn't Mr. Delaney say he wanted you to get this schooling?"

"Yeah, he did, but that's only because he wasn't able to go to school when he decided to be an electrician. He told me later that even if I didn't go to school, I'd still be a good electrician, it would just take a little longer is all." They drove along in silence for a few moments and then John said, "Father?"

"Yes, Son."

"Do you remember how disappointed you were when I told you I wanted to go to work for Mr. Delaney?"

"Yes, I do, Son. Why do you ask?"

"I just want you to know that I appreciated that you wanted me to work for you. I realize now that you were working hard to build your business so that someday I'd be able to take over and not have to struggle as hard as you had to, in order to build a business."

"Well, John," said his father, "When I first started out, I was doing it for myself. I had this dream of being independent, and it was quite a gamble at first. Red Pine was really struggling to survive when we moved here. But after awhile our business became fairly solid, as did most businesses in town. I was really proud of what I had done, especially after we started the resort. I never dreamed it would become as good a business as it has. I think that's when I started having thoughts about you taking over someday, and I suppose in a sense I really was doing it for you. It never occurred to me that those thoughts were rather selfish ones. I should have asked you sooner to see if you were interested."

"I was interested, Father. And I would have been proud to do just that, but when the opportunity came along from Mr. Delaney, I was so excited because it was a chance for me to prove that I too could start a career, just like you did."

"I know that now, Son. And thanks to Mary, everything worked out just fine." His father took his eyes off the road for a moment and glanced over to his son saying, "She's a very special woman, John."

A Homeplace

A smile appeared on John's face as he stared through the windshield, then said, "Yeah—she sure is."

They arrived at the train station and were unloading John's luggage just as the train arrived at the depot. After a handshake and final farewell from his father, John boarded the train and took a window seat. As the train left the station on its day-long journey to Minneapolis, John again found himself facing mounting apprehension about leaving Mary behind in pursuit of furthering his education. After all, this would be only the second time he had returned to the city since they moved to Red Pine twelve years ago. Three years ago, his family had returned for his cousin's wedding.

He had no concerns about his boarding arrangements, for he was as fond of his aunt and uncle as they were of him. His uneasiness stemmed from an uncertainty about what to expect at school. Then it began, that inner struggle, when the emotions and doubts from both sides of his decision started tugging with ropes of justification. Will I be able to handle the school work? Make new friends? Get a part-time job? What would be so terribly wrong with running a general store and a resort anyway? It's just a job. Everyone has to work at something to make a living. No, I probably won't be wealthy running a store. But it's not like I'll get rich drilling holes and pulling wire either. And as quickly as it began, his apprehensions gave way to common sense and the realization that he was worrying about things he had no control over. He found comfort recalling that Mr. Delaney said he would do just fine in school. Besides, he thought, if it doesn't work out, what's the worst that can happen? I'll go back to Red Pine and who knows? Maybe I will go to work for my father. That job really isn't so bad. Anyway, I'll be with Mary who loves me just the way I am. And I'll be at home, back in my home place.

He put his head back and tried to get some sleep. He thought about Mary and how lucky he was to have her in his life, and he was looking forward to the time when he could start building their home. As he thought about how much work they had accomplished preparing the building site, he remembered Ray's statement to Mary about how progress does have a price. Then he wondered how long it took Minneapolis to become the size it was, and if it would continue to grow forever. He remembered overhearing many discussions from guests at

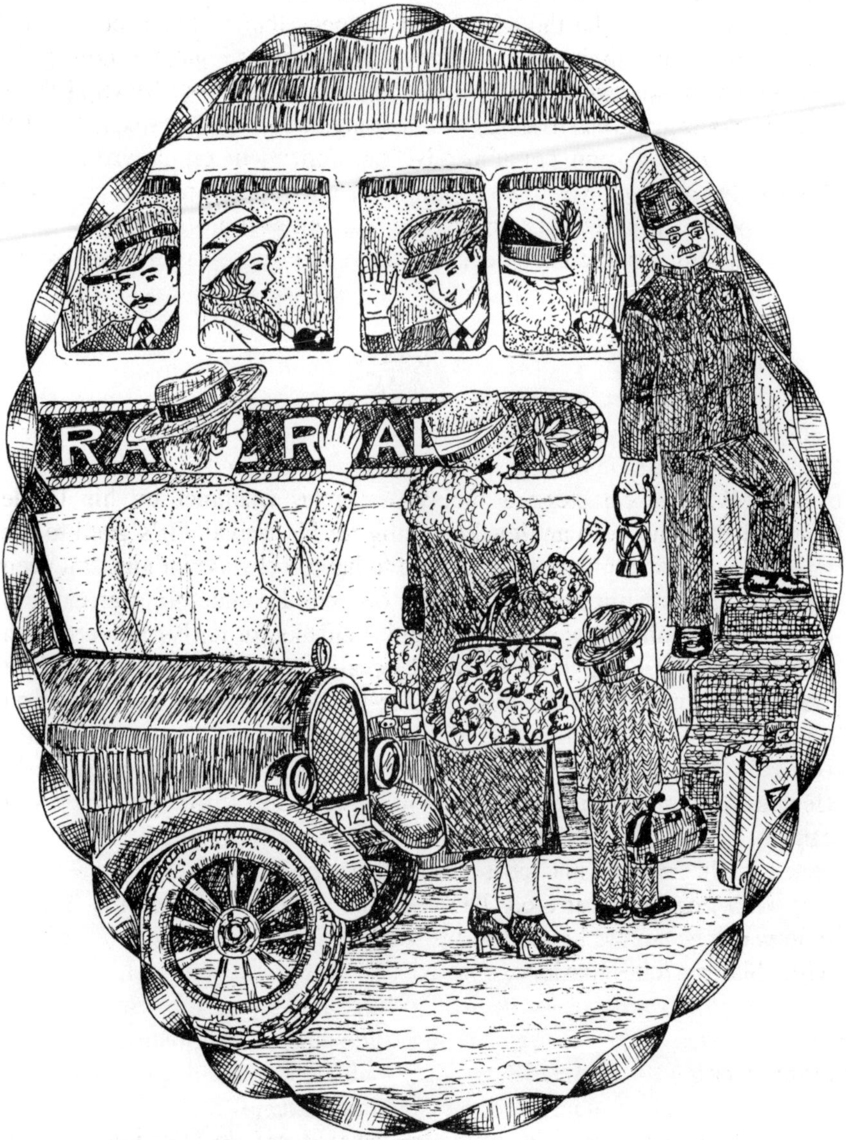

A Homeplace

the resort regarding how good it felt to get away from the city. I wonder why they say that, he thought. What happens that makes a person feel that way about their town? Was it the congestion, the noise, the numerous smoke stacks billowing streams of black soot? More of those drawbacks to progress that Ray was talking about, I suppose. And what about the career I am pursuing? Isn't it dependent on progress? New homes, businesses? Mr. Delaney said the country is growing rapidly. I just hope Red Pine will never become like Minneapolis is today. I don't ever want my town to become an irritation that I need to get away from.

When John stepped off the train he was met by his Uncle Richard who had been anxiously waiting for his arrival. "It's good to see you, John. Your aunt and I are excited to have you stay with us. It's been so quiet around the house now that our children are all married and gone." John smiled and shook his hand. "Thanks for letting me stay with you, Richard. I don't think I would be able to go to school here if it wasn't for your generous offer. I don't know how I'll ever pay you back."

"Well, we're all family and you don't have to pay us back. Besides, I hear you're engaged so you'll need to save all the money you can."

John laughed and said, "Yeah, that's true enough."

When they arrived back at the house, supper was ready. Afterward, he settled himself in his room, and before he went to bed, he wrote his first letter to Mary.

Dear Mary,

I've just settled in my room here at my uncle's house and I thought I'd write you. I have to admit I'm as nervous as a long-tailed cat in a room full of rocking chairs. Don't know quite what to expect when

Back to School

school starts, but I'll give it a good try anyway. Uncle Richard gave me a good lead on a part-time job at one of the restaurants close to the school. It sounds like I'll be able to work every night after school and on Saturdays. He knows the owner of the restaurant very well because he has been delivering supplies there for several years.

I've forgotten what it's like to live in the city. It's so different from Red Pine. I know that I'll never take the peace and quiet of the country for granted again. It's a fun and interesting place to visit, but I don't think I could ever live here permanently anymore. Please know that I love you very much and I pray that we will see each other again soon. I promise to write you at least once a week.

Love John.

The time seemed to go by so slowly for Mary. She and John exchanged letters nearly every week. One week before Thanksgiving she received a letter that read:

Dear Mary,

Seldom a moment goes by that I don't think of you. I love you very much, and at times I think I even get homesick. The good news is that at least I keep busy, what with schoolwork and my job at the restaurant. School is getting a little easier now, and I have made several friends. I am able to put a little money away even after my expenses. My uncle and aunt insist that I don't pay for groceries but I still buy some occasionally because it just doesn't seem right if I don't.

The bad news is, I won't be coming home for Thanksgiving as I will be needed at the restaurant, and at this point, I am afraid to ask for time off for Christmas because I haven't been working here very long and I don't want to make a bad impression.

A Homeplace

You wouldn't believe how many stores there are here, especially downtown. The other day I went into one of them and saw so many different things I wish I could give to you for a Christmas present.

I love getting letters from you so please don't stop sending them. They are a pleasant reminder of why I'm here, and help me stay committed to finishing school so that when I come home to you I'll be a good provider. Keep your fingers crossed that I can find a way to get home for Christmas.

Love John.

Mary began to cry when she read about his uncertainty of coming home for Christmas. She missed John so much and had been looking forward all along to when they could be together for the holidays. This would mean that they wouldn't see each other until he was out of school next spring, and the thought deeply saddened her. She wrote to him right away.

Dear John,

I love you so much that it hurts to think I won't see you for Christmas. Every day that goes by makes me realize how much I need to be with you because of the emptiness inside me. I have so many things to say to you and talk about with you. I was hoping we could set a date for the wedding if you were able to come home for Christmas. You can't believe how hard it is for me to go to school each day and concentrate on my studies. When I look up the hill to our land, all I can think about is building our home and spending the rest of our lives together. I pray every night that somehow I will be able to see you soon.

Please don't spend any money on me for Christmas. The best gift you could ever give me is to hold me in your arms again. Please try to come home for Christmas if you can.

Love always, Mary

Late on a Friday night after working at the restaurant, John lay on his bed with his head propped up with his hand and reread the last part of her letter over and over. He sat up and folded her letter, then looked out the window into the blackness of night, "Dear God, please help me find a way to get home and be with her."

That same night, Mary was invited to spend the night at the home of her best friend, Diane Larson, and she shared some of her love letters with her. Diane said, "I'm so envious of you, Mary. You're so lucky to be in love and engaged to such a nice man. I wish Ray would be more interested in me than he is. What can I do to help him get the hint that I would like to be more than just friends with him? We always have fun when we're together or see each other at church, and I know that he likes me, but he just doesn't seem to want to advance our relationship. For heaven's sake, he has never even tried to hold my hand!"

Mary could see that Diane was frustrated and close to being in tears. "I don't think that there is a lot you can do to push him into love," said Mary. "I know Ray has always been very shy around girls. He is probably afraid to take a chance for fear of being rejected or embarrassed if you were to decline any of his advances. One thing I have noticed though, is that you two are hardly ever alone. You've never been able to walk to or from school together because you live opposite directions from town. When you're at church, there's always a crowd around. I think you should try to get alone with him and give him an opportunity to be brave."

"Any suggestions?" asked Diane.

Mary thought for a moment and said, "Try this. On Sunday, after services are over, tell him that you feel like taking a walk, especially if it's nice outside, and ask him if he'd like to join you. I'm sure he'll say yes because he loves the outdoors. Then, just walk a few blocks and try to get him to talk about something he likes. Ask him if he's done any fishing lately or maybe ask him about his job. When you return from your walk, just thank him for coming with you and tell him how much you've enjoyed his company. He may just open up if you give him a chance. I guess all you can do is plant and water the seed. You can't force it to grow."

"That's sounds like a really good idea," said Diane with a rekindled spirit. "And I don't think it would be very forward to suggest simply taking a walk together, do you?"

"No, not at all," said Mary reassuringly. "He'll never know what hit him. Some men need a little hint—some need a big push." They both shared a devious laugh.

A Homeplace

Before falling asleep that night, Mary stared out the window, thinking about the letter from John that cast some doubt on the possibility of his coming home for Christmas, and her prayers included a request that somehow he could find a way.

Monday at school, John was having lunch with one of his friends who revealed that he was having some financial difficulty, and if he couldn't find a part-time job he would have to drop out of school. After they talked awhile, John had an idea that he thought might work. As they walked back to the classroom, he asked his friend, Scott, if he would be interested in sharing a part-time job with him washing dishes at the restaurant he was working at.

"That would be great," said Scott. "I just need little more money each month. I thought I had enough money saved for school, but the room and board is adding up to more than I had planned for."

John replied, "Let me talk to my boss tonight and I'll see if we can work something out. I work every night and on Saturdays, but I would like to get back home over Christmas to be with my girl. I'm afraid I might lose my job if I asked for any time off, but maybe he would let us share the duties. That way you could work while I'm gone over Christmas and I will have a job when I get back."

"Well, all you can do is ask," said Scott. "Let's hope for the best."

That evening John explained to the owner of the restaurant what he wanted to do. "Let me think about it for awhile and I'll let you know after closing," said Mr. Davis.

After the restaurant closed and John was in the kitchen scrubbing some pots, Mr. Davis approached him and said, "I've thought about your idea John, and I'll agree to it under one condition. You'll have to train him in at no cost to me. I have already taken the time training you in for this job and I don't want to have to do it again. You've always given me an honest night's work, and I trust your friend will be the same way. If he'll agree to those conditions, I'll let you two work this out."

"That sounds fair enough to me, Mr. Davis. I'm sure my friend will agree to that. Thank you."

The next day John told Scott the arrangement and he agreed. The next two nights they went to work together, and John trained Scott in on all the responsibilities of their job. From then on, they alternated each night and Saturdays. It worked well and John would now be able to get home for Christmas. He wrote to Ray and made arrangements to pick him up on Christmas Eve at the train station in Agate Falls, asking him not to tell Mary or his parents so that he could surprise them.

On Christmas Eve, John was waiting impatiently for Ray at the train station in Agate Falls. It was just starting to get dark, the snow was coming down hard, and the wind was steadily increasing. Finally, the blurred yellow beacon of headlights from Ray's truck came into view through the snowy darkness.

"I was beginning to think you forgot about me," said John as he closed the door on the truck and brushed the snow from his shoulders.

"Well, I was beginning to think that I wouldn't make it. I got stuck twice on my way here. The snow isn't so deep, but it's hard to see where you're going at times. You will have to help me watch the power lines on the side of the road so I don't go into the ditch again. When the wind kicks up, the only way you can tell where you are is by the position of the power poles."

When they arrived back in Red Pine and drove down Main Street toward the general store, they noticed several cars and horse-drawn sleighs and cutters in front of the Lutheran Church. "Looks like we're late for services," said Ray as he glanced at his pocket watch.

"I hope we didn't miss much," said John. "Won't Mary be surprised when we come in?" he added as they hurried up the long flight of steps to the church. As the two of them approached the door they could hear the choir singing "Silent Night." They quietly opened the door and John looked to see if he could see Mary. He saw his parents and sister, Rose, sitting near the front. Then he spotted Andy and Ellen on the other side of the aisle about the same distance back. He was puzzled when he didn't see Mary sitting with them, and then he spotted her in the front of the church singing with the choir. He pointed her out to Ray and whispered to him, " Well I guess I won't be able to sneak in and sit next to her like I planned."

"Not unless you want to join the choir right now," Ray chuckled.

A Homeplace

"Oh, well, let's go sit down, Ray." They walked down the aisle, and at first Mary didn't pay much attention. She wasn't expecting to see John, and just figured it must be someone who had come in from the country, late because of the snow. John and Ray sat in the first empty pew about halfway down the aisle. As the choir sang, Mary casually scanned the congregation. She looked to where the two men had sat down, and saw John sitting with Ray. She recognized his big smile right away, and after the initial shock passed, tears of happiness filled her eyes. She was so overcome with emotion that the words to the song would not pass her lips.

Her mother, who had been watching her sing, noticed her reaction. When she looked back and saw John she poked Andy with her elbow and whispered to him, "Look behind you."

He turned around, and seeing John, gave him a big smile and a wink. Andy faced forward again and noticed his daughters display of emotion. Leaning over to Ellen who was also dabbing the corners of her eyes with her handkerchief, he whispered in her ear, "Memories in the making."

Sarah, who was distracted by Ellen's white handkerchief, also looked back and saw her son and Ray sitting together. She looked at Mary, and seeing her emotions, leaned over to Rudy and whispered, "Our son is here; it looks like Mary just received her Christmas present."

When the services were over, the two families and Ray were talking in the back of the church. John had his arm around Mary and was explaining to her how he was hoping to surprise her by sneaking in and sitting next to her. "I didn't know that you joined the choir," said John.

"I joined after you left for school. They needed some more members, and it gives me something to do on Thursday nights. That's when we practice."

Andy McCulloh interrupted the conversation saying, "Folks— Ellen suggested we all head over to the hotel and have some hot cider and cookies. It's just the kind of night that'll make the cider taste extra good."

Ray answered, " I hope you have a room available for me. I don't think I want to try to get home the way it's snowing now. We were lucky we made it from Agate Falls when we did."

"Don't worry, we've got a room for you, Ray," Andy said. "And considering the nice gift you brought our daughter, there'll be no charge." Everyone laughed as they walked out of the church and down the street to the hotel.

The evening passed, and as the Nelsons left for home John said to his parents, " I'll probably be home very late, so don't wait up for me. We'll have a nice talk in the morning."

Then Andy said, "If you'd like, you can spend the night here, John. You can sleep on the couch or share a room with Ray if you want. I know you two have a lot to talk about and I'd hate to see you walk home in the cold so late at night."

"Thanks, Mr. McCulloh. I think I may take you up on that. I'll see you in the morning," John said, addressing his parents as they headed for the door.

"Alright, son. It's good to have you home for Christmas," said Rudy as he, Sarah, and Rose walked out the door.

Mr. and Mrs. McCulloh turned in early, and Ray went to his room. Everyone respected that John and Mary wanted some time together. John explained that he would have to return to Minneapolis in two days so that Scott, who was covering for him at the restaurant, would be able to have a couple of days off before school started again. "That was so nice of Mr. Davis to let you two share that job together," said Mary.

John agreed and went on to say how everything seemed to be working out well for him; staying at his uncle's house, the job he had at the restaurant and the job opportunity with Mr. Delaney. "It's like it was meant to be," he said as he sat down in a large living room chair.

Mary sat on his lap and covered themselves with a heavy quilt. The snow was coming down hard in front of the street lamp and it was very peaceful in the room. She looked to John and asked, "Do you think we should set a date for our wedding before you go back?"

"I was just going to ask you that very question," he said. "I've been thinking about the last Friday in August. How would that be?"

"That would be okay with me," she said, trying to hide her disappointment. Mary was really hoping it would be sooner. "What made you decide on that day?" she asked.

"Well, I figured that by then our house would be ready to move into and we wouldn't have to rent a place."

"Okay," said Mary. "Let's make it a date. Even if we don't have the house quite ready to move into, I'm sure my folks would let us stay at the hotel."

A Homeplace

"That'll be extra incentive for me to get the house done," he said with devious grin.

"Why do you say that?" Mary asked, surprised that John would object at such a generous offer.

"Because, I'm not sure I'd feel comfortable doing what I want to do with you under the same roof as your father." Mary pondered his remark, then responded with a playful giggle and kissed him on the cheek and nuzzled to his chest.

"Its getting late, Mary!" came her mother's voice from the bedroom at the end of the hall. Her parents had left their door slightly ajar, a subtle reminder for Mary and John to keep their attraction to each other under control, especially after John's three-and-a-half month absence.

"Yes, Mother!" Mary replied with an eye-roll and a tone of irritation. They talked for a while longer until Mary noticed John was struggling to keep his eyes open. She sent him to the couch where she covered him with a blanket. She sat beside him on the floor and watched him as he went back to sleep. She ran her fingers through his thick brown hair and said a silent prayer of thanks as she considered all the wonderful things that were part of her life, her parents and future in-laws, and this wonderful man that would soon be her husband. Then she kissed him on the cheek and went to bed.

The winter was going by quickly for John because he was so busy, but not so quickly for Mary. One day in mid-February, John received a letter from Mr. Delaney requesting that if at all possible, would he be able to leave school and come back to work by the end of March. The letter explained that he needed John's help with a big electrical project in Agate Falls in the spring. The town had awarded Mr. Delaney the project of installing electric street lighting in a new development of the town. It would take the two of them most of the summer to do the job, and the contract stated that it must be completed by August 1st. John informed his instructors at school about the situation. They gave him permission to leave, and because of the special circumstances, he would be allowed to return to school the following year and resume his studies.

Back to School

From the Red Pine Weekly Herald, Thursday April 5, 1923

News from in town:

Last Saturday, John Nelson, son of Rudy and Sarah Nelson of Red Pine, returned home from Minneapolis where he was attending trade school for electrical construction. He was home just in time for Easter and plans to start construction of a new home.

The House

On a warm, muggy Friday afternoon on the last day of August, just four hours before his wedding was to begin, John was still working on the new home that he had started nearly six months earlier. He had taken the day off from his job as an electrician and had finished his responsibilities with the wedding arrangements earlier in the day. He thought that by starting to install some of the woodwork he would also release some of the nervous tension that had been building the last few days. He had hopes of being finished with the house before he moved in with his new bride after their honeymoon, but in spite of his diligence, delays caused by weather and material availability left him two weeks behind schedule. The master bedroom was finished, but the remainder of the interior still required the installation of the woodwork and painting. The weather would no longer be a factor, and all the materials needed to finish were on site.

The sun was hot, and John decided to rest for a while, taking advantage of the shade under one of the large oak trees in the backyard that Mary had requested to spare when they cleared the building site. He sat down at the base of the tree, dried his brow with a handkerchief and took a long drink of water. Closing his eyes, he rested his head against the tree, and began to reflect on all the events and accomplishments of the last year.

It was barely one year ago that he and Mary had become engaged. John was now in his second year as an apprentice electrician and Mary, who had turned nineteen in June, would continue working at her parent's hotel. He thought about how fortunate he and Mary were to receive such a generous gift of land from his parents. The view of the town and lake from atop the hill was even more picturesque than they dreamed it would be, and the heavily-wooded building site provided all the lumber that was needed to frame and sheath the entire house. The rest of the materials were paid for with money John had saved up over the years and a small loan from his father.

He was glad he had taken the advice of his father last fall and spread a thick layer of straw on the ground where he would begin digging the basement in the spring. The straw, along with an early, heavy snow, prevented the formation of frost and allowed him to begin digging the basement and footings in early April.

The House

The basement portion—excavated by hand with shovels and picks—was just under six-feet deep and 12-feet square; large enough to accommodate the boiler, the coal bin, and the root cellar. The rest of the area beneath the main floor was crawl space. It took John and Ray nearly three weeks to complete the excavation of the basement and footings.

Throughout the summer, John and Ray spent nearly all of their free time building the house. They were limited to working in the evenings and on Saturdays, due to the obligations of their regular jobs, and he recalled his frustrations about the slow rate at which the project seemed to progress at first. He remembered how desperately he wanted to work on Sundays after the church service, but knew that it would upset his parents as well as Mary if he did so. Both his parents and Mary's, rigidly adhered to keeping Sunday a day of worship and relaxation. And even though the café at the hotel would offer a noon dinner, ("A necessary evil in order for their business to survive," according to Andrew McCulloh) it only required a couple hours of their time, and as soon as the dinner was over, Mary's parents took the rest of the day off..

As spring gradually advanced, the increasing amount of daylight allowed John and Ray to make great progress. By the end of April, they had completed the rock and mortar foundation and had all the sub-flooring installed for the main level. By mid May, all exterior walls of the first floor were in place as well as the floor joists for the second floor. There were four evenings and a Saturday lost to rain, and two evenings lost to take advantage of the good spring fishing. Once the framing and the roof rafters were in place, John was able to do most of the remaining construction himself.

The days and weeks went by, and by the middle of August, John was ready to have the hardwood floors installed. He hired a man by the name of Sven Holmgren, who farmed just outside of Agate Falls, and who for many years had supplemented his farm income by doing carpentry work. John had met Sven when he and Mr. Delaney were wiring a new home several weeks prior and was very impressed with his craftsmanship. While the flooring was being installed, John was able to focus his efforts on painting the exterior of the home after he and Mary had finally come to terms on a color scheme. They were in agreement on painting the siding white, but couldn't decide on the color of the trim. After much discussion, and John's recollection of Mr. Delaney's advice about keeping the women happy, they settled on dark blue trim, Mary's favorite color.

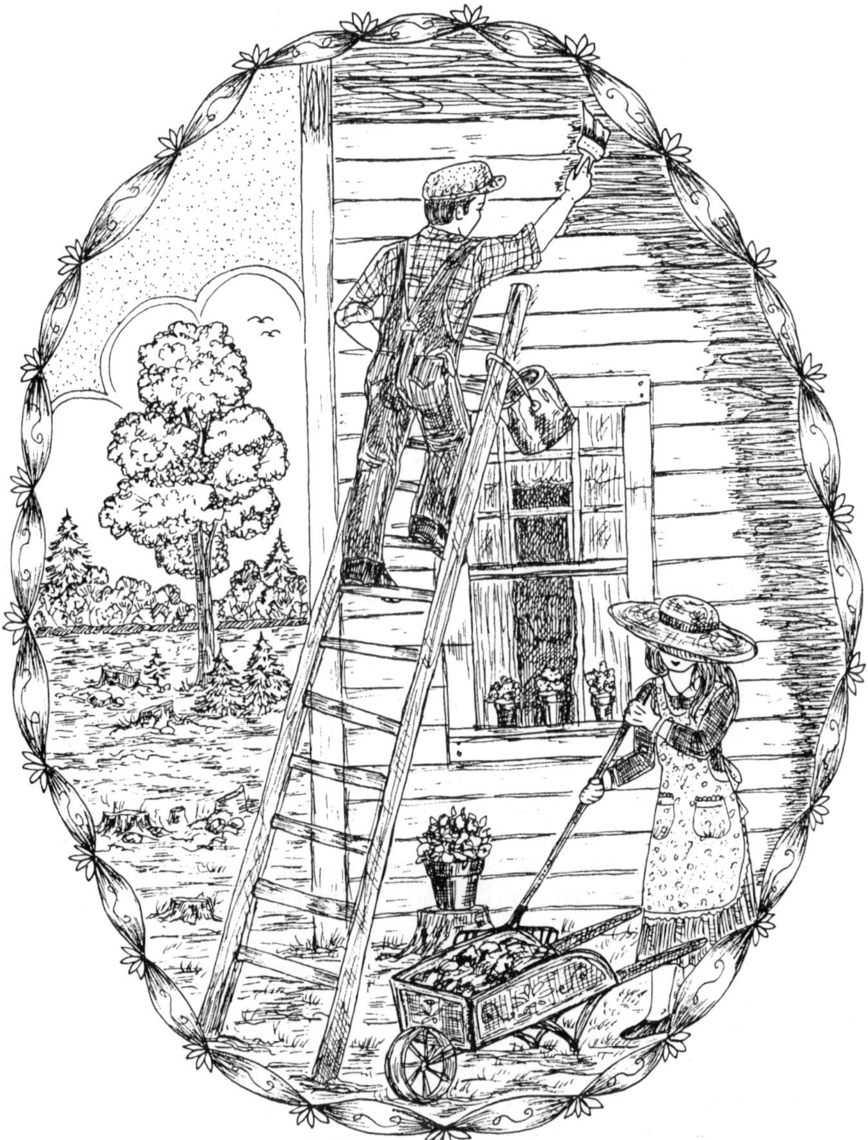

The House

During the summer, while John and Ray concentrated their efforts on the construction of the house, Mary spent most of her free time working on the yard and landscaping. She spent many hours picking rocks and roots, raking the dirt level and reseeding the grass. The enormous amount of work involved in preparing the soil in their new yard was more strenuous than Mary was used to, but she had learned long ago how to pace herself by taking her time and resting frequently. She even started a vegetable garden and transplanted some of her favorite wildflowers from a meadow down the road.

A light breeze swept across John's face and he could feel himself getting drowsy. He stood up, stretched for a moment, then carried the two saw horses up the stairs and into the bedroom with the other tools and woodwork. He had just set up the miter box to begin the installation of the woodwork when he heard the "ahoooogha" of a horn. He looked out the window, and saw Ray, leaning on the fender of a brand new delivery truck holding up a bottle of soda. "I've got a cold one for you if you can pull yourself away from this house," he shouted. "Besides, you'll have to stop anyway and get cleaned up for the wedding."

"I've already got everything ready for the wedding, and it will only take me half an hour or so to clean up and get dressed," he replied. "I'll be right down."

As John walked towards the truck, Ray met him halfway up the walk and handed him a cold bottle of soda saying, "What do you think of her?" turning his attention to the new delivery truck.

"Mighty nice rig," John replied as he walked around the truck in admiration. "The lumber business must be doing very well."

"We needed a little more horsepower and a heavier suspension. With this truck we should be able to get through anything now," Ray declared. "Here's the good part, though, John." He climbed in and sat behind the wheel, pushed a button and the engine turned over and started immediately. Smiling from ear to ear Ray said loudly, "Auto start! No more cranking!" Ray shut the engine off and stood in the road next to John as they continued to look the truck over while enjoying their sodas. After awhile they walked back toward the house and Ray said, "Let's see how you're coming along, John."

"We're getting close," he answered, "We were able to get the master bedroom trimmed out and painted like we had hoped to. I guess

A Homeplace

we'll have to wait 'til after the honeymoon and take on one room at a time."

"Nothin' wrong with that," said Ray. "At least you'll be able to move in when you get back."

They proceeded up the front steps, and while standing for a moment in the shade of the covered porch, Ray commented on the nice view of the town below and of the lake. "Just think" said Ray, "Nine months from now you may be sitting out here in your rocking chair with your new baby," he chuckled.

"Now hold on, Ray! I'm not even married yet and you've already got me rocking a baby?"

"Well, you were just telling me the other day that Mary said she wanted to start a family right away. I just figured that a healthy, young couple like you two would probably get down to business tonight, and by next May or June you'll be out here on those warm summer evenings rocking your little baby." Ray nudged him with his elbow and continued his good-natured teasing by adding, "In fact, old buddy, with this nice view of the lake, you'll be able to see me out in the boat while I'm anchored over our honey hole pulling in one walleye after another." They both laughed as they turned and walked through the front door and into the foyer.

Once inside, John and Ray sipped their sodas as they strolled admiringly through the living room, dining room, kitchen and back to the foyer where the foot of the stairs led to the second floor. As they passed through the sunny, vacant rooms, their footsteps on the hard maple flooring echoed off the gray, newly-plastered walls. Each of the generously-sized windows in the dining room along with the front porch and bay windows in the living room, offered their own unique view of the beautifully-landscaped yard.

The kitchen was small, allowing only a small table next to a window overlooking the back yard. The rest of the space was dedicated to cupboards, an ice box, and a large black Monarch cook-stove. The kitchen sink was fastened to the wall below a window overlooking the side yard, and a short curtain that hung below the sink concealed the plumbing and two small shelves.

As they toured the upstairs, Ray said, "It's obvious to me that an electrician is going to live here. There must be three or four outlets in each room besides the ceiling light! Why so many?"

The House

"Well" said John. "It's a whole lot easier to put them in before the lathe and plaster goes on. It may seem like I over did it, but I'll bet someday people will wish they had more outlets in their homes than they're getting now. In trade school, they referred to them as convenience outlets. Seems to me they'd be even more convenient if there were one on each wall."

"Maybe so" said Ray.

John and Ray were coming down the stairs and as they finished up their sodas, Ray said "If you want I can drop you off at your folks' so you can get ready for the wedding."

"Oh, that's okay, Ray, there's plenty of time for me to get ready. I'll just close up the house and walk home. It's only two blocks away, and down hill at that, but I'd appreciate if you could pick me up on your way to the church."

"You bet," said Ray. "What time are we supposed to be there?"

"Well" said John. "Mary wants us to be there an hour before the ceremony starts, so pick me up at six."

"Okay then, John, see ya later." Ray hopped back into his truck and drove off toward home. John returned inside, closed all the windows and the big front door, then walked to the edge of the road where he turned back to admire the front of the house. He was very proud of the work he had done and how fast everything had come together, especially considering they only worked on the house in the evenings and on Saturdays. He thought to himself how lucky he was to have such a good friend as Ray. He had given so unselfishly of his time, and the only compensation he wanted was a reciprocal effort next year when he built his house. Ray had spent many evenings helping John frame up the house and install the narrow lap siding and cedar shakes, saving him considerable time and money. John did his own wiring, which left only the plumbing, plastering, and flooring to be hired out.

It was about four-o-clock in the afternoon as John started to walk down the hill into town when he saw Mary running towards him. He noticed how she seemed to glow with excitement in anticipation of their wedding. As they met they put their arms around each other's waists and walked back toward the house. "Are you nervous?" asked Mary with a giggle, trying to catch her breath.

"A little," said John. "But not as much as I thought I'd be. What were you running for?"

A Homeplace

"I slipped out of the house and didn't want my mother to see me. You know, you're not supposed to see the bride before the wedding. She went down to the church to check on things, and I knew you'd be up here. I just had to see you, John."

"I'm glad you did, Mary. Now, how about you?" asked John. "Are you nervous?"

"Not a bit" she replied. "Mom has everything under control."

They walked up to the porch together, and John opened the front door and glanced back to make sure they weren't seen. He took Mary by the hand and quickly led her inside shutting the door behind them. "I guess the next time we walk through this door I'll have to carry you in."

"Yes you will, Mr. Nelson," said Mary. "And the next time we come in here I'll be Mrs. Nelson."

Mary put her arms around his neck and on her tiptoes gave him a long, passionate kiss. "I love you so much, John. And I am so proud of you to be able to do so much of the work on the house yourself. It still seems like a dream that we're able to move into a new home right after our wedding."

"I love you too, Mary. I just wish I could have been completely done. We'll just have to finish one room at a time."

"That doesn't bother me one bit," she said. "We don't have any furniture anyway except for my bedroom set." John returned her embrace and began kissing her on the mouth. His lips slowly moved to her neck, sending waves of tingling goose bumps down her back. He held her tightly in his arms and could feel her excitement grow. She returned his kisses and as their lips met once again, John could feel the warmth of her passion radiate from her face. She felt his warm, callused hands move down her neck and over the surface of her clothing, then, whispering softly in his ear she said, "John, we've waited this long, we can wait a few more hours."

His lips continued to caress her neck for a moment and then he sighed. "You're right, Mary. I can see now that you'll be the prudent partner in this relationship."

Still with her arms around his neck, she affectionately rubbed his nose with hers saying, "I promise that tonight you'll see it was worth the wait," said Mary.

"I'm going to hold you to that," he replied with a smile.

Mary adjusted her clothing and her hair as they walked out the front door and onto the front porch. John closed the door and they both

The House

stood on the porch to admire the view of the town and the lake below. John held Mary's hand and chuckled saying, "Ray was here earlier and said that nine months from now, I'll be able to see him from here out on the lake fishing from his boat, while I'm rocking our new baby."

Mary replied, "Don't you worry, John, baby or no baby you'll still be able to go fishing."

Then he said, "Come with me, Mary, I want to show you something." He took her hand and they walked down the steps and around to the back yard to a large oak tree. John pointed to a carving he had made in the tree. He had removed the bark from the tree in the shape of a heart and carved the words, "Mary & John, Aug. 31, 1923."

"Oh, John, it's beautiful. When did you do that?"

"Last evening. I'm glad you talked me into leaving this tree here," he said, looking up into the branches admiringly. "It's so shady that I sat down to rest a while ago and darn near fell asleep." Then he said with a chuckle, "Besides, now when I look out the kitchen window and see the carving, I won't forget our anniversary."

Mary smiled at him and said, "Don't worry, I won't let you forget."

They walked down the hill together toward town. John reached for Mary's hand, and she quickly put her arm around his waist. They walked along the side of the road to the intersection with Main Street, where she turned to John and said "I had better get home and start getting ready. Mom has a house full of company, and even though she insists that everything is under control, I should see if she needs help."

"Okay," said John. "I should probably get home too. My folks may need some help bringing the food and some ice down to the church kitchen. Dad and I set up the tables and chairs for the reception earlier this morning, so there really isn't much left to do." Mary gave John a peck on the cheek, then started across the street and said, "Now you won't change your mind and leave me standing at the altar will you, John Nelson?"

"Are you kidding?" replied John. "I'd rather have a tooth pulled than face my folks if I backed out now. How about you, Miss McCulloh? Any chance you'll change your mind?"

"Guess you'll just have to wait and see, Mr. Nelson!" Mary shouted, as she carefully backed up the stairs to the front porch of the hotel. Their eyes were concentrated on each other, and neither one wanted to break the connection. Mary kept watching from the open

A Homeplace

doorway to the hotel as John slowly crossed the street to the general store. John never blinked an eye, and as he stepped onto the porch his toe caught the edge of the stoop, and he went down with a thud. Mary covered her mouth as she gasped, but her concern was quickly replaced with laughter when she saw him quickly jump to his feet and brush his hair back. His face was red with embarrassment, and as he glanced back towards Mary, he was relieved to see that she was not looking. She had quickly gone inside the hotel and shut the door as John was getting back to his feet, knowing he would be even more embarrassed if he thought she had watched him fall. Mary giggled as she hurried up the stairs to her room, when she unexpectedly met her mother in the hall. Ellen asked, "Mary! what's so amusing?"

She replied with a dreamy sigh, "Oh nothing, Mother. I just love that man!"

"Oh, Mary, please don't tell me you let John see you before the wedding? You know it's bad luck!"

"Oh, don't worry, Mother, everything will be just fine, you'll see." She sat at the table by her bedroom window and opened her journal.

August 31, 1923

In just a few hours, I will be Mrs. John Nelson. This is such an exciting day. I've always heard that weddings are frequently times of nervousness, fear and flaring emotions. Thank goodness I seem to have been spared that, so far anyway.

John and I walked through the house together this afternoon. I could tell he is disappointed that he didn't finish completely before we move in, but I will be perfectly content to move in and finish our home as time and money permit. Something tells me, though, that there will be more time than money, for a while anyway. The house will certainly seem spacious as we scarcely have any furnishings. Mom and Dad allowed me to take my bedroom furniture, and John's folks gave us a kitchen table and two chairs. It certainly won't take us long to move in.

The Wedding

John stood in front of the mirror above his dresser, fastidiously combing his hair, when he heard the horn from Ray's truck below his bedroom window. He leaned out the window and shouted, "Be right down, Ray."

As he left his room, he was met in the hall by his parents and sister. His mother approached him and said, "Turn around, Son, so I can have a good look at you." He slowly turned in place before his mother and felt her hand as she brushed down against the back of his suit coat, as if to remove some nuisance lint or thread. Completing his turn, he faced his mother and said, "Well, what do you think?"

He noticed the tears form in his mother's eyes when she replied, "I think you are the most handsome young man I have ever seen, and I am very proud of you."

"We're all proud of you, Son," added his father while his mother kissed him on the cheek and hugged him. Then his father embraced him, and he noticed that the feeling of strength and solidity in his father's arms and chest still felt the same as it did when he received a hug as a young boy. Then John turned to his younger sister, Rose, who was already wiping the tears from her eyes. "Hey, little Sis, don't cry. I am not going away, I am just getting married."

"But you won't be living here with us any more, John," Rose replied.

"That's true, but our house is just two blocks away. In fact, if you move into my old bedroom, you'll be able to see it from the window. Besides, you can come and visit us anytime you want. Now wipe away those tears, because we don't want our flower girl to have wet cheeks when she comes down the aisle." Rose chuckled as she dried her eyes. John gave her a kiss on the forehead and said, "I have to get going now before Ray gets antsy." Immediately the horn from Ray's truck sounded again.

"Too late," Rose shouted, as John scurried down the steps.

"I swear, Ray is more nervous about this wedding than I am," John mumbled as he went out the door.

The Wedding

As John hopped into the truck, Ray said, "Let's go or we'll be late."

"It's just now six o-clock and we're only two blocks from the church. What are you so nervous about, Ray? I'm the one who's getting married."

"Because this is the first wedding I've ever been in, and I just want everything to go well."

"It'll be just fine," he insisted, rolling his eyes at the sight of Ray's white knuckles on the steering wheel.

Ray's truck pulled up into the churchyard, and they could see the McCullohs' car parked in the back near the basement door. John and Ray stepped out of the truck and climbed the long flight of stairs to the front door of the church. When they entered, Pastor Adams had just finished opening the windows in the nave, and was about to prop the doors open in the narthex in order to displace the accumulation of warm, stuffy air in the church. When John felt the uncomfortable atmosphere inside the church, he was glad his mother had sent him out to the island cabin early in the morning to open the windows. "Good evening, gentlemen," said the pastor with a cheerful voice and big smile.

"Good evening to you, Pastor," replied John. Ray acknowledged the pastor with a nod and a smile. The three men exchanged handshakes, and then John asked, "Is there anything Ray and I can do to help you get the church ready?"

"I think everything is taken care of," said the pastor. "Your bride to be and her mother and the rest of the ladies are downstairs getting dressed. I was just getting the church aired out when you two arrived."

"Boy, it sure is warm in here," said John. "I should have come earlier and opened the windows".

"Oh, that's not necessary," said Pastor Adams. "This place really airs out quick once the doors and windows are opened, especially the way the breeze has picked up this evening."

While the pastor was talking, the sound of footsteps on the wooden stairs echoed throughout the church as Mary's father, Andrew, approached them from the stairway leading to the church basement. With a big smile he said, "Well, John, I see you didn't change your mind about matrimony," he chuckled as he put his hand on John's shoulder.

John returned the smile and said, "How are the ladies doing, Andy?"

"Oh, you know how women can be when it comes to their appearance. Everything has to be just perfect or else! By the way, my wife told me to remind you it's bad luck to see the bride before the wedding, so you better not go downstairs."

John smiled and said, "Did your sister and her husband arrive from Jamestown okay?"

"Yes they did, John. I picked them up at the train station in Agate Falls late this afternoon. They said they couldn't believe how warm it was here. Back in North Dakota it was only about sixty degrees when they left for Red Pine."

"I suppose that weather will be here by tomorrow," said John.

"Yeah, well, this *is* the last day of August, and I can remember many a time when we've had a frost in the first week of September," Andy replied. "I sure hope you've put up some firewood out at that cabin you two are staying at tonight."

"There's enough for a couple of days anyway," said John. "I was out there last Sunday and brought out some supplies and made sure everything was in order for us to stay out there."

Three weeks ago, John and Mary had rowed out to the island cabin on a Sunday afternoon and decided that it would be a very romantic place to spend their wedding night. The cabin wasn't scheduled to be rented for the rest of the season, and they chose not to travel very far for a honeymoon in order to allow them to be back on Saturday afternoon so they could begin moving into their new house.

It was now about six-thirty, and people were steadily entering the church. Nearly a hundred family and friends were expected to attend the ceremony in the little Lutheran church that had seating for only about 120 people. John and Ray, along with John's and Mary's parents, were greeting people as they entered the church. John's anxiety heightened as the ceremony quickly approached, and at five minutes to seven, Pastor Adams gave the signal for Mrs. Carlson to begin playing the piano.

As the music began, the noisy visitation of friends and relatives seated in the pews quieted, and John and Ray took their positions at the front of the church, just as they had practiced the night before. John stood behind Ray and they both faced the rear of the church in anticipation of the procession that was to start. Upon a signal from Pastor

The Wedding

Adams, Mary's father had gone down to the basement of the church to tell the ladies that the ceremony was to begin.

As soon as John's sister, Rose, appeared in the doorway, Mrs. Carlson finished the last stanza of the song she was playing and began to play "The Wedding March." Rose started down the aisle and distributed the cut wild-flowers from her basket to each side of the narrow white runner as she progressed to the front of the church. When she was nearly to the front, Mary's maid of honor, Diane, started down the aisle. Like Rose, she wore a dark blue full-length gown with a white bonnet and a bouquet of daisies in her hand. As Diane passed the front pew, Ray stepped out into the aisle and offered his arm to her. They then proceeded together up the three steps to the altar area and separated, taking a position on each side of Pastor Adams who was facing the congregation.

John stepped forward to the edge of the aisle, and out of the corner of his eye he could see Mr. McCulloh and Mary appear in the doorway at the back of the church. He felt a bead of sweat trace down the middle of his back and, with his heart pounding, he glanced over at the front pew where his mother and father were standing. His father smiled and winked at him while his mother forced a smile as she carefully blotted the tears from her eyes with the corner of her handkerchief. He turned to focus his attention on Mary as she proceeded down the aisle. His nervousness suddenly vanished as his concentration shifted to her splendid beauty. The cadence in her stride, the confidence in her smile, left no doubt of her desire to become his wife. She was easily the most beautiful woman he had ever seen. Her long black hair in contrast with the white dress was accentuated each time she passed through the colorful beams of sunlight shining through the tall stained glass windows of the church. As they approached the front pew, Mr. McCulloh released Mary's arm. He gave his daughter a kiss on the cheek and joined his wife in the pew.

Mary turned to John, and he offered his arm to her. They walked up the short flight of stairs and knelt down in front of Pastor Adams. With a big smile on his face, the pastor gestured for everyone to be seated and began to speak. It was customary for Pastor Adams to give a short homily before the wedding ceremony began, especially when it concerned two long-standing members such as Mary and John and his close friendship with their two families.

"My dear friends in Christ," he began. "Without a doubt, two of the most precious and rewarding aspects of my service to God are the baptism of a child into the Christian faith, and the joining of a young Christian man and woman in holy matrimony. Today, we are assembled here to witness, celebrate, and support, John Nelson and Mary McCulloh, who have chosen to live the rest of their lives together as man and wife. I find it especially rewarding to join these two young people, who have regularly attended this church since they were young children. We know that they have the tools for a successful marriage because of their strong Christian upbringing. Their support has come not just from their parents and relatives, but also from their congregation. My friends, this gives them a huge advantage for a long happy marriage.

Now, we all know that there will be disagreements between them. We know that they will be faced with hard times as well as good times. We know that if they are blessed with children, the joys, as well as the sorrows that they will be faced with when raising them. But—my friends, we also know that John and Mary have the two most important tools they need to help themselves through the difficult times as well as the good times. Those tools are *FAITH*, and *PRAYER*. Faith is the tool we use as Christians, that gives us the strength and confidence we need to place our most difficult problems in the hands of our Lord. It is very comforting to know, that no matter how desperate our situation may seem, God is always with us and ready to help. We are never alone if we have faith.

Prayer is the tool we use as Christians to communicate to our Lord for His help, and to give Him thanks. I would like to remind John and Mary, and all of us for that matter, that through prayer, we should always give thanks to God for the things He has given us. You know—we teach our children at a very young age the common courtesy to thank someone when they have done or given us something good. Should we not extend our Lord the same courtesy?

My friends, before we witness the vows of holy matrimony between John and Mary, let us all rise and bow our heads before God and give Him thanks." Pastor Adams turned to face the front of the church while the congregation stood and bowed their heads. John and Mary remained kneeling and held each other's hands as the pastor continued. "Dear God, we thank You for this wonderful evening in which to celebrate the marriage of John and Mary. We thank You for the safe passage of friends and relatives who have come from near and far for this celebration, and we ask for their safe return home afterwards. We thank You for the parents and relatives of John and Mary, and also for the members of this church who have contributed, not only by instruction, but also by example, to the good Christian upbringing of these two young people. Amen."

Pastor Adams then turned back to face John and Mary and the rest of the congregation. He smiled, as he gestured for Ray and Diane to take their positions beside the bride and groom, and opened his book to recite the vows of matrimony as the ceremony continued.

"In the Name of the Father, and of the Son, and of the Holy Spirit. Dearly Beloved! Marriage is a holy estate instituted of God Himself for the preservation of the human family, and for the mutual help of those who enter into this sacred bond, to lighten the burdens of life, to alleviate its unavoidable cares, and by careful nurture to provide for the happiness of posterity.

This is a holy institution; its obligations and objects are likewise holy. It is the duty of a husband to love and honor his wife, and by careful consideration for her welfare ever seek to deepen her love for him. It is the duty of the wife to love her husband, share with him tenderly and faithfully the cares of the household, and at all times so conduct herself as to be his true helpmate. They should both carefully consider that they have entered into an estate in which their mutual happiness is dependent upon fidelity to their marriage vows, and, by due regard to their persons and their duties, they should seek to make themselves worthy of mutual esteem and love, and always set for each other a good example of a godly life. Wherefore it behooves them to pray earnestly for a virtuous helpmate who appreciates the duties of the marriage as well as the blessedness which comes from fulfilling them. So shall the marriage begin and continue according to the will of God, and the highest happiness be thereby secured. To this end we pray Almighty God for His blessing on this man and this woman."

He turned to John and said, "Before the omniscient God and in the presence of these witnesses, I ask thee, John Nelson, wilt thou have Mary McCulloh to be thy wedded wife, to love her in prosperity and adversity?"

He answered, "I do."

The pastor then turned to Mary and said, "Before the omniscient

God and in the presence of these witnesses, I ask thee, Mary McCulloh, wilt thou have John Nelson to be thy wedded husband, to love him in prosperity and adversity?"

She answered, "I do."

Mary and John then handed Pastor Adams their rings, and he continued to pray.

"Almighty God, Who with a holy, wise and beneficent purpose....." Pastor Adams' voice faded into the background as Mary began to ponder the words he spoke earlier about their duties to each other and leading godly lives. Still kneeling, she focused on the large wooden cross that hung in front of the church, and about the important role the church had played in their lives, not only as a center for worship, but also as a place of family support.

She thought about the many years that she and John were part of the Sunday School program, the time that they played Mary and Joseph in the Christmas Pageant and the many years that their mothers had taught Sunday school in their quaint little church. Finally, she reflected on how fortunate she was to have grown up in the loving home provided by her parents, and how she was determined to mold her new life with John in the same manner.

As the pastor continued his readings, Mary glanced at John, and they exchanged a brief, nervous smile. Behind those smiles, were the hidden fears about what lay ahead in their lives together. There was no doubt of their love for one another, but there was an apprehension of the trials that would eventually arise, those trials that would test their bond with each other and their faith in God, the faith that had been so patiently and durably built over the years as they transformed from children to adults.

John's thoughts were also occupied by the realization of his good fortune of being brought up under the loving guidance of his parents. When he thought about the words Pastor Adams spoke regarding the joys and sorrows to be encountered when raising children, it reminded him of the occasions in his life when his parents had to discipline him, and he remembered how he told himself then, "I'll do things differently someday when I have children of my own." But as he reflected on his entire childhood from his current mature perspective, he realized that the perfect template for parenthood already existed in the example set by his parents.

The service continued as Pastor Adams handed John Mary's ring, which was then held by both John and Mary while John repeated after the minister, "I, John Nelson, take thee, Mary McCulloh to be my wedded wife, to love in prosperity and adversity, and as a token thereof I give thee this ring." John then placed the ring on Mary's finger.

The minister then handed Mary John's ring, which was then held simultaneously by the couple, and Mary repeated after the pastor, "I, Mary McCulloh, take thee John Nelson, to be my wedded husband, to love in prosperity and adversity, and as a token thereof I give thee this ring." She then placed the ring on John's finger.

Pastor Adams then continued, "In the name of the Father, and of the Son, and of the Holy Spirit. Amen."

Pastor Adams continued from his book, "Forasmuch as ye now have been joined in holy wedlock, I, as a servant of Jesus Christ, before God and these witnesses confirm your marriage covenant in the name of the Father, and of the Son, and of the Holy Spirit. Amen."

For the first time ever, after performing a matrimonial ceremony, Pastor Adams then turned to the congregation, and with Mary on his right and John at his left side, and an arm around of them, said, "It is with great pleasure that I introduce to you, Mr. and Mrs. John Nelson."

Mary and John then stepped down from the altar area, and as they had secretly planned, went to the pews where their new in-laws were standing. Mary gave both Mr. and Mrs. Nelson a kiss on the cheek, as John kissed Mrs. McCulloh and shook hands with Mary's father. It was an unexpected and emotional moment for everyone, and tears of joy were visible on all the parents as they followed the newlyweds to the back of the church.

After the wedding party and the parents had left the church, Pastor Adams said, "I've been asked to announce that everyone is invited for food and refreshments in the church basement after you pass through the reception line."

John and Mary, together with their parents and the rest of the bridal party, formed a reception line just outside the door of the church and on the large landing above the steps that led to the street below.

There was a noticeable change in the weather as they stepped outside. The breeze was now from the northwest, and the humidity was much lower. It was a very refreshing change because even though the church windows were opened well before the service had begun, the large number of people in the church had offset any noticeable cooling to occur inside. John could still feel beads of sweat running down his back as he greeted the well-wishers from both families as they filed past. He loosened his tie and collar, as did most of the men, allowing some relief from the discomfort that had built up inside their shirts.

After awhile, everyone moved to the church basement for sandwiches, cake, coffee and ice cream. It was much cooler in the basement area where the church had a small kitchen and serving counter. The tables that John and his father had set up earlier that morning were now decorated with white table cloths. Small blue vases with cut wildflowers were placed in the center of each table. The air was filled with conversation and laughter, and the aroma of freshly-perked coffee blended with tobacco smoke from the cigarettes and pipes enjoyed by some of the men. Most of the adults sat at the tables, but many of the children went outside to run and play in the cool evening air; their laughter could be heard through the open basement windows.

Because they wanted to be sure to be out at the island cabin before it was dark, John and Mary did not sit and eat. Instead they chose to visit their friends and relatives, thanking them for being a part of their celebration and for their gifts.

It was less than an hour before dark when Mary said to John, "We had better change clothes and get ready to leave, John. Let's take turns getting changed so we're not both gone at the same time, I think it would be rude if we both just vanished. We can each say our good-byes while the other is changing."

"Sounds like a good idea to me, Mary," he said. "Why don't you go first, and I'll have Ray drive the truck around to the back door. He'll give us a ride down to the dock with our belongings." Mary went into the women's changing room to remove her wedding dress in favor of a casual dress, blouse, and sweater. Her mother came in momentarily and helped her out of the delicate, sentimental gown. It was the same dress that her mother had worn on her wedding, and Ellen was delighted when Mary asked her if she could wear it for hers.

Mary was busy brushing her hair when her mother turned to her, gave her a hug, and smiled saying, "You'd better get going, you don't want to miss your boat."

"Don't worry, Mother, something tells me the boat won't leave without me," said Mary, as she winked an eye at her mother and they exchanged a roguish chuckle.

The Wedding

When they returned to the fellowship hall, she noticed that John had already changed out of his suit and into his casual pants and a flannel shirt. He was standing next to the back door of the hall with his father, Andy and Ray. He saw her and gestured with his hand for her to come quickly. She noticed a look of concern on his face as she approached them.

"We better go in a hurry," said John. "When I put my bag into Ray's truck that there was a little lightning in the western sky. I think that the change in weather that your relatives from Jamestown were talking about is coming soon."

"Do you think we can get out to the island before it starts raining?" asked Mary.

"Oh, I think we'll have time if we leave right now," John replied.

Mary turned to her father and gave him a hug and said, "I guess we better get going. Thank you so much, Dad. Everything turned out just like I hoped it would. I love you and Mom very much."

"We love you too, now get going or you'll get drenched," he warned.

She turned to Mr. Nelson and said, "Thanks, Rudy. You and Sarah have been so kind and generous to us. I couldn't have asked for better in-laws".

"Well, we're equally as proud to have you for a daughter-in-law" replied Rudy. " Now you kids best get going, or I believe Andy's right about getting drenched."

As Ray, Mary and John walked out to the waiting truck, several people formed a line on each side of the walk way and showered them with rice as they made there way to the truck.

John put her bag behind the cab, and the three of them squeezed into the seat and left for the dock behind the general store where the little row boat was tied up. It was only three blocks from the church to the dock, and they were there in less than a minute. John carried their bags down to dock as Ray maneuvered the boat into the water. John entered the boat first, and steadied it tightly against the dock. Ray held one of Mary's hands, and John the other, as she stepped into the boat. Ray handed each bag to John, and he placed them on the floor in the bow.

John sat in the middle seat, and Mary sat in the stern seat facing him. He slid the oars into the oarlocks and looked up at Ray and said,

A Homeplace

"Ray, I can't thank you enough for all the help you've given us, both on the house and with the wedding. How can I ever repay you?"

"Don't worry, John," said Ray. "You'll have plenty of opportunity next year when I build my house."

John replied, "You better know I'll be there."

"And I'll see to it that he is," said Mary.

Ray untied the rope that held the boat to the dock and said, "I guess I'll see you two tomorrow afternoon if you need any help moving into the house."

"I don't think so," said John. "We really don't have much to move, just Mary's clothes, her bedroom set and some bedding."

"Hey, wait, that reminds me," Ray said excitedly. "I almost forgot to give you two my gift." He ran back to the truck and reached behind the seat and pulled out a brown paper package wrapped with string. "I don't know if it's the color you like, Mary, but I know it's warm," he said as he handed Mary the package. She untied the string and opened the paper wrapper. Her face was filled with joy as she held up the heavy wool blanket. "It's a Hudson Bay!" said Ray, beaming from ear to ear.

"Oh, Ray, its perfect" said Mary. "Thank you so much. I think we'll probably be able to use it tonight the way the weather seems to be changing."

Mary folded the heavy blanket and put it in her lap as Ray pushed the boat away from the dock. "Good luck you two," he called. John glanced back over his shoulder and positioned the bow of the boat in line with the island and began to row. The flashes of lightning in the western sky were becoming more frequent, and the wind was beginning to pick up. John pulled with all his might, and the bow of the boat rose out of the water momentarily with each thrust of the oars. As they made their way closer to the island, the sounds of conversation and laughter coming from the church gradually faded away. Neither one talked for a while, preferring to savor the peace and quiet that was present on the lake. The small splash made by the oars was followed by the gurgling sound of water as it rushed passed the side of the boat, and the tremolo call of a loon could be heard from across the lake as if it were calling for its mate. Mary took a deep breath, looked up into the sky and then turned to John with a sigh, "What a beautiful evening! It seems so peaceful out here compared to all the noise and activity back at the church hall."

The Wedding

"Yes, it sure is," replied John. "And it looks like we'll make it to the island just in time to get our belongings into the cabin, then we can sit on the porch and watch as the storm comes in. I just love to watch a thunderstorm, don't you?"

"Yes, I do too."

The sky continued to darken, and the yellow twinkle of lights from the town were visible as the front of the boat scraped up against the rocky shore of the island. John jumped out of the bow of the boat and instructed Mary to hang on tightly while he pulled the boat farther onto the beach. Mary handed him their bags; he placed them on the grass and extended his hand for her to hold while she stepped out of the boat. She started up to the cabin with their belongings while John pulled the boat completely out of the water and then flipped it over to prevent it from filling with rain. He ran up the little bank and caught up to Mary just as she stepped onto the covered porch. He took the bags from her, and when she opened the door and stepped inside, they noticed how cool it was inside the little cabin.

John asked, "Where shall I put our bags?"

"Oh, just set them on the bed for now," she said. "I'll get the lanterns lit if you want to close up the windows and start a fire in the stove. It's cooler in here than it is outside."

John agreed and carried in several armfuls of firewood and set them beside the stove. In just a matter of minutes he had a good, hot fire going. He reduced the draft slightly to retard the flame, and as he stood up he said to Mary, "Do you want to go sit out on the porch while the cabin warms up?"

"Yes, I'll be right there," she answered. "I just want to pull the curtain back so the bedroom area warms up too.

"Bring that new blanket with you when you come out."

John went out on the porch and sat down in one of the large wooden chairs that he had made a year ago from a pattern he had sent for in a magazine. It was a very comfortable chair with a deep, wide seat, broad armrests and a steep backrest.

Mary came out onto the porch and closed the door to the cabin. She looked out over the lake and said, " You were right, John. We made it just in time. I can see the rain working its way toward us from across the lake."

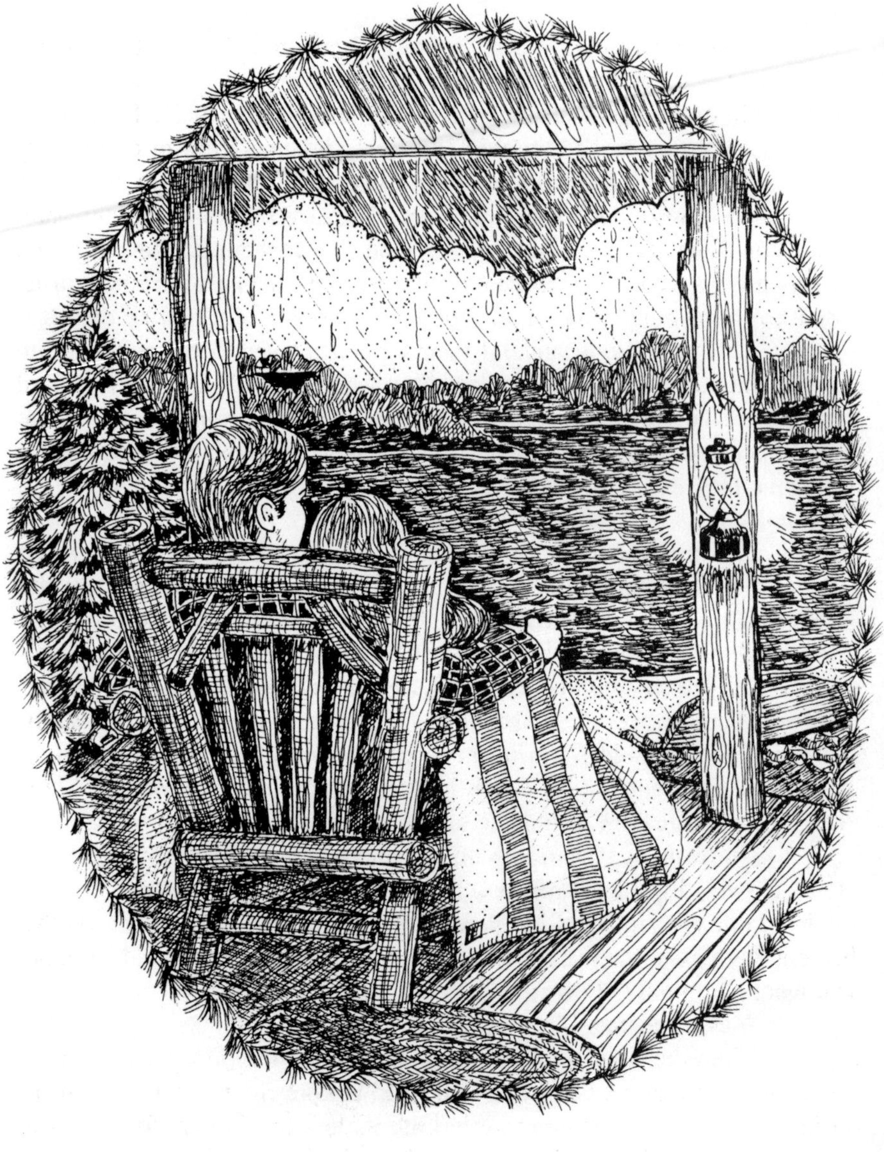

The Wedding

The thunder and lightning were now much closer, and the wind was starting to gust. Whitecaps began to form on the lake, and the sound of the large waves slapping the rocky shoreline could be heard from the porch.

Mary sat down on John's lap and covered them both with the large blanket. They huddled beneath it with only their heads visible, just as the rain drops became audible against the porch roof. He held her in his arms as they watched the rain and lightning and listened to the sharp cracks of thunder. The storm was right over them, and the rainfall was so heavy that a continuous sheet of water rolled over the edge of the roof. They could feel the cool mist against their faces with each gust of wind. It was not a severe storm because there were no dangerous winds gusts, but it evolved into a heavy downpour with a brief mixture of hail.

Their eyes met, and John said to her, "I love you, Mary." She looked intently into his eyes for a moment and then pressed her lips hard against his. His kisses moved down her neck and, closing her eyes, she tilted her head back encouragingly. He cradled her face with his warm hands as they continued to kiss. Without a word spoken, she stood up, took hold of his hand and led him into the cabin.

He stopped and stood in the doorway as she went to the bedroom area and closed the curtain behind her. It was now dark enough in the cabin that the yellow light from the lantern on the nightstand projected Mary's silhouette against the sheer curtain.

While she prepared for bed, he went to the stove to check on the fire, added more wood and adjusted the damper. It had become toasty warm inside the cabin now, but he wanted to be sure that the fire could go unattended for a while. When he looked up he could see that Mary was sitting on the edge of the bed brushing her long hair.

The rain was still coming down, though not as hard, and the storm slowly drifted to the east. John sat on one of the chairs by the kitchen table and took off his shoes. Mary pulled the covers back on the bed and lay down, feeling the cool, soft sheets against her skin. "John, do you want me to put out the light?"

"Yes, go ahead, Mary."

When the light went out, John took one end of the curtain and pulled it open against the wall. "I'll keep it open so we get some heat during the night." It was completely dark in the cabin except for the little flicker of flame that could be seen through the opening in the stove damper.

A Homeplace

With her hands at her side, and goose bumps multiplying with each passing second, Mary watched with nervous anticipation while John undressed for bed. His dark figure moved about beside the bed, highlighted by an occasional flash of lighting through the windows. He slid beneath the covers beside her, pulled the blankets up just under their chins and they turned on their sides facing each other. She moved closer to him and kissed him passionately on the lips.

Kneeling over him, her long hair fell to each side of his face like a curtain, behind which they exchanged a barrage of kisses. The rumble of thunder continued to fade away as they made love, and the wind through the pine-tops returned to a placid whisper.

Lying on their backs in the darkness, Mary's faint sniffle revealed her emotions. John rolled onto his side, moved her hair aside and asked, "What's wrong, Mary?"

She turned to face him and said, "Nothing, John. Everything is just perfect. I'm so happy for this day, John. I'm happy that we are married and that we waited until now to make love to each other. I know how tempting it has been for both of us to do this before, and I must confess that the urge was becoming unbearable. But it is so special now. I feel so comforted, so rewarded, and I will treasure this feeling and this night for the rest of my life."

With his thumb he cleared her tears away saying, "I'm happy too, Mary. And I want you to know that I will always love you and take care of you." Then he kissed her and they cuddled together on their sides with her back nuzzled tightly against her husband's chest. Lying in the security of his arms, she fell asleep while he caressed her face to the soothing sound of raindrops tapping on the roof, the occasional crackle from the fire, and shadows projected by the flickering flames in the wood stove, dancing against the knotty-pine walls.

From the Red Pine Weekly Herald, Thursday September 6, 1923

News from in town:

A very pretty wedding was solemnized at Emmanuel Lutheran Church last Friday evening. John Nelson and Mary McCulloh were united in Holy Matrimony at a well-attended service that began at 7 o-clock.

The Wedding

The bride wore her mother's white wedding dress while the maid of honor, Miss Diane Larson, and flower girl, Miss Rose Nelson, wore dresses of peacock blue messaline. The groom and best man, Ray Hanson, wore dark blue suits. A light meal was served in the church basement hall with nearly 100 friends and relatives present and a great many beautiful and costly gifts were received. The newly weds will take up housekeeping in their new home atop the hill on Second Avenue. The Weekly Herald joins with their many friends in extending congratulations.

Honeymoon's Over

Morning saw a temperature struggling to stay above forty degrees. Water droplets sustained by the hazy drizzle, held precariously to the tips of every pine needle, and the low, thick cloud cover hung like a veil between the island and nearby mainland, concealing any sign of the town. Mary, who woke to go to the outhouse, looked back at her soundly-sleeping husband whose head was barely visible above the thick layer of blankets.

She quietly made her way outside, wrapped only in their new Hudson Bay blanket. The dense, wet cushion of pine needles on the forest floor silenced her footsteps as she moved through the mist like a phantom. The cool, moist air outside the cabin was fresh with the scent of pine from needles and twigs broken during the brief burst of hail in last night's thunderstorm.

When Mary returned to the cabin, she stopped at the stove to add wood to the feeble embers left from last night's fire. After adjusting the damper she returned to bed, snuggled up to her husband and kissed him, waking him from his tranquil slumber. Within moments, she had rekindled the fire in the stove and last night's tender passion. The remainder of the drowsy morning hours were spent beneath the covers in romantic conversation and sleepy, sensual touching.

By noon, the dense fog had dissipated, and the cloud cover was beginning to break up as Mary and John approached the dock behind the general store. They were met by Mary's parents who were washing windows on the hotel porch and observed their boat leave the island.

"For a while there, I was beginning to think that you two would have to spend another night out there," said Andy. "The fog was so thick we couldn't even see the island 'til an hour ago. Did you make it through the thunderstorm without any problems?"

"Yes, we got there about ten minutes before the rain started," said John. "It sure came down hard for a while, there was even a little hail, but at least the wind wasn't bad."

"Did you stay warm last night, Mary?" asked Ellen. "I can't believe what a difference there is in temperature between yesterday and today."

"Yes, it was very cozy in the cabin. The wood stove gave plenty of heat, and there were lots of blankets on the bed. See the nice Hudson Bay we got from Ray?" she said, holding up the new blanket.

"Oh, it's beautiful," said her mother. "Those are such nice blankets, I really love them. It'll go very nicely with some of the other bedding you two received as gifts yesterday. You should see all the wonderful gifts that people gave you. We brought everything back to the hotel last night and put them in your room."

"Thank you, Mom. We'll bring everything over to the house as soon as we have something to eat. We're starved."

"Well, didn't you two have any lunch?"

"No, Mom. We didn't have breakfast either."

Immediately John blushed with embarrassment after Mary naively volunteered the information about their scant eating habits. Mary looked on as John dropped his head and winced with chagrin, just as her father removed the pipe from his mouth and burst into laughter—so loud that it echoed throughout the bay.

"What in the world is so funny about that, Andrew?" asked Ellen.

Mary too, looked at him in bewilderment by his sudden outburst.

"Don't you remember," he paused to laugh, "what it was like, my dear? When we were their age we tried to live on love too."

Then the women understood and their faces reddened. He continued to laugh out loud until his wife had heard enough.

"For heaven's sake, Andrew, do you have to draw attention from the whole town. Put your pipe back in your mouth and help carry their bags back to the hotel."

"Oh all right, Ellen. It just struck me as funny, that's all." Andy's pipe returned to the corner of his mouth, and gripping it tightly in his teeth, he continued to chuckle as he carried his daughter's bag while the four of them walked back to the hotel.

After a lunch of soup and leftover ham sandwiches from the reception, John and Mary looked through all their wedding gifts. Afterwards, Andy and John brought them to their new home along with Mary's bedroom set and her personal belongings.

John and Mary thanked her parents for all their help, especially for the wonderful wedding, and walked back to their new house.

A Homeplace

Ellen watched as the newlyweds walked up the hill to their new home. Andy put a comforting arm around her after noticing the emotion fill her eyes.

"We're very lucky, Dear. At least they will be staying in town. We'll be able to see Mary every day when she comes down to help with the hotel."

"I know, Andy," she said as she rested her head on his shoulder. "I feel so blessed that Mary has found love with such a nice man. I can't imagine what I'd do if she were to move away."

The bond between Mary and her parents was a warm and devoted one, as would be expected in the case of an only child. But Ellen's motherly instincts that told her Mary's bout with rheumatic fever as a young girl left her with an impairment affecting her stamina, heightening the motherly concern for her daughter. Ellen felt truly blessed that Mary had married someone whose career would keep them near their home, at least for now—especially when it seemed that the popular choice for so many young adults these days was to leave for the big city after graduating from school.

As John and Mary walked up to the front door of their new home, Mary stopped and said, "You know, John, someday our children will call this house the home place."

He smiled at her, scooped her up into his arms, and carried her across the threshold. Once inside, he turned her so she could close the door with her foot and they began to kiss. John let her down to her feet, wrapped his arms around her waist and spoke softly in her ear, "What do you say we haul the bed upstairs and put it back together?"

Mary replied with a fervent smile, "What do you say we just bring the mattress upstairs and deal with the rest of the bed later?"

"I like your idea better," said John. They giggled mischievously as they scampered up the stairs, dragging the mattress behind them and into the bedroom, letting it flop onto the floor where they continued their honeymoon.

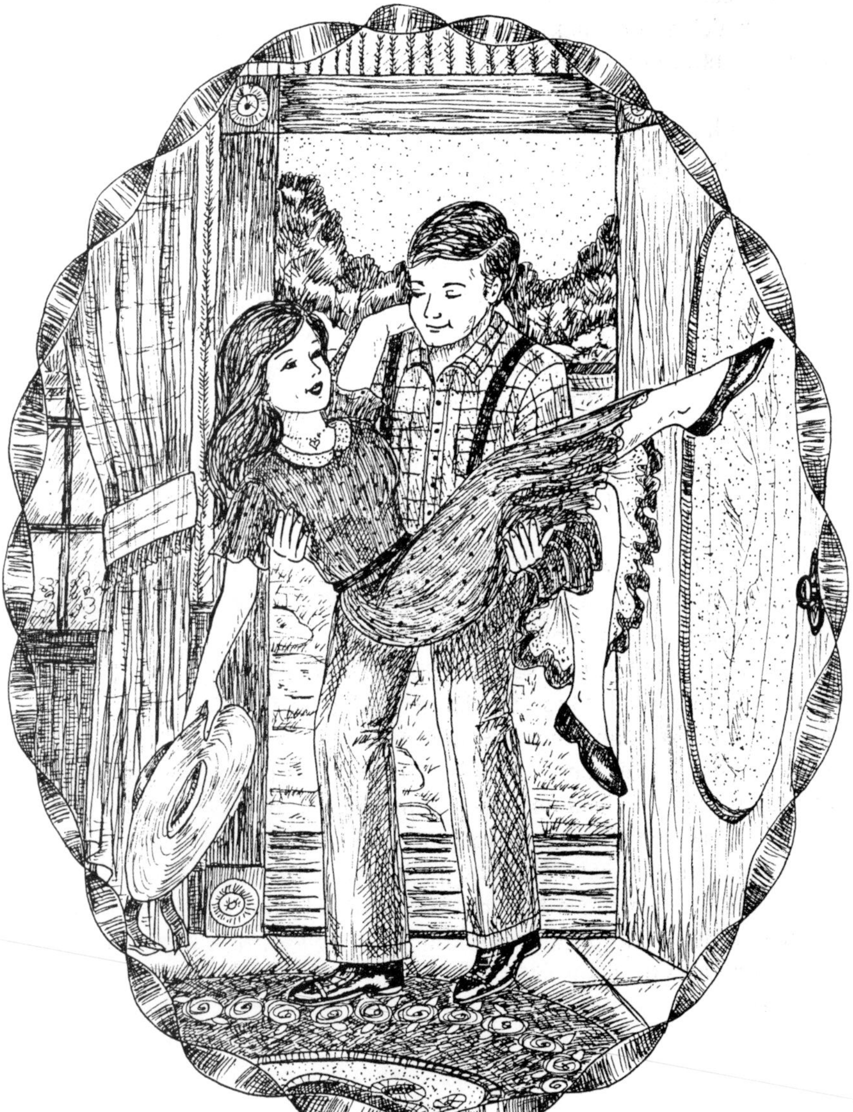

A Homeplace

Late in the afternoon, lying on their backs on the mattress, Mary said, "We better think about putting some curtains on the windows before it gets dark."

"Yeah, there's a lot of things we should get started on in this place," John answered. "I suppose I should get busy and start installing the woodwork. What room would you like me to start in, Mary?"

"I think *we* should do the kitchen first."

"What do you mean, we?" asked John.

"This is *our* house, Mr. Nelson. You've worked so hard all summer building it and finishing the outside. The least I can do is help on the inside."

John rolled to his side and looked into Mary's eyes, "I love you, Mrs. Nelson. It will be fun having you help me. Let's get dressed, go to my folks' store before they close and pick out some paint for the kitchen."

"It's a date, Mr. Nelson."

"I'll bet by tomorrow night we'll have the kitchen painted," said John.

"I'll bet we don't," she said.

"Why not?"

"Because tomorrow is Sunday. I don't work on Sunday and neither do you." John knew this would be a sensitive subject with Mary, but he thought he'd try to bargain with her anyway.

"How about we work on Sundays, only until the house is done, and then I promise you we never will again."

Mary rolled to her side, facing John with her elbow on the pillow and her head cradled in her hand. Looking into her husband's eyes, she ran her fingers through his hair and replied, "John, we're not in any hurry. It'll get done just the same. We can work evenings and Saturdays, and before you know it, we'll be finished. Ever since we were children in Sunday School, we've been taught to keep Sunday as a day of rest. Both our families have always lived that way, and I think it's important that we continue to practice that for the rest of our lives too. Please, John! I can't explain why, but I just feel very strongly that God intended for us to have one day a week when there is no excuse for families not to be together and enjoy each other's company. He knows how busy our lives are and I believe He wants us to spend time as a family and enjoy His creation. I've always looked forward to Sundays when I was growing up because Dad would spend so much time with me. He'd read me stories or

Honeymoons Over

we'd go on a walk or a picnic. He was always so busy during the week that he didn't have time to spend with me, but I could always count on him being with Mom and me on Sunday."

John leaned forward and gave Mary a kiss. He knew she was right and her explanation left him feeling guilty for even making the suggestion. She's so sensible about these matters, he thought. She's right. If we start working on Sundays now, it will make it that much easier to justify doing it all the time. "You're right—again!," he said.

When they left the mattress, Mary concealed herself with a blanket as she tiptoed passed the window and into the corner of the room where she started to dress. John, unabashed by the uncovered window, stood to get dressed when Mary scolded him affectionately. "John!" she said, giggling with a smile. "Aren't you afraid someone will see you?"

"Nope," was his only reply.

As they dressed, John noticed the dark blue dress with the white collar that Mary had made nearly two years ago hanging in the closet and said, "I wish you'd wear that dress more often! It's so beautiful. I remember the first time I saw you in it, when we were going to the church festival. I thought I was standing with an angel."

Mary smiled and said, "Oh, I don't know. I suppose it's because we haven't gone anyplace lately where we need to dress that fancy. I wore it to church several times when you were away at school, but now, it seems like all we've been doing in our spare time is working on the house and in the yard. Besides, I don't think it's in style anymore."

"Well, that's a darn shame," John replied. "It really is a beautiful dress, especially when *you're* in it."

"If you don't stop sweet talking me John, we won't get to the store to buy our paint before it closes," she said with a suggestive look.

He acknowledged with a smile, glanced at his pocket watch and with his foot, he thrust the mattress across the floor to the corner of the room where Mary stood. Unbuttoning his shirt, he approached her and said, "We've got an hour before they close."

Hand-in-hand they walked into the general store where John's mother was anxiously waiting for details on the wedding gifts they had received. John and his father discussed what they were doing next in the house. Mary made her paint selections for the kitchen, living room and dining room. All the ceilings in the house would be white, she decided, with different colored walls in each room.

The weeks went by and nearly every night John would install more of the wood trim, and Mary would paint. There were many evenings that John would not be home from work until almost dark and would be too tired to work on the house. Mary would also rest on those evenings. She continued working for her parents at the hotel during the day and lately, it seemed, she was always tired. By the end of October, the kitchen, bathroom, and dining were completed, leaving only the foyer, the living room, the stairway and two upstairs bedrooms left to finish.

On a Friday morning in November, on her way to the hotel where she continued to work for her parents, Mary stopped in at Dr. Stevenson's office.

"Oh, good morning, Mary," said Diane with surprise as Mary slowly opened the door to the office. While still in high school, Diane had met with Dr. Stevenson and discussed her interest in learning to become a nurse. She had been working for him as a receptionist since her graduation in the spring.

"Good morning, Diane," she replied with a smile and a blush. "Is Dr. Stevenson in yet?"

"Why no, not yet, Mary. He went over to the hotel for breakfast as usual, but he should be here in just a few minutes. His first appointment isn't for another half an hour. Did you need to see him, Mary?"

"Well," she said. "I know I don't have an appointment, but I thought I'd see if you could fit me in this morning."

"I'm sure he could, Mary, are you feeling ill?"

"Oh, no," she said emphatically and with a smile. "I just thought I'd better confirm something."

After studying the grin on her face and the blush in her cheeks, Diane said with excitement, "Oh, Mary! Do you think so?"

By now Mary was beaming from ear to ear and said, "Well if not, I'm terribly late."

Diane got up from her desk and came over to give Mary a hug just as Dr. Stevenson came through the door.

Seeing the big smiles on the two women he said, "Well, good morning, Mary. How's married life been treating you?" he asked while removing his hat and coat.

Still blushing, Mary replied, "Well, Doctor, that's what I've come to find out, if you have time this morning, that is."

All three exchanged a short laugh at Mary's reply and then Diane said, "You've got a half an hour before your first appointment, Doctor, if you want to see Mary now."

"Well good, good. Come on back to the exam room, Mary, and let's see what we can find out for you." He put his arm around her and escorted her into the room, closing the door behind them.

During the course of the examination, Dr. Stevenson listened to Mary's heart for what seemed a rather long time and then asked, " Have you been feeling tired at all, Mary?

"Maybe a little more than usual I think. Why?" Her concern was growing at Dr. Stevenson's questions and the persistent frown followed by his concerned 'hmmm.'

"You have an abnormal sound in your heartbeat, Mary, but because you don't have any established medical records, there's no way of knowing how long you've had this. Have you ever had rheumatic fever?"

"Yes, I think I was about six or seven years old when I had it. Why, Doctor?"

"Well," he said. "It's possible you could have had some heart damage from that fever. I'm not saying that you did, but that's something that can result from that particular illness. I wouldn't worry too much about it now, but we should probably keep checking it for a while and see if it changes at all."

As he concluded his examination he said with a smile, "Well, Mary, let me be the first to congratulate you. It seems you have an extra heart beat inside there." He told her to set up another appointment with Diane, and as they walked out of the exam room, Dr. Stevenson said, "Tell John congratulations for me, Mary."

A Homeplace

"Thank you doctor, I will," said Mary happily.

Diane said to Mary, "I hope you tell John right away tonight, Mary, because I don't know how long I can keep this good news inside of me."

Dr. Stevenson laughed and said, "Well, Diane, I hope you can hang on long enough so that John hears the news from his wife and not at the post office or on the street somewhere. Remember, we live in a small town and that kind of news will spread like a grass fire."

They all laughed and Diane and Mary exchanged a hug before she went out the door and walked to the hotel. She was so overjoyed about being pregnant that she gave little consideration to what Dr. Stevenson had told her about her possible heart condition. Other than the change in my body from the pregnancy, I really don't feel any different than I ever have, she rationalized.

That night John came home late and said, "Let's take tonight off and relax. We can put in a long day tomorrow."

"That sounds good to me Dear. I'm rather tired myself."

Mary had held supper for her husband and as they sat at the kitchen table he asked, "What room should we do next, Mary, my love?"

"Well, Mr. Nelson. I think we should do the other two bedrooms."

"Really!" he said. "I thought for sure you'd want to do the living room."

"No, I think not. I bought the paint today for the two bedrooms. Two cans of light blue and two cans of pink." John's attention was divided by the reading of some mail and didn't notice Mary smiling at him.

"Why do you want to do those rooms next?" he questioned, still unaware of the look on her face.

"Well, because that way we can be sure that they will be done before the baby arrives." John didn't comprehend what she had just said, and as he stood up to clear his dishes she rolled her eyes in disgust.

He started to run the water for doing dishes like he did every evening. They always did the supper dishes together before getting started on the house projects. While standing together at the sink, John suddenly stopped and looked at her and said, "Did you say baby?"

Mary continued looking down into the sink turning her head slightly away from him trying to hide her smile.

Honeymoons Over

"The baby! Did you say the baby!?" John held her shoulders and turned her to face him. When he saw the joyous smile on her face, and the sparkle of emotion in her eyes, he held her tightly in his arms. "Oh, Mary, I love you so much. When did you find out?"

"I stopped by Dr. Stevenson's office this morning and made an appointment. I had an idea that I was pregnant, but I wanted to find out for certain."

"When is the baby due?"

"Well, after discussing it with him, the doctor figures about the end of May."

John was still grining with delight when he said, "Well, it's a nice evening. Why don't we walk to town and tell our parents the good news?" They put on their coats and walked down the hill into town to visit the grandparents to be.

Everyone was excited, especially John's sister, Rose. Her eyes lit up when Mary asked her if she could count on her to come up to the house and help with the baby once in awhile. "Do you really mean it?" said Rose.

"Of course," said Mary. "You're plenty old enough. It will be fun to have you around to help me with the new baby. Just think, you will be the baby's only aunt." Rose smiled and beamed with pride as she reflected on what Mary had said.

"I can hardly wait 'til the baby is born," said Rose.

By mid-December, the inside of the house was completed. Work was starting to slow down now for John, and some weeks he only worked three days. When he was off, he would help his father at the store or Mary's parents at the hotel. The week before Christmas, Mr. Delaney told John that there wouldn't be any more work until spring. He was expecting that to happen and took the news in stride. He knew that Mr. Delaney kept him working as long as he could. It was winter now, and in the construction business that usually meant time off.

Since finishing the inside of the house, Ray and Diane, who had been dating regularly now for several weeks, would come over to Mary

A Homeplace

and John's for dinner on Friday nights. Even though they ages were the same ages as John and Mary, their love for each other was much slower to blossom.

Diane was finally able to get Ray to lower his guard revealing a very sensitive and affectionate man. Once they started dating, Ray fell head over heels for her, and they were together nearly every evening.

On the Friday night before Christmas Eve, when Ray and Diane were over for dinner, the conversation that was usually centered around Mary and John's house projects or the approaching birth of their child was about to change. First, they were half-an-hour late for dinner. And from the moment Diane and Ray entered the house that evening, Mary sensed something different about the couple. Diane seemed more spirited than normal, and Ray was obviously hiding something. She witnessed several kittenish glances between the couple followed by Diane's quick coquettish smile.

As they sat around the kitchen table, Mary had finally had enough and said, "Alright you two, what's going on?"

Diane looked at Ray for a hint of approval and when he smiled, she quickly held up her hand displaying her engagement ring. "Oh my goodness!" said Mary. "I'm so happy for you two. Congratulations! When did this happen?"

"On the way over here," Diane said with a smile, as John and Ray exchanged handshakes. "You should have seen Ray before he asked me," laughed Diane. "When he picked me up at the house tonight, I thought he was sick. His face was as white as snow and he could hardly drive. When we drove by the schoolhouse, he pulled over to the side of the road and stopped the truck. He just sat there, staring out the windshield and I asked him if he was alright. He answered, 'No, not exactly. Diane, this is so hard for me, but I've been wanting to tell you something for several days now, and I can't seem to find the right words.' I asked him what it was, and he said, 'Diane, we've been dating quite awhile now, and I've discovered that I no longer want to be your boyfriend.'"

"Well, when he said that my heart just sank, and I was stunned. I sat there for a moment and then I said, 'So what do you want to do?' He reached into his pocket pulled out the ring and said, 'I want to be your husband.' I didn't know whether I should slap him silly for scaring me like that, or kiss him because I knew how nervous he was to ask me. Lucky for him I decided to kiss him."

"And even luckier for me, she said yes!" added Ray with a wide grin.

"So when is the wedding?" Mary asked.

"Well, that's what we need to talk about," said Diane. "I want you to be my maid of honor, but I thought you would probably want to wait until you have the baby."

"I would love to," said Mary, "but the baby isn't due 'til the end of May. Are you two sure you can wait that long?"

"I guess we'll have to. Hopefully I won't change my mind before then," Ray replied teasingly as he winked at Diane.

Then Mary said, "I don't mind being in the wedding when I'm pregnant if you want to try for an earlier date. How about April? Let's see," she said as she stood to study the calendar on the kitchen wall. "How about Saturday, April twelfth, that's the first Saturday after Easter."

"Oh, Mary, that would be wonderful, if you're sure you don't mind."

"Well, okay, it's settled then. April twelfth," said John. "Now you two ladies can start talking wedding plans, and Ray and I will start talking about building your new house."

"Hey, I like that idea," said Ray. "Do you have any house plans lying around that we can look at for ideas?"

"I have three or four up in the closet that might interest you," said John. "I'll go get them."

Their evening get-together lasted until nearly midnight with all the excitement of wedding talk and building a new home. Then Ray mentioned to John that if he wanted to come and work for him and his dad for a couple months he could. "We have a lot of timber to cut this winter, and we could use the help. And, if the weather stays cold, we'll be harvesting ice in the middle of January, I suppose. We can always use the help for that. Dad gets a little stiff once in awhile, and it would be nice if he could stay home some of those mornings when he isn't feeling so well."

"That would be great, Ray, thanks. I think I'll take you up on that. Lord knows we'll need the money with the baby coming and all."

A Homeplace

On Christmas Eve, John and Ray sat together in church while Mary and Diane sang in the choir. The mild weather allowed for a large turnout for the Christmas Eve service. Pastor Adams said he couldn't remember the last time there was such a full church for the evening service. After the church services were over, Mary and John invited a group of their church friends and family over to their new house for Christmas cookies and hot cider. Mary and John's parents were there as well as John's sister, Rose. Ray and Diane were also present along with their parents. The new house was alive with laughter and conversation. The men and women segregated into different rooms, and the conversation among the women was dominated primarily by the upcoming wedding. The discussion between the men centered around an outpouring of advice regarding the new home to be built for Ray and Diane. It had just begun to snow as everyone left that night. There was no wind, and the big fluffy snowflakes fell gently from the sky, creating the perfect Christmas ambiance.

John started working for the Hansons after Christmas. He and Ray made some minor repairs on the long wooden trestle for skidding the large blocks of ice up to the icehouse, and except for Saturdays and Sundays, he worked for them steady until the first week in March. Soon after, Mr. Delaney notified John that his services would be needed again, as electrical work was steadily increasing.

Diane and Ray confirmed their wedding date to be the second Saturday in April which was less than six weeks away. Their new home was to be built on a secluded part of the quarter section of land owned by Ray's father. It was where his parent's house and sawmill were located, but far enough away from the mill, and among a dense stand of trees to offer a private and peaceful setting in which to live. Ray and John had already removed the necessary trees to allow for the house. There was still a foot of snow in the woods, and the potential for some heavy snowfall still existed. But the amount of daylight was slowly increasing and the sun was getting noticeably stronger. As soon as the ground thawed and was dry enough to work, Ray and John would begin construction in the evenings and on Saturdays, just as they did when building John and Mary's house. In the meantime, after their wedding Ray and Diane would live with Ray's parents until the house was finished.

Mary was now well along in her pregnancy but still working at the hotel. Her mother was very selective of the work she allowed her to do, even though Mary stubbornly insisted she was fully capable of performing her regular tasks.

Diane continued working for Dr. Stevenson, who divided his time equally between Agate Falls and Red Pine. He alternately worked three days one week and two days the next between the two practices. Diane took care of the bookwork and scheduling on the days that Dr. Stevenson spent in Agate Falls. Occasionally, she would have to call the doctor at his other office so he could drive over for an emergency. When the doctor was in his Red Pine office, Diane also served as his nurse. Dr. Stevenson was "a very kind and compassionate man as well as a good teacher," Diane often said. She was learning a lot from him, and hoped that someday she would be able to go to nursing school. She always assisted him in the office with patient's broken bones and cuts, and on many occasions, assisted him on house calls and baby deliveries. She was looking forward to helping Dr. Stevenson deliver Mary's baby.

Tragedy

The sun was noticeably stronger by mid-March, but on this day, its efforts were no match for the relentless northwest wind that had been pushing hard since day break. By mid-morning, the bright sun had surrendered to an ever-thickening cloud cover, and the temperature continued to drop.

Dr. Stevenson's schedule had him in Agate Falls that day, and Diane was busy with bookwork in his Red Pine office when the telephone rang. "Good morning, Dr. Stevenson's office, can I help you?"

"Yes, Diane, this is Dr. Stevenson. We have a little problem over here this morning."

"Oh, no," Diane replied, genuinely concerned. Her spirits had been riding high this day because it had been a pleasantly uneventful week at the doctor's office, and she was looking forward to being with Ray at their usual Friday night get-together at Mary and John's that evening. It was so exciting to discuss the wedding plans with Mary, especially now that the wedding was less than a month away. She hoped Dr. Stevenson's dilemma wouldn't intrude on their evening plans.

"What's wrong, Doctor? Is there something I can do?"

"I hope so, Diane," he replied. "Emily, woke up very ill today and won't be able to come to the office. We have a patient that has just started laboring, and unfortunately it appears there will be some difficulties with the birth. I'm reasonably sure that she'll deliver by early afternoon, and I could really use some help with this one. Do you think you could find someone to bring you to Agate Falls as soon as possible?"

As she was listening on the phone, Diane noticed Ray was making a lumber delivery across the street at Harold's filling station.

"Yes, Doctor, I think so. I can see Ray is delivering some material across the street at the filling station. Just a minute and I'll ask him." Diane set the phone down, went out the door and called for Ray, gesturing him to come to the office.

The expression of urgency on Diane's face sent Ray sprinting toward the office. "What is it Diane?" he asked, panting slightly from his run across the street. "What's wrong?"

"Dr. Stevenson is on the phone and he has an emergency at the office in Agate Falls. He wants to know if I could get over there right away. His nurse was too sick to come into work today, and he expects to

Tragedy

have a complicated delivery to perform this afternoon. Would you be able to bring me there?"

It was just beginning to snow when Ray finished unloading his delivery and it was a relatively slow day at the mill.

"Yes, yes I can," said Ray. "Just let me fill the truck with gasoline and I'll be right back. Ask him if it's snowing in Agate Falls."

"Yes, Doctor," she said with relief. "Ray said he'd be able to take me. He wanted me to ask you if it started snowing in Agate Falls yet."

"No, not yet," he said. "Why, is it snowing there?"

"It's just starting to," Diane said. "Ray went to put gas in the truck and he's coming right back to get me. Do you want me to bring anything when I come?"

"No, Diane, I have everything I need here. We may have to stay the night if problems arise, but I can put you up at the hotel if need be. Ray can head right back home if he needs to, and I'll bring you home tomorrow in my car."

"That will be fine," said Diane, hiding her disappointment. "I'll see you in a little while. Goodbye, Doctor." As she hung up the telephone she noticed the snow was coming down harder, and during the wind gusts, she could barely see across the street. She put on her coat and posted a note in the office window explaining the early closing hour.

Ray drove the truck in front of the office just as she was locking the door. Diane climbed into the truck and closed the door. Once inside, she removed her scarf and brushed the snow from her shoulders saying to Ray, "Are you sure we can make it to Agate Falls?"

"Oh I don't think we'll have any problems," he replied. "Did you ask Doc Stevenson if it's snowing there yet?"

"Yes, I did, and he said it hasn't started yet."

"Well, then we shouldn't have any trouble. It's only fifteen miles away, and as long as I can see enough to stay on the road we'll be okay. This old gal can go through anything," he said, referring to the truck with a boyish grin as he affectionately patted the steering wheel. Diane sat close to Ray as they drove off. She told him that Dr. Stevenson said he would get a room for her at the hotel because she might have to spend the night if there were complications with the patient.

"I was so looking forward to our evening with Mary and John," said Diane. "I'm really sorry about dragging you into this, Ray."

"Oh heck, don't worry about it. These things happen," he said reassuringly. "This could be a serious emergency, and I'm glad I can help out. Besides, this way I can still spend a little time with my girl." He smiled and put his arm around her. "When I get back I'll just explain to Mary and John what happened, they'll understand."

"Why don't you stay overnight too?" said Diane.

He looked at her with a smile and said, "What are you trying to do? Get me in trouble? Remember what happened the last time we were alone together. Don't make it harder on me than it already is," he chuckled. Diane just smiled and rested her head on his shoulder as they drove along.

The snow was beginning to accumulate quickly, and during the wind gusts it was often hard to follow the winding road. It snowed hard all the way to Agate Falls, and when they arrived at Dr. Stevenson's office, there was two inches on the ground.

When Diane and Ray entered the office, Dr. Stevenson was busy gathering some necessary medical supplies for the delivery.

"Oh, thank goodness you're here, Diane. The baby is coming much quicker than we anticipated, and we have to go right away." As he was putting his supplies into his bag, he looked to Ray. "Thank you very much, Ray, for bringing Diane here so quickly. Why don't you get a room at the hotel, and tell them to put it on my account. Diane and I may be gone several hours, and you shouldn't try to go back this afternoon." Looking out the office window he said, "Goodness, it looks like a full-scale blizzard out there."

"Oh, that's awfully kind of you Doctor, but I really need to get back home. I never told my folks I was coming here, and they're probably wondering where the heck I am."

"Well, why don't you call from my office and at least let them know where you are?"

"Thanks, Doctor, I believe I'll do just that. Do you need a ride to the patient's house?"

"No thanks, Ray. Its just down the street. We can walk there very easily. Speaking of which, Diane, we had better go right now."

Tragedy

"I'm ready," said Diane. "Let's go." As Dr. Stevenson went to the door, Diane gave Ray a kiss and whispered, "Please stay the night."

"I really have to get back; Honey, but it does sound tempting," he said giving her a wink. "I'll see you tomorrow."

She gazed romantically into his eyes for a moment, and in a low luscious whisper said, "I love you, Ray," and then turned for the door.

"I love you too, Diane," he replied as the door slowly closed on their affectionate exchange of words and glances. After she left, Ray tried to call his parent's house, but there was no answer. He looked out the window at the falling snow and thought, oh heck, I can make it. I'll just take my time, and when the wind kicks up I'll stop until I can see the road again. The snow can't be that deep yet. He went out, started the truck, and re-lit the lantern that was kept on the floor for heat. After letting it warm up several minutes he turned around and drove out of town toward Red Pine.

The numerous buildings in town had a buffering effect on the raging wind, and gave a deceivingly tame impression of the ferocious, fast-moving storm compared to what was happening out in the country. The strength of the wind stirred the falling snow with a fluffy accumulation that had fallen earlier in the week.

When Ray approached the edge of town, he noticed that the wind and snow had already erased any sign of the tire tracks he had made coming into town. The poor visibility limited his pace to a crawl, but he was able to follow the road by using fence posts and power poles to gauge his position relative to the ditch. The wind continued to intensify, and as his truck emerged from the heavily-forested landscape along the road and into the windswept, open meadowland, the white-out conditions made it impossible to navigate.

He stopped the truck while waiting for a lull in the wind and rubbed more salt on the windshield, trying to prevent the formation of frost on the glass. When the wind momentarily subsided, he put the truck into gear and eased out the clutch. The truck moved ahead only slightly before the tires lost traction and spun. Ray put the truck into reverse and slowly backed up in his tracks to take a run at the drift that had formed on the road. He put the truck in forward and accelerated steadily toward the drift in an attempt to punch through. As the front of the truck made impact with the drift, a wave of snow curled up and over the cowl, and the truck came to an abrupt halt, killing the engine. He was able to restart it, but when he put it in gear the wheels spun freely in both directions.

A Homeplace

The snow was so tightly packed beneath the chassis that it had lifted the tires away from their traction with the road, and they hung uselessly beneath the fenders. Ray lowered the door window, leaned his head out the opening and observed the rear tires as they spun with a high-pitched whine. He sat behind the steering wheel in frustration while the engine continued to idle.

The first waves of regret for leaving Agate Falls came over him as a strong gust of wind shook the truck. He knew that he was close to Red Pine, but with the poor visibility, it had been impossible to recognize any landmarks. He figured the open meadowland that bordered both sides of the road where he was stuck was about half a mile from the little bridge that crossed the Agate River near the schoolhouse. I can't be more than three quarters of a mile from town, he thought to himself. Ray sat for awhile, staring through the windshield trying to decide whether to start walking or stay in the truck. He watched as each gust of wind created ghostly swirls of snow that floated across the meadow single file and disappeared over the hill. It would be a waste of time and energy to dig the truck out just to advance to the next impassable drift, he reasoned, noting that the tops of the fence posts along the pasture were barely visible above the drifts of wind-driven, hard-packed snow.

As he continued to ponder his dilemma, he recalled several snowstorms that took days before the roads were made passable. "If I stay here, I'm sure to freeze to death. If I leave here I could get lost in the blizzard and freeze to death, but I'm sure I could make it to town," he said, trying to convince himself. As he peered out the small opening in the frosty windshield, and noticed the lantern was now out of fuel and his breath was visible in the cab of the truck, he made his decision. I'd rather die trying, he thought. I know that if I go north from here, in just a few hundred feet I'll come to the river and then I can follow it all the way to town. It'll be hard to see, walking straight into the driving snow, but if I get to the river as quickly as I can, I'll be able to duck out of the wind behind the some of the big oak trees along the bank.

It was a good plan. He knew that there would be more walking involved by following the meandering waterway, but he had to weigh that against the very real possibility of getting disoriented in the white-out conditions if he attempted the shorter distance by road. He also knew that the trickiest part would be to try and walk a straight line north to the river. As long as the wind is in my face, I will be going mostly north, he

Tragedy

figured, and by following the river to it's source, he'd be less than a quarter mile from the warmth and safety of Nelson's General Store.

Ray buttoned his coat as high as it would, raised his collar, and wrapped a blanket that was stored behind the seat around himself. When he opened the door and felt how quickly the bitter cold wind penetrated his thin layers of clothing, the first hint of fear challenged his normally composed demeanor.

He left the truck and started walking in the direction of the river. The depth of the snow varied between his knees and waist, and after only a minute of walking, his breathing was labored and his thighs burned from trudging through the deep snow. When he turned around to look for the truck, it was gone. He was lost in a whirlwind of white where there was seemingly no left or right, or up or down. "Why didn't I stay in Agate Falls?" he mumbled to himself.

Panic began to infiltrate his decision making. Ray was now truly fearful for his life. He stood in the middle of the white, wind-whipped meadow, slowly turning in place, looking for some sign or reason to go in a certain direction. Then he remembered, head into the wind and keep walking. He continued to push his way forward; his breathing again became heavy, and the burning sensation returned to the muscles in his legs. As he peered through the small opening in the blanket around his face, he could see what appeared to be a tree line. "I knew it! It has to be the river."

His spirit was renewed and his pace quickened as he headed toward the trees. The gusts of windy snow temporarily obscured the sight of the trees, but he lowered his head and continued hard in that direction until his shoulder unexpectedly slammed into a small popple tree, knocking him back into the snow. When he returned to his feet, he could see large areas of dark, open water in the river in contrast with the snow. He walked partway down the bank and rested at the base of a large tree ten feet from the river's edge. A sense of relief came over him as he caught his breath and realized he had completed the first step of his journey to safety. The feeling was short lived, however, when he noticed he had no feeling in his forehead as he adjusted the portion of the blanket that was wrapped around his face.

When he stood up to continue his trek, his legs buckled like a newborn fawns, and he staggered forward to a little tree where he propped himself up, and then to the next, and the next, until he fell

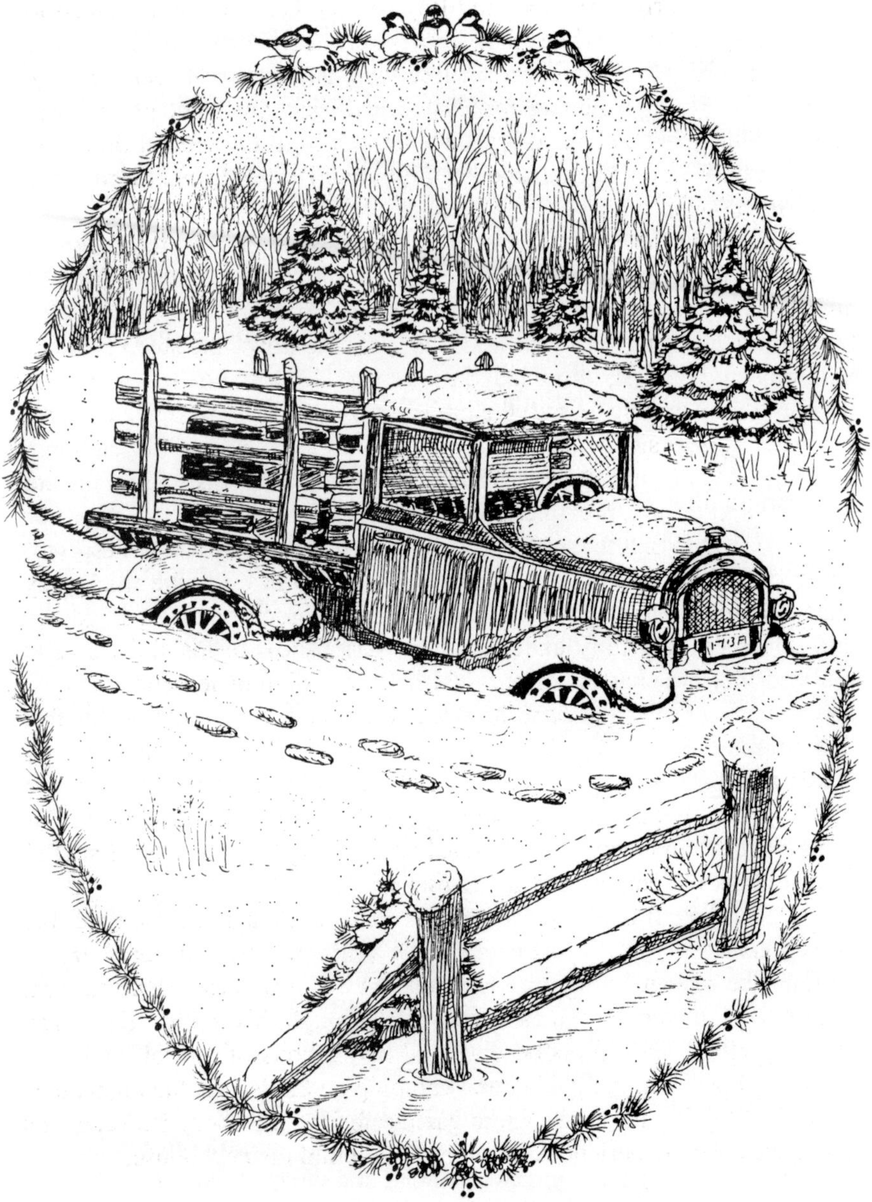

Tragedy

forward, completely exhausted, face-first into the snow. After a moment he lifted his head and crawled to the base of another tree and rested again. It was nearly dark now, and Ray sensed that the storm seemed to be gaining strength while the temperature continued to drop. The persistent north wind roared in the tree tops, and he could feel the large trunk of the tree he rested against, move with each gust. The ground was littered with small limbs and branches broken from the violent thrashing of the wind. If I don't get up and keep moving, I'll never live through the night, he thought.

Fearing the possibility of getting turned around in the darkness and blowing snow, he followed close to the river's edge using the numerous saplings along the bank as crutches. Suddenly, he tripped on a branch hidden beneath the snow and fell, sliding down the steep bank on his stomach, feet first, into the dark, icy river. He slid into the water up to his chest but was able to grab the branches of a small bush preventing his complete submersion. The frigid water quickly penetrated his clothing, sending waves of muscle-constricting shocks through his body that sent him into a thrashing, breathless panic.

He held tightly to the handful of brush and in a last desperate surge of energy, he was able to pull himself up through the thick gray slush on the riverbank where he crawled to the base of another large tree and sat down. Ray fully understood the seriousness of his situation and realized that his chances of survival had now diminished considerably. His shivering intensified, and he wanted desperately to climb to his feet and continue, but he was completely exhausted. The plunge into the icy water and the struggle to pull himself out with his encumbering wet clothing quickly tapped his remaining energy, and he could hardly lift his arms. Within minutes, his water-soaked clothing became frozen stiff in the plummeting temperature and raging wind.

Panting frantically, he put his head back against the tree and closed his teary eyes. "I just need to rest a minute," he whispered, trying to fight the strengthening urge to sleep. As his awareness began to fade, many fond memories quickly scrolled through his mind. He began thinking about his childhood days and had visions of himself and John as young boys fishing together and camping on the island, the nights they spent just talking for hours while gazing up into the starry heavens, and the more recent experience of helping John build his new house.

A Homeplace

Ray could no longer hear the wind and had no sensation of being cold. His shivering had ceased, and a darkening grayness slowly encroached on his dreamy apparition of Diane with her warm smile. He could smell her perfume and could hear her last words to him as she smiled and went out the door at the office, 'I love you, Ray.'

"I love you too, Diane. I'm so sorry. Please forgive me for this," he whispered, then his consciousness slipped away.

John and Mary had given up waiting for Ray and Diane and sat down to eat supper without them when the telephone rang. Mary answered, "Hello."

"Hello, Mary. This is Pete Hanson, is Ray over at your place?"

"Oh, hello Mr. Hanson. No he isn't here. He and Diane never showed up, why?"

"Well, Alice and I are a little concerned that we haven't seen Ray since late this morning. He went out on a delivery and should have been back by lunch time. We thought that maybe the roads got bad, or if he had trouble with the truck, he may have decided to stay at your place."

John noticed the look of concern on Mary's face and asked, "What's wrong?" Mary held her hand out at John, gesturing for him to be quiet as she listened intently to Mr. Hanson. John rose from the table and went to her side as she spoke.

"No, I haven't seen him all day," she went on. "Just a minute and I'll ask John if he has." Mary told John about Ray not returning home after the morning delivery and asked if he'd seen him today.

John took the phone and said to Pete, " No, I haven't seen him today, Pete. Where was his delivery at?"

"It was at Harold's Garage," said Pete. "It was just a small order for some shelving that Harold wanted to build at the station, and he said he'd be right back. We're just concerned because if Ray was near a phone, he would have called us. The fact that he hasn't called makes me wonder if he's stuck or broke down out in the country somewhere. I'm afraid a person wouldn't last long in this storm without a good shelter."

"That's true enough," said John. "I suppose it's possible that he is out at the Larson's farm. I know that they don't have a phone out there."

"Well, let's just hope that's the case," said Pete.

Tragedy

"I'll tell you what, Pete, I'll walk down into town, and see if anyone knows anything or has seen Ray today. I'll call back later and let you know what I find out."

"John, use your own judgment. The wind is howling to beat hell out here. I can't even see our barn, and its only a hundred feet from the house."

"Well it's windy here too, Pete, but not like it is out in the country. It's only two blocks to town, and I can warm up at my folks place if need be. Besides, now you've got me worried. I'll call you back in awhile. Goodbye, Pete." John hung up the phone and told Mary he was going to check in town to see if there was any sign of Ray's truck or if anyone had seen him.

"Be careful out there, John," his wife insisted. "Wind like this can give you frostbite very quickly." John bundled up and went out the door as Mary watched until he was out of sight.

She returned to the kitchen and finished her supper. As she sat alone at the table, the gusts of wind rattled the window above the sink. Mary understood very well that the relationship between John and Ray was special, and that John was terribly concerned for Ray. They were like brothers she thought, and said a silent prayer for Ray's safety.

As John walked into town, he noticed the lights were still on at Harold's Garage. He went inside to find Harold working in back of the repair shop. "Hello Harold," said John. "Working late tonight I see."

Harold was busy building some additional shelving for his inventory of auto supplies when he replied, "Yep, with crappy weather like this nobody is out driving around and buying gas, so it gives me a chance to catch up on things like this. Speaking of horse-shit weather, what the hell are you doing out on a night like this? It's colder than a well digger's ass out there!"

John chuckled. "Well, Harold, Pete Hanson called earlier and wondered if anyone had seen Ray. They haven't heard from him since he left to deliver you some lumber this morning. I was wondering if you knew where he might be, or if he said anything to you that would help us locate him."

Harold scratched his head under his hat and said, "The last thing I knew is that he was going to take the Larson girl to Agate Falls for Doc Stevenson. Seems his nurse over there couldn't work today, and there was some kind of emergency that he needed help with. Ray told me

A Homeplace

about it as he gassed up his truck. He drove out'a here like a bat-out'a hell and that's the last I saw of him."

"Thanks Harold," said John. "That explains a lot. Maybe he's staying in Agate Falls someplace where there isn't a telephone."

John left the filling station and headed toward home. He felt more at ease now that he knew where Ray had gone after his delivery. He figured the emergency with Doc Stevenson was the reason why Ray hadn't called his folks. Knowing Ray, he'd call his folks as soon as he was able to.

When John returned home and walked in the back door, Mary was sitting in the living room working on some knitting. "Did you find out anything?" she asked.

"Yes. Harold Nyberg said that Ray had to take Diane to Agate Falls because Doc Stevenson had some sort of an emergency. His regular nurse wasn't able to work today. I figure that as soon as he is able to he will call his folks."

"Well, that should put his parents' minds somewhat at ease. At least we can account for where he went after his delivery, and he *was* with Diane." After John took off his boots and coat he called the Hanson's and Pete answered.

"Hello, Pete. This is John. I think I have some good news." He explained to Pete what Harold Nyberg had told him and how he felt a little better now that he knew where Ray had gone after his delivery.

"Well," said Pete. "I just got off the telephone with Diane, and she's staying at the hotel in Agate Falls. She called here to talk to Ray, and I told her that he hadn't come home yet. She said that Ray left for home about three o'clock this afternoon."

John's heart sank as Pete shared the conversation he had with Diane. Mary saw the anxiety return to John's face. He lowered his head in dejection as he concluded his conversation with Pete. "All we can do now is wait 'til morning and see what the weather does, Pete. He probably found his way to a farm house or old hunting cabin and is just waiting out the storm. Even if he got stranded in the truck, Ray is tougher than nails and if it's possible for anyone to survive out there, he can do it. I'll call you in the morning, and we'll discuss what to do next. Good night, Pete."

John hung up the telephone and went to his wife's open arms. She could tell by John's conversation that Ray could be in serious trouble if he wasn't able to get out of the weather. John explained the phone

Tragedy

conversation with Pete and said, " The only hope he has is if he made it to some kind of shelter. All we can do now is wait 'til morning and hope that the weather gets better. God help him if he tried to walk very far."

Mary and John went to bed and prayed together for Ray's safe keeping. Mary eventually fell asleep, but John stayed awake the entire night listening to the surging wind and driving snow as it pelted the window panes like handfuls of thrown sand.

John was dressed and making breakfast before daylight. He checked the thermometer outside the kitchen window, noting the eighteen-below-zero reading. The wind was noticeably quiet now except for an occasional light gust. The moon and stars were still visible but the eastern sky was beginning to lighten. John turned on the light by the back door, but it was hard to determine just how much snow had fallen. In some areas of the yard, the grass stubble was visible through a skiff of snow, and in other parts there were three-foot drifts.

The telephone rang as John sipped his coffee. "Hello. Hi, Pete. Any word?"

Mary had come down the stairs unnoticed by John as he listened intently to Pete. She put her arms around her husband from behind and rested her head against his back. When John hung up the phone, Mary asked if there was any word of Ray.

"No, not yet," said John in a dejected tone of voice. "That was Pete. There are seven of us who will be meeting at the store in about two hours. Pete is hitching up his team and going to try to make it into town. I need to find my snowshoes and get down to Dad's and see if he's got enough snowshoes in stock for the search party to use."

Mary could see the distress in John's eyes, and as he went out the door, she stopped it from closing completely. He looked back to her and she said, "John, I'll keep praying for him until you return, but you must promise me that you will too." He turned to leave again, but Mary continued, "And John," he looked back again, "Please know that I love you."

John turned and walked away without a word as Mary slowly closed the door, hoping he would turn back and acknowledge her. As the door shut she began to cry, sensing that John knew Ray's chances for being found alive were very slim unless he found a way to keep warm.

At nine o'clock, all members of the search party were gathered at the General Store. Gustav Schmidtke, Charles Goshea`, Henry Schroeder,

A Homeplace

Harold Nyberg, Philip Lewis, and Samuel Hopkins all stood behind John and his father, as Pete Hanson explained the details of his search plan, and informed everyone that there was another group from Agate Falls that would be starting toward Red Pine at the same time.

Everyone was in agreement with the plan devised by Ray's father and Rudolph Nelson. Knowing that Ray had indeed left for Red Pine yesterday afternoon, he had to be somewhere in between. The search party, equipped with shovels, snowshoes, and a toboggan, climbed into the back of Harold Nyberg's truck, except for Pete Hanson, who rode in the cab with Harold.

The sun was shining brightly, and its strength at this time of year pushed the temperature to zero by mid morning. The beauty of the brilliant blue sky against the snow-covered pines was overshadowed by the sobering task of the group. The search party encountered the first big drift in the road near the school house. The men got out of the truck and waited along the side of the road and watched as Harold lowered the make-shift plow. He returned to the truck and accelerated into the drift. After three ramming attempts, the truck broke through to the other side where yet another drift awaited them just thirty yards away.

Harold and Pete got out of the truck and addressed the rest of the party. " I'm sorry men, but my truck just won't hold up to this kind of battering for very long," said Harold, shaking his head with disappointment. "It has enough power to clear the snow away at the filling station, but if I have to keep doing this for very long, it'll pound the son-of-a-bitch to pieces. This is a job for a damn big team of plow horses."

John's father spoke up saying, "We can't wait that long men. Let's put on the snowshoes and start following the road toward Agate Falls. We'll spread out in a line and keep our eyes peeled for Pete's delivery truck. They all agreed and started down the road. The snow was so hard packed that some of the smaller men didn't need to wear snowshoes. After about half-an-hour of walking, John shouted, "I think I see something—right over there," he said, pointing down the road.

"Where?" asked Pete.

"Straight ahead. The sun is reflecting on something just ahead about two hundred yards." John continued to point as he shielded his eyes with his hand. Then Pete saw it and some of the other men too. "Could be a windshield," someone yelled. The pace quickened toward the small, exposed piece of glass. John arrived first about twenty yards

Tragedy

ahead of the rest of the group. The truck was totally embedded within the drift and only one corner of the windshield and part of the cab was visible.

"This is it!" he shouted. He got down on his knees and started to dig down toward the drivers side door. Within moments everyone was kneeling and digging with their hands.

Seconds later, John slowly stood up, and with a look of dejection, turned to Pete, saying with a somber voice "Its empty. He's not here."

Pete, who was now obviously distressed, looked around in every direction for some sign of his son.

Rudy said, "He hasn't been here for hours. If he was, there would be some sign that he tunneled out, and we would have noticed some footprints in the area. I'd say, judging by the depth of the drift, that he left the truck yesterday, maybe late afternoon."

"Left for what!" Pete asked in a voice filled with anxiety with his arms above his head.

"I don't know, Pete. Let's stop and think things out for a moment. Turning to John, Rudy asked him, "What would Ray do in this situation, John? You know him probably better than anyone here except for Pete." Rudy knew that Pete was not thinking rationally right now and was relying on John's years of friendship with Ray to help decide the next course of action.

John rubbed his forehead in thought for a few moments, then he looked up to his father and said, "The river. He headed for the river. I know he did!"

"Why would he go to the river?" asked Rudy. "There's no shelter or safety there."

"To follow it toward home," said John. "He couldn't see very far ahead in the blizzard, but if he stayed along the river he knew he wouldn't get lost. He told me that many years ago when we were just kids. We were walking along the banks one day, and I said 'We better turn around before we get lost.' He replied, 'We can't get lost if we stay in sight of the river, because we know that it starts right in town.'"

"I believe he's right, Rudy. I remember telling him that when he was just a young boy," said Pete.

"Okay then, lets head for the river and start walking toward town, men," said Rudy. "When we reach the river we'll spread out in a line and walk slowly along the banks.

A Homeplace

The group started toward the river, and each member of the party made a three-or four-foot probe from tree branches when they got to the tree line near the river bank. They spread out in a tight line and started toward town. John was farthest from the river and Harold Nyberg was as close as he dared get to the edge of river because of tripping hazards concealed below the snow.

They continued, slowly scouring the bank of the river and probing the drifts and humps in the snow-covered ground. Other than Pete occasionally shouting Ray's name, no one spoke a word while they searched. The only sounds heard were the distant calls of a crow and the heavy breathing coming from the members of the search party as they labored through the deep snow.

The combination of the recovering temperature and strenuous walking compelled the removal of coats and hats by some of the men. John veered off from the rest of the party to investigate an unusual hump in the snow when he heard someone shout, "Over here!" When he turned to see where the shout came from, he saw Pete kneeling at the base of a tree with several of the search party members gathered around him. John immediately started to forge through the deep snow toward the group, but stopped abruptly when he saw the look of anguish on his father's face.

Rudy looked directly into his son's eyes and slowly shook his head in dejection, confirming their worst fear. John's eye's filled with tears as he slowly walked toward Pete, who was now sitting in the snow and embracing his son. Out of respect, everyone moved a short distance away to allow Pete to be with his son. After several minutes, Rudy and Harold approached Pete with the toboggan. Harold said, "We best get started back, Pete, there's nothing more we can do."

The three men loaded Ray's body onto the toboggan, and Pete used his coat to cover the expressionless gaze on his son's face before securing his body to the toboggan with rope. Harold, Pete and Rudy took hold of the rope and led the way back to the truck while the rest of the search party followed behind.

It was a very sobering trip back to town for John. This was the first time in his life that the reality of death had been this close to him. This time it wasn't just some distant acquaintance mentioned in church, or someone's name in a newspaper. This was his very best friend. His life-long buddy who was like a brother. There had never been a cross word or ill feeling between them. Never.

Tragedy

During the short drive back to town in the back of Harold's truck, the reality of Ray's passing began to sink in with John. He could not rid his mind of the sight of Ray's frozen face and his gray lifeless eyes peering through the frosty, narrow openings in his eyelids. When he thought about the finality of his relationship with his best friend, Ray, whose wedding date was quickly approaching, he was struck by the realization that his life would never be the same again, and he became sick to his stomach and relieved himself over the side of the truck.

When the search party arrived in town, they moved Ray's body to the examination room at Doc Stevenson's office. Rudy looked at his grief-stricken son and said, "Go home now, Son, and be with your wife. There is nothing more you can do here."

John walked home and when he came through the door, Mary, who was working in the kitchen hurried out to meet her husband as he removed his coat and hat. When he turned to face her, and she saw the tears in his eyes and his quivering chin, she knew. They embraced each other tightly as they wept.

"He's dead, Mary. Ray is dead." There was nothing that could be said or done that would stop the hurt right then, and neither one tried. After their long embrace, John said, "I'm going to take a hot bath and go to bed. It seems like forever since I've slept."

"Don't you want something to eat, John? I've saved some lunch for you."

"No thanks, I'm not very hungry right now." John slowly walked up the stairs to the bathroom and started his bath water.

Mary went to the rocking chair in the living room and opened her Bible. Her strong faith had taught her to always turn to the Scripture in times of crisis. She had already begun a daily Bible reading sin becoming pregnant and recalled reading some passages recently that thought she could share with John to help them over this tragedy. was looking for answers to the questions that she had and knew that J would have as well. Why? What did Ray and Diane do to deserve Why would a loving God inflict this kind of tragedy on his fai servants? She also prayed for Diane who still wasn't aware of wha happened.

Nearly half an hour had passed before she heard John mo their bedroom and get into bed. A few minutes later she went upst be with him, but when she entered the room, she found he was a asleep. He was so physically and emotionally drained that he slept through until morning.

Renewal

When Mary pulled the curtains aside, the orange rays of early-morning sunlight filled their bedroom, transforming the shiny maple flooring into an amber pool. She looked down at her husband who was still sound asleep beneath the layers of blankets, and the feelings of sadness returned when she saw Ray's wedding gift, the Hudson Bay blanket. The heavy colorful blanket, used as extra bedding during the winter months, became visible when Mary rolled back her covers to get out of bed, inspiring a vivid recollection of the big proud smile on Ray's face as he stood on the dock and handed Mary the blanket.

"Time to get up for church, John." He slowly raised his head, squinting in the brightness. Sitting up with his back against the headboard, he focused on Mary standing in the doorway drying her tears with a handkerchief.

"Are you sure there will be church today?" asked John. "I doubt that the roads are open yet in the country."

"I'm sure they're not," she replied. "But services will be held for people in town. With the parsonage so close, Pastor Adams said h would always hold service if anyone can make it to church."

The reality of Ray's death returned to cloud the joy of waking a new day as John rubbed the sleep from his eyes. Mary sat beside hi on the bed resting her head against his chest. "I was hoping to just wa up and discover it was all a bad dream," he said, caressing her back they sat together. "Did you talk to anyone last night after I went to bed

"Yes. Your mother called to see how you were doing."

"Anyone else?"

Mary hesitated for a moment, searching for the strength to re the sorrowful conversation she had with her best friend. "Diane c; last night from Agate Falls. She had called the Hansons' late ir afternoon asking about Ray, and they told her what happened." trembled slightly as she cried on his chest. John rested his head against the wall and sighed as one of Mary's warm tears slowly down his bare chest. "Her heart is simply broken, John. She's bl herself because she asked him to take her to Agate Falls. She just she would have tried harder to convince him to stay the night ins driving home. She and Doctor Stevenson had to hurry off to h woman deliver her baby, and she didn't have time to convince stay. Even Doctor Stevenson offered to put him up in the hotel if he wanted to stay the night."

"That sounds like Ray," said John. "The worst fault he had was that he always thought he was invincible. As soon as anyone said 'that's impossible,' or, 'it can't be done,' Ray would try to be the one who could do it. That, and the fact that he put too much faith in that damn truck," John said as his chin began to quiver and tears formed in the corner of his eyes. "Ever since..... they bought that new delivery truck, he'd always say, 'She'll go through anything.' "

"That may be part of it," said Mary. "But Diane seems to think that Ray didn't want to put themselves in a position of temptation again."

"What do you mean?"

"Last night on the telephone Diane told me that about three weeks ago, Ray stopped out at their farm on his way back from a livery. Her parents had just left for town and wouldn't be back for a couple of hours. They were alone and she said one thing led to another before they knew it, they were in her bedroom." Mary added, "You promise not to say anything about this, John."

"I promise," he said, annoyed at her requirement to make such a

"Diane said they were so deeply in love and were going to get soon anyway, they just figured why not?"

John shook his head in disgust as he got out of bed, confused and by thoughts of the seemingly wasteful loss of his best friend's e went into the hall toward the bathroom, he turned back to in a sudden, angry tone said, "I find it very difficult to go to give thanks to a God who has allowed so many lives to be e this. Ray never had an evil bone in his body. He was a good son, soon to be a good husband, and maybe someday, He was cheated out of the best years of his life."

hn went into the bathroom, he slammed the door shut, with his sudden display of bitterness and anger. She had this type of behavior in John before, but when she magnitude of the tragic loss of his best friend, she cern.

ist finished making the bed when he came out of the dressed, still bearing an expression of pain and hesitant voice she said, "John, do you really blame ? How do you know he had the best years of his life

A Homeplace

ahead of him? Remember Pastor's sermon a few weeks ago? Our lives don't really belong to us, they are a gift from God. We are His instruments and no one knows the plans God has for our lives. It's times like this that we need to rely on our faith, John. In Pastor's sermon he reminded us that God tests our faith in many ways."

John whirled around and glared at Mary, "It's one thing to have your faith tested, it's another thing to have it crushed! I'm sorry, Mary, but I don't accept that crap. Tell me: Why does everything about God have to be such a mystery? Ray went to church nearly every Sunday for his entire life, just like God wants and look where it got him! He was going to be married to a wonderful woman. I've never seen Ray happier in his life than he has been lately, and now he's gone—gone forever. And you expect me to just shrug my shoulders and say, 'Oh well, must be God's will.' Well I'm sorry but I can't do that. Now, if you don't mind, I'd rather not be lectured anymore about His wonderful plans for us. It appears to me that you're born, you live and then you die. Period."

Mary sat on the bed, frightened into tears by his outburst. John had never raised his voice to her before. He finished dressing and stormed down the stairs and out the door. She watched from the window as he took a snow shovel from the shed and furiously began slicing away cubes of hard-packed, drifted snow from the sidewalk. She dressed for church and after breakfast went out the front door and walked alone down the snow-covered street. When she reached the bottom of the hill, she was joined by Rudy and Sarah who waited when they saw her coming. "Where's John?" Sarah asked.

"He's not coming to church today," she said, notably disappointed.

"Why not?" asked Rudy. "Is he ill?"

"No," said Mary. "He's having a difficult time accepting Ray's death—and it's causing him to question his faith," she added with a tearful look of despair. Sarah and Rudy extended their arms around her in comforting support as they continued to walk to the church.

"He'll get over it in time, Mary," said Sarah. "He's lost his best friend, and it was so sudden and tragic. It's a normal response, I would think."

"I hope so," said Mary. "But he's so hurt, and he's raising questions about God that I can't give answers to. He's just not finding any comfort in anything I have to say."

"Maybe we should see if Pastor Adams would speak to him after church today," said Sarah.

"I disagree," Rudy said with authority. "I think we should wait a while. It sounds to me like he's too angry right now, too angry and too hurt to listen to reason anyway. Let's give it a few days. Wait until after the funeral and we'll see how he's doing then. I've always believed the best thing to do in these situations is to give a person a chance to work through it alone first. There are no magic words of comfort for something like this. Like they say, 'Time heals all wounds.'"

As they walked into the church they were greeted by a somber Pastor Adams. It wasn't the same smiling, energetic welcome that was so customary every Sunday. The news of Ray's passing spread quickly and had left everyone stunned. The people in Red Pine died of old age, or expectedly from a diagnosed illness. Not a single member of the community had been wounded or lost their life in the recent war. No one could remember such a tragic loss as this.

There were only a dozen members present in the church compared to the normal sixty on a fair-weather Sunday. As Pastor Adams shook hands with Rudy and Sarah, he sensed there were problems with Mary and John by the redness in her eyes and John's unusual absence, but decided not to inquire about his whereabouts. Mary saw her parents sitting near the front of the church, and they joined them in the pew with Mary between her mother and mother-in-law.

Pastor Adams glanced at his pocket watch and looked outside the large front door of the church. Seeing that no one else was coming toward the church, he closed the door and proceeded to the altar where he turned to address the congregation.

"My dear friends in Christ. As I am sure you have all heard by now, our congregation and our town, has suffered a terrible loss in yesterday's passing of Ray Hanson. Our heartfelt sympathy and prayers go out to the friends and family of Ray Hanson in their time of grieving and sorrow. I spoke with Ray's father last evening and the funeral will be this Wednesday morning at ten o'clock. Let us now begin our service on this fifth Sunday of Lent with the singing of the appointed hymn.

When the service was over, Pastor Adams bid good day to the members of the congregation as they left the church. When Mary started to leave, Pastor Adams held Mary's hand and said, "I take it John is

A Homeplace

having a difficult time accepting Ray's death, Mary. Is there anything I can do to help?"

"Not right now, Pastor, but thank you for asking. He's very bitter this morning, and I think he'll need some time to accept what has happened. Right now he is so upset that he won't even consider any words of comfort. I've never seen John so disturbed before. It scares me. I worry that he will turn away from the church."

"Well, Mary, you're probably right about giving him some time. You can also pray for him that he will come to accept this tragedy. There is only so much we can do, though. It's not like we can use our finger to stop the leak and pour the faith back into him. It has to come from within himself. In time, I'm sure his heart will soften. He's a good, strong Christian and comes from a good Christian background. It is a very difficult inner struggle that John is going through right now. I can't remember ever seeing two friends who were so close for so many years. They did everything together."

"Thank you, Pastor. I appreciate the kind words and advice. I'll tell John you said 'Hello.'"

Mary and her in-laws walked toward home together, and when she started up the hill toward her house, Sarah said, "Rudy, you'd better walk with Mary up the hill in case she needs help. It's very slippery this morning."

"Oh thanks, Sarah, but I'll be okay."

"Just the same, Mary, I'd feel better if Rudy went with you. As slippery as it is and in the condition you're in now, we don't need any more unnecessary tragedies."

"Okay, Sarah, you win," Mary smiled. "Call me when you get more details about the funeral, and let me know if there is anything I can do to help. I'd be happy to bake something if need be."

"I'll let you know, Dear. Goodbye." Mary and Rudy walked together up the hill and between the neatly carved mounds of shoveled snow along the sidewalk leading to the house. As they climbed up the stairs to the front porch, John met them with an open door and a concerned look on his face.

"Are you alright, Mary? Is anything wrong?"

"Sure I am," she said. "Why?"

"Well, when I saw my father helping you up the street I though maybe you were hurt."

"Damn it anyway, John!" said his father, in a voice blended with anger and disappointment that sent John back on his heels in surprise. "You should be ashamed of yourself for letting Mary walk to church alone in the condition she's in. I know you were raised better than that." Rudy then turned to Mary and in a tone dripping with graciousness, fully intending to further John's humiliation, said, "If you need to come to town, Mary, give us a call and Sarah or I will help you."

"That won't be necessary, Father," said John. "I get the message."

"Well, I sure as hell hope so, Son. There's no telling what kind of problems would arise if your wife would happen to slip and fall in the condition she's in now. You know, John, we're all upset about Ray's death. It hurts me to think about it just as much as it does you. But that's no damn excuse to treat your wife like that. You're a married man—now start acting like one."

His father turned and walked away as John slowly closed the door, astonished and humiliated by his father's lambasting in the presence of his wife. Mary was embarrassed for John, but at the same time she felt a sense of vindication; comparing Rudy's scolding of his son's unintentional lapse of courtesy, to the harsh manner in which John had addressed her earlier that morning.

John closed the door and put his hands on Mary's waist while she hung up her coat. When she turned to him, his face was still red with embarrassment. "I'm sorry, Mary. I didn't mean to raise my voice to you earlier this morning. And I certainly don't want you to think that I don't care if you fall and get hurt. I'd never forgive myself if anything happened to you on account of my stupidity. I just wasn't thinking clearly this morning. Please forgive me. I love you very much."

They embraced each other tightly for several minutes and Mary said, "I love you more than anything, John. It just hurts me to see you so angry with God over Ray's death. I hope you can find it in your heart to ask His help in dealing with this."

John released his embrace and walked over to the windows overlooking the front porch. He leaned forward bracing himself with his hands on each side of the window and his head between his arms, staring through the glass at the piles of snow and the white frosted evergreens across the street.

"Pastor Adams announced that the funeral will be Wednesday morning," Mary added.

A Homeplace

John bowed his head and closed his eyes after she spoke but said nothing.

Sensing a need to change the subject, Mary said, "I've got a roast to put in the oven for dinner, Dear, does that sound okay to you?"

After a moment of silence John replied, "Yes…..yes that does sound good. I'm very hungry."

"I think I'll get it started and then go upstairs and lie down for awhile. I feel very tired today."

"Okay," John said as he moved away from the window. "Do you want any help?"

"It would be nice if you peeled some potatoes for me while I get the roast ready."

"I can do that," he said softly. "How many do you want me to peel?"

"Probably four if you're as hungry as you say you are."

John sat quietly at the table next to his wife as he peeled the potatoes and carrots for their dinner. The simple task of preparing a meal together proved to be a pleasant diversion from the recent tragedy. Although John was far from accepting the loss of his friend, the bitterness that had surfaced within his heart had begun to subside and the slow process of healing could now begin.

It was late Monday morning before the roads were passable and Doctor Stevenson and Diane were able to return to Red Pine. As they approached the town in Doctor Stevenson's car, they passed a group of men beside the road who were helping Pete Hanson dig the Model T delivery truck out of the snowdrift where Ray had left it at the height of the blizzard. As their car slowly went around the activity beside the road, Pete saw the expression of horror from Diane through the semi-fogged car window as she covered her mouth with her hand and quickly looked away when she realized who the truck belonged to.

The following two days were mixed with anxiety and sorrow for the family and friends of Ray Hanson as they made arrangements for his funeral. Diane spent most of her time in her room, unwilling to see or talk to anyone but her family. On Tuesday evening, after a desperate request by Mrs. Larson, Mary and John came to visit Diane. John waited in the living room with Mr. and Mrs. Larson while Mary entered her bedroom. Diane was sitting up in her bed, clutching a framed photograph of Ray. When she turned and saw Mary, she immediately started crying. Mary quickly went to her side and the two women embraced each other for several minutes before any words were spoken. Finally, Diane had gathered herself enough to converse.

"What am I going to do, Mary?" she asked.

"I'm afraid I don't have any words of wisdom for you, Diane, except to keep praying for strength. I've discovered with John, that there just isn't anything a person can do or say to stop this kind of hurt except to pray for strength and comfort." They continued to hug one another and Mary added, "I sure wish you would've let me know when you got back to Red Pine on Monday, Diane, so we could have talked. The worst thing you can do is to shut yourself up in your room. In times like this you need to surround yourself with your friends, that's what friends are for. Hasn't anyone been able to say anything to you these last few days that gives you any comfort?"

Diane looked up at Mary, and wiping her eyes she said, "I know one thing that I don't ever want to think about or hear again and that is, 'Don't worry, Diane, someday you'll fall in love with another man and everything will be just fine.' My dad said that to me yesterday, and it's the most hurtful thing he ever could've said. I know he meant well and was just trying to comfort me, but the thought of spending my life with anyone else but Ray just seems horrible to me."

They released their embrace and both started to dry their tears. Mary sat beside her on the bed and held her hand as they continued to talk. "Mary," Diane said. "I honestly think I want to live the rest of my life in Ray's memory. I know that sounds crazy and you probably think I am just saying that because I'm feeling sorry for myself right now. But I have been doing a lot of thinking the last few days, about what it means to be married. Even though our engagement was very short, it feels as though we've been married in a way. After all, a sign of a good marriage is to feel that your spouse is your best friend—right? Goodness, Mary, Ray and I have been friends since we were just children. Just like you and John. He was the kindest, gentlest man I ever knew."

Somehow, it seemed, Diane was now able to talk about Ray without coming to tears; her words could flow more freely and there was a noticeable lifting of spirit and sense of acceptance in her voice. Even though Diane's statement about never getting married seemed rather irrational to Mary, it obviously helped her to be able to vent some of the thoughts and feelings that had been racing through her head the last few days.

"There is something I'm confused about though, Mary," she continued. "Remember when I told you that Ray and I gave in to temptation a few weeks ago." Mary nodded. "I find myself asking God to forgive Ray and me for doing that, but on the other hand I find myself thanking Him for the only opportunity that we ever had to express our love for each other in that way. Do you think it's wrong for me to be thankful for that? I mean—I realize that we're supposed to wait until we're married, but at the time it seemed so right and so natural, and I don't feel there was anything evil or dirty about it. We never even thought about right or wrong or whether we were married or not, it just happened, and I have no regrets," she said trying to convince herself.

Mary thought for a moment, then decided that she was not comfortable entering a debate about right and wrong with Diane, given the high level of emotions from the recent tragedy. Cautiously, Mary answered, "I don't know what to tell you about that, Diane. Personally, I think you should look at it as two separate matters. If you feel that you need to ask for His forgiveness, then do it. If you are thankful for something that He has done in your life, then praise Him. But I am not your judge, Diane. This is another one of those examples where we must put our trust in God, that the plans He has for us are to serve Him in ways only He can know."

Mary continued her comforting conversation, but Diane was unwilling to get dressed and come out into their living room to talk with John. In her conversation with Mary, she was well aware of John's difficulties in accepting the loss of his best friend and feared that seeing him right now would send them both tumbling back into emotional disarray.

The day had come for the family and friends of Ray Hanson to say their final goodbye. The last five days had sent the entire community of Red Pine through a whirlwind of emotions: the agonizing concern over Ray's whereabouts during the storm, the uncertainties and stress of the search effort and the stark reality of his passing, the ensuing grieving process. It was the grieving process that had the most powerful and humbling effect on John—powerful because of its ability to stir to the surface the sobering reminder of his own mortality and the preciousness of life. It was as though God had picked him up, shook him like a rag doll and scolded him saying, 'How dare you take your life for granted!'

Every seat in the church was taken when Pastor Adams began his homily. "When I first learned of our loss, I was saddened—I was hurt, and I was confused," said Pastor Adams. "My friends—most of us have experienced these particular emotional elements of death before with the passing of a friend or loved one. And you will find that no matter how many times you encounter these feelings from grieving a loss, it doesn't make it any easier to accept. Indeed, it is even more difficult when someone such as Ray is taken from us. He came from an outstanding Christian family and had kept his faith strong. He was physically strong, hard working, unselfish, and there was nothing he wouldn't do to help his fellow man. His tragic death gives testimony to that fact. He responded to help meet the needs of a young woman in Agate Falls who was having difficulties with childbirth. I'm told that the young woman and her newborn daughter are doing just fine.

"Do you realize what has happened here, my friends? Ray unselfishly risked his life so that a new life would be possible. He didn't even know who this woman was. He didn't have to think about whether to help or not, he knew it was the right thing to do. That was Ray. Always eager to help. Unconditionally! And when we take inventory of all these wonderful characteristics of his personality, we can't help but ask, why? Why would God allow someone this good to be removed from our midst? Why would God want to deprive us from someone who was such a beautiful example of Christian love, and caring, and faith?

My friends, I don't have the answer to those questions. No one on this earth has the answer to those questions. And I'm afraid, my friends, that to try and figure out the answer with our human minds would leave us even more confused than we are feeling right now. We simply must surrender to the fact that God has a plan for all of us. He knows just what He's doing and He is never wrong. God shapes our lives in many different ways. Some of His ways bring us great joy. Some bring us great sorrow and suffering. He is not obligated to reveal to us

A Homeplace

why He does what He does. Someday we will know why He has chosen to take Ray from our lives. It may become clear to us tomorrow, a week from now, a year, or possibly many years from now. It may not be known to us until we meet with our Father in Heaven, but He has a reason. And until we can understand why, we must rely on our faith.

"As you all know, Ray and Diane were to be married in just a few weeks." Pastor Adams held his arm out toward Diane and smiled as he continued. "A couple of weeks ago, Ray and I were in the church together taking some measurements and discussing the design for the new communion railing. Then we started talking about his upcoming wedding. Oh—he was so excited and happy knowing he was getting married! He just smiled from ear to ear when we talked about it. Somehow, we got on the subject of faith and I asked him what his favorite verse in the Bible was concerning faith. He told me that his favorite story was from Mark, Chapter 10, beginning with the thirteenth verse. Now, my friends, you may recall that in this particular chapter in the New Testament, Jesus was teaching in a village near Galilee and it had been a long tiresome day. Some mothers were bringing their children to him so he would touch them, and when the disciples saw this they stopped them from bringing their children. Jesus scolded his disciples and said, 'Let the children come to me, and do not hinder them; for to such belongs the kingdom of God. Truly I say to you, whoever does not receive the kingdom of God with the faith of a child, they shall not enter it.'

"When I asked Ray why that particular verse was so meaningful to him, he explained it to me this way. 'When I think about what Jesus is telling us in those verses, it helps me to get through trying times and keeps my faith strong. It reminds me of when *I* was a child and would ask my mother or father a question. Even though I may not have fully understood their answer, I still believed what my parents told me. I didn't doubt them or question them because I knew they loved me and wouldn't deliberately deceive me. I think that is the message God wants us to understand. Even now, though we are adults, compared to His wisdom and strength, we are still His children, and we should believe in Him with the faith of a young child. I find it very comforting to know I can put the things I don't understand in God's hands.'" Pastor Adams paused for a moment and used his handkerchief to dry his eyes.

"My friends," he continued with a waver in his voice, "I was honestly jealous of Ray's firm understanding of that verse. It is, without a doubt, the best example that I have ever heard of the kind of faith we need to have. Now, I don't know if Ray was that knowledgeable about the rest of the Bible, but it seems to me, that if you were to only remember one message from the Bible, that would be a good one to hold onto—Amen."

The service inside had concluded, and everyone was now gathering in the little cemetery beside the church. The events of the last several days had left John emotionally and mentally drained, and while the graveside rites were being spoken, he was oblivious to anything that was happening. He stood next to Mary as if in a trance, gazing around the cemetery and, for the first time in his life, he realized what a beautiful and peaceful place it was.

Ray's final resting place would be next to some plots owned by his parents. John thought how the gentle elevation of the ground reminded him of a sloped floor in a theatre or show hall and how it were as though the gravestones of the deceased would be the audience to an unobstructed view of the sunsets over Crystal Lake and the little island.

A gentle breeze made a mournful sigh as it moved through the tops of the tall pines, and he imagined how it could be the voice of Ray's spirit letting out a sigh of relief, like a person lying down in a soft bed after a strenuous day. The late morning sun warmed the air so that the little mounds of snow that clung to the branches high up in the evergreens began to break up and fall sporadically, filling the air with a sparkling crystalline powder, anointing the gathering in the cemetery like a sprinkling of frozen holy water from heaven.

Late that night, as John tossed and turned in his sleep, Mary left the bed and moved downstairs to the kitchen table with her journal.

March 19, 1924

I was just a little girl then, but I can remember as if it were yesterday. John and his family were moving into their new home above the general store. I watched from the front porch of the hotel as they carried their belongings up the long stairway behind the store. The Hansons, also new in town, walked across the street and introduced themselves to the Nelsons. In just moments, John and Ray ran off together to play near the lakeshore—the beginning of a dear friendship.

Ray was laid to rest today. And the way in which he was taken from our midst, so sudden and tragic, makes it difficult to believe he is really gone. John, I'm afraid, is finding Ray's death difficult to accept. He seems so distant from me these last few days, like a part of him is gone. At times I can almost feel the anger and bitterness that simmers within him and I fear that it will take nothing less than a miracle to restore his faith.

I, too, have been touched by this tragedy. It has aroused an awareness within me of the preciousness of life, especially the life that grows within me. There is so much danger in this world—both natural and man made. It causes me to worry about what lies ahead for the little person that grows in my womb. I can only pray that God will soon bestow a comfort on John and me regarding these matters.

From the Red Pine Weekly Herald, Thursday March 20, 1924

Card of Thanks

Words cannot express our appreciation and thanks for the many kind and thoughtful expressions of sympathy rendered us over the tragic loss of our beloved son, Raymond.

Pete and Alice Hanson

The next several days after the funeral found the close friends and relatives of Ray Hanson bound in a shroud of emotional numbness. But as the days became weeks, the tasks and obligations of everyday living gradually lifted the encumbering effects from their spirit, allowing smiles, laughter, and thoughts about the future to return to the tight-knit community.

The lifting of spirits was aided by the natural feeling of renewal as winter lost its grip on Northern Minnesota. The snow pack was gone, and the ice on Crystal Lake was black and honeycombed. The water flowed high and swift within the banks of the Agate River and faint specks of green foliage began to appear in the landscape, coaxed by the spring rain and strengthening rays of the sun.

Due to his wife's pregnancy, John had notified the trade school in Minneapolis that he would not be returning to finish his classes in the spring as he had previously arranged. The loss of his good friend, combined with the upcoming birth of his first child, had subtly bridled his youthful, invincible spirit, and heightened a feeling of togetherness and a desire to be home with his family and loved ones. His sense of urgency to become an electrician and prove that he could establish a career on his own had cooled, and now seemed rather trivial to him.

The April twelfth date that was set for Ray and Diane's wedding had come and gone, temporarily dampening the spirits of those who would have participated as they struggled with thoughts of what might have been. John had resumed his attendance at church each Sunday, but Mary could tell by his half-hearted participation in the service, that he was still struggling with his faith, and realized that his attendance was probably more out of a sense of duty to her and to avoid another confrontation with his father, than an earnest desire to give thanks and praise.

Mary's time to deliver was upon her now, and each day was filled with a mixture of fear and impatience. Every morning before leaving for work, John told Mary where he would be working and called home whenever he could to check on her.

On the morning of May thirtieth, 1924, John and Mr. Delaney were working at Hanson's Sawmill, installing new lighting fixtures in one of their storage buildings. Shortly after eleven o'clock in the morning, Mr. Delaney left for Agate Falls to pick up the lighting fixtures and a small material order for another job. Before leaving, he laid out enough work to keep John busy while he was gone. "You can finish drilling the holes before your lunch break, John," said Mr. Delaney. "I should be back shortly after lunch." Pete Hanson had left on a lumber delivery about half an hour earlier and wasn't expected back until one-o-clock in the afternoon.

Mary called Dr. Stevenson's office at eleven fifteen in the morning, informing Diane that her water had broken. Diane assured her that she and the doctor would be right there and hurried to the hotel where Dr. Stevenson was enjoying a cup of coffee with his newspaper, informing him of Mary's condition. Mary's mother joined them as they

A Homeplace

quickly walked up the hill to the house, leaving Andrew to mind the café alone. Rudy and Sarah saw what was happening from the store window, and moments later, Sarah was headed up the hill as well. Dr. Stevenson and Diane, along with Mary's mother, went into the bedroom with Mary while John's mother waited below in the living room. Diane relayed Mary's request to Sarah to call the Hanson's and notify John.

When Alice Hanson rushed into the storage shed, John was eight feet up on a ladder and watched as she clutched her chest with a look of panic, trying to catch her breath from the brisk run from the house. "John," she gasped. "Your mother just called—Mary is having the baby."

In an instant he dropped from his perch on the ladder to the dirt floor below, and without a word, shed the tool pouch from his waist, and ran outside the building where he stood for a moment, anxiously trying to decide the quickest way home. Knowing he would have to travel by foot, he eased into a casual run down the driveway to the road, and when he finally focused on the mental image of his intended route, he left the road and broke into a sprint.

By going cross country, he figured he could shave half a mile from the normal three mile trip to town by road. His shortcut would lead him through an open pasture, around the wet, spongy edge of a vast cattail slough, through a thick and hilly woodland, and across a large hayfield severed by a rain swollen creek.

He hurdled the fence separating the pasture and hayfield and as he approached the creek, he accelerated to the edge of the water, and with the grace and ease of a majestic buck, cleared the 12-foot-wide waterway. His legs churning against the tall thick grass in an awkward, high-stepping gait, took a heavy toll on his stamina, and he tired rapidly as he began to ascend the wooded hillside.

When he reached the top, he stopped and bent over slightly with his hands on his knees, panting heavily, while thoughts of love and fear for his wife raced through his mind. When he looked up and wiped the sweat from his brow, the sight from his lofty vantage point instilled a fresh burst of adrenaline. From here he could see the Red Pine water tower, and the white, sun-lit cross atop the steeple of the Lutheran Church rising above the tree tops, and just to the left, the faint outline of the roof of his own home. At the base of the hill lay a narrow strip of meadow bordering the road into town.

With less than a mile to go, he started down the steep incline, twisting and weaving between trees, struggling to control his momentum. He was nearly to the bottom of the hill when suddenly, he lost his footing on the loose mat of pine needles covering the forest floor, sending him tumbling out of control into the base of a small pine tree. When he bounced off the trunk with his back, the force of impact knocked the wind out of him. He lay on the ground in a breathless panic, desperately trying to replenish his lungs. Within minutes, he recovered enough to sit up, and moments later he was back on his feet.

His brisk-paced walk gradually returned to a run as he made his way through the narrow strip of meadow. When his feet landed on the firm dirt road, free of the resistance of the tall grass, he surged past the school house, down Main Street, and up the hill toward home, while bewildered onlookers watched him race through town.

When John arrived at the house, he was thankful to discover that Mary was still in the beginning stages of her labor. Sarah informed Mary that John was home, and he waited downstairs with his mother. While he kept his anxious vigil, his nervous pacing was accentuated with each vocal outburst from the bedroom.

For several hours, the intermittent groans from the struggle upstairs could be heard throughout the house. John had moved to the front porch where he sat on the railing, nervously wrenching his hands while observing a pair of loons gliding through the sparkling water on the lake below. Once again her struggle could be heard, and moments later, the soft cry of a baby. John quickly climbed the stairs, two at a time, followed by his mother. They were waiting outside the bedroom door when Diane slowly opened it and looked at John with a big, teary smile saying, "Come and see your new son."

As he passed through the doorway, John beheld a sight that would have a profound impact on him for the rest of his life. He stood at the foot of the bed, oblivious to anything except the sight of his wife lying in bed with their infant son wrapped in a little, white blanket cuddled next to her face in peaceful slumber. At that precise moment, the words of a familiar phrase from Ray's funeral passed through his mind.

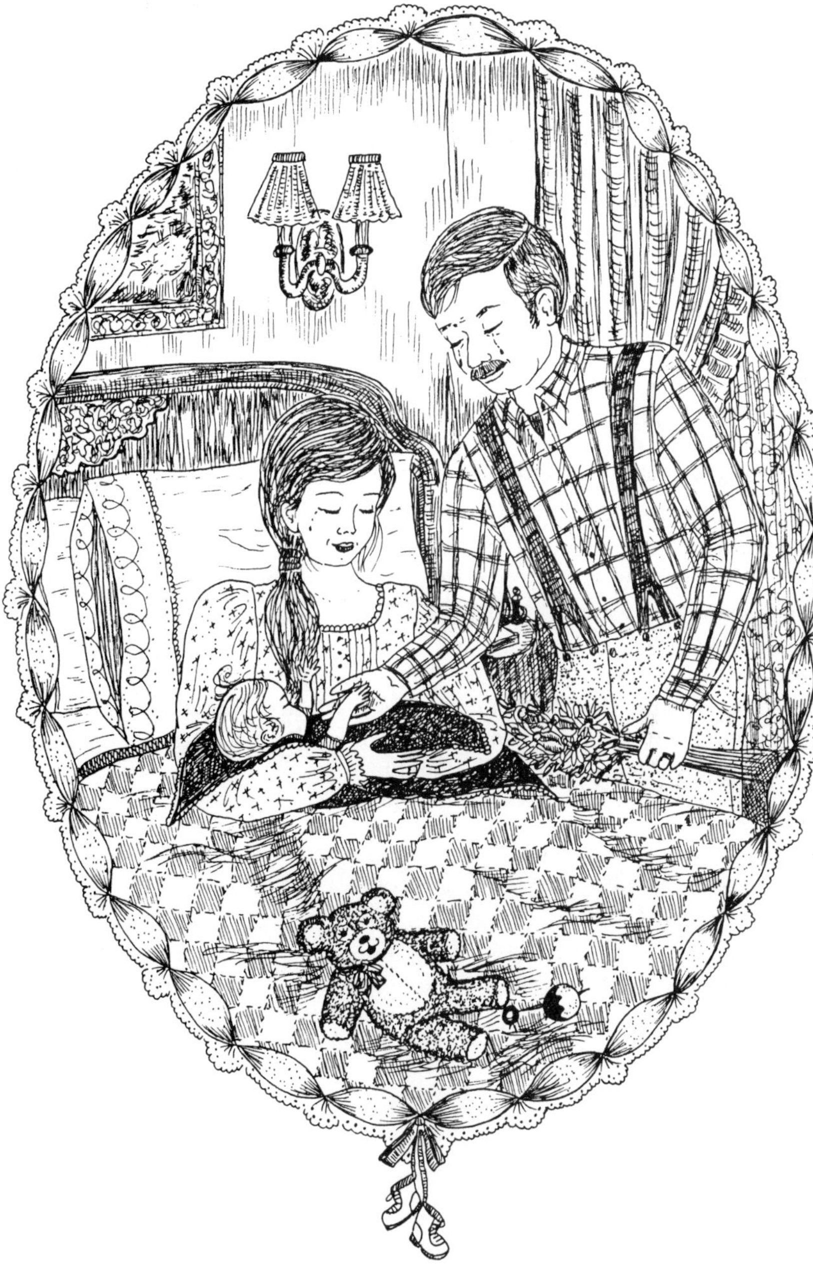

Renewal

"Let the children come to me, and do not hinder them; for to such belongs the kingdom of God. Truly I say to you, whoever does not receive the kingdom of God with the faith of a child, they shall not enter it."

At first, tears of guilt-ridden shame filled John's eyes as he thought about his recent anger with God. Then, as he stared down at the fresh renewal of life that lay in the bed beside his wife, an overwhelming feeling of love and pardon filled his heart, replacing the dark veil of doubt that had challenged his faith for so long. He knelt beside the bed, kissed his wife, and looking into her eyes said, "We have to think of a special name to give him."

"I already have," said Mary.

"What is it."

"John Raymond Nelson," she replied smiling with a glisten in her eyes.

After a long pause in which John struggled to overcome the emotional tightness in his throat, he could only whisper, "Perfect."

From the Red Pine Weekly Herald, Thursday June 5, 1924

News from in town:

Congratulations to John and Mary Nelson on the birth of their baby boy. John Raymond was born last Friday afternoon, May 30th. Mother and son are doing just fine. Reportedly, the father was treated for muscle cramps in his face from a chronic smile.

Changes

Mary sat in the rocking chair by the living room window with her infant son at her breast. She rested her head against the back of the chair and closed her eyes as he established his nursing rhythm. A warm spring wind softly whispered with each gust as it passed through the window screen, swelling the sheer white curtain, and filling the room with the fragrance of freshly cut hay from Mr. Younghans' field that bordered their property. The soft cooing of a mourning dove perched in the oak tree outside the window and the distant singing of red-winged black birds added tranquility to the lazy day.

Gradually, her son's vigorous sucking slowed to an intermittent pace, and he drifted off into a peaceful slumber, induced by his full stomach and the warm security of his mother's bosom. Mary too, began to succumb to the serenity until she heard the sound of footsteps on the front porch, and saw Diane peering through one of the little panes of glass in the front door. She started to knock softly on the door until she noticed Mary motioning her to come in. Diane quietly entered and slowly closed the front door so as not to startle the baby. "Is this a bad time?" Diane whispered." You look as though you were sleeping."

"No, no, come in," Mary whispered. "He's just finished nursing and ready to go to sleep." Mary carefully broke the seal of her infant on her breast, and the little baby continued his sucking response for a moment as she place him in Diane's outstretched arms.

"Oh, he's so cute," whispered Diane as she took the baby from Mary, cuddling him next to her face.

"Let me put him in the cradle, and I'll make us some lunch," said Mary. "Please tell me you can stay for lunch, Diane. It's been two weeks since the baby was born, and I haven't seen you since. It's so good to see you, please stay."

"Yes, yes, I can stay, Mary. But only on one condition."

"What's that?" Mary asked.

"That you let me hold the baby a while longer."

"Please do," said Mary. "He'll sleep for quite a while now. At least that's been his pattern the last few days. Come out into the kitchen so we can talk while I start some lunch for us. I should tell you that John and I decided to call the baby, Jack. John is still his legal name but we

Changes

thought it would prevent a lot of confusion in the future. Besides that, John didn't want to call him junior" she said, looking back as Diane followed her into the kitchen.

"That's probably wise," Diane said.

"How did you manage to get a Friday off?"

"Well, just the afternoon," said Diane. "Dr. Stevenson is going to a convention in Minneapolis this weekend, and the office work is all caught up. He gave me an examination this morning and told me I deserve to have the rest of the day off.." Mary was preparing some soup on the stove and glanced over her shoulder at Diane with a look of concern on her face.

"What did you need an exam for? Aren't you feeling well?"

"I feel just fine, Diane said with a hint of hesitation. "I just wanted the doctor to check on something that I've suspected for some time now."

"And what would that be?" said Mary as she continued to prepare their lunch.

"Mary—I'm going to have Ray's baby." Mary spun around to face her with a look of shock as Diane cuddled Jack in her arms. She looked up at Mary with an unreadable expression on her face and an emotional sparkle in her eyes. Mary stood speechless for a moment, watching as the look on Diane's face seemed to waver between overwhelming happiness and utter heartache. Then she said, "I hope you're not upset with me for saying this, Mary, but this is the happiest day of my life. It's true. I've been praying for this ever since Ray's funeral."

Mary sighed with relief knowing that Diane was joyful about her situation, and they embraced each other for several moments. "I'm so happy for you, Diane. I'm happy that you're happy. Have you told anyone else?"

"You and Dr. Stevenson are the only ones to know so far. He asked me right away if Ray was the father and I said yes. I was so nervous about what Dr. Stevenson might say, but I think he knew I was glad to be pregnant. He even told me 'congratulations.' We talked for a while and I asked him if he felt any differently towards me and if I could continue to work for him. He said, 'Of course you can continue to work for me, Diane. I don't know what I'd do without you.' He explained that he wouldn't normally approve of this type of situation, but he thought that under the circumstances, it would be inappropriate for him to pass judgment on me. He went on to say, 'You're obviously happy about it, and I wouldn't think of tarnishing your joy with some fatherly lecture. I'm sure you realize that it won't be easy trying to raise a child by yourself, but I'll help you in any way that I can, and I am sure that you'll find your friends and relatives will do the same.' He is such a nice man to work for. I am very lucky to have such a good job."

Mary continued to prepare lunch as they talked, and when it was ready, she took the baby and put him in the cradle while they ate.

"I think I would like to find a place in town that I can rent after the baby is born," said Diane.

"Why," asked Mary with concern. "Do you think your parents will ask you to leave home?"

"No, it's not that," said Diane. "I just feel like getting out on my own. I think that if I stay at home, my parents will probably spoil the baby. Also, I'm not sure how Ray's parents will react to my having his child, but I want them to feel included in the baby's upbringing. I think that if I stay at home, they might feel left out. If I live in town, I will be close to work and about the same distance away from both sides of the family."

"It sounds like a good idea if you can afford it," said Mary. "John and I will keep our ears open to find a place for you."

"Where is John working today?" asked Diane.

"He and Mr. Delaney are in Agate Falls working on the new gymnasium at the high school. It sounds like they will be very busy this summer. In fact, John said that Mr. Delaney would like to hire two more men so that they would have another crew."

"I think the whole country is busy these days," said Diane. "Dr. Stevenson said that the last time he was in St. Paul there were construction projects going on everywhere he looked."

"Well," said Mary. "John's father likes to invest in the stock market a little bit, and he was saying the other day that he thinks President Coolidge really has the economy running well. He's not sure how long it can keep going like this, though. His father likes Coolidge because he learned about business while growing up and helping in his father's store, just like he did"

"Speaking of John's father, how's his back? I know I shouldn't say anything because he is a patient of ours, but everyone knows his back gives him trouble. He came in to see Dr. Stevenson on Tuesday, but I don't know what they talked about. They were in the exam room for nearly half an hour just talking."

"He doesn't say much about it when John or I ask him how his back is," said Mary. "He'll just say 'Oh, some days are better than others.' I was talking to Sarah last week and she said she found Rudy in the back storeroom one day just holding his lower back, and it looked like he was nearly in tears. We've noticed that on days when the delivery truck comes, and he has a lot of merchandise to put away, by the end of the day he can hardly stand up straight."

"It must be frustrating for him to have to be so careful with his back. He's always been such a hard worker."

"I'm sure that it is," said Mary. "In a way though, he's his own worst enemy. He won't even let Sarah help him stock the shelves. He just tells her to go back up front and mind the store. 'This is a man's work,' he says—the stubborn old coot."

"Well," said Diane. "He'll eventually have to get some help or his back will just get worse."

Diane started to chuckle when she finished talking and Mary asked, "What's so funny."

"Oh, nothing. This talk about bad backs reminded me of something funny." Diane continued to chuckle and Mary said," You better tell me what is so funny, Diane, or I won't let you hold the baby anymore." Her giggling had now become contagious and Mary was starting to chuckle. "Come on, Diane, tell me what's so funny. Please."

"Okay," she said. " It probably won't seem funny to you , but at the time I thought it was. You know old Mr. Younghans who lives on the farm next to you."

"Yes, I know him. The poor old man is so hunched over that he can't even look up anymore."

"Yes, I know" Diane giggled. "Two Sundays ago, Mom, Dad, Carol, and I were in church when Mr. Younghans and his wife came in and sat in the pew in front of us. Mom and Dad visited with them a little until the service started. Mrs. Younghans had removed her white gloves and set them in the pew next to her purse. Mr. Younghans didn't realize it, but he sat on his wife's gloves."

Diane was now laughing so hysterically that Mary could hardly understand her. The tears rolled down her cheeks and she was holding her stomach as she continued. "When it was time to stand for the opening hymn, Mr. Younghans stood up—and one of the fingers of his wife's glove—was pinched in the crack of his pants." For what seemed like an eternity, Mary and Diane laughed so hard that it hurt, and each time their eyes met, resulted in a fresh outburst. "I can still see old Mr. Younghans—hunched over the pew—with that glove dangling by a finger from the seat of his pants," Diane added, wiping the tears from her eyes.

Eventually the humor passed, and the redness left their faces along with the tears of hysterical laughter, and the two ladies were able to finish their lunch. Diane had decided to walk home rather than wait for a ride from her father. "It's such a nice day," Diane said as she picked up her purse and folded her sweater over her arm. "It will give me a chance to think about how to break the news to my parents. I'm not too worried about what they'll say, but I am somewhat nervous about how Ray's folks will feel."

"Good luck," said Mary as Diane walked out the door. "I'm sure everything will be all right. Thanks for coming over today, Diane. It was really good to see you again. Please come again soon. I wish you had a telephone on the farm so you could call me tonight. I just have to know how it turns out."

"We'll talk at church on Sunday morning," she said as she went down the stairs.

Mary slowly closed the door and watched Diane walk down the street. She thought how good it was to see her laughing and smiling again. She was concerned about how some of the townspeople would react to Diane's unorthodox situation, but her happiness about being pregnant was obvious, and Mary could see that this was just the diversion Diane needed to help her through the recent tragedy. Hopefully, she thought, people will realize that Diane has suffered enough hardship with the loss of her future husband, along with the prospect of raising a child alone, and allow her to live in peace.

It was shortly after six p.m. when John walked up the back stairs and into the kitchen. He was greeted by the pleasant, aromatic blend of roasting chicken, baked potatoes, and a pot of green beans simmering on the stove. The little oak table next to the kitchen window was set as always. The plates, bowls, silverware and drinking glasses in perfect position atop the blue and white checkered tablecloth. In the center, a small white vase with a fresh cutting of lilac blossoms adorned the table setting, a quaint and fragrant representation of the flora of late spring.

"I'm home, Dear."

"I'll be right there, John," said Mary from the cellar. John sat in a chair by the table and removed his work boots. He went to the stove and opened the oven door to verify the source of the homey aroma.

"It'll be another half-an-hour—longer if you don't keep that door shut, my love," said Mary as she closed the cellar door. He hadn't heard her come up the steps, and her remark startled him. He quickly closed the oven door and turned to greet his wife with a sheepish grin on his face. Mary set a jar of peaches on the table and went to embrace her husband. On her tiptoes she wrapped her arms around his neck, and he around her waist as they performed their evening romantic greeting ritual—a long tender kiss followed by an exchange of "I love you."

"It smells so good in here Mary. You're making my favorite meal, and it isn't even Saturday. What's the occasion?"

"Oh, John," she said with child like excitement. "Diane stopped by this noon and we had lunch together. She was as happy as I'd ever seen her, and it made me feel so good to see her that way again. She had the most wonderful news to tell. After she left I kept thinking about what she said, and it made me so happy that I just felt like making something special for dinner."

"So what's her good news?"

"I'll tell you at dinner," she said teasingly. "Why don't you go upstairs and clean up before supper?"

"Sounds good," said John. "Where's my little boy?"

"He's sleeping right now, Honey. I just fed him about an hour ago so he'll sleep for a while yet. Try not to wake him, John, so we can have a nice, quiet meal together."

"Okay, Dear, but I just want to take a peek at him. It seems he changes so much from day to day. I hardly get to see him when he's awake except on the weekends. Sometimes I wish I had a job that allowed me to be home during the day so I could spend more time with you two."

A Homeplace

John returned to the kitchen after his bath just, as Mary set a platter with the steaming hot chicken on the table. "You're just in time, John. Would you please carve the bird while I mash the potatoes?"

"Mmmm, smells real good, Mary. Do you want white meat or dark?"

"White, please. I'm surprised you have to ask yet, John. We've been married almost ten months now." John looked at her, guiltily at first, then realized by her roguish smile that she was teasing him.

"One of these days I'm going to get even with you for all this teasing, Mary."

"Oh, you poor thing," she said facetiously. "You'll just have to get used to it, John. I can't help myself. You're always so serious, anyway. It's a good thing you married me, or you'd never have any fun."

"I'm sorry, Mary. I guess I have a lot on my mind lately. We're so busy at work. Today Mr. Delaney said we may have to start working longer hours and possibly Saturdays too. He's having trouble finding experienced men to hire for another crew."

"Well, I suppose that if you have to, you have to. You know how winters can be so slow. At least you can make enough money during the summer and fall to hold us over for the winter."

"Yeah, I know, but now that I'm married and have a little son, I want to spend a little more time at home with you two."

"It makes me feel good to hear you say that, John. I wish you could be home more too. Let's pray that Mr. Delaney can find someone to hire soon so that you won't have to work long hours for very long."

John and Mary held hands and bowed their heads as they said grace over their meal.

"So, what was the special news you were going to tell me at supper?"

Mary leaned forward toward her husband across the little table and said in a low, secretive voice, "Diane found out today from Dr. Stevenson that she is pregnant with Ray's child."

John abruptly stopped the fork full of green beans from entering his mouth. "She's pregnant!" John looked at her in disbelief. "She's really pregnant!? I can't believe it!" Mary nodded her head affirmatively while chewing her food. She daintily wiped the corners of her mouth with her napkin, then said excitedly. "John, you should have seen the look of joy on her face as she told me. Her prayers have been answered, she said."

Changes

For a moment, John stared out the window contemplatively, then turned to her and said, "Do you realize what this means?"

"What?" she asked nervously, unable to tell if the expression on his face was that of joy or disappointment.

"Ray will continue to live on, in a way that is." John's excitement continued to grow as he ate and contemplated the news that Mary had just revealed. Relieved that John shared her happiness about Diane's situation, she explained to him Diane's initial concern about her future employment with Dr. Stevenson, as well as her desire to find a room to rent in town after the baby is born, because she wanted Ray's parents to feel they could actively participate in the raising of their grandchild.

They continued their conversation as they washed dishes together until the sound of Jack crying in his room meant John would be finishing the chore alone. Mary tended to the needs of the baby while John put away the last of the dishes. All the while, he was consumed by the news of Diane's pregnancy and thoughts about how God truly does work in mysterious ways. Ray would be denied the opportunity to see and raise his own child. Yet Diane, who had hoped and prayed that she had conceived since Ray's funeral, appeared to have had her prayers answered. Surely it would have been better had Ray lived to help raise his child, it wouldn't be easy to raise a child alone.

Then he began to reflect on the cherished friendship he had with Ray and the countless hours of time that Ray had so freely given him when building his home. He began to think about how he would never be able to repay him, now that he was gone. Then it hit him, "Hell," he mumbled to himself. "This *is* my opportunity to repay him. Mary and I will do everything we can to help Diane with her child," he said decisively. "It's the least we can do at this point." He quickly ran upstairs and into the bathroom where Mary was crouched over the tub, bathing their little son. John knelt beside her and laughed as Jack kicked and splashed in the water.

"Isn't it funny the way he carries on like that," Mary said. "He just loves the water." John put his arm around Mary's shoulder and said, "You know, Mary. It just occurred to me that we are going to be raising another child in a few months, in a way that is."

"What do you mean?" asked Mary, puzzled by his statement.

"Well, I was thinking about all this while I finished up the dishes. You know how much Ray helped us when we built our house."

A Homeplace

"I certainly do."

"Well, remember the conversation we had with Ray on our wedding night? We were on the dock, and he helped us load our things in the boat. I thanked him for all his help, both with the house and the wedding, and said I didn't know how I could ever repay him. I can still hear his words today when he said, 'Don't worry, you can help me next year when I build my house.' Obviously that isn't going to happen now. I don't know about you, but I feel very obligated to help Diane any way we can. If it wasn't for Ray, we would still be pounding nails on this house. In fact, I don't think we would have even been able to build it if it wasn't for Ray's help and his family's generous offer of trading our standing timber for their lumber. That saved us a lot of money."

"You're absolutely right, John. I agree with you completely," said Mary as her eyes moistened with emotion. "The first thing we have to do is find a place in town for Diane to live that she can afford."

Mary finished bathing Jack and went into the bedroom to nurse him. John lay on the bed next to his wife and studied the look on his son's face, as his eagerness to nurse quickly transformed into an expression of contentment as the milk began to flow. John smiled at his wife and said, "Doesn't take much at this age to make a child happy, does it?"

"Nope. Just a warm meal and dry pants," said Mary.

After his feeding, John took his son down to the living room and rocked him in the chair for over an hour. After fussing for several minutes, he gave in to the repetitive squeak in the floor, and the pacifying motion as the chair rocked back and forth, and fell asleep cradled in the warmth and security of his father's strong arms and soft, flannel shirt. Mary was seated at the table writing a letter to her aunt and uncle in North Dakota when she noticed John's eyes were getting heavy. "Do you want me take Jack and put him in the cradle?" Mary whispered.

"No, not yet," said John softly. "Let me hold him for a few more minutes. Then I'll put him to bed. I was thinking of going to bed soon anyway. I'd like to get up early and catch some walleye for supper tomorrow. Might be the last Saturday I can do that for a while if we can't get caught up at work."

"Walleye sounds good John. We haven't had any for so long."

"I know. It just isn't the same going fishing without Ray, but I guess I'll just have to get used to it. My dad said they've been biting pretty good the last few days. If he's right, I'll be home before eight in the morning. What did you have planned for tomorrow?"

"Well, I just thought maybe we could work in the yard a little. It looks like the grass we planted last fall is about ready to be cut."

"Well, my dear. It just so happens that I figured on cutting it anyway."

Mary went back into the kitchen to answer the telephone. "Hello. Oh, Hi, Diane," Mary said with surprise. "Where are you calling from?"

"You'll never believe it," said Diane. "When I got home this afternoon the phone company was here installing the new phone my dad ordered. He ordered it three weeks ago and kept it a secret all this time."

"It's Diane," Mary whispered to John. "They had a phone put in today."

John acknowledged her with a smile and rose from the chair, walked into the kitchen and gave his wife a kiss on the lips while she listened intently to Diane on the phone. He gestured with his head that he was going upstairs and she nodded affirmatively, still listening to Diane. After he tucked his son into his cradle, he went to bed so he could get up early and be on the lake before sunrise. Experience had taught John that low light conditions were the best time to catch the timid walleye in the clear water of Crystal Lake.

The stars were still visible when John walked out the back door and went to the shed for his fishing tackle. He strolled down the narrow brick sidewalk, making his way to his father's dock. Rudy, who was already up and working, came over to help him right one of the little wooden rowboats on shore. A slight fog rose from the warm lake water into the cool morning air, and a distant call of a loon echoed across the water.

"Morning, Father."

"Morning, John. I don't recall seeing you fish at all this year until now."

"Well, you're right, Dad. I've just been busy with the house and yard this spring. That and the fact that it just isn't the same for me now that Ray is gone. It kind'a takes the fun out of it anymore."

A Homeplace

"Yes, I'm sure it does, John."

"You'd better let me turn the boat over myself, Father. You know how tender your back is."

"Yes, I'm painfully aware how tender my back is. I have to learn to take it easy nowadays, but damn, it's not easy when I've been able to work hard all these years. Say, John," said his father as he watched him turn the boat upright. "Would you stop up to the house when you get back from fishing? Your mother and I have a favor to ask of you."

"Sure. I'll stop back. If they're biting as good as you say, it won't take me long to catch a meal." John rowed out to the island and anchored in a spot about thirty yards from shore and perfectly in line with a towering red pine tree on the island and the outlet of the Agate River. It was a honey hole that he and Ray had discovered when they were just kids. If the fish were biting, it always produced, and this morning was no exception. In less than an hour, he had four nice walleyes on the stringer and was rowing back to the dock.

Sarah and Rudy were in the stock room as John began rowing back. "That sure didn't take him long," said Rudy.

"No, it sure didn't, Sarah replied. "Is he going to stop up to the store when he gets back?"

"Yes, he is."

"Are you going to tell him about your job offer in St. Paul?"

"I don't think I will yet, Dear. Let's wait 'til I get back. Even though the job sounds good, I still need to go down and look things over before you and I can make a final decision. No use raising any concern 'til need be."

John rolled the boat over on the beach and carried his catch up to the wooden table behind the store where he was met by his father.

"I may as well clean them here if you don't mind."

"No, not at all, Son. That's what it's for."

As Rudy and Sarah watched, John started to clean his fish on the wooden fish cleaning table that was built for the guests at the cabins. "What did you want to ask me, Father?"

"Well, Son. I'm going to go to St. Paul on Monday for a couple of days. There is some business I need to do, and I thought I'd visit your Uncle Richard while I'm down there. I just wanted to ask you if you'd stop here before and after work to see if your mother needs any help with the store or the resort. Rose is very helpful, but there are some things about this business that require some heavy lifting. Some of the guests may need help with the boats or things like that."

"Sure, I'd be glad to. I never thought I'd feel this way, but I kind of miss working around the resort."

Sarah and Rudy exchanged glances of delight after John's remark. "Well, thanks, John. I sure appreciate your helping me out. It's a lot easier for me to leave if I know the ladies have some help if they need it. What do you and Mary have planned for today?" asked Sarah.

"Well, I think we'll work in the yard today. She loves to do that, but it's hard for her to get out during the day when I'm at work because the baby needs a lot of attention right now. I think I'll watch Jack while she gets out and works in the yard."

"Tell her to come down and visit us, John. We live so close, but you'd think we were miles apart, as often as we see each other."

"I know," said John. "That's exactly what *her* mother says too. You two are always so tied down with the store, and her folks are busy with the hotel, it doesn't leave much time for visiting."

"It seems the only time we get to see our grandson is in church on Sunday," Sarah complained.

John finished cleaning the fish and gathered the rest of his fishing gear and left for home. "See you tomorrow in church," he said as he started back up the hill.

Mary was just getting out of bed when John came into the kitchen. He could hear the water run in the bathroom sink and decided to start breakfast as soon as he had rinsed the fish fillets.

Mary was still in her robe when she entered the kitchen. "Coffee and bacon sure smell good, John. Thanks for starting breakfast." She noticed the large fillets in the sink and said, "Oh, good, looks like fish for supper tonight."

"Yep," said John. "They were really biting good this morning."

"Same place as always?" Mary asked.

"Yep. Is our son still sleeping?"

"No, he's awake. You should have seen him. I went to check on him when I got out of bed and he was just lying there with his eyes open and sucking his thumb, just as content as he could be."

"Well, I hope he's going to be like that all day," said John. "I want you to have some time for yourself today. Work in the yard, visit your folks or whatever you feel like. I realize you'll have to be here to feed him, but the rest of the time is yours."

A Homeplace

Mary put her arm around his waist and they exchanged a long kiss. "Thank you, John. That's really nice of you. I think I will visit my parents this morning, but when Jack takes his afternoon nap we can work in the yard together. I'd like to spend some time alone with you, too, you know."

"Okay, it's a date—an afternoon together in the yard. How many eggs do you want for breakfast, Mary?" Jack started to cry, and as Mary left the kitchen to tend to him, she smiled at John and said, "We've been married for ten months now, my dear. You should know how many eggs I have for breakfast." John smiled as she disappeared through the doorway, and added another egg to the pan.

Mary returned to the kitchen and sat at the table with the baby in her lap. "You didn't feed him already did you?"

"Nope. Just changed him." John placed his wife's breakfast in front of her, then sat next to her with his. After their prayer of thanks John said, "By the way, what did Diane have to say last night?"

"Well, she's very happy. Everything turned out okay and she's relieved to have it off her chest. She told her parents yesterday at dinner, and then she called Ray's parents last night. Her parents were a little shocked at first, but then they were happy for her when she explained how happy she was to be having Ray's child. Her dad was disappointed, though, when she told him she wanted to move to town after the baby was born, but he finally agreed.

Ray's father was still out working in the mill when she called the Hansons. She said Mrs. Hanson broke down in tears when she told her. She said Alice was so happy that a part of Ray would now live on, just like you said. It sounded as though Pete has been very depressed since the funeral and that it's a good thing the sawmill is so busy because it helps him take his mind off things. She thinks that this is just the thing that may help him get over their loss. She said Alice could hardly wait to hang up the telephone so she could walk down to the sawmill and tell Pete the good news. Anyway, Diane is happy because everyone who's close to her is being very supportive."

"Well," John said. "We have to realize that there are those in town that will still raise their eyebrows because she got pregnant before she was married. I know how much in love those two were, and that the baby inside her was conceived out of pure love for each other."

"I agree," said Mary. "Besides, no one on this earth has the authority to pass judgment on her."

"Oh, by the way, I almost forgot to tell you," John said. "My father is leaving for St. Paul on Monday for a couple of days and asked me to stop at the store before and after work to check on Mother and Rose. I just thought you should know because if they need any help, I may be a little late coming home Monday and Tuesday evening."

"What is your dad going to St. Paul for?"

"Something to do with business. He's also going to visit my Uncle Richard and his wife."

"Did he say what kind of business he was going for?"

"No, he didn't and I didn't even think to ask him. It's probably for some new item he wants to start carrying in the store. He's always been very cautious about adding new products.

"I have a strange feeling that this isn't an ordinary business trip," said Mary.

"What do you mean."

"Has your father ever gone to the city for business before?" asked Mary.

"Not for several years anyway. I can't remember for sure. I think it was before we started the resort business."

"I just think it's strange that he didn't tell you what it was about. He's always been so quick to volunteer information about his business. You know, sometimes I think he still hopes that you will take it over someday."

John shrugged his shoulders. "We'll just have to wait and see when he gets back," he said, not sharing her suspicions. "I'm sure that if it's anything important, he'll tell us right away."

After they finished their breakfast, John tidied up the kitchen while Mary fed Jack. She left for the hotel to visit her parents while John stayed home and looked after his son. That afternoon John and Mary did their yard work together, cutting the grass for the first time since seeding it last fall. They started the installation of a picket fence along the sidewalk in front of the house.

John had been making the pickets in the evenings and weekends as time permitted, while Mary had been painting them out in the yard on nice days during the week when Jack was napping. By the end of the day, John and Mary had all the posts in place and the top and bottom rails were fastened to the posts ready for the installation of the pickets.

The house and yard had become a labor of love for the young couple, especially for Mary. Next to her husband and son it was her pride

A Homeplace

and joy. She loved to experiment with flowers and shrubbery when growing up at home and was always receiving compliments from the guests for the colorful flower gardens that she tended around the hotel. She was equally successful in the vegetable garden, growing all the vegetables and many of the herbs used for meals served at the hotel dining room. Mary had always had a deep interest and love for nature, and her bedtime prayers usually included words of thankfulness for the world outdoors.

It was nearly seven o'clock when John got home from work on Tuesday evening. He entered the back door and received his usual loving reception from his wife and son. "I'm sorry I'm so late, Dear. I stopped at the store, and Mom needed some help with one of the boats."

"Oh no, what happened?" Mary asked.

" One of the guests didn't pull it up onto shore far enough, and the wind took it away. Luckily it beached out on the island or it would have drifted clear across the lake."

"Oh well, it could have been worse," said Mary. "Your father should be home tonight anyway. How was work today, John?"

"Busy, but I have some good news." He sat down in the chair to remove his work boots and then held his arms out to receive his son.

Mary placed Jack in his arms and asked impatiently, "Well, what's the good news, John?"

"You'll be happy to know that Mr. Delaney hired two men to start next week. They're men he used to work with in Duluth. One of them is originally from Agate Falls and wants to move back. The other is just a good friend of Mr. Delaney and agreed to come and work for him. Doesn't look like I'll have to work Saturdays now. As long as we can keep up, that is."

"Oh, John, that is good news. Thank goodness he was able to hire someone so quickly."

"That's for sure," he replied. "Mr. Delaney said he would've hired a couple of men from around here, but there just aren't any with experience, and we're too busy to take the time to train someone. The two men he hired have enough experience so he can send them off to another job right away."

"I am so thankful for that, John," Mary said with sincerity, putting a pan of well-risen dinner rolls into the oven. "Supper will be ready shortly, John, so you'd better get washed up."

"Yes, Dear."

Mary and John were reading quietly in the living room when John jumped up to answer a knock at the front door. Mary noted the 9:30 display on the wall clock and said, "Who could be here at this time of night?"

John opened the door, surprised to find his parents standing on the front porch. "Mother, Father, come in. Is something wrong?" John quickly grew concerned by a rather nervous expression on their faces. "Where is Rose? Is she all right?"

" Yes, yes, everyone is just fine," said Rudy reassuringly. He released a sigh of anxiety and said, "Mary, John—we realize it is getting late, but your mother and I have something to tell you and it's rather important."

"What is it, Father?" asked John.

"I returned from my trip to the city about an hour ago, and I have some news to share with you two. As I told you last week, John, I went to St. Paul for some business. What I didn't tell you was that I went to interview for a job opportunity. Let me back up a little." Mary and John sat down at the table together and listened intently as Rudy continued.

"As you know my back has been giving me a lot of problems lately, and about a week ago I had a long talk with Dr. Stevenson about it. He said that about the only way I'll be able to keep working without ruining my back completely is if I stop all heavy lifting. Now, I'm sure you two realize that it's impossible to run our business without doing any heavy lifting. It isn't the first time Dr. Stevenson has told me this, and I had mentioned this to your Uncle Richard about a month ago.

"Well, last week Richard called and told me about a management opportunity at a large grocery store chain in St. Paul. He has become good friends with the owner of that chain, because he has been delivering produce to them for several years now. Anyhow, he set up a meeting with the owner, and that's where I went yesterday. He really seems to want to hire me, but I'd have to start right away. They are opening a new store in three weeks, and the person he was going to have manage that store decided to move back to Chicago. I've decided to take that job, John, and that means your mother, Rose, and I are going to move back to the city. I'm going to move back down and live with your uncle until I can find a house, and then I'll send for your mother and Rose.

"What we wanted to ask you, John, is this: Do you think that you and Mary would be interested in taking over our business? I would sell it to you with very affordable terms. In fact, I would give you the resort business because you've done so much of the work to build it up anyway. The general store is running smoothly, and you already know a good deal about it too. I know you're in a good position financially because you were able to pay cash for most of your house, and you don't have very much left to pay me on your house loan. I think it's just under three hundred dollars. I would be willing to make the payments for the store very easy for you because I really would like to see it stay in the family.

"Until you decided to become an electrician, John, you helped your mother and I make this business what it is today, and you deserve a chance to have it if you want it. Now, John, before you give me an answer, I want you to know that I will understand completely if you don't want to do this. We had a good talk about that when you decided to pursue a career as an electrician, and I will respect whatever decision you make. I just want to offer it to you first. I'm sure that I won't have any trouble finding a buyer if you're not interested, Son, so don't let your decision be guided by a notion that you need to help your mother and I make our move. That simply isn't the case."

Mary and John exchanged stunned expressions by the sudden decision before them. "I don't quite know what to say, Father. I'm a little shocked by all this information all at once. When did you say you were leaving?"

"I told the owner that I could start next week. He was relieved when I told him because he thought it would take me a couple of weeks to get things in order up here. Like I said John, I don't expect you two to make a decision tonight. Take a couple of days to think about it. If you're not interested just let me know. There is a man in St. Cloud named Carlson, who's stayed at the resort. I can't recall his first name right off, I'm sure you'd know him. Anyway, he's stayed here two or three times, and the last time he was here he mentioned that if I ever wanted to sell the business to let him know. He owns a small hotel there and seems to think that resorts will someday be a very good business to be in. I'm not sure if he knows what he's talking about, but I know that our little business has grown steadily every year. It's getting to be that there's hardly ever a week when the cabins aren't full. I did get the impression, though, that he was more interested in the resort than the store."

"Are you sure that somehow we can't find a way for you to keep your business where you don't have to strain your back? Maybe you could hire someone to do the heavy work," said John.

"I've thought of that already, John, believe me. The fact is, most of what I do around here is bull work, so to speak. If I hired someone to do that, your mother can handle everything else in the store, it would leave me to stand around or push a broom. I'm too young to just start fading away into the shadows, John. I have a lot of retail experience with everything from groceries to hardware, and now I have an opportunity to start using my brain instead of my back. It's like when you wanted to try the electrical field. If you hadn't tried it, you'd have forever wondered, what if?"

"We should go now, Rudy," said Sarah. "It's late and these two have a lot to think about. Just remember one thing," Sarah added. "Don't just think it over. Pray about it. It's a big decision and it will definitely change your lives."

"Thanks, Sarah," said Mary. "We will." Rudy and Sarah left, and as John closed the front door he turned to Mary with a look of bewilderment and said, "Now what do we do?"

"What do *you* want to do, John? I would be happy with whatever decision you make. The only question I have is that if we decide to take over the business, would we be able to keep our house too? We have so much into it besides money. We have our hard work, our pride, our memories, especially the memories of Ray. Most of all, it's where our son was born."

"Let's go up to bed and think on it," said John. "It's getting late." They went upstairs and neither one spoke as they dressed for bed. Mary came out of the bathroom, turned out the light, and climbed into bed. John lay on his side next to her with his head propped up with his hand. Mary was lying on her back and watching her husband as he thought about their new opportunity. He gently brushed the stray strands of hair from her eyes saying, "Remember what I said last Friday—about wishing I had a job that allowed me to be home so I could be with you two?"

A Homeplace

"Yes, I remember," she answered.

"It's like God is listening to everything we say."

"What do you mean?" asked Mary

"He's giving me a chance to be home with you and Jack. Not only that, if we did decide to take over the business, you'd still want to keep this house, wouldn't you?"

"Yes," said Mary. "If at all possible."

"Well, that would leave the whole living quarters above the store unused."

"So what do we do with it?" Mary asked.

"Who do we know that is looking for a place to live in town?" John asked with a smile.

John watched her as she pondered what he had said and noticed the sparkle of bright moonlight coming through the window gather in the corners of her moistening eyes. "You're right, John. It's as though He is listening to everything we say."

"Not only listening, but answering," John added.

The decision had been made. The choice was very easy. The excitement, however, kept them up all night. Ironically, though, this was the first night that Jack would sleep the whole night through. It was like a heavenly sign of assurance by God, through their little infant son, that the right decision had been made. A symbol of peacefulness and contentment from above to reinforce and reward their faithfulness, and to show them that even through all the recent changes in their lives, everything would be alright.

The next morning John informed his father of their decision to accept his offer and gave Mr. Delaney his notice. He was thankful that Mr. Delaney was able to hire two new men, which made his resignation easier to deliver. "I hate to see you leave, John," said Mr. Delaney. "But I don't blame you a bit. In fact I'd have to question the intelligence of any man who would pass up an opportunity to make a living while staying home with his family. But if it doesn't work out Lad, come and see me. I've always got room for a good man like you."

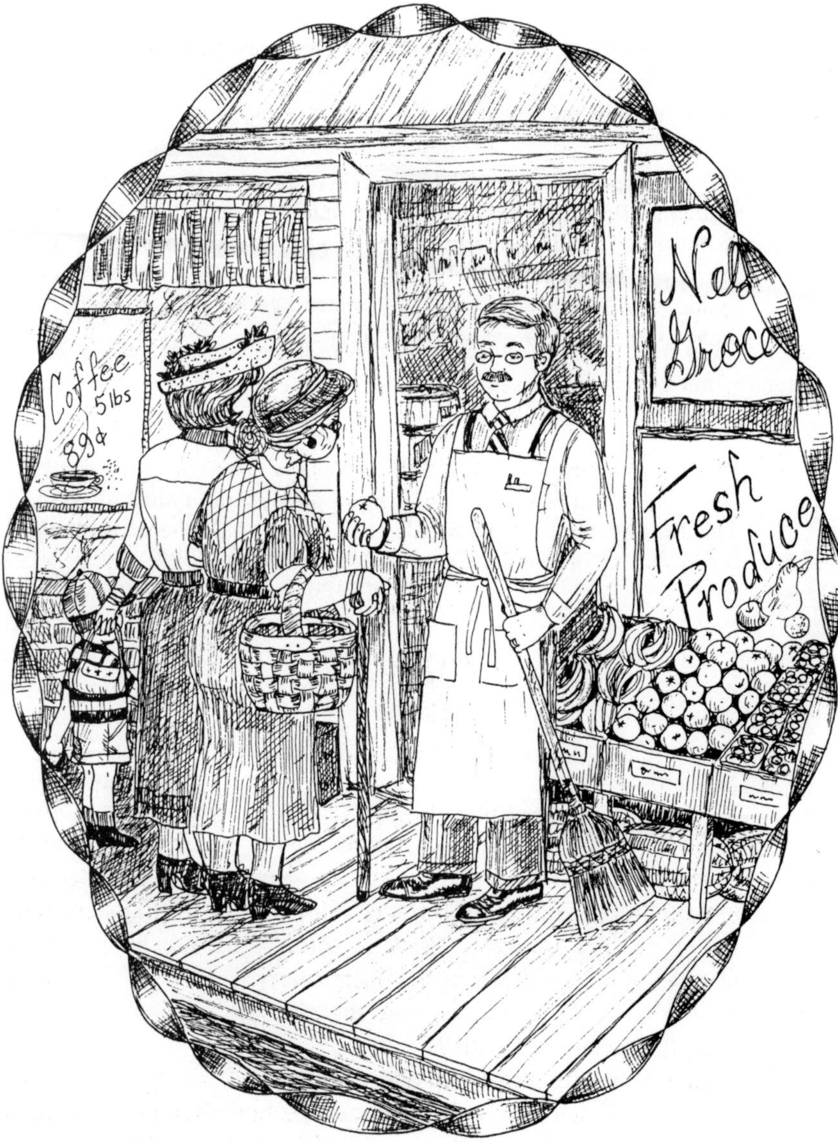
Coffee 5lbs 89¢
Fresh Produce

A Homeplace

From the Red Pine Weekly Herald, Thursday July 31, 1924

News from in town:

Mr. and Mrs. Rudolph Nelson and their daughter Rose, left last Saturday, the 26th for their new home in St. Paul where Rudy will be assuming his duties as manager of a new grocery store chain in the cities. Nelson's General Store and Resort has been purchased by his son, John. Rudy was a fine citizen and business man for many years in Red Pine and will be missed.

From the sheriff's report:

William Rutger, of rural Red Pine, was convicted in U.S. District court in Duluth last week for being in possession of alcohol mash. The Judge verbally reprimanded the jury who deliberated all night for taking so long to decide on such a clear case.

On a Saturday morning in August, Diane walked into Hopkins Bakery to buy some bread while her mother was at the library. When she entered the door, she overheard August Rutger's wife, Beatrice, gossiping with Madeline Nyberg, as Laura Hopkins was filling her order.

"It's a perfect example," Beatrice said, "What can happen when you monkey around like that before you're married. Now she'll have to raise a child alone. My goodness, who'd ever want to marry a woman with an illegitimate child anyway?!"

When Madeline looked up and saw Diane standing behind Mrs. Rutger, she cleared her throat in a desperate, but obvious, attempt to silence Beatrice. Beatrice turned around and immediately blushed when she saw Diane standing behind her. For what seemed like an eternity, they stared at each other in a state of mutual shock.

Changes

Laura quickly tried to suppress the sudden hostile atmosphere saying, "Well good morning, Diane! It's so nice to see you. What can I help you with?"

It was far too little and too late for redemption. Horrified by the hurtful words spoken by Mrs. Rutger, Diane turned and walked out the door as tears filled her eyes. She started to run toward the library when she was met by Mary, who was walking toward her. The look of distress on Diane's face was obvious, and Mary grabbed her as she tried to run past.

"Diane, my goodness what's wrong? Why are you crying?" When Diane explained what had happened, Mary's long subdued Scottish blood began to boil. "Why that gossiping old biddy! She's the last person on earth to be criticizing *anyone* after what I read in the paper on Thursday."

Diane continued on to the library to meet her mother as Mary stormed into the bakery just in time to hear Beatrice end her lecture on moral behavior.

"It must be just an awful embarrassment to her family," Beatrice concluded as the screen door on the bakery snapped shut.

"Good morning Mrs. Hopkins, Mrs. Nyberg, Mrs. Rutger," Mary said, nodding to each of them.

Mrs. Rutger's verbal rambling fell suddenly quiet as she turned to see Mary Nelson standing behind her. The three ladies returned a rather submissive greeting to Mary, and then Laura took her order. The normally festive atmosphere in the bakery was awkwardly quiet as Laura Hopkins filled Mary's order. Everyone knew how close Mary and Diane were.

After Mary paid for her baked goods, she turned to Beatrice, put her hand on her shoulder and said with piercing condescendence, "Oh, Mrs. Rutger. I was so saddened to read the article in the paper about your son's conviction for being in possession of alcohol mash. It must be terribly embarrassing for your family." Then she looked at all three women and with a big smile said, "Good-day ladies."

Mrs. Rutger stood with her chin dropped in silent, red-faced astonishment and watched Mary walk out the door as Laura Hopkins and Madeline Nyberg covered their muffled snickers with their hands.

A Homeplace

On December 6, 1924, at seven o'clock in the morning and at her parents home, Diane gave birth to a healthy boy. Her mother and sister, Carol, along with Dr. Stevenson stayed by her side throughout the nine-hour struggle. Diane was completely exhausted after the delivery and slept much of the day. It was shortly after six p.m. when Mary and John came to visit. When they arrived, everyone gathered in Diane's bedroom after she finished nursing her son. Her parents and sister, Pete and Alice Hanson, John and Mary all stood around her bed where she proudly displayed the sleeping, content little newborn. Emotions reached a climax when Diane placed the little infant into Mrs. Hanson's arms, already in tears at the sight of her deceased son's offspring.

From the Red Pine Weekly Herald, Thursday, December 11, 1924.

News from the country:

Early last Saturday morning, Diane Larson of rural Red Pine gave birth to a beautiful baby boy, Raymond John. Mother and son are doing fine.

The Growing Years

The next several years were prosperous ones for Red Pine, as well as for the rest of America. The country enjoyed a time of growth. Businesses generally did well, and incomes grew accordingly. Each year, the population of the little community increased by four or five, and in September of 1927, John and Mary made another contribution to the populous by adding a daughter to their family. She was named after Mary's grandmother, Caroline, whom she had never known except through a photograph.

Diane and her son, Ray, lived comfortably above the general store. John and Mary kept her rent affordable and helped her raise her son. She continued her employment with Dr. Stevenson, whose practice flourished in Red Pine and gate Falls. Diane enjoyed the convenience of living in town and above the store. She was able to walk to work each day to the doctor's office just a block away, and to come home at noon and enjoy lunch with her son, Mary and John, and their children.

From mid-May to mid-September, John walked down to the cabins early in the morning and took care of some of the responsibilities associated with the resort before it was time to open the store.

John was much like his father—he loved to get up early and enjoy the peace and tranquility during what his father always referred to as, "the best part of the day." One of the first chores that could be done without disturbing the guests was emptying trash cans. Normally this was an easy task, but an occasional night visit by a bear or raccoon would add complications by scattering the contents of a trash can throughout the resort grounds. He always made sure that the fishing boats were bailed out if it had rained during the night so they would be ready for the early-rising fisherman. His other duties included cleaning the outhouses each morning and raking the beach front free of any weeds or driftwood that may have washed up during the night.

His father had taught him that taking care of the little things resulted in an appreciation by the guests that kept them coming back. Their growing list of repeat customers proved he was right.

A typical day for Mary started with feeding the children and getting them dressed before walking down to the store to help John open. The store opened at eight o'clock every morning, Monday through Saturday, and closed at five. Diane would bring her son, Ray, to the store each morning before she went to work. Mary had organized a small area in the back store room for the children to play and nap.

After the store was open John could resume his duties as required by the resort. By mid-morning he would be able to accomplish some of the more disruptive maintenance needs like grounds-keeping or building repairs that would have otherwise disturbed the sleeping guests.

After lunch, when the children were fed and Diane returned to the doctor's office, Mary brought the children back up to the house for afternoon naps while John finished the day working at the store. After closing the store, he made a final round at the resort, making sure the needs of the guests were taken care of before going home, usually by six o'clock.

All of the cabins were of the housekeeping variety, requiring very little attention until checkout time on Saturday mornings. Change over time was very hectic, but fortunately Diane was able to watch the children and mind the store for a few hours while Mary helped her husband clean the cabins and change all the bedding before the new guests arrived.

The general store was closed on Sunday and the guests were encouraged to make any purchases they needed on Saturday when they checked in. Sundays were set aside for worship and family just like their parents had raised them, and John and Mary continued to run the resort in the same tradition.

On Sundays after church services, John would stop at the resort on the way home and check on the guests while Mary and the children continued to walk home.

John grew to love the business, mostly because of his ability to be home with his family, but also because it allowed him to see his friends each day as they came into the store for groceries or hardware items. Summer was a very busy time for John and Mary, but when fall and winter arrived, and the only responsibility was the operation of the store, it was like a vacation for them. During this time, Mary would usually stay home during the day because John could easily manage the store alone.

Both businesses continued to grow each year. John kept in close contact with his father who frequently called from the cities and kept John and Mary abreast of new products and trends in the grocery business.

A Homeplace

Every year, the occupancy rate at the resort was at nearly full capacity, largely due to a loyal customer base. It was common for guests to make reservations for the following summer when they checked out at the end of their stay. In mid-September of 1928, after closing the resort for the season, John began thinking about whether or not to expand the resort by adding more cabins.

On a warm Sunday October afternoon, on their way home from church services, Mary decided to have a picnic lunch down by the lake. After putting a lunch together, they returned to the resort grounds and let their children play while they talked. Mary and John sat on a blanket with Caroline in the shade of the same sprawling oak tree where John had proposed to Mary, while Jack was busy climbing among the white hulls of the overturned boats on the beach.

"What would you think of adding three or four more cabins over the next few years, Mary?" asked John. "I've been thinking it over lately, and I'd like to know how you feel about it."

Mary, surprised by his sudden entrepreneurial flare up, thought for a moment, then smiled at him when she asked, "Do we really need more cabins, John, or are you just satisfying an itch to build something?"

He returned a boyish grin and said, "You know me pretty well. I do admit to having a desire to build, but we also have to remember that for the last two years now, the resort has had close to 100 percent occupancy during our season. It's getting hard to find time slots for all of our repeat customers, much less any new ones. It seems like a good opportunity to expand the business. I don't think we'll have any problem keeping them full if we do build them, and we can always use the extra income."

"Well, okay, Dear. I'm curious. Show me where we could put four more cabins."

"I was thinking there is a lot of room between cabins three and four, and also between six and seven. I think we could put one cabin in each of those locations without people feeling they're on top of each other. Then I thought about putting one or two more out on the island."

The Growing Years

Before he finished his sentence, John noticed Mary's quick frown of displeasure. "What's the matter?" he asked.

"I'd go along with the first two you mentioned, but I really hate to see us build up the island, John." She recalled how disappointed and guilty she felt when they had to harvest the large stand of red pine in exchange for the lumber used in the construction of their home. She couldn't bear the thought of tarnishing the beauty of the island and the view of the virgin pines that somehow escaped the indiscriminate timber harvest of the previous century.

"Why?"

"Because, John, it's so beautiful to look out there and see the tall pines. It looks the way I imagined it did 100 years ago. It's such a special place right now with only one cabin on it, and from here you can't even see it because it's hidden so nicely among the trees. I think we should keep it that way. Perhaps we should advertise it as a special honeymoon cottage," she said with a smile and a suggestive twinkle in her eye.

John returned the smile with a reddened face, acknowledging her hint of the romantic pleasures of their wedding night in the little island cabin. "Yes, I see what you mean."

"Besides," said Mary. "In a few more years, we'll probably want to start making some improvements to the first cabins that you and your father built. Maybe we should even think about putting electricity in them, and indoor plumbing."

"Well, okay! You're the boss," said John. "We'll just build two more and then start fixing up the older ones like you said."

"I don't want to be the boss," she said. "I want you to be the boss. But it pleases me when you ask my advice, John. I'm thankful that you include me in our business matters." Mary knelt in front of her husband who was still sitting on the blanket. Caroline, who had recently learned how to walk, was busy mastering the technique of standing up and sitting down and taking a few clumsy steps on the uneven ground. Her father held her hand to steady her as she stood beside them.

"Well," he said. "For someone who doesn't want to be the boss, you sure have a way of explaining things that makes you get your way a lot. Just remember now, it's your fault if we're short of money some day," he said with a teasing manner.

"Being rich has never been one of my goals, Mr. Nelson. Besides, you're already the richest man in town," Mary replied with a playful grin.

John let out a loud chuckle. "How do you figure that?"

"Because! You have a gorgeous wife and two wonderful children." She thrust herself forward against him knocking him onto his back and started to laugh. Caroline joined in the fun, and when Jack saw what was happening, he too came running, and they all hog-piled onto their father laughing and giggling.

During the remainder of that fall, as time allowed, John installed electricity in all of the cabins except for the one on the island. The "Honeymoon Cottage," as it affectionately became known, would forever be a rustic, quaint, and private retreat for guests who didn't mind using a wood stove for heat and kerosene lamps. John and Mary decided to wait until the following fall before starting construction of another cabin. It was a decision, however, that would continue to be put off for several more years.

The stock market crash in the fall of 1929 sent the business climate into a tailspin all across the country. John and Mary were fortunate to have just made the final payment to his father on their house loan and to have had such a manageable payment plan set up with his father for the purchase of the store.

Red Pine struggled along with the rest of America for the next several years. John and Mary were no exception, but they were luckier than most. It was difficult to watch friends and relatives desperately fight to maintain a meager existence year after year. Yet it was even more difficult to witness others lose their battle. For many, it was a time of uncertainty and learning to do without that would profoundly shape the financial dealings and attitudes of millions of Americans for the rest of their lives. For the next ten years, business at the resort and general store never exceeded their best year of business in 1929.

Diane's parents became casualties of the depression in 1933. Farmers had been excluded from the prosperity of the Coolidge Administration and for many, the depression nudged them over the edge financially. Diane's parents moved in above the store with her and Ray after losing their farm. Two years later, her father found a job in St. Cloud and relocated there.

During these times of struggle, however, a special bonding and sense of community began to grow among the residents of Red Pine, as it did in most towns across the country. An attitude began to develop of people helping people, along with a sense of appreciation and contentment for the basic necessities and simple pleasures of life.

One Saturday morning in December of 1935, Mary brought the children down to the store to stay with John while she helped her parents decorate the hotel for Christmas. John kept his children occupied with chores like sweeping the stock room and cleaning the glass on some of the display cases, rewarding them with a nickel each for their efforts.

"Can we buy some candy, Dad?" asked Jack.

"Yes, you can do what ever you want with it. Just don't eat a whole nickel's worth of candy before lunch or you'll spoil your appetite, and your mother will get after me."

"We won't," Jack replied.

Mary returned to the store where they all enjoyed lunch together, sitting at a small table in the back room where John could keep an eye on the door when customers came in.

While they were eating, Mary said to John, "I think it would be nice if we could clear a large skating rink on the lake for the children in town. Don't you agree?"

John looked at her with surprise saying, "Well, sure I do, but do you realize what a big job it would be to remove that much snow? My

A Homeplace

goodness, Mary, it would take several people all day to clear away a decent size rink."

"I thought about that too," she said. "Why don't we ask Harold Nyberg if he'd bring his new plow-truck down to the lake and move the snow for us."

John chuckled with a hint of sarcasm. "Good luck," he said. "You know how tight fisted old Harold is as well as I do. Trying to get him to do something for nothing is 'Like trying to push butter up a bobcat's ass with a red-hot poker,' to use one of his expressions."

Jack snickered at his father's remark, inciting a frown of displeasure from Mary, "John, you don't have to talk like that in front of the children."

John winked at his young son and said, "I'm sorry, Dear, but it just seems like you're asking for the impossible. I'll ask him," he said half-heartedly, "but I can already tell you what he's going to say."

"Never mind," said Mary. "It was my idea and I'll ask him. We'll stop at the filling station on our way back home, and see what he says."

Mary's disappointment in his lack of faith and pessimistic response was glaringly obvious, sending John scrambling for redemption. "Okay, Mary I'll tell you what. If he'll do that, I'll open one of the cabins close to the lake every Saturday and on Sundays after church. The children can use it as a warming house. How's that?"

"It's a deal," Mary replied happily. "I hope he says yes! It would be just wonderful for the children, and who knows, there may even be some parents interested in taking up skating again."

Mary and her two children stopped at the filling station on their way home. They entered his shop, undetected by Harold who was busy beneath the hood of Henry Schroeder's Studebaker. He was stretched far over the fender, noisily pounding on his wrench against a stubborn, rusted bolt. Not wanting to startle him, Mary waited, nervously wondering how the gruff old mechanic would respond. She continued to rehearse the wording of her request, patiently waiting for him to quit pounding when she would subtly clear her throat to get his attention.

Suddenly, his wrench broke loose with a loud clang, causing him to split the skin on his knuckles. "OUCH! You DIRTY, ROTTEN, SON-of-a-BITCH,!" he yelled, standing up abruptly and backing away from the engine compartment shaking his hand. Still gritting his teeth and mumbling with his injured hand cradled in the other, he turned to face the doorway where Mary and her two children stood white-faced, wide-eyed with chins dropped. Both parties stood motionless for several seconds, just staring at each other. Then Mary stooped over, and like a mother hen gathered her children together and was about to guide them out the door and tell Harold she'd come back at a better time. Harold's face turned bright red with embarrassment and he said, "I'm terribly sorry Mrs. Nelson. I didn't realize you and the children were standing there. Is there something I can do for you?" he asked with a painful wince.

She hesitated for a moment, weighing the chances for the successful granting of her request against the obvious mood of Harold Nyberg. "Oh, well, that's okay, Mr. Nyberg. I can see that you're very busy today. Maybe it would be best if I came back at another time."

Harold, still red with embarrassment, and now desperate to redeem himself after his vulgar outburst, pleaded with her, "Please, Mrs. Nelson, I'm really very sorry you and the children had to hear that. I'm not all that busy right now. What is it I can help you with?"

"Oh, umm—very well, Mr. Nyberg. ....The reason I'm here is to ask for your assistance in clearing a skating rink on the lake for the community. My husband and I thought it would be a good idea, and we have decided to open one of our cabins for use as a warming house on Sunday afternoons. You're the only one in town with a snowplow, and we hoped that maybe you'd help by using it to clear the snow away for us."

Knowing full well he could hardly refuse her request after what he had just subjected them to, he started scratching his head beneath his hat and in his mind cussed himself out for being in this predicament. "Tell you what, Mrs. Nelson. I'll plow it next week some evening after I close up," he said with an averse tone. "And if it gets used enough, we'll see, maybe I'll keep doing it."

"Oh, thank you so much," Mary said joyfully then gave him a kiss on the cheek. "You're such a nice man to do this for the community. I can't thank you enough."

Harold was flustered by her enthusiastic response and tipped his hat as he bid her good-day. He chuckled and shook his head in disbelief as he watched her walk down the street with her children. "Guess I'll have to get a damn bell for my door," he mumbled while crawling under the Studebaker for his wrench.

A Homeplace

That evening, while sitting at the supper table, John asked Mary if she had any luck convincing old Harold Nyberg to help her with her idea. "Of course," she said confidently. "He's a very sweet man, and I think perhaps you've gotten the wrong idea about him."

"Mommy gave him a kiss," blurted Jack.

John chuckled. "Well, that explains everything. You cheated and took advantage of the poor fellow."

Mary smiled at him and said, "I didn't cheat, John. He agreed to do it before I kissed him." Then she explained what happened.

John laughed and said, "Nevertheless, my dear, he didn't have a chance standing face-to-face with a pretty young woman."

Smiling with a mischievous spirit Mary said, "Well, I can't help that. The important thing is that I got the job done. Now you'll have to live up to your end of the agreement. He said he'd plow next week, so you better make sure you move some firewood close to the cabin before next Saturday."

"Don't worry, I will. In fact I'll do it tonight after supper before the snow gets any deeper."

That evening, while John and the children moved some firewood near the cabin that would be used as a warming house, Mary sat at the kitchen table with her journal and enjoyed a peaceful cup of coffee.

Saturday, December 14, 1935

Christmas is quickly approaching and hopefully by next Saturday, the people of our town will be able to enjoy ice-skating on the lake. I think what I enjoy most about this little town is the peacefulness. Even during the middle of the day at this busy time of year, at the height of activity on main street, there exists a quiet quaintness that is so dear to me.

I have often considered the effect that the different seasons of the year has on the town; reminds me of our own cycle of life. During the winter, the deep snow covers the towns like an infant peacefully asleep beneath a soft blanket. Spring—a time of newness and growth, is like a child in school discovering another wonder of the world. Summer—a season of long hot days and hard work is like an adult in the prime of life. In autumn—my favorite season, I think of an old man or woman enjoying the fruits of their years of labor as they nap in a rocking chair on a sunny porch in the cool autumn air.

When I consider all the simple pleasures I receive from living in this little town, I am aware, more than ever, how important it is to give something back to the community, no matter how small, in order to ensure that the life we enjoy will continue to be enjoyed by our children and grandchildren.

Mary's idea for the skating rink was a huge success and grew to the point where many of the parents took turns bringing hot cider and cookies down to the warming house to share with everyone. They could watch their children skating and sliding down the hill on their toboggans while enjoying each other's fellowship in the warmth of the little cabin.

From the Red Pine Weekly Herald, Thursday December 26, 1935. News from in town.

A special thanks from the community to Harold Nyberg for his help in clearing the snow on the lake for the skating rink. It was such a delightful winter scene to see so many children and adults enjoying themselves on the moonlit ice surrounded by sparkling snow-covered pine trees last Saturday night, especially right before Christmas.

The families and businesses of Red Pine continued to evolve in step with technological advancements as the years passed by. Harold Nyberg's two oldest sons, Eldon and Victor, were helping him full time at the garage now. They were capable of doing most of the repair work,

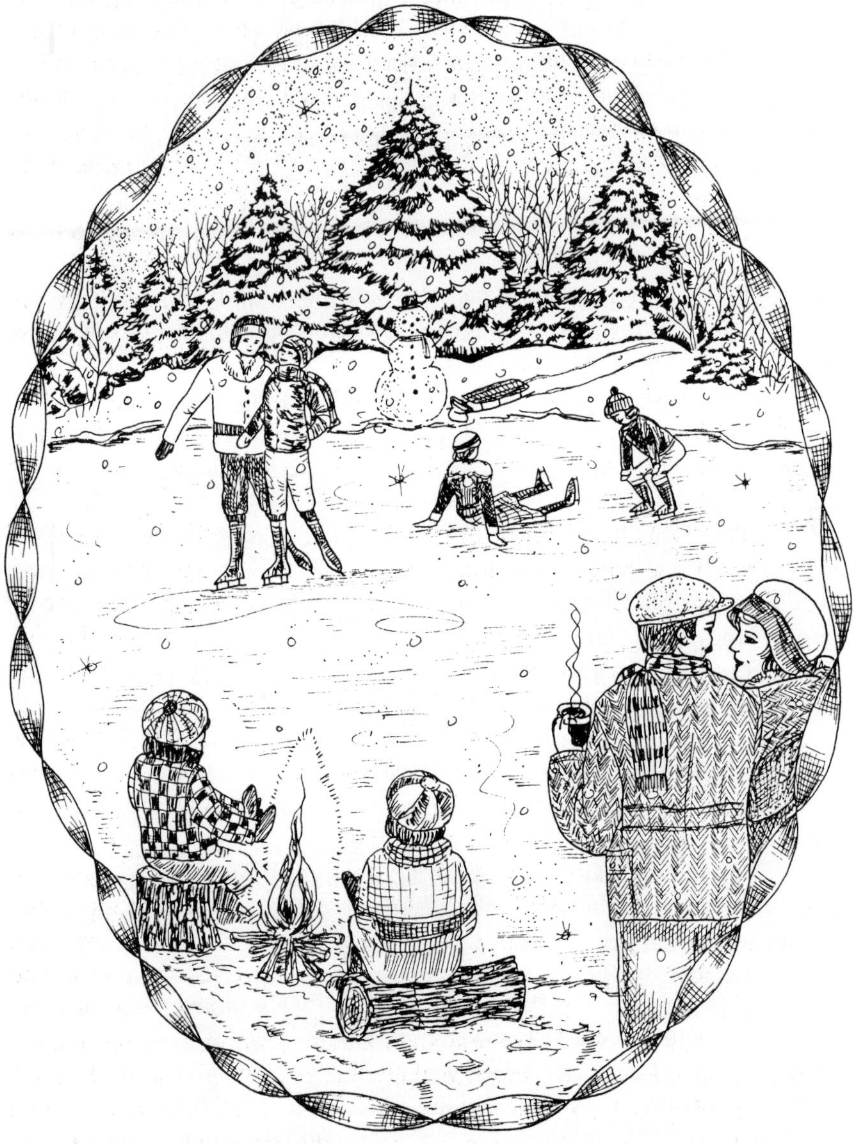

The Growing Years

allowing Harold to spend more time with the customer relations part of his business—pumping gas, washing windshields, checking oil, and just general chitchat. Harold's friends and neighbors knew that behind his gravelly manner was a kind and caring man, and were able to see past his occasional slips of uncouth language and knew that his heart was good. He was dedicated to his family, and was very active at St. Gabriels Catholic church. His dedication to the community led to his third term as mayor, this time unopposed.

Harold's oldest son, Eldon, had recently become engaged to Elizabeth Hopkins, and a June wedding was planned. There was talk that when Eldon and Elizabeth were married, Laura and Samuel Hopkins wanted them to learn the bakery business and help them as they grew older.

The increasing number of automobiles and trucks finally led to the sale of the livery stable by August Rutger. He sold his building and vacant lots to Pete Hanson who decided to move his lumber business off the farm and into town.

Pete Hanson no longer did any logging or milling and sold all of his saw mill equipment. He, too, was feeling the effects of aging and decided to simplify his life by concentrating strictly on the retail sale of lumber and other building materials. He ceased operations of his ice business in 1939 because of the declining need for storage ice due to the popularity of the electric Frigidaire. There had been many rumors circulating throughout the town lately that Harold Nyberg was considering the purchase of the icehouse building from Pete Hanson and converting it into a roller rink, to be run by his third oldest son, Leonard, who had no interest in working at the garage.

Vi and Henry Schroeder's Meat and Dairy business had undergone changes as well. Vi's homemade chocolates, fudge, and peanut brittle had been famous throughout the area for years. After much encouragement by friends and neighbors, they converted their meat and dairy business into a full-line candy store. The gamble was a huge success, and after completely remodeling their store front to resemble a ginger bread house, they renamed their business, "The Candy Shack." Word spread quickly, and in just a few months their business became a well established tourist attraction. It was nearly impossible to pass by the front of the building without succumbing to the aroma of fresh chocolate and roasted nuts.

A Homeplace

Phillip Lewis and his wife, Millicent, continued to enjoy the success of their newspaper business. Besides assisting her husband with the paper, Millie shared the duties of librarian with Mrs. Carlson. Despite having none of her own, her love of children inspired her to start a reading program at the library. Every Tuesday and Thursday morning, the young children were invited to attend a story hour which grew in popularity in a very short time.

From the Red Pine Weekly Herald, Thursday November 10, 1938. News from in town:

The following is a list of new books in the library.
Adventures of Buffalo Bill-----Col. Wm. F. Cody
The Boys Book of Magic-----Carrington
The Radio Amateurs Handy Book-----Collins
Tarzan the Terrible-----Burroughs
The Wolf Hunters-----Curwood
Anderson's Fairy Tales-----Hans Christian Anderson.

The town of Red Pine continued to progress as well. More curbs and sidewalks were added each year along with the paving of streets. The tourist industry continued to be the mainstay of the town's economy and grew each year. The last several years had seen a notable increase in the number of people from Iowa and Illinois taking advantage of the beauty and serenity of the lakes and woodlands of northern Minnesota.

By the end of the decade, the depression had gradually released its grip, but not before testing the resolve of millions of Americans.

On a sunny Sunday afternoon, in September of 1941, the Nelsons and Larsons were having a picnic lunch behind the general store. John, and his son Jack, now seventeen, carried a picnic table from the resort area to the shade of an oak tree behind the store. Caroline was now a blossoming young woman of fourteen with a secret and growing

The Growing Years

affection for Ray. Mary and Caroline were setting the table as Diane and her son came down the exterior stairway from their apartment above the store. Ray carried a large roaster down the steps, and his mother followed with a pitcher of lemonade.

"What's in the pan, Ray?" asked Jack

"Mom fried up a big batch of chicken yesterday," replied Ray.

"Ooohh, that sounds good! I'm really hungry."

"Jack," said his mother with a tone of futility. "I can hardly remember a time when you weren't hungry. I honestly don't know how you two boys can eat like that and stay so slim."

Ray spoke up seeing an opportunity to tease Mr. Nelson, "That's because your husband works us so hard at the resort and store, Mrs. Nelson."

John laughed loudly, "Well," he said. "You two do work hard. *Almost* as hard as your dad and I did when we were your age, Ray."

Jack and Ray affectionately scoffed at John's remark. "What do you mean almost?" Jack questioned.

"Well, I'll tell you what I mean, boys."

Just then, Diane said, "It's time to eat now, everyone. Sit wherever you like at the table. There's fried chicken, potato salad, bread and butter, lemonade and chocolate cake for dessert."

"Everything looks delicious, Diane," said Mary.

"Yes, just wonderful," said Caroline. John sat between his wife and Diane on one side of the table, while Caroline sat between Ray and her brother on the other side. After giving thanks for their meal, Ray turned to John, while buttering his bread, and said, "You were about to tell us what made you and my dad such hard workers compared to us."

John noticed his son and Ray exchange a smile as if to encourage him to brag about the good old days. "Ya, Dad, we're listening."

"Okay, boys, I'll tell you why. First off, all eight of these cabins were built by me and your father," he said as he pointed toward the lake. "My father helped us with the first one so we could learn how to build them. The rest we built mostly by ourselves. We did everything too. Dug the footings, framed them up, roofed them, put up all the pine paneling inside and painted them. It was hard work, but we enjoyed building them.

When we decided to build the cabin out on the island, I hauled all the lumber out there by myself in one night's work, and it took me all night to do it too. Rowing out there and back to bring each load. Seems

A Homeplace

to me it was about twelve loads." Mary affectionately kissed him on the cheek in acknowledgement of his sacrifice from years ago, as he continued to boast of his accomplishments. "Then," he said as he turned his attention to Ray, "Your father and I built that house by ourselves in one summer during evenings and Saturdays," pointing up the hill at their house as he spoke. "We dug the entire basement by hand. Put in the foundation, too. The only jobs I hired out were the plumbing, heating, plastering and wood flooring." John boasted, shaking his finger at the two young men as he spoke, hoping to get a rise out of them.

Mary and Diane could see what he was trying to do, and Caroline caught a glimpse of the two women as they tried to conceal their roguish grins. Mary winked at her daughter as if to invite her to share in the humor as her father egged the two boys on.

"Well," said Jack, "I'll bet Ray and I could do the same if we had the chance."

"Yeah," said Ray. "We just don't have the same opportunity as you and my dad had."

Mary turned to John and said, "Well, Dear, perhaps this fall would be a good time to start building one of those new cabins we've been talking about for years. The boys could work on it after they get home from school and on Saturdays."

"Yeah, Dad!" said Jack excitedly. "Show us how to build them just like grandpa taught you."

"Okay, boys," said John "I believe I'll take you up on that. If your mother will watch the store for a few hours tomorrow, I'll dig holes for the footings and have some lumber delivered. There's something I want to make clear though," he added with seriousness. "You still have to keep up your school work, or I'll stop the project if you start falling behind. There's something you two need to remember. When Ray and I built these cabins, we were going to school right here in town. Now that the high school is in Agate Falls, you'll have nearly an hour less of daylight to work because of the time lost traveling home. Do you understand?"

"Yes, Mr. Nelson," said Ray. Jack nodded affirmatively.

"Would it be okay to work on Sundays if we fall behind?" Jack asked.

Simultaneously, as if it was rehearsed and cued by a band conductor, Mary said, "Absolutely not!"

Diane, "No way!"

John, "Forget it!"

Jack cringed in reaction to the resounding response of the adults, ducking his head between his shoulders.

"I'll watch the store tomorrow, John," said Mary." But why not let the boys dig the holes? They said they wanted to learn how to build."

"I know they do, Mary, but it will save valuable time if I get them dug. Besides, there's not a whole lot to learn about digging a hole." John turned his attention back to the boys and said, "If the weather cooperates, and you two work hard, we can have the outside finished before the heavy snows come. Then we'll put a wood stove in so you two can work on finishing the inside over the winter months. When spring arrives, all that will be left is to paint the siding, move the furnishings in, and it'll be ready to rent. At least I think it will," he teased. "I know that Ray and I were able to do it, but we'll see about you two."

"Don't worry, Dad, we can do it just as well as you did."

"Time will tell," John said, teasing them with a tone of doubt. "Tomorrow we start. If all goes well, we'll do it again next fall."

"Why can't we just keep building during the summer?" asked Ray.

"Well, I've thought about doing that too, Ray, but I think it would be too disruptive to the guests. They spend good money to come up here each year to relax and enjoy themselves. I wouldn't want to take a chance and spoil it for them."

"I see," said Ray. "I didn't think about that. I suppose it would be annoying listening to hammers pounding all day long."

After everyone was finished eating, John and Ray asked to be excused so they could go fishing.

"I'd like to go fishing, too," said Caroline. "I like to fish just as much as you two do, you know."

"Okay, Caroline, you can come with," said John, halfheartedly.

"Yeah," said Ray with a mischievous smile. "We need someone to bait our hooks for us and row the boat."

Caroline stuck her elbow into Ray's ribs as they started toward the boats. "I won't have time to bait your hooks because I'll be busy pulling fish into the boat," she said confidently.

As the three of them walked toward the dock, the adults enjoyed a cup of coffee before they started to pack away the leftovers and clear the dishes.

"Have you noticed lately what I've noticed, Diane?" asked Mary.

"Yes, I believe I have," she replied.

"What are you two talking about?" asked John.

"You mean you haven't noticed that Caroline has a little spark for Ray?" said Diane.

"Can't say I have. Does Ray have any for Caroline?"

"I don't believe so," said Mary.

"The poor girl," said Diane. "It's so hard to have feelings for someone and not know if they're mutual. I know just how she must feel. His father never gave me the time of day when we were that age."

When they finished their coffee, Mary and John stood up to clear the table. Diane stopped them for a moment with her arm, trying to speak through her sudden display of emotion. Mary noticed the tears right away and asked, "Diane, what's wrong?"

She looked at John with watering eyes and said, "I just want to say how much I appreciate all that you and Mary have done for me and Ray, John. When Ray was born, I was so worried about how difficult it would be to raise a son without a father. But it has occurred to me that he has had one all along. You've been as much of a father to him as any man could have. I just know that if Ray could be here he'd tell you the same thing."

John held Diane tightly in his arms and Mary put her comforting arm around her shoulder. Then John said, "I know that Ray would have done the exact same thing for me, Diane. Your son is growing up into a fine young man, and his father would be just as proud of him as all of us are."

Ray, Caroline and Jack rowed one of the little wooden boats out to the island and anchored in the same spot where their fathers used to fish. As they sat and fished, Ray turned to Jack and said, "It didn't sound like they cared for your idea about working on Sunday."

They all burst into laughter and John finally said, "No, that's for sure. But that's okay. We'll get the job done just the same. And we'll do it just as good as they did. I can't wait to start—it should be fun."

"Yeah, me too," said Ray.

The adults heard the laughter from their children echo across the water. They all turned and looked out toward the boat and Diane said, "What a nice group of kids they turned out to be."

The Growing Years

John replied, "Yep, we're really lucky to have such nice children."

"Luck has nothing to do with it," said Mary with a smile. She stood between John and Diane, and with one arm around each of them said, "I'd like to think *we* had something to do with it."

The next day, while the children were in school, John dug the footings and ordered the lumber from Pete Hanson. Pete drove up to the building site just as John finished digging the last footing. As the truck came to a stop, Pete leaned his head out the window, took the pipe from the corner of his mouth and said with a smile, "It's about time you built another one. You've been talking about doing it for three years now, haven't you?"

John returned with a smile, "Actually, Mary and I talked about doing this back in '28, but when the economy turned sour we decided to hold off. We've just been waiting for the business to get stronger."

"Are you going to build them or hire it out?"

"I'm going to have my son and your grandson do most of the work on these next two. I just intend to get them started and help them out here and there."

"Well that's a darn nice thing you're doing for those two boys. It's just what they need, to learn a skill and some craftsmanship. This is the kind of responsibility that turns them into men."

"To tell you the truth, it all started when I was bragging how hard Ray and I worked at their age. Now they feel they have something to prove. They don't know it yet, but I intend to pay them by the hour for building them."

"Are you really going to build two of them?" asked Pete.

"I think one this fall and one next," John replied. "That will give us a total of ten cabins, and believe me, when they're all occupied, we'll have our hands full during the summer. Mary and I figure that'll be just the right amount. There'll still be plenty of space between each one so the guests will feel like they still have some privacy. Once we get these next two built, we'll start to make improvements to one or two each year. There'll always be something to do around here."

A Homeplace

"Well, I'm glad you're letting the boys build them. It's good for them. They sure are growing up fast."

"They sure are, Pete. Yesterday we were down here having a picnic lunch, and after we ate the two boys and Caroline took a boat out to the fishing spot where Ray and I used to fish. Seeing them out there sure brought back memories. Good memories. It seems like it was just yesterday when it was me and Ray out there."

Pete and John continued to reminisce as they leaned on the fender of the truck and looked out toward the island. "Ya know, Pete, I'm sure it's the same with you, but not a day goes by that I don't think of Ray. Seems like almost everything I do reminds me of something we did together when we were young. Fishing, camping, hunting, even building these cabins. We did so much together. I sure do miss him."

"I know what you mean, John. Alice and I still catch each other in tears every once in a while because of something that has reminded us of Ray. Every thought I ever have about him is a pleasant one. I guess that's one of the good things about memories, they just stay with you forever." Pete wiped his thumb near corner of his eye and started to unload the lumber from the truck.

"Speaking of memories, how are your folks doing down in the cities?"

"They're doing just fine, Pete. I got a letter from Rose the other day. She and her husband, Dave, still visit them every week. She mentioned that Dad said he was thinking of working another year or two and then retiring." John and Pete worked together unloading the truck as they continued their conversation.

"Do you think they'd move back up here when they retire?"

"I doubt it," said John. "They really like their house and neighbors. Besides, I think they enjoy being close to Rose and her children. Her young ones are a lot younger than mine and easier to spoil." Pete chuckled. "They'll be coming up here for a few days over Thanksgiving this year. We'll have to have you and Alice over then for a good visit."

"Well, he's earned his retirement, John. I'm thinking of retiring myself, maybe next spring. Keep that under your hat, though, I haven't decided for sure yet."

"You've sure enough paid your dues, too, Pete. Would you sell the house and move into town?"

The Growing Years

"Nope, I'd probably just sell the business in town and stay on the farm. Maybe raise a little beef or some chickens, just to keep busy. Alice would never think of selling the house. Too many memories, if you know what I mean."

"Oh, yeah, I know exactly what you mean. There is something about a house after you've lived in it for a while. Especially when you've built it yourself. It's almost like it becomes part of you. Like a member of the family. I can't imagine the circumstances that would cause us to want to move out of our house. You'd never get Mary out of there now. We've put so much of ourselves into it, plus the fact that both our children were born in that house. Yep, we're really rooted in pretty good."

From Boys to Men

As the days of autumn grew shorter and colder, John assisted his son and Ray in the construction of the new cabin. It was difficult for him to resist helping them beyond his limited role as an instructor because of his love of construction. More than once, he was affectionately scolded for getting involved beyond his original agreement with the two young men, to just show and tell, rather than do.

"Please, Dad, Ray and I are trying to do this ourselves. You were just going to show us what to do and let us do the work, remember?" was his son's frequent reminder.

By early November, the little structure was weather tight. All the windows were in place, and the single entrance door from the covered porch was installed. The only task remaining on the exterior was to paint it in the spring. John helped install the wood stove and the overhead electrical drop to the new cabin and some temporary lighting. The inside could now be finished over the winter months, in the comfort of toasty wood heat.

John had kept pressure on Ray and Jack to complete the exterior before the heavy snows came, so that all of the building materials and tools could be conveniently stored inside the shell of the cabin and out of the elements.

Still fresh in everyone's mind was the Armistice Day Blizzard the year before. That fierce November storm, the worst in recent memory, had quickly swept through the Midwest and taken the lives of many people who were caught unprepared for the rapidly plunging temperature and deep, drifting snow. The unusually warm temperature on that morning, had lulled many hunters into wearing lightweight clothing that offered no protection from the effects of the raging storm.

That storm was a grim reminder for Ray of the type of conditions that claimed his father's life. The Armistice Day Blizzard was a storm of much greater magnitude than the one in which his father had died, but the elements of danger were identical.

From Boys to Men

In the early morning darkness, Saturday, the sixth of December, John walked down to the resort to start a fire in the stove of the new cabin so that the interior would be warm before his son and Ray arrived to start working. It would be half an hour before he had to prepare the store for opening, and he wanted to layout the wiring of the cabin before he had to leave. At the bottom of the hill he paused for a moment to take in the faint, homey fragrance of fresh pastry from Hopkins' Bakery drifting throughout the town on frosty air currents. As he approached the cabin, he stopped abruptly, cocked his head and smiled as he listened to the groaning of thickening ice from beyond the blackness across the lake. "I'd better get my spear house ready," he said to himself.

From the kitchen window Ray noticed the smoke rising from the chimney of the cabin as he and his mother finished their breakfast. He put on his coat, said goodbye to his mother, and started toward the cabin where he was met by Jack.

"Happy birthday, Ray," said Jack.

"Thanks!" he said with a smile. "What are we going to work on today, Jack?"

"Dad said we should do the wiring next. It will be a lot easier to wire this cabin than it was the others. He had to remove some of the paneling in the other cabins in order to conceal the wiring within the walls."

"Is he going to let us wire them too?"

"Yep. He said it's easy. Just a few lights and switches and four or five outlets. He said it won't take us long. Then we can start putting the paneling on."

They walked into the cabin, which by now was toasty warm. The frost was beginning to puddle on the window sills, and John was already working in his shirt sleeves.

"Good morning boys!" he said.

They both returned the greeting.

"I've just installed all the metal boxes for the lights, switches and outlets, and over in that box are the staples and a roll of cable," he said, pointing to the corner of the room. "I'll show you how I want you to install the wiring before I have to go and open the store, but if you two have any questions come on up and ask. I'll be back at lunch time to

A Homeplace

check out the wiring before you cover it with paneling. If you get the wiring done before lunch, you can go ahead and start paneling where there isn't any wiring."

John showed them how to install the wiring and then left to work in the store. He returned at noon and joined the three of them for lunch, while Mary watched the store.

"Here you go, boys," said John as he handed Ray and his son a basket with their lunches inside. "Your mother made us a nice lunch so we could stay here and eat instead of going up to the house."

John closely inspected the wiring installation while Jack and Ray made a make-shift table from a pair of wooden planks between two saw horses. "Looks good you two. After the store closes, I'll connect the wires to the fuse box, and we'll be done with the wiring for now. You can go ahead and start the paneling after lunch."

"Sure feels like it could snow," said Ray, as he returned from a trip to the outhouse.

"It's starting to cloud up a little in the west, I see," said Jack, as he wiped the condensation from the window pane.

"Well, let it come," said his father. "We're right where we want to be with this project. Everything we need to do now is inside so it can snow all it wants to."

"I'd like to see the ice get thicker on the lake before we get too much snow," said Ray. "It'd be nice to have a good four inches thick before we set up the spear-house."

"Yeah, me too," said Jack "That water is mighty cold if you fall through this time of year."

"Where did you two figure on putting the spear-house this year?" asked John

"We thought we'd put it in the same place as last year," Ray answered. "Over in that shallow bay where the river starts."

"Yeah, that's as good a place as any," replied Jack. "We speared four 20-pound pike there last year and lots of ten pounders."

John began to chuckle as he took a bite from his sandwich.

"What's so funny, Dad?" asked Jack.

"Oh—I was just thinking about the time your father and I," he said, nodding toward Ray, "were spearing over in that same place that you two like to go. We had just set up the spear-house, chiseled our hole open and cleared the ice out. I remember your father saying, 'There won't be any fish near here for awhile, after all that noise. Let's go get some more firewood for the stove and our spears and decoys. Maybe by the time we get back things will have settled down a little and we might get a chance at a pike.' I agreed, and so we lit the stove so it would be warm when we returned, and went to get our gear and some more wood.

"When we came back, Ray lowered his decoy into the water. He was kneeling down, kinda hunched over the hole and I heard him say, 'Looks like there's a small log or a fence post sunk down there. It's hard to tell what it is 'cause the water's a bit cloudy.' He continued to adjust his decoy when all of a sudden I heard a splash, and Ray rolled backwards across the floor hitting his head against the wall. He stood up and looked at me with a face that was still dripping wet and white as a ghost and said, 'Damn! that was the biggest pike I ever saw.'"

All three of them burst into laughter as John finished his story, and John laughed so hard he had tears in his eyes as he recalled the adventure of his younger days.

"I take it the fence post was really a fish?" asked Ray.

"It sure was," said John. "He had lowered the decoy right down on top of the fish when it turned and grabbed the decoy, nearly pulling him into the water." He continued to chuckle and said with a sigh, "Oh my, those were the days."

After their lunch was over, John returned to the store while Ray and Jack started the installation of the paneling. They began on the long wall facing the lake. There were two large windows and a door to work around, which required a lot of cutting and fitting. "Once we get this wall done, the other three will be a lot quicker," said Jack. They continued to work, painstakingly measuring, cutting and fitting each length of paneling perfectly into place.

It was dark when John locked up the store and made his way toward the cabin. The air was cold and heavy with the smell of snow. The muffled sound of hammers pounding inside the cabin echoed throughout the resort grounds and as he approached the cabin, he could see Ray and his son through the window, diligently working in the yellow hue of light inside.

When he entered he said, "That's it for today, boys. We'll get back to it next Saturday." He installed the wiring into the fuse box, and made the connections as Jack put their tools away. Ray swept the sawdust and small wood scraps into a pile that would be used for heating the stove the next week. John took several minutes to inspect what they had accomplished during the afternoon.

"You two are doing a real fine job," he said. "Your joints are nice and tight, and they're straight as an arrow. Looks just like the high quality work that your dad and I used to do," he said, patting Ray on the shoulder.

Ray and Jack put their coats on and took one last admiring look at their work. John turned the lights out, and as the three of them walked out the door, they were greeted with a shower of large feathery snowflakes. The air was calm, and the soft, airy flakes piled up quickly. The freshly-fallen snow squeaked beneath their feet as they walked away from the cabin, and the lights of the town were barely visible through the dense veil of falling snow. They walked side by side toward the store with their shoulders hunched up around their necks to prevent the large snowflakes from falling behind their collars.

As Ray walked toward home, he looked back and said, Goodnight, Jack, goodnight, Mr. Nelson.

"See you at church tomorrow, Ray," John answered. Jack acknowledged with a wave.

While walking home, Ray contemplated Mr. Nelson's words of praise about their workmanship on the cabin, inspiring a smile and an overwhelming sense of pride.

The next morning, the Nelson family was met at the base of the hill by Diane and Ray for their usual stroll to church services. They usually attended services together, along with Mary's parents, and frequently shared Sunday dinner as well. The McCullohs joined the group on their way to church as they passed by the hotel.

As they approached, Ellen said, "I hope you can all come over after church today and have dinner with us; there are no guests at the hotel this weekend, so it's a good chance for us to have all of you over. I'm going to ask Pastor Adams to join us if he can."

"Sounds good to me," said John

"Yes, we'd love to," said Diane.

"That'll give us a chance to listen to that new radio you bought, Andy," said John.

"It's a nice one!" replied Andy with a proud smile on his face. "Wait 'til you hear the nice, rich sound it has. I'm told it's the best one Zenith makes."

"Oh, we just love it," added Ellen. "The color of the wooden cabinet goes so well with the rest of our furniture. And it really does have a nice sound to it."

"It takes a little longer for the tubes to warm up than our other radio did, but it sure pulls the signal in strong," Andy boasted. "We can even pick up some overseas broadcasts!"

"Well, I can hardly wait to hear it," said John.

Ray, Caroline and Jack, annoyed by the pokey pace, accelerated ahead of their parents as Andy continued to describe the features of the new radio. Caroline glanced over her shoulder at the adults, then commented to her brother and Ray in a low, secretive voice, "Remember when Dad and Mom used to tell *us* not to lollygag when we walked to church?"

Jack and Ray acknowledged her with a snicker as the three of them climbed the stairs to the church.

When the services were over, Pastor Adams greeted the congregation as he usually did when they left. He accepted Mrs. McCulloh's invitation to Sunday dinner and said he would join them as soon as he had greeted everyone and closed up the church. Pastor Adams was very well liked by the members of the congregation, young and old alike. He was five years older than John and had come to Emmanuel Lutheran Church of Red Pine one year before Mary and John were wed. Emmanuel was his first church, and lately there were rumors he was considering a call at another church in southwestern Minnesota. Although everyone understood the church's reasons for moving its pastors to new ministries from time to time, it was still hard for some to accept, especially when someone with the passion for his work like Pastor Adams had, came along and did such a wonderful job.

Everyone was gathered around the table in the dining room. Caroline took her usual seat next to Ray, still hoping that he would eventually acknowledge her interest in him. Ray was always kind to Caroline, and her attraction did not go unnoticed by him, but thus far, his interests were dominated by his love of nature and work on the cabin with her brother and father. For now, his relationship with Caroline was casual and comfortable. In many ways, Ray was much like his father, and whenever they were caught up with their chores, Ray and Jack spent their free time hunting, fishing, and most anything to do with the outdoors.

After Pastor Adams led the grace before meal, the room was instantly filled with the sounds of fellowship—conversation, laughter, and the clattering of spoons and forks against the fine china platters and bowls as the food made its way around the table.

After dinner, Ray, Jack and Caroline helped their mothers with the dishes, while Pastor Adams, John and Andy went to the living room to see and hear the new radio that Andy was so eager to demonstrate.

Late in the afternoon, everyone was relaxing and enjoying each other's company. Andy and John sat next to the radio smoking their pipes while Pastor Adams shared coffee at the dining room table with the ladies. Jack and Ray lay on the large braided rug next to the window that overlooked Main Street, and casually paged through the latest edition of Sports Afield. A light snow had started to fall and was now visible in the glow of the street lamps outside the window.

The conversation at the dining room table centered around the possibility that Pastor Adams would be leaving to accept a new call. "All I can say is that I've been considering a call at another church," he said. "On one hand, it's a difficult decision. I've been here almost 19 years now, and I'm surrounded by people I have grown very fond of. I am truly blessed to be the spiritual leader of a church that is so well attended and supported. On the other hand, the decision is easy because it is my calling to help spread the word of God and to use my skills to enable His ministry where it is most needed. If I decide to accept this new call, I can do it with the satisfaction of knowing that the church I leave behind is a healthy, strong congregation that will help and support its new pastor and make his adjustment an easy one."

He paused for a moment to compose a sermon-like analogy that would further explain his reasoning. "Think of it this way, ladies," he said. "It would be very selfish and foolish for someone who loves gardening, to concentrate their efforts on one single flower, for example, to keep cultivating, fertilizing and watering one plant, while letting the rest of the plants in the garden fend for themselves. It's a much more glorious sight to behold an entire garden of healthy, vibrant flowers than one single flower against a background of dried withering and dying plants—don't you agree? The same holds true for the church. If God speaks to my heart and wants me to spread my talents somewhere else, I must go and do it. That's why I chose to be a pastor."

"It makes sense when you say it that way, Pastor, but it doesn't make it any easier to accept that you may be leaving," said Diane.

The intimacy and comfort of the conversation with Pastor Adams as they sat around the table, filled Caroline with a sense of maturity, and she enjoyed the feeling. It was as though the barrier of her young age was suddenly removed, allowing her to rise to an equality with the other adults at the table. Her new status inspired the courage to inquire about a situation that she had wondered about for a long time. "Pastor, why is it you aren't married?" she asked.

Her mother and Diane froze for an instant, caught by surprise by such a forward question, especially when directed at their pastor. Instinctively, her mother watched Pastor Adams' reaction, preparing to quickly change the subject if she detected the slightest hint of discomfort caused by her daughter's inquiry.

"Well," he said, smiling at Caroline. (A smile that released the lump in Mary's throat). "I'm surprised that after all these years no one has asked me that question, Caroline, and it's something that I enjoy thinking about. In a way, my story is a lot like yours," he said, turning his attention to Diane. "I had fallen in love with a beautiful young woman during my last year of studies at the seminary. Her name was Marie. We had been seeing each other for about two years, and our love for one another had grown very strong.

"I came home to visit her for a few days one Christmas and we started casually talking about marriage and made many plans together for our future. I'm almost certain that she was hoping for a proposal then, and I nearly did. But at the time I felt it would be better to wait until summer, after I was ordained. About two weeks after I returned to the seminary, I received a phone call from her parents stating that she was hospitalized with a very serious illness and had requested that I come to see her. I went to be with her as quickly as I could, but it was too late. When I arrived at her parents' home, I learned that she had passed away just hours before I arrived.

"As you may well imagine, I was devastated and very confused for a time. I began to struggle with my faith, and I decided to take a short leave from my studies. It was such a shock to me that she was taken so quickly, and I was always sorry that I didn't propose to her sooner. Once

I was able to accept her passing, I returned to my studies and directed my full concentration on doing His work."

Pastor Adams smiled as he recalled a childhood memory. "My father used to tell us children, 'If you find a job you really love, you'll never have to work a day in your life.' And you know, he was right. I thoroughly enjoyed what I was doing.

"Meanwhile, the years continued to slip by and I kept myself very busy being a pastor. Several years later, I did have an opportunity to pursue another relationship, but I chose not to. I had such fond memories of Marie that I was afraid I would gauge my new relationship on the standards I had developed with her, and that would hardly be fair. It was as though I had built a shrine around my cherished memories of our brief relationship. I guess you could say that I decided to live the rest of my life in her honor, and I can honestly say that I've never regretted it."

The women had hung on his every word, evident by the emotional glisten in their eyes as he finished. "Oh, that is such a touching story," said Mary

"It most certainly is," added Ellen. "What was it that took Marie's life?"

"Spanish Influenza, is what they called it," Pastor Adams replied.

Ellen went to the kitchen and returned with the coffee pot. She was about to pour some coffee into Pastor Adams' cup when Andy suddenly spoke up loudly. " Listen! Quiet everyone. Come listen to the radio."

Andy and John were sitting forward in their chairs as everyone gathered around the radio. Andy turned the volume up as a special bulletin was coming across the air waves.

The news of Japan's attack on Pearl Harbor was beginning to unfold. Bits and pieces of information were released as they became available. The small gathering of friends and family listened intently as the reports trickled in, telling of the severe damage to the naval base and the enormous loss of life. The atmosphere for the remainder of the afternoon was a somber one, but by the time everyone left for home, the initial feelings of fear and sadness were replaced with those of anger and determination, as the realization became clear of the cowardly manner Japan chose to engage the United States in war. The tiny flickering flame of patriotism glowing in the hearts of Americans would now be fanned into a roaring inferno.

As the United States continued to ramp up its war machine, the feelings of patriotism and sense of duty to God and country grew steadily. The appeals by the government to collect tin, scrap iron, and rubber for building planes, ships, tanks and other military hardware received an enormous response all across the nation. The production of automobiles came to an end, and those factories were converted to the manufacture of military goods. Commodities such as gasoline and sugar were rationed. As the war progressed, the information about various battles in every theatre of the war was made available through the newspapers, radio, and news reels in the show halls across America. The news releases continued to feed the growing appetite of the nation to rise to the challenge and ensure that Good would win out over Evil.

On a warm spring evening in May, 1942, just one week after Jack had graduated, and three days before his eighteenth birthday, he and his father went out for an evening of fishing on Crystal Lake. They anchored in their favorite spot near the island, and John barely had his line in the water when he caught his first walleye. He smiled at his Jack and said, "See, the old man still has it!"

His son smiled back. "You'll never lose it, Dad. Just try to remember to leave a few for the guests."

They exchanged chuckles, and while his father gently released the fish over the side of the boat, Jack said, "Dad, I'm really glad we could come out here together for a while. It seems like it's so hard these days to find time to spend together like we used to."

"Yeah, it sure is, Son. It's too bad too, I really enjoy this. The resort and store keep us very busy. We'll just have to take the time to do it more often. If you let it, the business will always keep us too busy to get away. I think once in awhile a person just plain has to say, 'Well, it's time to go fishing,' and just do it. Work will always be there when you get back." His father lowered his bait back into the water and lit his pipe.

"Dad, I have to tell you something."

A Homeplace

"What is it, Son."

"It's just a few more days until my eighteenth birthday, and, well—I've decided to join the Army."

His father was silent for several moments—stunned by an onrush of emotion. Jack watched him intently, waiting for a response and could see the orange glow of the setting sun reflect in the moist corners of his father's eyes.

"The Army!" his father said with a crackle in his voice. "What made you decide on the Army?" he asked as he turned to face his son. "I figured you'd want to join the Navy, being that you've been around water all your life."

"That's just it, Dad. In the Navy, I figured that water's all I'd see for days on end," he chuckled. The several seconds of silence that passed seemed like minutes, as Jack nervously waited for a further response from his father.

"Well, your mother and I knew this day would come eventually," he said, clearly dejected. "I thought I would be prepared for it, but I realize now that you can't prepare yourself for something like this."

"Will you come with me when I tell Mom?" asked Jack.

"Yes, I will, Son, but I think we should wait for the right opportunity to tell her. It'll be mighty hard for her to hear this news, Jack. Let's celebrate your birthday together as a family without having the worry of you going off to war looming over your mother and your sister. It might be better if we wait until the day you go to enlist. Besides, that'll give us time to figure out what to say."

"I already know what to say when she asks me why Dad. I've been thinking about it for a long time."

"What are you going to tell her, Son."

"The same thing I was going to tell you tonight, Dad. First of all, by law I have to register for the draft anyway, but I don't want to wait that long. Dad, I love you and Mom and Caroline. I love my friends, my town, and my country. I love my way of life and the freedoms that go with it," he said as if reciting from a book.

"Take tonight for example. We can just decide to hop in a boat and go fishing at a moment's notice. If we don't win this war, all of our freedoms will be gone. I love all these things enough to fight for them and die for them if I have to. I'm so used to my way of life that if I can't have it this way, I'd rather be dead, anyway. Maybe if we fight hard we can stop the war before it comes to our country."

John was silent for several moments, reflecting on his son's words. He was proud of the unselfish and intrepid attitude his son had developed toward his family and his country and his way of life. He looked at his son with a teary-eyed smile and asked, "How long you been working on that speech?"

His son, who also allowed his emotion to show, returned the smile and said, "Two days."

At two o'clock in the morning, the day of Jack's birthday, John woke to get a drink of water and realized that Mary was not in bed. He walked down the hall to the bathroom, and noticed his son's bedroom door was open. When he looked into the moonlit room, he saw Mary sitting on the floor in her robe facing the head of their son's bed. He walked in and touched her shoulder. "What are you doing, Mary?" he whispered.

Mary stood up, and silently they walked out of the room and closed the door. Mary's eyes were full of tears as they went back to their room. She handed John a piece of paper, a hand-written letter listing their son's reasons for joining the armed forces.

"Where did you get this?" he asked.

"It was under his bed," said, Mary. "I found it yesterday when I was dusting in his room." John handed the note paper back to Mary. "Aren't you going to read it?" she asked.

"I already know what it says, Dear. We were going to tell you this morning at breakfast. Jack and I talked about it the other evening when we went fishing together."

Mary sat on the corner of the bed and looked up at her husband. "What are we going to do, John?"

He sat next to her and put his arm around her saying, " Did you understand what his note said Mary?"

"Yes."

"Then we're going to do the only thing we can do. We're going to support him, love him, and above all, pray for him. Every reason he mentioned in the little speech he gave to me the other evening was exactly the right reason to go to war. There wasn't a single hint of doubt in his belief about what he wants to do. He's going to get drafted anyway, so he might as well go into the branch of service that he wants to serve in."

They went back to bed and John held Mary in his arms as they lay in silent contemplation. Finally John asked, "What were you doing in his room when I found you in there?"

"I was just watching him sleep and listening to him breath—like I used to when he was a baby."

The next morning, John told his son that his mother already knew of his intentions, and they all sat together at breakfast and talked about his plans. Caroline took the news very hard and ran back to her room in tears. After several minutes her brother came into her room and sat on the bed next to her.

"Don't cry, Caroline, everything will be okay. Please come down and finish breakfast with us."

"It's just not fair, Jack. It's not fair that America has to go to war. Why can't those other countries just mind their own business and try to get along with the rest of the world."

"I don't know the answer to that, Caroline. Maybe if America fights hard and wins we won't ever have to go through this again. Maybe then they'll think twice before they try to pick a fight with us. And that's exactly why we have to go and fight, Caroline. To show the rest of the world that the United States cares about its people and we love our way of life enough to fight for it."

"I know you're right, Jack, but it's so dangerous, and you'll be so far away from us if something should happen to you."

"Don't worry, nothing is going to happen to me. I promise to be careful and use my head all the time. Besides, I want to come back and build that last cabin with Ray."

"That is, *if* Ray comes back too," Caroline said sharply. "He told me that when he turns eighteen in December he wants to join the Navy."

"I know he does, Caroline. We've been talking about this ever since the war started. Try to understand why we're doing this. We don't want to go to another country to fight and possibly get hurt or killed, but we can't just let the Germans and Japs take away everything that we've worked so hard for. If they aren't stopped, you can say good-bye to our way of life."

"I know that, Jack, but it still makes me angry that we have to fight to protect something that belongs to us in the first place."

Caroline stood up from her bed, and she and Jack walked down the hall together. As they walked down the stairs Jack put his arm around his sister and said, "Ya know, the best thing you can do for me and Ray is to support us and pray for us every day. And don't forget to send us lots of letters like they say in the news reels at the movie house. Oh, and by the way, I may as well let you in on a little secret if you promise not to say anything."

"What is it Jack?"

"Do you promise not to say anything?"

"Yes, I promise, now tell me what it is," she said impatiently.

"Ray asked me the other day if I minded if he were to date my sister when he comes back from the war."

"Are you serious, Jack!? Did he really ask you that!? Really!?"

"Yes, he did, Caroline. I wouldn't tease you about that."

"Oh my gosh, I can't believe it!"

"Well, you better, because he asked me."

"What did you say to him?"

"I told him that he better not date you or I'd never talk to him again." Jack turned his head slightly so that Caroline couldn't see the mischievous smile on his face.

"You said what!?" Caroline shouted as she pulled on his shoulder trying to turn him to face her. Jack couldn't keep a straight face and burst into laughter.

"I'm just teasing, Caroline," he finally admitted. "I told him that I would be proud to have him date you. He's a good friend, and you won't find a kinder person."

Caroline gave a sigh of relief, "Geez, Jack, you really had me worried there for a moment. If you only knew how long I've been trying to get him to notice me."

"Well don't worry, he's known for quite awhile now."

"Have I been that obvious?"

"Yes, yes you have," he smiled.

"Oh well," she said. "I don't care. I really like him, and I wanted to make sure he knew it."

"Well, he knows. He just wasn't ready to have a girlfriend yet, I guess. Just don't tell him I told you what he asked me. Anyway, I think

UNCLE SAM
I WANT YOU
U.S. ARMY

it's best to let him take the next step. Just be patient, Caroline, he'll open up eventually."

"Thanks for telling me, Jack. I really needed to hear that. And please be careful and return home as quickly as you can."

"I will, Sis. I will."

Jack and Caroline returned to the kitchen and finished their breakfast with their parents.

Jack followed his heart and in June of 1942, two weeks after his birthday, said farewell to his family and friends and went off to war. After basic training, he became part of the Sixth Army and was sent to the Pacific Theater. The frequency of his letters gradually tapered to a trickle as his company became more engaged in the war.

Ray also followed through with his plans. Shortly after Christmas he entered the Navy. He, too, was assigned to the Pacific and was a seaman aboard the USS Hornet.

And so it was, the two life-long friends, who had grown up more like brothers because they shared the fatherly love and guidance of John, were transformed from boys to men and rushed to answer the call of their country.

The Greatest Gift of All

On a Saturday evening in late October, 1944, the faint honking from a flock of Canada geese could be heard as their formation passed across the velvety orange sunset over the lake. Ghostly plumes of smoke from scattered piles of burning leaves throughout the town drifted upward in the windless twilight sky, filling the air with the familiar autumn fragrance. John, Mary and Caroline had just finished raking in the last section of the back yard. Mary entered the house and returned with two cups of coffee for her and John to enjoy while they tended the last pile of burning leaves.

John emptied the last bushel basket on the pile and said to Caroline, "Would you go around to the front porch and get that box of matches I left on the front steps?"

"Sure, Dad," she replied. She walked around to the front of the house and watched as a tall man in a military uniform closed the door on a car parked in front of the house. He approached Caroline through the front gate of the picket fence, saying, "Good evening, Miss, I'm looking for Mr. and Mrs. John Nelson. Is this their home?"

"Yes it is, Sir. Just follow me around to the back of the house. My parents are working in the backyard."

"Thank you, Miss," he answered solemnly.

Mary and John were sitting on the back steps with their coffee when Caroline and the soldier walked around the side of the house. Mary stood up and smiled at the man as he approached them and removed his hat, but when she looked back to her husband who was standing behind her, she saw the look of fear in his eyes, and immediately went to his side and held his hand.

The soldier introduced himself as Sergeant James Anderson and exchanged handshakes with John. "Mr. and Mrs. Nelson, I am terribly sorry to have to inform you that your son Jack was killed in action on October 23rd during the battle for Leyte Island."

Mary covered her mouth with her hand, made several gasping cries, and returned to the back steps where she sat down in a state of shock. Caroline rushed to her father and buried her face into his chest as

The Greatest Gift of All

he embraced her. The tears began to flow freely as the initial shock wore off. The soldier sat next to Mary with his arm around her as she bowed her face into her hands and wept profusely. After several minutes, John escorted Caroline and his wife into the house, sending them upstairs and telling them he would join them after he talked with the sergeant.

Standing in the doorway he gestured with his arm, saying, "Come in, Sergeant, and sit down for awhile. Would you like a cup of coffee?" he asked with a crackle in his voice.

"Thank you, Sir, that would be very nice."

John dried his eyes with his sleeve as he poured a cup of coffee for the sergeant. He sat down across the table from him and asked if he knew Jack.

"No, Sir, I didn't know him. I was sent home after I was wounded in Guam, but I do have some information from his lieutenant concerning the circumstances of the battle in which he died." He handed John an envelope and said, "I am very sorry for your loss, Mr. Nelson. This is not an easy job for me."

"I know it isn't," said John. "My family and I appreciate your condolences, and I realize it must be a terrible thing to have to inform a family of this type of tragedy." John and Sergeant Anderson continued to talk for nearly an hour and made arrangements to have Jack's body sent home for burial.

Ten days passed before the flag-draped coffin containing Jack's body arrived by train in Agate Falls and was then transferred to Red Pine by hearse. The next morning, when the funeral began, every pew was full inside the little Lutheran church. Mary and John were surrounded by the love and support of their parents and friends. Diane sat next to Mary in the front pew along with John and Caroline. The young new pastor, Daniel Nordstrom, began the ceremony, and when it came time for the eulogy, he introduced Pastor Adams, who had driven up to Red Pine the night before to comfort his long-time friends, Mary and John, during their time of grief.

"My dear friends. It doesn't seem that long ago, but it has been slightly over twenty years since Mary and John Nelson brought their

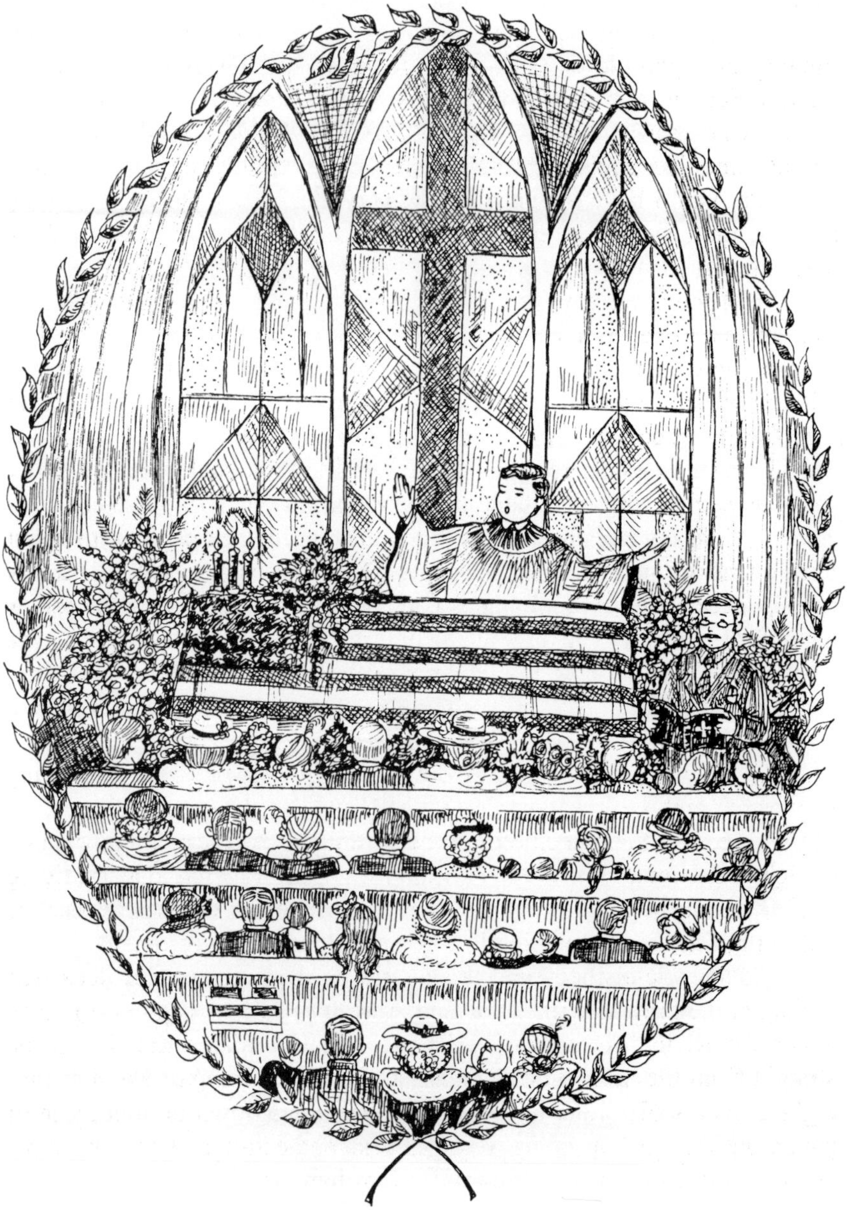

infant son Jack into the front of this very church to be baptized into the Christian faith. As he grew older, he was instructed in the ways of the Church.

"Many of us here today can remember Jack as a young boy, running and playing in the streets and on the playground, attending Sunday School, and enjoying the fishing and hunting that he loved so much as he grew older. He grew up under the loving guidance of his parents and his church community to be a strong, energetic young Christian man. I have the privilege of knowing his grandparents and his parents, and I can testify to the good solid Christian background that Jack comes from.

"Today, we say goodbye to a young man who has made the supreme sacrifice for his country, and it saddens us to think about it. His mother shared something with me last night and I would like to share it with all of you, something that should make us all feel very proud of the man Jack had become."

Pastor Adams took an old worn and wrinkled sheet of paper from his pocket, unfolded it and started to read.

"I've learned from his parents, that when Jack decided to enlist in the Army he spent several days struggling over what to tell his parents to help them understand why he wanted to enlist in the service as soon as he was of age, rather than wait to be drafted. Here is part of what he wrote. 'I love my mother, my father, and my sister.'"

Mary wept loudly when hearing the recital of her son's words, and rested her head on John's shoulder as the eulogy continued.

"'I love my friends. I love my town and my country. I love my way of life and the freedoms that go with it. If we don't win this war, all of the freedoms that we enjoy will be lost. I love all these things enough to fight for them and, if necessary, die for them. I can not imagine living a life without the freedom I have known. To me, life without freedom is not living, it's merely existing.'

"My friends, stop and think for a moment about what Jack was feeling at the time he wrote this. Does it make you feel as proud to be an American as it does me—to hear the sincerity and dedication come straight from the heart of such a young man? Jack was just about to turn eighteen years old when he wrote these thoughts down on this piece of paper, but the wisdom in his words and the dedication and bravery in his heart comes from a man many years wiser than that.

A Homeplace

"Yes, it is a sad day for us today, but the good news, my friends, is this: as long as there are so many people in this country who have this kind of dedication to their parents, their family and friends, and to their homeland, America will forever be blessed. God has truly blessed our lives by giving us the gift of John Nelson Jr. There are, however, no guarantees as to how long we will be able to enjoy the gifts God has given us in our lives, whether they be family, friends, or the material wealth of this world. Jack answered his country's call for help, and unselfishly gave us the gift of his life that we might be free. And that, my friends, is the greatest gift of all."

From the Red Pine Weekly Herald, Thursday November 9, 1944

Card of Thanks

We wish to thank all those who were so kind to us during our time of sorrow at the tragic loss of our son and brother. Words cannot express our appreciation for all the expressions of comfort given to us. May God bless all of you and may God bless America.

John, Mary and Caroline Nelson

It wasn't until three days after the funeral that Ray had learned of Jack's death. He was terribly saddened and shocked by the loss of his best friend, and while pondering what Mary, John, and Caroline must be going through, he struggled with his own strong yearnings for home. The increasing activity and viciousness of the war, however, continually refreshed his sense of duty, eventually replacing his intervals of sorrow, pouting, and self pity, into a strengthening of his resolve.

The next several weeks were very difficult for the Nelson family. Thanksgiving and Christmas, a season that traditionally brings families together for love, fellowship, conversation and laughter were tarnished by the loss of Jack.

The Greatest Gift of All

On Christmas Eve, Mary was in the bedroom getting ready to go to the evening service. Caroline and her father were waiting impatiently for her downstairs with their coats on when John finally called up the stairway to his wife, "Mary, are you ready yet? We're going to be late if we don't get going right away, Dear."

He waited for her response for a few moments, but when there was no reply, he went up the stairs and found Mary sitting on the edge of the bed drying her tears.

When John appeared in the doorway she looked up at him and said, "John, I don't think I can go to services this evening. I just can't bear the thought of sitting in such a joyous place when the loss of our son is still so heavy on my heart."

He knelt down in front of his wife and said, "I know it's hard, Dear. I have to admit that for the first time in my life the spirit of Christmas just isn't in my heart. In fact, I, too, was ready to ask you if we should just skip going to services this Christmas, but then I remembered how strong your faith was when our friend, Ray, died so many years ago, and how important it is to just keep praying and keep our faith. Eventually we will find comfort. Do you realize that since I moved to Red Pine when I was just seven years old, that I haven't missed one Christmas Eve service? Even when I was going to trade school in Minneapolis I found a way to get home and attend church, remember?"

He lifted her chin and wiped the tears from her cheek with his thumb. "It was snowing awfully hard that night, and Ray and I barely made it from the train station in Agate Falls in time for the service to start."

Mary looked up at him, sniffled with a teary smile and said, "As I recall you were late. Remember, you and Ray came in when we were singing "Silent Night."

They stood up together and embraced as they recalled the circumstances of that particular Christmas Eve. John held her for several moments and then spoke softly in her ear, "Just remember Mary, we're not alone tonight. There are tens of thousands of parents who are going to church tonight who have lost their sons in this terrible war. Even though it saddens us to think that Jack is gone, we must not forget that one of the reasons all these fine young men have given their lives for this country, is so we may continue to enjoy our freedom, especially the freedom to worship God as we choose. I think it would be a terrible dishonor to our son's cause if we stayed home from church tonight, don't you agree?"

"Yes, John, you're right," she said as she dried her eyes. "Thank you for helping me see that." As they left the room together, Mary stopped John in the doorway and put her arms around him. "I love you, John. I don't know how I'd get through this without you."

"And I love you too, Mary. I always will. No matter what happens we will always have each other. And Jack will always be alive in our hearts."

The three of them walked to church together in the subtle glow of the streetlights and the peaceful beauty of the crisp air and sparkling snow. They walked along the white picket fence in front of the cemetery where Jack was buried and could hear the faint singing of "Hark! The Herald Angels Sing" coming from within the church. They paused for a moment, gazing at the gravestone of their son protruding through the deep snow. Mary rested her head against John's shoulder as they reflected on the finality of his death.

"Dad, do you think that as time goes by people will remember the sacrifice that was given for our country by all the people that gave their lives in the war?"

"I don't know, Caroline, I certainly hope so," said her father, sighing with despair. "I think that it's up to the family and friends of those who died to make sure that future generations realize the price that was paid to protect our country. I know that the three of us will never take our freedom for granted. Never."

Very early on Christmas morning, while John and Caroline were still asleep, Mary left the bed and quietly descended the stairs to the kitchen with her journal.

Monday, December 25, 1944

It has taken many weeks to find the courage to make an entry into this journal. Truly, my life has been torn apart with the loss of Jack and it has taken until now to sort through my feelings about our loss so that I may record them in a rational manner.

The Greatest Gift of All

Our family has had its share of visits by death over the years;. our good friend Ray many years ago, and now our son. Once again we have been humbled. Once again we struggle with the pain, the sorrow, and the memories. Once again we find ourselves searching for answers with our feeble human minds.

Time eventually eases the pain and sorrow. The memories, however fond they may be, will begin to dim, and the search for an answer still ends the same—faith.

On our way to Christmas Eve service last evening, we stopped in front of the cemetery for a moment of prayer and reflection. It became obvious that Caroline, too, is still struggling with the loss of her brother. She is concerned that the future generations of our country will forget the sacrifice that was made to ensure our freedom. Although it is painful for me to think about that, I am afraid that it is inevitable. Fifty years from now, this war will be condensed to a few pages of interesting reading in some history textbook, similar to the way we read about the Civil War today. If only there existed a way to preserve the horror, the fear, the sorrow and the scarring of families and loved ones—maybe then the future generations would realize the investment that was made for our freedom.

When I consider all of the young men lost in this war, it troubles me to think how this terrible loss might have changed our future. How many doctors, scientists, teachers and leaders have we lost on the battlefields? How many cures for disease and suffering have washed up on the beaches? How many hopes and dreams lie unfulfilled at the bottom of the sea because of this awful scourge?

I will never forget the words Jack wrote when he decided to join the Army. He was so dedicated to preserve our freedom, and he said he'd rather be dead than to lose his way of life. He did die to keep our freedom, and I pray that somehow God enables the spirits of all those who have fallen, to know how much we appreciate what they have done.

John has been so strong and comforting for me since Jack's death, and I don't know how I'd ever get through this without him. But even he cannot hide the effect our loss has had on him. He looks a little grayer now. The sparkle in his beautiful hazel eyes has dulled a bit and his soft spoken voice is noticeably softer. As recent as yesterday I caught him struggling with his emotions as he worked alone remodeling one of the cabins—there are so many memories.

A Homeplace

Feel the Warmth

After the war ended, Ray's mother and friends anxiously waited for his return. In his last letter he informed his mother that he would certainly be home before Christmas, but that was as close as he dared predict.

On the third Sunday of Advent, 1945, Ray walked up the back stairs to his mother's apartment above the store. As he entered the kitchen door, he was greeted by the aroma of freshly-baked cinnamon rolls. "Hello!" he shouted, "Mother, I'm home." There was no answer. He took off his coat and looked around the apartment, absorbing the sights and the smells of the home he missed so much. She must be at church, he thought.

He returned to the kitchen and removed the heavy cloth napkin covering the cinnamon rolls, cutting away a large section and putting it on his plate. "Mmmm, still warm," he said with heightening anticipation as he licked the gooey frosting from his fingers. He sat at the table and spread a generous amount of butter on the warm pastry. He took a bite of his mother's homemade roll, and just like he remembered, it melted in his mouth almost instantly. "Oh, gosh it's good to be home," he said with a sigh, closing his eyes and leaning back in the chair. After savoring his first bite, he decided to pour himself a glass of milk.

On his way to the refrigerator, he passed by the window overlooking the roof of the old icehouse, and could see that the front doors of the church were just opening and the service was letting out. Without a moment's hesitation, he quickly went out the door, down the back stairs, and ran down Main Street toward the church.

He stopped and stood in the middle of the street watching as the congregation continued to exit and saw Mary, John, and Caroline exchange greetings with Pastor Nordstrom. Next, his mother appeared in the doorway, and as the four of them descended the long flight of stairs in front of the church, someone yelled, "Hey! Isn't that Ray Larson?"

Feel the Warmth

Diane looked down the block and saw her son standing in the street. "Oh my G..!" she cried, covering her mouth with her hand. For a moment she stood in shock and disbelief. "It's my son!"

Everyone on the stairs looked to Diane and then in the direction she was looking. Ray started to run toward his mother and she too surged through the lingering crowd. As they embraced each other in the street, tears of joy and shouts of "Welcome home" flowed from the on-lookers at the heartwarming sight of mother and son. Caroline was next to run and greet Ray with a hug and a barrage of kisses. Mary and John were right behind her, and they all gathered around him in the middle of the street.

"It's so good to see you, Ray," said John.

"Thank God, you're home," said Mary.

At first, Diane was so overwhelmed emotionally that every attempt to speak resulted in hysterical sobs. Finally, she turned to the Nelsons and said, "I don't have much prepared at home, but I would like it if you all would come over for some coffee and rolls."

"We'd love to," said Mary, "but wouldn't you rather spend some time alone with your son?"

"There'll be plenty of time for that later," she replied. "Besides, we're all family."

"I have a confession to make, Mom," said Ray. "You were at church when I came home, and when I walked in the door and smelled the cinnamon rolls, I couldn't resist and I got into them."

John burst into laughter at Ray's confession. "I'll tell you what, Ray," he said. "After all you've been through, you oughta be allowed to eat the whole darn pan if you want."

They walked toward the apartment, Ray in the middle with one arm around his mother and one around Caroline. John and Mary followed behind and when he noticed that his wife's tears continued, he put his arm around her. It was a difficult moment for the Nelsons, balancing feelings of joy and sadness as they walked along—sadness because they would not be able to celebrate the war victory with their son, but joyful for the safe return of Ray, who in many ways was like a son to them.

John tried to divert Mary's thoughts away from their loss and said, "It certainly appears as though Caroline is happy to see Ray."

"Yes, it does," Mary replied as she dabbed her tears with her handkerchief, "And I'm very happy for her. I just hope that Ray feels the same way."

"Something tells me he does, my dear. Something tells me he does."

They all went to Diane's apartment and enjoyed the rest of the afternoon together. Ray shared some of his stories of the war, but he was mostly anxious to catch up on the news in Red Pine and get his life restarted.

During the previous October, after the resort was closed for the season, but only one week before the Nelsons were informed of their son's death, John had installed the foundation for the last cabin, in response to an excerpt from a letter he received from Jack earlier in September.

'The fighting is tough and slow but eventually we are beating them in every battle we fight. I really feel we are going to win this war, but it's hard to say how much longer it will take. I just wanted to tell you to go ahead and put the foundation in for the last cabin if you have time, just in case the war ends and I come home in the winter months. I'm anxious to get home and start on another cabin, and I'm sure Ray is too.

Love, Jack.

Early Monday morning, Ray stopped in at the store and had a long talk with John. "So what are you going to do with yourself, Ray, now that the war is over?"

"I'm not sure yet, Mr. Nelson. I've thought about college, but I really don't know what I want to do yet. I was hoping to find a job around here, at least over the winter. That would give me some time to think about a career."

Feel the Warmth

"Well," said John. "I could put you to work right here if you'd like."

"Thanks, Mr. Nelson. What would you have me do?"

"Well, believe it or not, under that snow drift out there is the foundation for the last cabin," said John. "I was saving that project for you and Jack to do when you returned, but now it looks as though you and I will have to do it alone. It may be a cold job, but it's a job. If you're interested, that is."

Ray's face lit up with a big smile. "I sure am," he said eagerly. "When can I start?"

"I might be able to have the lumber here by tomorrow. That fellow who bought the business from your grandfather is awfully busy, but I'm sure he could deliver at least enough lumber to get started. How's that sound?"

"Sounds great, Mr. Nelson. I'll get a shovel and start clearing the snow away from the foundation right now." He started toward the back room where the scoop shovels were kept and then turned to John and said, "Mr. Nelson, would you mind terribly if I tried to build the cabin by myself? Perhaps you could just refresh my memory if I have any questions, just like John and I did on the other cabin that we built."

"Only on one condition," John said with a smile. "From now on you can drop the mister and just call me John. If you're man enough to fight for our country, you don't have to call anyone mister."

"It's a deal!" replied Ray with a smile. Ray put his hat and gloves on, and snatched up the shovel. He was just about to open the door and go out to the building site when he paused and turned back to John. "Just one more favor Mr. Ne…, John?"

"What is it?" he said.

"I'd appreciate your permission to ask Caroline for a date?"

John's face immediately beamed with joy. "You certainly may," he said. "And I'll let you in on a little secret."

"What's that, John?"

" I think she's been hoping you'd ask that for a long time," he said with a big smile.

"That's good," said Ray. "It takes a little pressure off me then." They exchanged a chuckle as Ray turned and walked out into the snowy outdoors.

John watched through the window as Ray made his way through the knee-deep snow to the building site and started to uncover the foundation blocks. He thought how lucky he was to have Ray back home and working for him, and although he would never be able to take the place of his own son, in many ways Ray would fill the void in his heart left by Jack's death. Just then the little bell on the front door of the store rang as a customer walked in.

As Ray worked at moving the snow away from the site, he thought about how beautiful a woman Caroline had become while he was gone. She had the same black hair and creamy-white skin as her mother, but she was taller and had a slightly larger build.

Caroline had been out of school for over a year and was working full-time as a cook at her grandparents hotel, where Mary also helped when she wasn't needed at the store. Age was catching up with Andy and Ellen, and they were having difficulty managing some of the tasks of operating the hotel by themselves. They had put it up for sale in September, and a young couple from St. Cloud had come to terms to buy the hotel. The sale was expected to be finalized in January. Once that occurred it was decided that Andy and Ellen would live with Mary and John during the winter months and rent one of the resort cabins for the summer.

John's father had retired in the spring of '43, and chose to stay in St.Paul. Their house was only seven miles from where Rose and her husband lived, and Sarah enjoyed the convenience of the close proximity to her daughter and two grandsons. Sarah and Rudy were frequent guests at the resort during the summer months. They enjoyed coming up for two or three weeks in the summer and helping John and Mary with the store and resort and a chance to get reacquainted with their old friends and customers from Red Pine.

Ray was busy moving snow, unaware that Caroline had walked up behind him. She had noticed him earlier when she was cleaning in the dining room of the hotel and decided to bundle up and come over to chat with him. "Whatcha doin there, good lookin'?" she asked.

Ray turned and smiled at her. "Trying to earn a buck, Miss, why do you ask?"

She returned a flirtatious smile saying, "What are you going to do with all your money, Mister?"

"Well, first thing I want to do is save enough to take this girl I know out on a date."

Feel the Warmth

The smile quickly left Caroline's face, and she said, "Oh, is that so! Anyone I know?"

"You just might, Miss. She's got long black hair, soft white skin, and a face like an angel. Do you know anyone who fits that description?"

Her smile returned and she stepped closer to him, "I think I might know that person, but how do you know she'll even go out with you?"

"Course I can't say for sure," he said. "But I'm told she has very good taste and is an intelligent young woman. I just figure a nice guy like me has a pretty good chance."

Caroline now stood directly in front of him, nearly toe to toe. Still smiling, she adjusted the collar on his coat and said, "You seem very confident, Mister, I sure hope she doesn't turn you down."

Ray took her in his arms and said softly, "Well, let's find out." He bent over slightly, and gave her a long, soft kiss on the lips. She closed her eyes and Ray could feel her tremble as he continued to kiss her. Her heartbeat quickened as he held her, and for a moment she felt as though her legs would give out.

When Ray broke away from her lips, he looked into her eyes and said, "I sure missed you when I was gone, Caroline. I thought about you every day when I was on that ship, and I'll bet I've rehearsed a hundred different ways of asking you on a date, but none of them even came close to this," he chuckled.

"Why, what's wrong with this way?" she asked.

"Well, nothing I guess. I just figured on something a little more romantic than standing knee-deep in a snow drift in broad daylight." They both started to laugh and then Ray said, "Do you think you'd want to take a chance and go out with me?"

Caroline was jumping for joy inside, but she very confidently smiled and said, "Well, this is your lucky day, Mister. It just so happens that I feel like taking a chance. Where shall we go on this date?"

"I thought about going to Agate Falls and taking in a movie. How does that sound to you?"

"Sounds real good. What's playing?"

"A show called 'The Bells of St. Mary's.' They say it's a good one."

"Do you have a car?" she teased.

"No, I don't, Miss. Do you?"

"No sir, but my father has one. You'll have to ask him if we can use it."

"I think I'll leave that to you, Caroline."

"Why me?"

"Because, within the last hour he's already given me a job and permission to date you. I think I'd be pushing my luck to ask him for use of his car to take his daughter on a date."

Caroline laughed and said, "I'll see what I can do. When do you want to go?"

"I thought this Friday night, if it's okay with you."

"Sounds good to me. It's a date then."

Their romance continued to blossom throughout the winter. They attended church together each Sunday and continued to date. Ray made good progress on the cabin considering the several days lost because of the extreme cold. When the first warm days of spring finally arrived, he was able to paint the exterior—white, with red trim, just like the rest of the cabins—and it was ready to use in May when the resort opened.

Ray and Caroline were very much in love, but Ray was growing increasingly restless about starting a career or going to school. He realized that part of his restlessness was because his best friend, Jack, was gone. A haunting absence kept suggesting that life in Red Pine just wouldn't be the same anymore.

On a warm spring day in early June, Ray and Caroline sat together at a picnic table on the resort grounds, enjoying their lunch. The lush green foliage beneath the forest canopy was garnished with flecks of white from trilliums in full bloom. The boisterous call between a mating pair of loons and the fragrant melding of lilac and apple blossoms drifting about on warm spring breezes, combined to stir the romantic feelings between the young couple. After they finished eating, they turned to face the lake and leaned back against the table. Ray had his arm around her and she rested her head on his shoulder. "You seem a little distant today Ray, is anything wrong?"

"Oh, I'm a little confused about some decisions I need to make is all. I'm sorry if I don't seem myself today." He gave Caroline a peck on the cheek and a smile.

She held his hand and asked, "What kind of decisions do you need to make?"

"Well," said Ray. "The most important one I need to make is when I should ask you to marry me."

Caroline spun around and faced him with a look of surprise, and as his words sunk in, she noted the serious look on his face. Beaming with joy she hopefully asked, "What's wrong with right now?"

Ray held both of her hands tightly and said, "Because I don't have anything to offer you right now. I have no job, very little training and no education beyond high school. That's one of the drawbacks of having to go to war, I guess. If it wasn't for that, I might have had a job or enough schooling by now to be able to get a good job."

Caroline could sense how he was anguishing over his concerns, and tried to offer her help. "Why can't you just keep working for my father? I'm sure he would keep you on. He loves you like a son, and if he knew that we wanted to get married I'm sure he would hire you permanently."

Ray looked intently into her eyes and said, "I'm sure that he would too, and I think that's part of my problem. Your father has been looking after me all of my life. I think its high time I start to fend for myself and earn some respect."

"But Ray," she pleaded. "You already have his respect. Mine too. Hardly a day went by during the war that he didn't mention how highly he thought of you and my brother and all the men who were fighting and making sacrifices for our country. Believe me Ray, he has a lot of respect for you."

"That may be, Caroline, but I'm talking about something different now," he pleaded. "I'm talking about the kind of respect that a person gets when they can accomplish something by themselves. Taking a chance, working hard, making a living in this world. Do you understand what I mean?"

A Homeplace

"Yes, I suppose I do," she said softly. They sat quietly for a few moments and gazed out across the lake. "So what do you have in mind then?" she asked.

"I'm going to go to the cities and try to find a job." Ray watched as she turned her attention away from him and lowered her head in disappointment. Quickly, he put his hand under her chin and raised it up.

"Don't you be that way Caroline, do you hear me? This doesn't mean the end for us."

Caroline started to get teary eyed as she continued to stare out at the water.

Ray turned her face toward his and said, "Look at me and listen Caroline. I love you very much and I'm going to marry you, do you hear me? Please try to understand. I have to get a good job and put some money away so I can take care of you, okay? When we get married I just want to be able to start off on the right foot. Come on Angel Face, what da ya say?"

Caroline put her arms around his neck and hugged him as hard as she could. "I love you Ray, I just wish you didn't have to go away again. When we get married are we going to live down in the cities?"

"I think that's where we'll have to live, Caroline. That's where most of the jobs are. Do you mind moving away?"

"I'll move to wherever we have to Ray. I just hoped that when you were away for so long during the war, that you hadn't lost your love for Red Pine."

"That will never happen Caroline. And the first opportunity we have to come back we will. I promise. Our town will always have a special place in my heart. You know, Caroline, after I was in the Navy for a while, a lot of us guys would sit around at night and talk about our home towns, and we practically made each other homesick," he chuckled as he thought about it. "I couldn't wait to get home and get back to my boyhood town. But lately though, I've found it isn't the town that I miss so much—it's my boyhood. It's just that, well, I don't know if it's because I miss your brother, or I just miss the good times we used to have together. Maybe a little of both," he said. "It's hard to explain, but I just feel the urge to get out on my own and get my life started. I've heard there's a lot of jobs down in the cities, and I want to go and see if there is something for me."

Feel the Warmth

Ray used some of the money he had sent home to his mother during the war to purchase his first car, a 1938 Chevrolet Coupe. He left for St.Paul and quickly found work as a carpenter with "Hitchcock Construction Co.,"a large residential developer. The skills he had learned while helping build the two small cabins in his home town quickly returned and proved to be all the experience he needed to get a job. Work was plentiful, and new homes were springing up everywhere, especially in the suburbs of St. Paul and Minneapolis.

Ray's skills continued to improve, and the good work habits and pleasant demeanor that were instilled while growing up in Red Pine, contributed to his quick promotion to foreman. Everyone enjoyed working for Ray because he was such a hard worker himself and never delegated the difficult jobs to someone else. He always remembered the words that John had spoken to him and Jack one day when they were building their first cabin. They were talking about fairness and respect and John had said, 'Never ask anyone to do something you wouldn't do yourself.' It was a motto that John learned from Rudy, and Ray continued to live by it. By fall of that same year, Ray was in charge of three carpentry crews in a large housing development north of St. Paul.

Ray returned home to visit his mother and Caroline as often as he could. When he came home in November to go deer hunting with John, he asked for Caroline's hand in marriage, and John happily consented. Later that month, John, Mary, Caroline and Diane traveled to St. Paul to celebrate Thanksgiving in the cities with Rudy, Sarah and Rose, her husband and three sons. During that holiday weekend, Caroline and Ray picked out a building lot in the development where he was working. Their plans were to be married in May of the following year, and then Caroline would join her husband.

After a brief honeymoon in Duluth, Ray and Caroline returned to St. Paul to live in the tiny apartment that Ray had been renting. In August of 1947, Ray and Caroline finally moved into their new home. The skills she had learned from working in her grandparent's hotel and café, helped

A Homeplace

Caroline gain employment as an assistant cook in the school district in their community.

When Caroline was off during the summer months, she and Ray returned to Red Pine nearly every Friday night and helped her parents with the resort and store over the weekend, returning on Sunday evening. At times, Ray was so busy with the construction company he worked for that he had to work ten hour days and on Saturdays. During these times, it was common for Caroline to spend a week at a time at her parent's home and help out since Ray was unable to get away.

Caroline and Ray had intended to start a family soon after they were married, but it wasn't until 1954 that Caroline gave birth to their first child. Mary Ann Larson, named in honor of her mother, was born on Thanksgiving Day, bringing a special meaning for that particular holiday. After patiently waiting seven years before finally having their first child, Caroline quit her job with the school district and focused her attention on raising children. They adjusted to the loss of income when Caroline quit her job, freely accepting the fact that they would have to do without some of the luxuries that they had become accustomed to. As parents, they recognized the importance of the task that lay ahead of them and chose to raise the children in the same tradition as their parents and grandparents had done. In September of 1956, their second daughter, Irene, was born.

The construction business continued to flourish, and the company Ray was with expanded into developing, which fit nicely with their rapidly-growing construction company. Ray's many years of hard work and dedication to the company did not go unrecognized, and in 1958 he was promoted to general foreman of all home construction. Nearly half of his time was spent in his office where he met with the customers and coordinated the construction of each new home.

These were precious times for the grandmothers, Mary and Diane, enjoyable times watching their children's children grow. John, too, grew fond of seeing the fresh innocence of his two little granddaughters each time they came to visit. "You know, Mary, we're so darn busy all the time with this store and resort, it does my soul good to see those two little kids running and playing without a care in the world," was one of John's frequent revelations to his wife.

Feel the Warmth

Every year since Caroline and Ray left Red Pine, they returned home to celebrate the Thanksgiving and Christmas holidays with Mary, John and Diane. It was here that the memories continued to be made, memories of the many Thanksgiving dinners when everyone gathered around the large oak table to give thanks and share a meal amidst the sounds of laughter, conversation, and silverware clattering against fine china plates.

The most cherished memories for Mary were those of Christmas. For her, it was a time when the feelings of love and belonging were heightened by the special meaning of the season. She loved walking home from the late Christmas Eve church service surrounded by her family, past the warm, yellow light in the frosted window panes of their friends' and neighbors homes, while large feathery snowflakes fell from the darkness into the soft glow of streetlights. And when they returned home, she and John would stand back at the edge of the room, with their cups of hot cider, and watch with joy as their granddaughters sat around the Christmas tree, excitingly opening their presents in front of the warming embers in the fireplace.

Hard work was never a stranger to John and Mary, but as they grew older, it became increasingly difficult for them to manage all the responsibilities of the store, the resort, their home and yard. For many, many years, Nelson's Crystal Lake Resort enjoyed a nearly 100 percent occupancy rate from Memorial Day to Labor Day. With nine cabins behind the store, and the little "Honeymoon Cottage" on the island, the Saturday changeover time was so hectic that Mary and John never stopped for lunch. A checkout time of 10 AM and check-in time of 3 PM left such a small window of opportunity to accomplish the enormous amount of work. Diane was still minding the store for them on Saturdays during the summer, while the Nelsons changed the bedding, scrubbed the floors and tidied up each cabin for the next customers.

A Homeplace

In the spring of 1966 John and Mary made a decision to hire a young man to help run the general store, Sandy Nyberg, Harold's oldest grandson. He was working his way through college at the University of Minnesota in Duluth, trying to get a business degree. Mary was especially pleased to have him in their employ, because he was so reliable, and courteous to the customers. This enabled Mary to help her husband more with the demands of the resort.

On the last weekend in September of that year, Ray and Caroline and their two daughters came up on Friday night to help John and Mary get ready for winter. The resort had been closed for two weeks, and John had done most of the work involved in preparing the resort for the long, cold winter months. Caroline and Ray helped Mary clean and install the numerous heavy storm windows on their old house, while John and his two granddaughters rowed out to the island to close up the little cabin. "How did this cabin get named the "Honeymoon Cottage," Grandpa?" asked Mary Ann.

John looked down at her and smiled saying, "It was your grandmother's idea, Honey." He paused for a moment and looked around admiringly inside while he lit his pipe. "There is quite a story behind this little cabin, my dears."

"Tell us the story, Grandpa," said Mary Ann.

"Yeah, Grandpa, tell us the story," added Irene.

"Okay girls, I'll tell you the story. Let's go out on the porch and sit down. It's too nice a day to be inside."

They went out onto the covered porch, and John began his story while the little girls listened intently. Mary Ann and Irene always pestered their Grandpa to tell them a story whenever they were together, and truth be known, John was just as eager to accommodate them. He began by telling them when he was just seventeen, how eager he was to build this cabin and how their grandmother had gotten so angry with him for forgetting about taking her to the church fall festival. He explained how bad he felt about forgetting his commitment, and how he worked all night long bringing the lumber out to the island so he could take Mary to the festival the next day.

"Do you girls remember that beautiful blue dress with the white lacy collar that grandma has in her closet?" he asked.

"Yes, I know the one!" Mary Ann said excitedly as Irene nodded affirmatively.

"Well girls, your grandma made that dress just for the fall festival, and I remember the first time I saw her in it," he smiled and said yearningly, "She looked just like an angel."

Mary Ann and Irene exchanged a grin of delight at their grandfather's heartfelt disclosure. Then he explained how he and Mary barely made it out to the island cabin on their honeymoon night before a thunderstorm moved in.

"So that's how it got it's name," said Mary Ann.

"Well almost," said John. "Many years later I wanted to build two more cabins out here and your grandma talked me out of it. She explained what a special and romantic place it is out here, and she thought it would be ruined if we added any more cabins. So she came up with the idea of advertising it as the "Honeymoon Cottage." And, like always, she was right. Everyone wants to be out here, even though there's no electricity, and you have to heat with wood and use kerosene lamps; people just love to be out here, especially the newlyweds."

"How did Grandma know that people would like it so much, Grandpa?" asked Irene.

"Because she is a smart lady, my dear. That's why I married her," he said with a smile.

It was now late in the afternoon, and after closing the last shutter on the cabin windows, John said, "We better get back now, girls, before Grandma begins to think we fell in the lake." As they walked down the trail to the boat landing the two little girls started bickering over who would get to row the boat back to the mainland. "Now, now you two," he said sternly. "There's no need to argue. You can each take an oar and Grandpa will just sit back and enjoy the ride. How does that sound?"

"Okay, Grandpa," they replied.

A Homeplace

Once his granddaughters were seated, John pushed the little rowboat out into the water and sat down in back of the boat. He filled the bowl of his pipe with tobacco, tamped it down tightly and struck a wooden match across the seat of the old wooden boat and lit it. At first, the little girls pulled awkwardly on the oars and out of unison with each other.

"You might have to ease up a little bit on your oar, Mary Ann. You have to remember that Irene isn't quite as big as you are yet, Honey, and we're starting to go in circles," he chuckled. They eventually found their rhythm and the boat slowly made its way back to the dock across the calm, glassy water.

Through the diminishing foliage on the trees, John could see that Mary, Caroline, and Ray were walking down the hill to meet them at the dock. They all arrived at the same time and Ray lifted his daughters out of the boat while Grandpa John steadied it against the dock. John pulled the boat up onto the beach and Ray helped him turn it over.

"Well, that's it, girls," John said to his granddaughters.

Mary put her arms around the two girls and asked," Did you get the little cabin all tucked in for a long winter's nap?"

Mary Ann spoke up, "It's not a cabin, Grandma, it's a honeymoon cottage."

Mary looked at John, and as a smile melted through her fabricated disgust, she shook her head. Smiling at her, John removed his pipe and said innocently, "They asked me how it got its name and I told them."

"Are you still angry at Grandpa because he forgot about the church festival, Grandma?" asked Irene.

Mary rolled her eyes and said, "I see you told them the whole story, Grandpa." She squatted down and looked Irene in the eyes, "Of course not, Dear. Your Grandpa worked so hard that night so that he could bring me to the festival the next day, I forgave him," she said with a smile and winked at her husband. "That's why I married him, he's such a hard worker."

"That's good," said Mary Ann. "Grandpa said he married you because you were so smart."

Mary stood up, laughing with the rest of the adults and said, "Oh, that Grandpa of yours sure likes to tell stories."

"John held Mary's hand as they all started back to the house and said, "I like to tell them stories, but I never tell them lies!" He kissed her on the cheek.

They returned to the house where they enjoyed hamburgers on the grill with potato salad and Mary's special homemade apple pie. The children and the adults eventually succumbed to the long, hard day's work in the invigorating crispness of the autumn air. By nine o'clock that evening, everyone was in bed and sound asleep except for Mary who sat at the kitchen table in her robe enjoying a cup of tea while making an entry in her journal.

Saturday, September 24, 1966

We've closed the resort for yet another season today and the house is also ready for winter. I honestly don't know how we'd have done it without the help of our children and grandchildren. Never in my life have I felt so old and tired as I have these last few days. It's a hard fact to face, but John and I are going to have to make some decisions this winter regarding the resort and store. We simply are getting too old to work this hard. It was so nice to have Sandy working at the store for us this year, but he will graduate from college next spring and I'm sure he'll be looking for work in his area of training. I doubt that I'll be able to convince John to consider complete retirement, but I'll have to urge him to hire some more help next year.

Mary and John woke early as always, and started breakfast for the rest of the family. It was a sunny, crisp, Sunday morning, and when breakfast was over they all walked to church together. Diane met them at the bottom of the hill and joined them on their way.

After the services were over, they all returned to the Nelsons, where they ate lunch and enjoyed a lazy autumn afternoon in the back yard together. The ladies sat on the back porch in the warmth of the afternoon sun, while Mary Ann and Irene played on an old wooden swing that hung from the large old oak tree in the backyard. John and Ray decided to take a walk in the woods to check the condition of their

A Homeplace

deer hunting stands. "I think I'll grab my shotgun, Ray, just in case we see a partridge while we're walking back there."

"Good idea," Ray said.

Mary added, "I'd love it if you'd bring a couple of birds back, John. I've been craving a good partridge meal for a long time."

"I'll do my best, Dear," he answered with a smile. John and Ray hopped into the old green '53 Ford pick-up truck used for the resort and drove off along the meandering roads to their hunting land on the other side of the lake.

While Mary Ann was taking her turn on the swing, she noticed the carving on the tree trunk in the shape of a heart. "Look, Grandma," said Mary Ann. "There's a valentine on your tree."

Mary walked down to see what her granddaughter was pointing at and when she looked she said, "Oh yes, my dear. Do you know who made that?"

"No," she replied.

"Your Grandpa carved that in there the morning of our wedding. Can you read what it says inside the heart?"

Mary lifted her granddaughter up to closely examine the barely legible markings and slowly read the inscription, "John and Mary, August 31, 1923," she said proudly.

"My goodness, I'd forgotten all about that. That carving is as old as this house is," she said. "Let's see now," she thought out loud, "We built in '23, so that would be…ohhhh…about 43 years old now. Goodness sake, time sure does fly by," she sighed.

It was late afternoon when John and Ray pulled up into the driveway. The ladies were enjoying yet another cup of coffee when John walked up the steps, proudly displaying two large partridge. "Oh, good," said Mary. "I finally get my partridge dinner." John dressed out the two birds while Mary prepared a light meal for everyone.

After supper was over, Ray and Caroline said goodbye to their parents and loaded up their station wagon to return to St. Paul. This was always such a sad time for John, Mary and Diane. They always looked forward to seeing their children and grandchildren and when it was time to leave, tears were shed by all. Mary Ann and Irene always begged to stay a little longer, but Mary would dry their eyes and say, "You girls write us lots of letters so we don't get lonely, okay?"

Feel the Warmth

The sun was just beginning to set as their car drove off beneath the autumn-colored dome of the tree-lined street. Mary, John and Diane stood in the road and returned the vigorous waves of their granddaughters until the car was out of sight.

"Gosh, it's hard to watch them drive off like that," said Diane.

"I think it gets harder every time," replied Mary.

"I wonder if they'll ever get the urge to move back up here," said John. "I know that Ray has such a good paying job, but I wonder if he's really happy."

"Why do you say that?" asked Mary.

"Oh, I don't know. Just the way he seemed to avoid talking about his job when I asked him about it today in the woods."

"Actually, I've been wondering the same thing," said Diane. "He seems like he's got something on his mind all the time. Like he can't relax."

"Caroline never mentioned anything was wrong when I asked her how everything was going at home," Mary said. "She said 'Everything is just fine, Mom.'"

"Well you know Ray as well as I do Mary," said John. "He's got the same personality his father had. He wouldn't say "crap" if he had a mouthful. Anyway there isn't anything we can do about it. He's old enough and smart enough to work it out by himself, if indeed there is anything wrong."

"There most certainly is something we can do for them, John," said Mary. "We can pray for them."

"Well, yes, Dear, I meant besides that," he said sheepishly.

John asked Diane if she would like a ride home.

"Oh, no, John, that's not necessary. It's a beautiful evening for a nice, slow walk. I'll be just fine." Diane said good evening, and turned to walked down the hill. John put his arm around Mary and they walked up the stairs to the front porch and sat together in the swing and admired the waning glow of an orange sunset.

"Do you want your sweater, Mary? I'm going in to heat up some apple cider for us, and I'll bring it out if you need it."

"Oh, thank you, Honey, that would be real nice. I'll sit out with you for a little while, but I feel awfully tired tonight. I think I'll go to bed early and maybe read for a bit. It was such a busy weekend, and I think it finally caught up with me."

A Homeplace

John returned with two cups of hot cider and her sweater draped over his arm. They sat on the porch swing and enjoyed the evening as the sounds of night filled the air. The stars were bright and a long, thin cloud drifted past the moon. A large dog could be heard barking far off in the distance, and the soothing, synchronous chirping of crickets was interrupted by the soft cry of a loon gliding through the shimmering gold band of moonlit water. They sat peacefully in the swing, reflecting on the accomplishments made around the house and resort over the weekend.

This time of year always found them with mixed emotions about their resort business. On one hand, the rigors of running the resort would be over for the winter, allowing them to spend more time with each other. But on the other hand, even though the effects of growing old hampered their efficiency, he and Mary still enjoyed the business because of the many friendships they had developed with their customers over the years.

John thought of how fortunate he and Mary were to have such helpful and caring children and grandchildren; they were such an enormous help over the weekend, and he wondered how much longer the two of them would continue to be so active in running their business.

"I sure hate to think of the day when we have to sell our business," he said. "Our family has put so much of ourselves into it. My folks got it started, and then you and I have watched it grow. Somehow we made it through the depression and then, as our children have grown, they too were a big part in making it what it is today."

"Yes, it is hard to think of, John, but we have to remember that we're 62 and 63 years old now. Before our folks passed away they were fortunate enough to be able to enjoy life a little. We should probably start thinking along those lines ourselves, my dear."

"I don't know that I ever want to completely retire," said John. "Next spring maybe we can hire a couple more college kids to help with the resort. That way you and I can just take care of some of the lighter duties or even take a few days off each week."

"I like that idea, John. We've got all winter to think about it, and perhaps we'll come across someone who would be interested in working at the resort for the summer. Heaven knows we can afford to hire someone. We haven't owed any money for twenty years now, we might as well spend some of it and make life a little easier for ourselves."

Feel the Warmth

Mary finished the last swallow of cider and got up from the swing. "I think I'll turn in now, John," she said. She stooped over to give him a kiss, and when she cradled his weathered old face with her soft hands, he noticed how cold they seemed.

"Are you feeling alright, Mary? Your hands are cold as ice."

"I'm just a little tired, John. I've been tired all week it seems, but other than that I feel fine."

"Well, if you still feel tired tomorrow, maybe we should take you to the doctor," he said firmly.

"Oh, don't worry yourself, John. I'm probably just coming down with a cold or something. Goodnight, Dear."

"Goodnight, Mary." He watched her as she walked toward the door and noticed a certain radiance about her. It was a familiar look. A look that reminded him of a time of innocence, back when they were just newlyweds. As she entered the doorway he said, "Mary."

She stopped and looked back at him. "Yes, John."

"I love you."

"I know you do. I love you too, John," she said with a smile before disappearing through the doorway.

A short while later, John went to the kitchen for another cup of hot cider and put on his heavy sweater. When he returned to the porch he sat in the old wooden rocking chair. He put the cup to his lips and gently blew on the steaming beverage. After taking a sip he placed the cup on the table, and rested his head back in the chair. He closed his eyes and shortly fell asleep in the cool, peaceful night air, slipping into a medley of fond memories of his younger days.

His dreams carried him back into times as a boy playing along the riverbank with his best friend, Ray; hunting and fishing in times of abundant game, walking with friends to the little one-room schoolhouse, and the time when he realized that he had fallen in love with Mary. He dreamt of the day he took Mary to the church fall festival and how she stopped him in the middle of the road to kiss him when she acknowledged the sacrifice he made for her the night before. As he continued his tranquil drift, he dreamt of moments of intimacy with his wife and her long passionate kisses, and he could feel her warm soft lips against his.

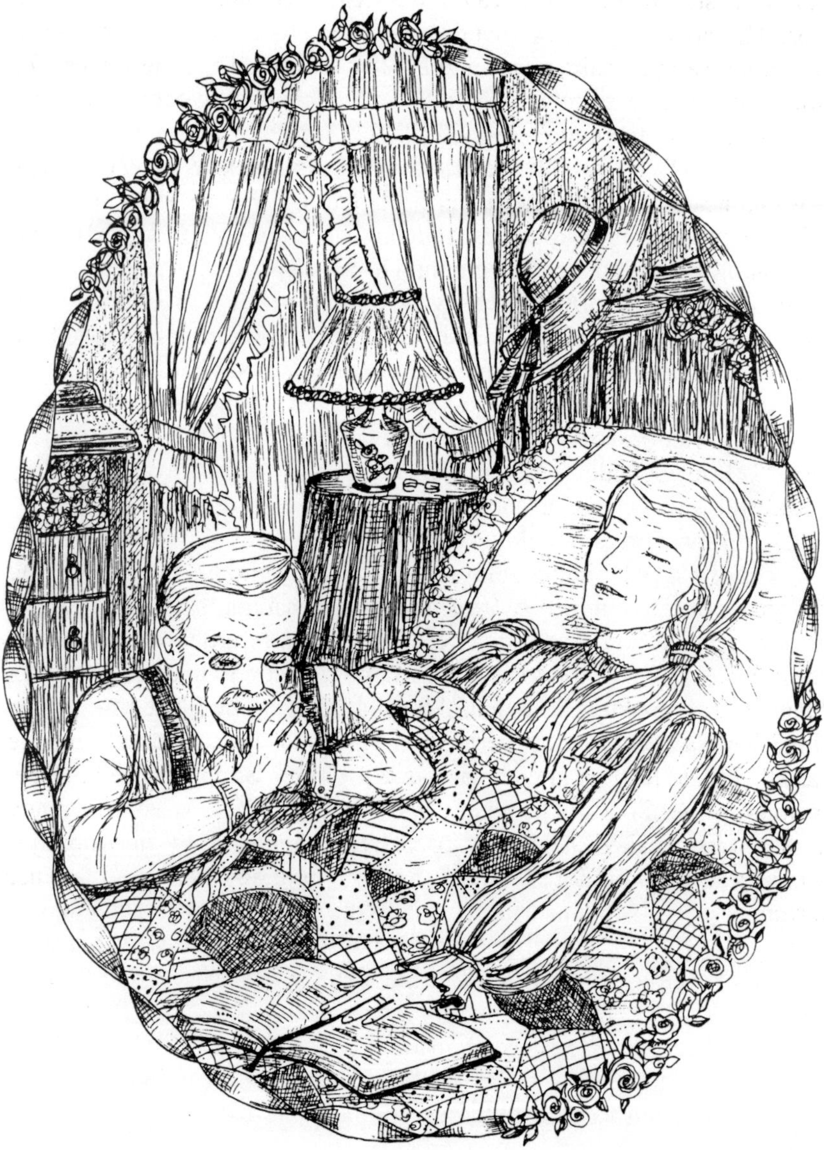

Feel the Warmth

He woke suddenly with a startling quiver. Glancing down at his watch, his eyes gradually focused on the 1 a.m. display. He stood up as a gust of cold wind stirred the fallen leaves that had accumulated on the porch floor. He noticed that his hands and face were cold except for a noticeable warmth radiating around his lips. He stood up, motionless for a moment, and as his drowsiness faded, a terrible feeling came over him, an empty and frightening feeling deep in his core.

"Mary!" he called loudly. "Mary!" As quick as his stiff legs allowed, he entered the house and started up the stairway to their bedroom and continued to call out for her. "Mary!—Mary!" he shouted, desperate for her response as he climbed the steps. When he entered the bedroom, he clutched his chest in anguish, then knelt beside the bed. "Mary!" he cried, trying to wake her. There was no response to the gentle shaking of her shoulders.

"Oh, Mary, please wake up," he begged. John pressed his face to hers and felt the tears leave his eyes and roll down her cool, lifeless flesh. "Please, God, don't take her from me now," he pleaded, looking up to heaven.

For several minutes John lay beside Mary and held her hand. She was gone now, he realized. With tears tracing past his temples, he lay on his back next to her wondering why. Why were so many of the people who were so close to him taken away so suddenly. "You never gave us a chance to say goodbye," he complained to God. A moment later, as he wiped his tears away with the back of his hand, he could still feel the warmth around his lips in contrast to the cool skin on the rest of his face. Then he remembered: The warm sensation, I've felt it before, many years ago, he recalled. And then it occurred to him. We did say goodbye, in my dream, right before I woke, she kissed me and I can still feel her warmth.

O Perfect Life of Love

It was nearly three o'clock in the morning when John picked up the phone to call Diane. After several rings, Diane answered with a raspy, "Hello."

He was certain that he had gathered enough composure to converse with her, but upon hearing Diane's voice, he realized he had not. A long moment of silence passed before John could speak. "Diane," he said in a soft, weepy whisper.

"Yes?" Despite the early hour and his soft tone, she recognized his voice. Clearing her throat, she repeated more clearly, "Yes, this is Diane."

"She's—she's gone."

"John, what's wrong?" Diane asked with increasing concern. She quickly roused from her sleepiness and listened intently while tightening the belt on her robe.

"Mary has passed away," he said with a weepy tone in his voice. It was an enormous emotional hurdle for John to speak those first words, but after a few moments, he was able to gather himself enough to converse more freely.

Diane sat down in a kitchen chair beside the phone, and in total shock and disbelief, she asked, "No! John, what's happened? Where are you?"

"We're at home."

"What happened?"

John explained the events of the evening after Ray, Caroline and the grandchildren left.

"John, give me a few minutes to get dressed and I'll be right over," she said.

"I really need you to be here, Diane," John said. "I called the hospital in Agate Falls. The ambulance should be here shortly."

Diane hung up the phone and dressed as quickly as she could. As she approached the top of the hill in the cold, windy darkness, the reflection from the red lights of the ambulance in front of the house whirled around within the confines of the tree-domed street. She stood on the sidewalk and looked up to the yellow glow in the bedroom windows, watching as the silhouettes of the ambulance crew moved about within the room. She ascended the stairs to the front porch, and through the opened drapes, saw John sitting in the living room rocking chair with his head back and a vacant stare on his face. Diane gently tapped on the door as she entered, and John quickly rose to greet her.

No words were spoken and they both began to cry as they exchanged a long supportive hug in front of the fireplace. Looking over her shoulder, he watched the as the two ambulance attendants carefully maneuver the gurney down the stairs, through the doorway, and onto the porch. His sorrow became more audible when it occurred to him that Mary was leaving the house forever, the house that they worked so hard together to build over forty years ago, the house that she cherished so dearly. And he realized the love and caring that she gave so freely to him, her children, and grandchildren, that transformed a mere house into a home, was now gone. Those thoughts were more than he could bear and he shook with grief as he tightened his embrace of their life-long friend.

It was six-thirty in the morning, and Caroline was in the kitchen making breakfast for her husband and daughters. Ray was just about to leave for work when the phone rang. "Ray, can you get that?" Caroline asked.

"Hello. Well, John!" he said energetically. "How are you this morning?"

"Not so good," he said softly. After a long pause, "Is Caroline there, Ray?"

"Yes she is, just a minute." Ray sensed something was wrong, and frowned with concern as he handed Caroline the phone. "It's your father," he whispered with a furrowed brow.

Caroline read the look on Ray's face, and because of the odd timing for a phone call from her father, she knew something was very wrong. "Hello, Dad, is everything alright?" she asked hesitantly. Ray watched nervously as a mixture of shock and sadness claimed the expression on her face. She sat down in a chair beside the kitchen counter. Her husband and daughters watched helplessly as tears filled her eyes.

"Why is Mom crying?" Irene asked with a look of distress.

Ray went to his daughters and said, "I don't know, girls. Grandpa John called with some bad news I think, but we'll just have to wait 'til Mom gets off the phone, okay?"

A Homeplace

After several minutes Caroline said, "We'll be up late this morning or early afternoon Dad, okay?" She wiped her eyes and said, "Dad—we all love you."

"I know you do, Caroline. I love all of you, too."

She hung up the phone and joined her family at the table. She held each of her daughters' hands and looked at Ray, "Grandma Mary died last night."

With tear-filled eyes Mary Ann looked at her mother and asked, "How could she die, Mom?"

"She just died in her sleep, Mary Ann. God must have really wanted her to come home to heaven."

"But we want her too," said Irene, who hadn't fully grasped the gravity of the situation. Caroline gave her a hug then turned to Ray's comforting embrace, completely releasing her emotions. It was the first time that the children had witnessed an emotional display of this caliber by their mother, adding even more anxiety to the quickly deteriorating events of the morning.

After a few moments, Ray looked up and said to his daughters, "You two better go to your room and start packing some clothes. I'll call work and let them know I won't be in for a few days. I'll call the school too. We're going to have to go back to Red Pine this morning, girls."

"Did Grandpa want us to come back?" asked Mary Ann.

"Yes, Dear," their mother replied. "He's going to need us very much for a while. He's especially going to need the love of his two granddaughters."

By late morning their station wagon turned off the highway and down the quiet, narrow street that led to her home place. Ray, Caroline, and their daughters, gazed out the windows in silent sorrow as the car slowly made its way towards the house. The only sound to be heard was the rustling of the crisp, fallen leaves being whisped to the side of the road by the velocity of the car. The vehicles of many friends offering comfort and consolation already lined both sides of the street in front of the house, requiring them to park near the end of the block. Diane, who had been receiving the steady stream of support at the front door, hurriedly descended the porch stairs and met Caroline on the front sidewalk with a hug. Caroline took a used tissue from her coat pocket and dried her tears asking, "How's Dad doing?"

"He's doing very well, I would say," replied Diane. "Thanks to all who have been stopping in this morning. It's just what he needs."

"Has Dad made any arrangements yet?"

"No, not really. The only thing we know so far is that the funeral could be as early as Wednesday, but Thursday would probably be better. Nothing has been confirmed so far. Your dad didn't want to make any arrangements without you."

They all walked together into the house, and when John saw his daughter and granddaughters, he excused himself from his conversation with the pastor. He crouched down to pick up Irene who had run to greet him and gave her a hug as Caroline, Ray and Mary Ann gathered around him in a loving, supportive huddle.

On a brisk Thursday morning in early October, the mid-morning sun sparkled brightly on the lake, and an occasional gust of wind swirled an accumulation of brittle, fallen leaves on the steps of the church. The little church was nearly full of friends and family who had come to say goodbye to Mary Nelson. John was seated on the aisle in the front pew next to his daughter, Caroline. Mary Ann and Irene sat between their parents, and Diane was seated next to Ray.

During the eulogy, Pastor Erickson revealed the little-known fact about Mary's weakened heart, a side effect believed to have resulted from a severe fever when she was very young.

"And even though her physical heart was scarred by the scourge of a worldly affliction," the pastor stated, "her spiritual heart was strong and pure. Her unwavering faith in God and dedication to her family are as good an example of Christian living as you will ever find."

As Pastor Erickson continued his tribute, Mary Ann and Irene turned their heads to the center aisle, distracted by the presence of a beautiful woman who stood by the pew next to their grandfather. The two young girls stared at the slender young woman wearing a long, blue dress with a white, lacy collar. Her shiny, black, shoulder-length hair glistened in the colorful rays of sunlight coming through the stained glass windows. The woman looked to them displaying a radiant smile, which they instinctively returned.

Irene turned to Mary Ann and whispered in her ear, "Who is that lady?"

"I don't know," she whispered back. "I think I've seen her before, but I don't know where."

Caroline took notice of her children's distractions and whispered to them, "What's the matter girls?"

Mary Ann whispered back, "Who's that lady standing by Grandpa?"

Caroline looked and saw nothing but the silhouette of her father against the bright colorful stained glass windows. She lowered her head towards them again, this time with a frown, and whispered, "I don't know who you're talking about, but you both know it's bad manners to stare. Just sit up straight and pay attention, and we'll discuss it later."

They obeyed their mother, but Irene couldn't resist taking one last look at the beautiful woman. Barely turning her head, and straining to look out the corner of her eyes, she saw the woman place her hand on her grandfather.

John slowly turned his head in response to a slight sensation of pressure and warmth on his shoulder, then returned his attention to the front of the church where Pastor Erickson continued with his kind and comforting words.

"It's difficult sometimes for a pastor to find the right words of comfort for the family and friends after the loss of a loved one. And being that I have only been here at Emmanuel for two years, I asked myself, how can I presume to know what Mary's life has meant to her family and friends? What words will I be able to say that could possibly bestow the kind of honor that this magnificent woman deserves?

"Two nights ago, when I met again with John and Caroline at their house to discuss the arrangements for Mary's funeral, I expressed this concern to them. John thought for a moment, then went upstairs and returned with several folders and handed them to me saying, 'These belonged to Mary, it's what she called her "life journal." I've never read it and would like you to return them to us, but perhaps you'll find something in here to help you.'

"When I returned home, I began paging through her journal, and it was so interesting that I was awake the entire night reading. I read excerpts about the joyous times in her life— the day she realized she had fallen in love with the man she would eventually marry, the joyous account of her wedding day, and the births of her children, just to name a few. I also read accounts of great sorrow and anguish—the death of a dear friend many years ago, Ray Hanson; the tragic loss of her son, Jack, during the war; and the loss of both her parents during the same year. I must say that this collection of such intimate thoughts was very moving for me. But there is one passage that really stood out for me that I believe beautifully captures the essence of Mary's life, and I would like to share it with you. This entry was made on Christmas Eve, 1940 and reads:

"John and the children have gone to bed, and I have just finished some last minute baking to prepare for Christmas Day. The house is silent except for the ticking of the clock. I look outside through the living room window at the mounds of snow sparkling beneath the glow of the street light, and a feeling of peace fills my heart, as it always does this time of year.

I was thinking earlier this evening as we walked home from church services, about how proud I am of our house and of my husband for building it. It was such hard work and he spent all of his free time working on it until it was finished. I have come to realize though, that there is a big difference between a house and a home. A house is just a structure made of wood and mortar and glass, designed and assembled to our liking. But it's the feelings of love and sorrow, the laughter and tears, the many Thanksgivings, Christmases and birthday celebrations that we have shared as a family that gives our house a soul and makes it a home. And I will forever thank God for that."

"My friends, Mary knew exactly what the important matters in life were, and she never let her personal possessions and goals obstruct the paramount obligations in her life—her family, her friends, and most of all, her Christian faith. Let us be mindful, though, that her exceptional insight to the important things in her life did not come about by accident. This wonderful characteristic of Mary was instilled in her by the same love and dedication of her parents. She and John recognized this very basic truth, and continued to live their lives consistent with their upbringing, and have successfully passed it on to their children as well.

"We have assembled here today, in this blessed little church that Mary loved so dearly, to tell her goodbye. This is the very church in which she began her life-long journey of faith with her baptism and continued with her first communion, her confirmation, her wedding—and now, after coming full circle, to be laid to rest in the comforting arms of our Father in heaven. She will no longer be a part of our physical world, but may I suggest this to you, my friends; her spirit will always be alive in our memory, as one of the main characters in what I think we would all agree is, a tremendous success story—Amen."

After the funeral, Mary was laid to rest next to her son in the little church cemetery on the hillside. John and Mary had made arrangements several years ago as their parents passed away so that all of their graves would be together.

At the conclusion of the graveside ceremony, the participants returned to the church hall for a luncheon and fellowship. John was seated at one of the long tables with his immediate family, and during the meal, many of his friends approached him to extend their support and condolences.

As the gathering gradually dispersed, Irene came to her grandfather, and took her favorite position on his lap. "Grandpa," she said. "Who was that pretty lady standing by you in church today?"

John turned to her with a smile and asked, "Now, what pretty lady are you talking about?"

Caroline overheard her daughter's question and said to her father, "I don't know who those girls are talking about, Dad. During the service they were distracted by some lady they said was standing by you, but I didn't notice anyone," she said.

John gave Irene a hug and kissed her on the cheek saying, "I don't know, my dear. What did she look like?"

Mary Ann was now standing next to her grandfather's chair and confirmed her sister's story. "She was the most beautiful lady I ever saw. Her skin was white as snow and her hair was black and shiny and went all the way down past her shoulders."

"Do you see her here now?" their mother asked.

The two girls looked around the church hall for a moment then Mary Ann said, "No, I don't see her now,"

"Honestly, Dad," Caroline added, "I don't know who they are talking about do you? I looked when they mentioned her during the service, but all I saw was the bright colors from the sun shining against the stained glass windows."

"Maybe that's it, girls," said John as he put his arm around each child and pulled them closer to him. "You saw a shadow or a figure from the church windows. Do you girls think that's possible?"

"Maybe," Mary Ann replied. Then she skipped away and joined one of her friends who had come with her mother to the funeral.

"How about you, Peanut," he said to Irene. "Do you really think you saw a lady standing by me?"

Irene nodded her head. "Yes, Grandpa," she answered softly. Sliding down off his lap she turned to face him, and with a look of total sincerity said, "She wore a long, blue dress with a white collar. Just like the one Grandma let us use to play dress up with. Didn't you feel her put her hand on your shoulder?"

John was stunned for a moment. He recalled the sensation he had during the service. "You saw her touch my shoulder?" he asked.

Irene nodded.

"Which shoulder did she touch, Honey? Do you remember?"

Irene thought for a moment and then walked around behind her grandfather who was kneeling on one knee facing her. From her position behind him she touched his right shoulder, saying, "This one."

Caroline looked on as her father kissed Irene on the forehead. He stood up slowly with an expression of a sudden, joyful realization and the sparkle of emotion in his eyes. Caroline asked, "Is something wrong, Dad?"

John took a handkerchief from his pocket and dried the corners of his eyes. "Do you realize what has happened, Caroline?" he asked, overwhelmed with joy.

"No I don't, Dad. What is it!"

"Those two little daughters of yours just gave a description of your mother when she was a young woman. She was there, Caroline. She was there in the church during the service. She stood right next to me."

"Are you serious, Dad? You're saying Mom was there at the church, standing next to you?"

"You bet I am," he answered, smiling with a glisten in his eyes. "I knew it the moment Irene told me which shoulder the lady touched me on.

A Homeplace

"Caroline—during the service I had this sensation of a slight pressure against my neck. Moments later I had a strange feeling of warmth on my right shoulder and I remember thinking that someone in the pew behind me was trying to comfort me, but when I looked—I saw nothing. Now, however, it all makes sense. You see, right before that happened, I'm sorry to say, I wasn't paying much attention to what Pastor Erickson was saying. My mind was occupied with concerns about running the store and the resort next year. Then, it was like I could feel her presence, and I could almost hear her comforting voice, telling me not to worry and that everything is going to be all right. I had this huge feeling of relief, but I don't know why, because I still don't know how I'm going to take care of everything without her help, but I'm just not worried about it anymore."

Caroline gave her father a hug and said, "Please don't worry about the business, Dad. We'll figure out what to do over the next few days, okay? Everything will work out somehow, just like you said."

"I know it will, Caroline. Like I said before, I'm just not worried about it anymore. I've never felt so peaceful inside, and now, after what those darling little grandchildren have revealed, I am more sure than ever that your mother is still with me—somehow."

From the Red Pine Weekly Herald, Thursday October 6, 1966

Card of Thanks

We wish to thank all those who were so helpful and comforting during our time of grieving at the loss of our wife, mother and grandmother. May God bless you all.

John Nelson and Caroline, Ray, Mary Ann and Irene Larson

A Homeplace

Coming Home

Ray and Caroline and their daughters decided to stay the rest of the week and through the weekend to be with John, and help him sort through some of Mary's personal belongings. On Saturday afternoon, John and Ray sat on the front porch together visiting in the warmth of the autumn sun, while Caroline was upstairs going through some of her mother's clothes with the help of her two daughters.

"So how's your job going, Ray?" asked John.

"Oh, it's okay I guess," he replied, half-heartedly.

"You'll have a hell of a time convincing me of that with that kind of enthusiasm," John returned. "Really, Ray, what's wrong? And don't say 'nothing' because I'm a lot smarter than that. I could tell the other day when we were checking our deer stands that you were less than enthusiastic about your job."

"Well, John, I've always liked my job, but now it doesn't look like I'm going to go any further in the company than I am right now."

"Why is that, Ray?"

"I've been passed up the last three times now for promotions that I really feel I should have had," he said with dejection. "I have consistently moved up the ladder ever since I went to work for the company in 1946."

"So what's different now?" asked John.

"About a year ago, the owner had some heart problems and decided to turn over the company to his oldest son, Ron. Ever since then, the promotions have been going to his friends or relatives who have only been there for two or maybe three years at best. It makes it really hard to keep my attitude in shape any more."

"Did you ever talk about it with the owner?"

"You bet I did!" said Ray. "Every time I missed a promotion I asked him why, and he said it's because I don't have a college degree. Can you believe that crap?" said Ray with a rising tone of irritability. He was now sitting forward in the rocking chair, and his knuckles were white as he gripped the front of the armrests. As Ray continued to vent his frustrations, John became more engrossed in the story, to the point that the smoke from his pipe increased in intensity, proportional to Ray's obvious agitation. "It was me and about three or four other guys who started with the company after the war ended," Ray continued. "We made that business what it is today. We were out there pounding nails in the heat and cold and catering to the customers' needs, and now, twenty years later, some snot-nose kid tells me I need a framed piece of paper in order to do a job that's ninety percent common sense anyway. The hardest part about all of this for me is the fact that if all three of those young hot shots put their heads together, they still wouldn't have enough brains to tell the difference between their asses and a hole in the ground."

At that, John removed the pipe from his mouth and burst into laughter.

"I'm sorry, John," Ray said with a chuckle. "I didn't mean to dump my problems on you like that. Lord knows you have enough to worry about, but it sure feels good to get it off my chest."

"Well, I'm glad for that," said John. "It won't do you any good to keep it stored up inside you, that's for sure. What does Caroline think about all this?"

"She doesn't know about it, John. I never bring work home with me."

"Well, she may not know anything is wrong, but I'll guarantee you that your mother knows something is bothering you, Ray. She even told me as much. And you know how those women get to talking."

"I suppose I should tell her. That way she won't be so shocked when I come home without a job someday."

"Do you really think it will come to that?" asked John, frowning with concern.

"I wouldn't be surprised," Ray said. "We've already lost quite a bit of work to our competition. I just can't see those young college geniuses being able to swallow their pride enough to let some of the older guys like me get more involved. That's saddest part about the whole thing. The old man worked his tail off over the years and built up a nice, solid little company before he let his son take over and throw it all away. It's a damn shame."

"Well, Ray," said John. "The only advice I can give you is what Mary would have said if she were here right now. Pray about it, Ray. Give it to God and let His will be done."

Ray looked to John and smiled, "Mary was so good at doing that, wasn't she, John?"

"She sure was. And every time I took her advice, and did that, I was never let down. That's why I'm telling you the same thing, Ray. Try it! It works, but keep something in mind when you pray about it, Ray."

A Homeplace

"What's that, John."

"Your prayers will be answered, but not always the way you want them to be. God knows what's best for us, and His plans don't always agree with our wants."

"Well, I'm going to do just that, John. Thanks!" The two of them sat back in their chairs, and John re-lit his pipe. "So, enough with my problems, John. What are you going to do, you know, with the business, I mean?"

John took the pipe from his mouth, tilted his head back and exhaled a long stream of smoke into the air, sat forward, and looking Ray in the eyes, said with a smile, "Pray about it."

Mary Ann and Irene sat on the bed as Caroline took each of her mothers' garments from the closet, carefully folded them and placed them in a large cardboard box. When she removed the long, blue dress that hung far back in the closet, and held it up admiringly in front of the girls, Mary Ann shouted joyfully, "That's it, Mom! That's just like the dress the pretty lady wore at Grandma's funeral." She quickly lowered the dress in order to see what her daughters were talking about. Irene smiled and nodded affirmatively at her mother as she pointed at the dress she was holding.

"This one?" their mother asked.

"Yes, Mom," said Mary Ann. "That's the dress she was wearing when she stood by Grandpa."

Caroline stood in shock for a moment, and then said, "Come here you two, I want to show you something."

Mary Ann and Irene followed their mother into the bedroom across the hall and watched as she opened a box containing several photographs. Caroline quickly shuffled through the large stack of pictures and stopped suddenly. Her eyes became moist with emotion as she stared intently at the photograph in her hand. She slowly turned it so that her daughters could see the faded black and white image. In front of them was a picture of Mary and John. As the girls studied the photograph, Caroline read a hand-written note on the back that read, Emmanuel Lutheran Church, Fall Festival, 1921."Is this the lady you saw at the funeral girls?"

She watched as their faces lit with joy and then Irene said, "Yeah, Mom, that's her! Isn't she beautiful?"

Coming Home

"And the man is so handsome, too," added Mary Ann. "Who are they, Mom?"

"Girls," she said softly. "This is a picture of Grandpa John and Grandma Mary taken before they were married."

"You mean the lady we saw in church was Grandma when she was a young girl?" asked Mary Ann.

"That's right, girls," Caroline said with a sniffle. She knelt on the floor and gathered her daughters to her side within her arms.

Mary Ann looked at her mother inquisitively and asked, "How come no one else could see her?"

"Oh, Honey," she answered with a weepy sigh, "That's what's known as a miracle." She continued to hold her daughters while she sat on the floor and stared at the photograph. Mary Ann and Irene rested their heads against her bosom, silently pondering what their mother had said.

On Sunday after church, everyone gathered at Diane's for the afternoon meal before Ray and Caroline left for the cities. It was a cloudy, blustery day, and the white caps rolled in rhythmatically against the shore of the resort. Diane and Caroline worked together in the kitchen, while Mary Ann and Irene set the table. John and Ray watched out the window as large flocks of bluebills glided in under the low, misty sky and gathered to raft on the less turbulent water on the sheltered side of the island. "I'd say winter is going to be early this year," John said.

"Think so?" replied Ray. "What gives you that idea?"

"Seems earlier than normal to see those ducks here. Don't usually see them until the end of October," he said with confidence.

"Now that you mention it, I believe you're right," said Ray. " Oh well, at least you've got everything ready for winter, John."

"Yeah, that's true," John replied. "Let it happen," he said with a chuckle.

They all enjoyed a quiet afternoon together, but the energy of the conversation was noticeably subdued by the awkward feeling of Mary's absence and the extra space at the dinner table. During the meal, Caroline questioned her father about her mother's heart condition and why no one ever knew about it.

"I don't really know why we didn't know more about it, Caroline," said her father. "All I know is that for as long as I have known her, she would tire rather easily when we did anything vigorously. I can remember when we were just young children at school, whenever we played in the school yard, she would never run very much or jump rope for very long. No one ever gave it much thought, I guess. You have to remember something else, too. Your mother never saw the inside of a hospital as a patient. You and Jack were both born in the house, and other than tiring somewhat easily, which she just accepted, I don't believe she ever had any reason to think something was wrong."

"It was before your family moved here, John," Diane added. "I think we were about five or six years old when she had a terrible fever. I remember her telling me how frightened her mother was and how she would kneel by her bedside and pray for hours at a time. That must have been when it happened."

After the meal, John and Ray volunteered to take care of the dishes while the ladies took the station wagon up to the house to load some of Mary's belongings that Caroline wanted to bring home with her. As the two men washed the dishes they reminisced about the days when Ray and Jack were younger.

"I have always wanted to thank you, John, for letting me help build those last two cabins. That's when I discovered how much I enjoy that type of work, and it eventually helped me get the job I have today."

As usual, John had difficulty taking credit for someone else's success. "Well, I'm glad you think I was an influence, Ray, but after what you told me yesterday, about how the new management is treating you, I'm not so sure you wouldn't be better off in another line of work."

"That has nothing to do with you, though, John," Ray said reassuringly. "I've never regretted my occupation, but sometimes I think it would have been less frustrating if I'd have stayed in the field as a carpenter, instead of getting into the office end of things."

There was a long pause in the conversation as the two continued their chore. John interrupted the silence and said with a serious tone. "You know, Ray, life is kinda funny in a way."

"How's that, John?" Ray asked, rigorously drying a dinner plate.

"Well, ever since you were born, I sort of felt like it was my duty to be as much of a father to you as I could, you know, being that your father was my best friend and then passing away before you were born and all. Well, now, ever since Jack died in the war, I find myself relying on you to be like a son to me. You know what I mean, Ray?"

Ray put his hand on John's shoulder and said, "Thanks for saying that, John. I'm glad you feel that way, because I've always thought of you as a father."

John smiled at him and said, "There's something else I want you to know, Ray. When it comes to your job, if push ever comes to shove, don't forget your roots."

"What do you mean, John?"

"Remember last night on the front porch when you asked what I was going to do with the business now that Mary is gone?"

"Yes, I remember," Ray answered. "You said you were going to pray about it."

"Well," said John. "That's just what I did. And this is what came to me. You've always got a home back here in Red Pine. I don't want to give advice on what to do with your life or where you should live, and I certainly am not trying to pressure you in any way. I just want you to know that if you're interested, the resort and the store is another option for you."

Ray was surprised by John's offer. He realized that John would probably need some help with his business now that Mary was gone, especially in the spring when the resort reopened. With a hint of astonishment, Ray said, "I don't know what to say, John. You've really caught me off guard with that one."

"I don't expect you to make a decision here and now, Ray. In fact I'd be disappointed if you did. This is something that you need to talk over with Caroline, and your children too, for that matter. I would imagine those two girls of yours are pretty well-rooted in at home, what with school and friends and the like. It would be a big step, Ray. You and Caroline have been gone for, what, about twenty years now isn't it?"

"Yeah, I guess it has been nearly twenty years, John. Caroline and I were discussing that very topic on the way up here on Monday. It doesn't seem that long, though. Time sure flies by, I guess."

"You don't have to tell me that. Wait 'til you're my age and you'll really see how fast it goes by." They exchanged a good laugh as Ray put away the last plate in the cupboard. He put the dishtowel down, leaned back against the counter with his arms folded and said in a quiet and sincere manner, "Thanks, John. I was really beginning to feel trapped with my job situation. You can't believe how good it feels just knowing I have an option."

John put his hand on Ray's shoulder and said with a smile, "Now it's your turn, Ray."

"My turn to do what?"

"Pray about it."

The last glow of daylight waned behind the heavy cloud cover as the headlights of the station wagon swept across the windows above the general store. "Looks like the ladies are back, Ray," said John as he sat up straight in the chair and peered out the window. He rose from the chair to shut the TV off as Ray lowered the copy of the St. Paul Pioneer Press he was reading.

"Well, John, I guess we'll be heading back home in a few minutes. I know Caroline will want to get the girls back home at a decent hour. They've missed a whole week of school, and they'll need to be good and fresh tomorrow morning. Why don't you let us give you a ride back up to the house on our way out of town?"

"That sounds good, Ray, thanks."

Diane entered the kitchen and said, "Your family is waiting for you in the car, Son." Ray gave his mother a kiss and said goodbye. "Have a safe trip home, Ray, and we'll see you in a month or so, if you're coming back for the deer hunting opener, that is."

"I've never missed one yet, Mom! And who knows, maybe you'll see me sooner than you think." John smiled from ear to ear at Ray's remark. It was the first hint that Ray was seriously considering John's proposal.

Diane frowned with confusion and said, "What do you mean by that?" Ray just smiled at her and started down the long staircase. She noticed John's big grin and said to him, "What did he mean by that, John?" He just shrugged his shoulders and started down the steps behind Ray. "What are you two up to anyway?" she asked, as they continued their descent. "John Nelson!" she said in an elevated voice as they reached the bottom of the stairs. When they disappeared through the doorway she shouted even louder "I know you two are up to something, and I won't give you any peace until you tell me what's going on."

John's head reappeared in the doorway and he said, "Stop in at the store tomorrow and I'll explain everything I know over a cup of coffee."

"You can count on it, Mr. Nelson," she said firmly.

The station wagon stopped in front of John's house, and when he got out of the car he leaned back inside the door and gave his granddaughters a kiss and a hug.

"We love you, Grandpa," said Mary Ann loudly.

"I love you too, girls. Now don't forget to write Grandpa lots of letters."

"We won't, Grandpa!"

Caroline rolled down her window and her father leaned his head inside and kissed his daughter on the cheek. Caroline's eyes were filled with tears as she returned his kiss. "We love you, Dad. Please take care of yourself and call if you need anything. We mean it—call anytime day or night, okay?"

"I'll be just fine. Don't worry about a thing."

"We'll get back up here as soon as we can, John," Ray said with a smile.

"I hope so," he replied.

John stepped back, slowly releasing the grip of his daughter's hand. The big station wagon pulled away and he stood in the street, returning their waves as they drove off. Caroline began to wipe her tears, and Ray tried to comfort her by placing his hand on her shoulder and saying, "Everything is going to turn out just fine, Caroline, you'll see."

"I know, Dear," she said. "It's just so hard to watch him stand there alone and wave. Mom and Dad were so much in love. I really worry about how he's going to get along. I don't think it's really hit him yet, you know? It doesn't seem like he really believes she's gone." As the car turned onto the highway, Caroline recalled the experience her father and daughters had during the funeral service. Maybe I'm wrong, she thought. Maybe Dad isn't going to be in for some delayed grieving experience. If he really believes that Mom was with him during the funeral and comforting him somehow—maybe he *would* be just fine.

A Homeplace

About an hour into their return trip, Caroline, Mary Ann and Irene had fallen asleep to the soothing drone of the car's engine and the relaxed selection of music on the "Hobb's House" radio program on WCCO. All the while, Ray was contemplating how he would sell Caroline and his daughters on the idea of moving back to Red Pine and taking over her father's business. He was reasonably sure it was the right thing to do, but to relocate their children and sell the house that had been their home for nearly twenty years, would be difficult. He continued to struggle for the proper justification for starting a new life.

The pros and cons kept scrolling through his mind as he drove along. It's going to be a tough sell, he thought. The schools are good. The neighbors are great. We have so many friends. Am I being selfish to want to move because of the uncertainties of my job? Certainly I could find another job in my line of work. Perhaps with one of our competitors, after all, loyalty is a two-way street. If my twenty years with the company suddenly means nothing to the owner, why should I give a damn? Then again, I could go through this all over again with another company. That settles it! I'm going to go to work for myself and be in control of my own destiny. Whether I succeed or fall flat on my face will be of my own doing.

Caroline was awakened by the car's change in speed as they approached the first of many stoplights at the outskirts of the city. "My goodness, I must have been sleeping hard," she said. "I can't believe we're almost home already."

The timing was perfect, Ray thought. The girls were still sleeping and it would be at least twenty minutes before they were home. Now's the time to reveal my plan. He reached to turn down the volume on the radio, and with a lump of apprehension in his throat, he was just about to speak when Caroline said, "Ray, I'd like to ask you something that I've been thinking about for a few days."

"Shoot," he thought. "Just when I gathered the nerve to ask her, she stops my momentum."

"What is it, Honey?" he answered.

"What would you think of the idea of moving back to Red Pine?"

Ray was utterly stunned for a moment, and looked directly at her as they waited at the stoplight. He shook his head back and forth and started laughing. "You've got to be kidding me!" he replied.

Coming Home

At that, Caroline became very upset and scolded him saying, "I'd like to know what's so funny about that!" She turned in her seat to face him more directly. "You seem to have forgotten a promise you made to me when we moved down here. You told me the first opportunity we have to move back home we would, and I can't think of a better reason than the one we have right now. My father is getting old, and now he's alone, and trying to figure out how he'll be able to run his business. Your mother is getting old, too, and she'll need more and more help as time goes on."

"No! Caroline, wait a minute, Honey!" Ray pleaded in a loud whisper trying not to wake the children. "I'm not laughing at your idea."

"Then what's so funny?" she insisted.

"Please let me explain. You're not going to believe this, but ever since we left, I've been trying to figure out a way to ask you that very same thing. What's funny is that I spent all this time worrying about how you would react to *my* idea of moving back home. Honest to goodness, I was just about to ask you the same thing when I turned the radio down, but you spoke before I had a chance."

He leaned toward her and put his arm behind her neck, drawing her closer, and kissed her on the lips. "I love you, Caroline," he whispered in her ear.

Their tender moment was interrupted by the impatience of the motorist behind them. Ray hadn't noticed that the light had turned green and was startled by the sudden blare of a horn. They quickly sat up straight in the seat, and Ray accelerated away from the intersection. Their embarrassment was furthered by the unkind one-handed gesture made by the driver of the car that sped past them, who was obviously put out by the brief delay at the intersection. Caroline, who was red with embarrassment, turned to Ray and said, "He probably thought we were a couple of teenagers."

Ray laughed and said, "Why don't you slide over here so he isn't disappointed in case we meet at the next stoplight."

Caroline sat next to Ray and rested her head on his shoulder. "So how do we tell the girls our plans?" asked Ray.

"What are our plans?" Caroline replied.

Ray started by explaining about the deteriorating situation at work and the conversation he had with her father while doing the dishes earlier that day. He told her how her father's idea came to him after he

A Homeplace

prayed about it. Caroline gave him a mild scolding followed by an affectionate lecture for shielding her from the troubles at work.

"Remember what our wedding vows said, Ray? For better or for worse. Some of our promises to each other include supporting and listening and working together to solve our problems. It won't do either of us any good to be silent martyrs."

Ray was genuinely ashamed after his wife's statements and apologized to her. "I'm going to give my notice at work first thing in the morning. Then I'll call a realtor and make an appointment for tomorrow night. I'll let you explain to the kids that we're moving to Red Pine," he said with a sinister grin.

"Thanks a lot," Caroline said, sticking her elbow into his ribs.

"Just kidding, Honey. We'll sit down together at the supper table tomorrow and explain it to them."

"I just don't know how they'll take it, Ray. They're so involved with school and their friends. I hope they're not too disappointed."

The next morning on his way to work, he mentally drafted a short oration that he would deliver as part of his resignation to his much younger superior, concerning the poor business decisions that had been made since his father gave him control of the company. He was even prepared to give a prediction of how much longer the company would be in business if the present policies continued. When the opportunity came, however, the smug and nonchalant manner that his employer exhibited in accepting his resignation irritated Ray beyond his ability to speak in a civil manner. When he left the owner's office he said to himself, "Now I know I've made the right decision."

Ray left work early so that he and Caroline could explain to their daughters about the decision to move, before the realtor came to list their home.

Caroline watched out the window as Mary Ann and Irene walked together down the sidewalk. "They're coming, Ray," she shouted.

"I'll be right up, Honey!" Ray replied from the basement.

The two girls sat down on the front stoop and began talking to each other. "What in the world could they be talking about out there, I wonder," Caroline said impatiently as she peeked out the window. Several moments later, the front door opened and the two girls entered to find their mother and father sitting on the couch together.

"Hi kids."

Coming Home

"Hi, Dad," they replied. "How come you're home already, Dad?" Mary Ann asked.

"Well, girls, I came home early because we need to have an important family meeting." The two girls looked at each other and exchanged a puzzled expression.

"What's it about?" Mary Ann asked as they sat on the couch next to their parents.

Caroline sat down on the floor in front of her daughters and said, "Girls, your dad and I have decided to move back to our home town so we can take better care of Grandpa John and Grandma Diane."

Fully expecting a reaction of disappointment and resentment, Ray and Caroline had prepared themselves for a firm but loving response. Instead, Mary Ann and Irene exchanged a look of surprise that quickly transformed into expressions of delight and smiles as their parents looked on in astonishment.

"Mom," said Mary Ann. "I can't believe it! We were just talking about that on our way home from school. Irene was crying on the bus, and when I asked her what was wrong, she said she kept seeing Grandpa John standing by himself in front of his house waving goodbye to us last night, and it made her sad to think he was going to be alone. I was thinking the same thing, and we decided to ask you and Dad if we could move to Red Pine and be with Grandma Diane and Grandpa John."

Caroline was so relieved that she gathered her children in her arms, kissing each one on the cheek.

"Let's call Grandma Diane and Grandpa John right now and tell them the good news!" Ray said with a smile. He handed Mary Ann the little book with family addresses and phone numbers and said, "Why don't you call Grandpa and then Irene can call Grandma."

She ran to the phone and quickly found the page with her grandfather's phone number and dialed. After waiting several seconds the big smile left her face and she said, "There's no answer."

Looking down at her watch she said, "Oh, he must still be at work. Try calling the store, the number should be right there on the same page, Dear."

Everyone gathered around the phone in anxious anticipation and watched as Mary Ann's face lit up when she heard her grandfather's voice. "Hello."

"Hello, Grandpa, this is Mary Ann."

"Well, hello there! How's my Mary Ann today?"

A Homeplace

"I'm fine, Grandpa. I have some good news for you."

"Well, hurry up and tell me, Dear," said John. "I just love to hear good news," he chuckled.

"We're going to come and live with you."

John had a fairly good inkling of what the call was about when he heard his granddaughter's voice on the phone with her good news, but he was still overjoyed and responded accordingly. "Oh my goodness!" he said. "That is the best news I've ever heard, Mary Ann. When are you going to move up here? I can hardly wait."

She looked at her mother and said, "I don't know yet, do you want to talk to my mom?"

"Yes put her on, Honey."

"Hello, Dad."

"Hello, Caroline," he said. "Are you as excited as I am?"

"I sure am, Dad. You wouldn't believe how this all transpired." She went on to explain how each member of the family was thinking about returning to Red Pine and the comical way in which everyone's desire to move back home was revealed.

Ray took his turn on the phone to explain the details of their move. "We'll be coming up this weekend and bringing a load of our belongings with us," he said. "I've given a two-week notice at work, so when I'm finished we'll concentrate on getting up there as quickly as we can. I talked to the realtor this morning, and he seemed to think our house would sell rather quickly. In fact he said he had three or four clients that he wants to show the house to already."

"Well, that's just great!" John said with excitement. "I have to tell you, Ray—I was thinking about the big decision you'd be making, and I honestly felt a little worried for you. But now, the way everything seems to be falling into place, you just have to believe that it was meant to be."

"Caroline and I were just saying the same thing," he said. "Well, I better get off the phone because it's Irene's turn to call my mother, and she's getting pretty antsy."

"Just so you know, Ray, your mother does know that you're thinking about moving back here. She came down for coffee this morning, and I had to tell her everything we talked about this weekend or she would have pestered me to no end."

Ray laughed and said, "Yeah, I'm sure she would have John. That's okay, though, she'll still be surprised. Goodbye, John. We'll be in touch daily."

"Sounds good, Ray. Goodbye."

Diane was equally delighted after hearing the news, and that evening she invited John up for dinner in order to discuss the exciting new changes.

The realtor placed a sign in the yard that evening and set up four showings for the coming weekend after they left for Red Pine. All plans continued to move forward smoothly, and on the third Saturday in October, Caroline, Ray, Mary Ann and Irene left their home in the cities and followed the large moving truck to their new home in Red Pine.

That afternoon, when they arrived in front of the old house, Diane, who had been preparing for their arrival while John worked at the store, greeted them at the curb with an emotional, "Welcome home."

They finished unloading the station wagon just before the large moving truck arrived. Most of their furniture was unloaded into the garage while the decisions of what would or wouldn't be kept were made. With the help of the two men from the moving company, the task of unloading the truck was accomplished rather quickly, and just as John arrived home from work, the truck pulled away and the move was completed. "Perfect timing, John," Ray teased.

That evening Diane served a roast beef dinner complete with mashed potatoes, gravy, corn, and homemade dinner rolls. When everyone was seated at the table, John led the blessing before the meal. "We thank You Father for all these gifts of food, and we are especially thankful to You for the return of our children and grandchildren who are truly the greatest blessing You have given me. Amen."

"Amen," everyone repeated. Outside, the daylight gave way to the cold autumn night, but inside the old house, the gathering around the table enjoyed the food, fellowship and smiles beneath the warm glow of light from the chandelier.

A Homeplace

The transition continued for the next several weeks as everyone settled into a new lifestyle. The girls made many friends at school the first day, largely due to some friendships with children in town that were established over the years when visiting their grandparents. Ray and Caroline quickly became involved in the store, allowing John to reduce his involvement in the business to just two or three half-days per week. So renewed was John's spirit, that for the first time in many years, he decided to fix up his spear house so it would be ready to use when the ice was safe.

On the Sunday after Thanksgiving, John sat quietly at the dining room table writing the annual Christmas greeting to each guest who patronized the resort during the year, a tradition started by his parents that he and Mary continued when they took over the business.

Dear friends,

Mary and I have always looked forward to this time of year when we can sit down and once again thank our customers for another wonderful season at the resort. The cabins are all closed up and Crystal Lake is now frozen tight beneath a blanket of snow.

I write this letter on my own this year with a mixture of sadness and joy. Mary, my wife of forty-three years, passed away suddenly on the last Sunday of September. She left very peacefully in her sleep, after we had tucked the resort away for the long, cold winter. You all know what an important part of our business she was and how terribly we will all miss the love and hospitality that she extended to each and every guest at the resort, from the first-time visitors, to those of you who have been regular guests for over thirty years.

The joyous news is that my daughter and son-in-law, along with their two lovely daughters, have returned home to Red Pine and will be taking over the duties of the resort and store, thereby ensuring our family tradition of making your stay at Nelson's Resort a pleasant and memorable experience.

Coming Home

May God richly bless you, and may you have a Merry Christmas and a happy New Year.

Sincerely, John Nelson

As John finished his last letter, the front door opened, and Mary Ann and Irene slowly backed through the doorway holding one end of a Christmas tree. Ray followed behind them with the top of the tree. They placed the tree in the stand and stood it up in front of the window overlooking the front porch. "Isn't it a beautiful tree, Grandpa?" Irene asked.

"It's one of the nicest looking trees we've ever had in the house," John said with a smile. "Where did you ever find such a perfectly shaped tree?"

"I noticed it on our hunting land last weekend," Ray answered. "It was right near my deer stand, and I thought that in a couple of years it would probably interfere with my shooting lane so I decided it would make a good Christmas tree."

Caroline slowly descended the stairs with a large box of Christmas decorations, and stopped for a moment to observe the expressions of joy and excitement of her husband and children from her lofty vantage point.

John stood back and watched from a distance as everyone started decorating the tree. The aroma from the freshly-cut balsam fir filled the room, and he thought how good it was to see the warmth and togetherness and to hear the voices of children and laughter, once again fill the rooms of the old house, just as it did so many years ago. He was gripped with emotion at the sight before him, and as he lowered a cup of hot cider from his lips, a tear gathered in the corner of his eye. His fond memories of Christmases past with Mary and their children began to scroll through his mind, when suddenly, a warm and familiar sensation developed on his right cheek—a deep warmth that radiated to the entire side of his face. He knew, now, that Mary was with him.

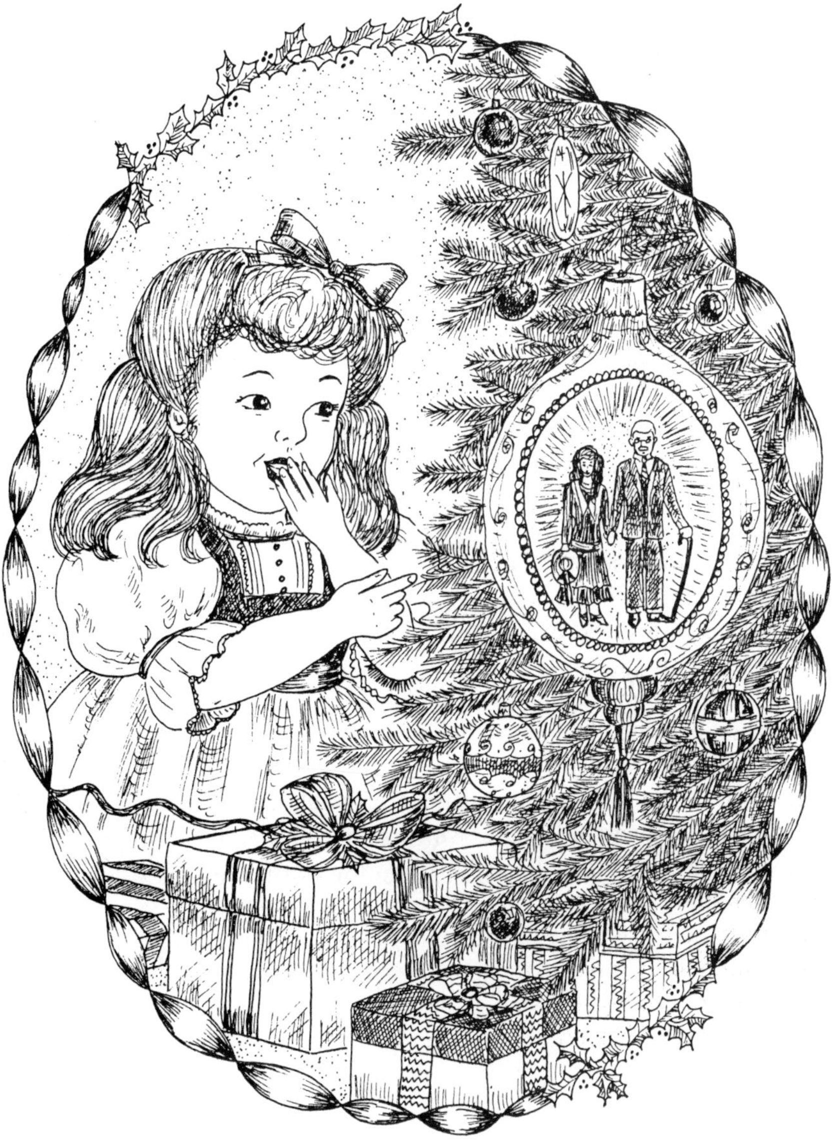

Irene carefully placed a round, shiny, silver ornament on the tree, and as she took a moment to admire it, she noticed the reflection of her grandfather standing across the room. A smile came to her as she observed her grandfather's image in the ornament, when next to him, holding his hand, appeared the beautiful young woman in a long, dark blue dress with a white, lacy collar.

Outside the window, perched in the soft branches of an evergreen, a dove with radiant white plumage suddenly sprang into flight. Rising higher and higher into the sky, it eventually vanished into the brightness of the sun.

THE END

Thank you for purchasing this book. I hope you enjoyed the story. It is my sincere wish that there is, or will be, a place in your heart that is filled with the fond memories of warmth and love and caring of a home place, and that you find it fitting to pass those same qualities of living onto the next generation. Truly, it is one of the greatest gifts we can inherit.

Steve Goshey grew up in St. Paul, Minnesota and now lives in Crosby, Minnesota with his wife and children. He has had articles published in *Country Extra* magazine and *Homespun,* a small local magazine.

A Homeplace is his first novel and in the next, *Home Town,* the story continues as the people of Red Pine become divided about the future of their town as the pressures from the growing resort and recreation industry bear down on the relatively untapped potential of Crystal Lake.

John Nelson struggles with loneliness after the death of his wife, Mary, and his son-in-law, Ray, becomes suspicious about the intentions of his former employer after spotting him in a neighboring town having discussions with the owner of a large real estate firm.